# Different
# Kind of
# Happy

# A Different Kind of Happy

## PART-TIME WORKING MUMMY

### RACHAELE HAMBLETON

EBURY
SPOTLIGHT

1

Ebury Press, an imprint of Ebury Publishing
20 Vauxhall Bridge Road
London SW1V 2SA

Ebury Press is part of the Penguin Random House group of
companies whose addresses can be found at
global.penguinrandomhouse.com

Penguin
Random House
UK

Copyright © Rachaele Hambleton 2021

Rachaele Hambleton has asserted her right to be identified as
the author of this Work in accordance with the Copyright,
Designs and Patents Act 1988

First published by Ebury Press in 2021
This paperback edition published in 2022

www.penguin.co.uk

A CIP catalogue record for this book is available from
the British Library

ISBN 9781529105193

Printed and bound in Great Britain by Clays Ltd, Elcograf S.p.A.

The authorised representative in the EEA is Penguin Random House
Ireland, Morrison Chambers, 32 Nassau Street, Dublin D02 YH68

Penguin Random House is committed to a sustainable future for
our business, our readers and our planet. This book is made from
Forest Stewardship Council® certified paper.

MIX
Paper from
responsible sources
FSC® C018179

*Betsy, Seb, Lula, Isaac, Edie & Wilby – watching you grow, each with completely different personalities, goals and dreams but at the same time showing loyalty, support and love to one another, especially when times are tough, makes me see I got something in life right. Thank you for teaching me new things every day. I adore all of you.*

*Joshua, for being such a huge part of who those six tiny beautiful humans are and the biggest reason I love you so much. You work so hard in your own career yet support mine constantly, making me achieve things that would be impossible without you by my side. Thank you for making me feel a love I never knew existed before you. I will never take for granted what we've created.*

*To the eight of us*

*This is a work of fiction. Names and characters are the product of the author's imagination and any resemblance to actual persons, living or dead, is entirely coincidental.*

# CONTENTS

# PROLOGUE

## THE EX

I'd just started writing in my book this morning when I heard them pull up.

I peer out the window before heading downstairs. It's grey out, the sky looks depressed and I sense the rain is going to start any second – and not stop for the day.

I see he's got another new car. Oh, he's gone for an Audi this time. Brand new. Black. Small and sporty, three-door – a perfect car for a forty-year-old father of three children. Dick.

The boot opens automatically, and he ushers the kids to pick up the handfuls of shopping bags, which are no doubt full of clothes and toys that he's treated them to. Total Dick.

I see Belle grab three small paper bags from MAC and one huge one from Hollister while Rex is laden with oversized bags from JD Sports and Game that he can hardly lift. Art isn't moving. He isn't collecting his bags, no matter how hard his dad is trying to persuade him. He's stood as still as a statue, leaning against the car with his head aimed down at the pavement. He's going to lose it. I can't even see his face, but I can just tell from his body language.

Here we go again …

I rush down the stairs and, as I get to the front door, it swings open and Belle flies in past me.

'He is SUCH a dick,' she bellows, as she storms up to her room with her headphones in, slamming the door behind her.

Rex follows. He tilts his head to the side as soon as he sees me, beams at me with his beautiful smile, showing his huge dimple in his left cheek. That boy – he instantly makes me melt whenever I see him. He says 'Hey Mum' then looks back, waves bye to his dad, turns back to me and whispers 'Art's about to lose it' in a small voice that reminds me he's still such a baby. He then drops his bags and walks straight past me into the kitchen and I can already hear him rummaging in the fridge.

I look round for a jacket to put on but everything is now packed in boxes, including my coat. I spot one of Jamie's old jackets on top of the stack of boxes that are waiting to be collected by the removal firm and quickly wrap it around me before going out to retrieve my heartbroken son. I'd hoped Jamie would be back before Mark turned up with the kids; he's so much calmer and more rational at dealing with Mark than I am. It's so typical that while he's gone out to grab us some lunch, this moron decides to turn up.

'Hey, buddy,' I say to Art, as I shut the front garden gate behind me and try to calm him down. By this point he's crying, repeatedly saying to his dad, 'But you always do this.'

My head is telling me to bite my tongue, even when faced with my upset child.

It's weird, I think to myself. I know immediately what each cry that one of my children makes means; it's our job as mums, isn't it? To immediately recognise whether your child is crying because they're in pain, crying in temper, anger or frustration, or whether it's a cry of genuine upset where their hearts are physically hurting. Right then, Art sounded like he was angry crying. I can hear his frustration, but both of these feelings are totally justified, and they come from the knowledge that his dad is yet again abandoning and rejecting him. The same old shit is flowing out of his mouth.

'Arthur, mate, I have to work. I promise I will make it up to you. I've bought you that new limited-edition game for your Xbox, and Sof is sorting your subscription as we speak so you can go online and play with your mates.'

*Bite your tongue, Jo*, I repeat, like a mantra in my head.

I try to intervene and do what I've done for the past five years, where I try to convince Art that his useless, narcissistic, lying piece of shit father isn't a useless, narcissistic, lying piece of shit.

'Baby, your dad has to go to work. Gran is going to come over and take you to the park while Jamie and I load the last few boxes, and then we will be ready to go,' I say, hoping to calm him down and take his mind off things.

Art tries to reply to me, but he's too far gone. He's inherited the same cry as me and he's now totally lost control.

He's choking back sobs and stuttering repeatedly while trying to get his words out. 'But … but … you, you said we were with Dad all weekend … all weekend until Monday be-be-be-because you and J-J-J-Jamie needed to move, and and and you wanted to get the new house sorted for us!' He stopped, let out a huge heartbroken wail and ended his sentence with, 'It's Saturday morning, Mum. We only went to Dad's last night. We haven't even seen him for one da-da-day.'

My heart aches. Still now, as I write this, it aches. It is actually a physical pain watching my baby feel so hurt because he can see that his dad doesn't want him and he knows deep down both his parents are stood here, blatantly lying to him.

*Bite your tongue, Jo.*

'Yes, babe, I did, but it's fine. Dad has to work.' I reassure him. 'Jamie will get all the beds up first and you guys can help unpack at the new house and put things exactly where you want them. I'll probably make your room look rubbish anyway if you aren't there to help me.' I want to reply with the truth and tell him that actually having three kids on top of trying to move hundreds of miles away to a new house is going to be really stressful and unfair, and I want to tell him his dad is a useless twat who is purposely trying to fuck this up for me yet again, but I don't. Instead I bite my tongue so hard it almost bleeds and I notice Mark slyly open his car door and slide into the driver's seat. He keeps the door open but starts pulling his seatbelt around him to prepare for his take-off.

I want to say, 'Are you not even going to give your son a cuddle goodbye? Are you not going to say sorry? Make another date? Wipe his tears away?' I want to tell him that he should be making the most of his time with the kids before there's a six-hour drive between them. I already feel guilty about moving them away, despite his uselessness, and I don't need his help to make it worse. Knob. Instead I bite my tongue ... again.

Mark starts to roar the engine of his brand-new Twat Mobile and says, 'Right, mate, I've got to shoot. Send me some pictures of your new room and let me know if you have any problems getting online with your game and I'll get Sofia to sort it.'

I want to scream as loud as I can: 'HELLO?? DICK-HEAD?? He's bawling. He isn't listening to a word anyone is saying because you have broken his heart yet again. Nothing is going in about the stupid game you've paid him off with, or the online pass your helpful girlfriend is sorting, or taking pictures of this new room he isn't interested in ... '

*Bite your tongue, Jo.*

As my mantra plays on a loop in my head, I instruct Art to go inside the house so I can quickly sort things out with his dad, and I spot Mark roll his eyes at me with irritation before he revs the engine. Again. Not for the first time I feel furious with myself for wasting so much effort involving him in our discussions the very moment this move became a possibility. I was so worried about moving the kids away from their dad, but if he doesn't care, why should I? Jamie and I are enough for them. They'll be better off.

When I see that Art has shut the front door I bend down, put my head through Mark's car window, and say, 'Just so you know, this shit stops now. I've spent the last five years watching you walk in and out of our children's lives as and when it suits you. Your daughter hates you, your youngest son sees you as some sort of weird rich uncle who swans in every few months to throw unnecessary gifts at him, and your middle son is totally fucked because he spent the first six years of his life having you kiss him goodnight most evenings, when you weren't out shagging around, for you to then disappear completely. For the last five years you've acted like he doesn't exist. If we're both being honest you *don't* have to go to work. You are lying, yet again. So, when you do go and collect your girlfriend now, if you're planning not to cheat on her like you did to us, then perhaps you could have a chat with her about making more of an effort with the children you can't be bothered with. You've been together for over five years now ... Maybe she could actually spend some time with them, get to know them. She didn't meet a single bachelor; she met a married father of three children. Maybe you two could think about behaving more like a family, more like parents, rather than constantly communicating to your children that they are a total inconvenience to the pair of you. You either start being a proper dad to make this move work like you said you would or you fuck off all together. I am not allowing you to cause any more damage to our children than you already have.'

'Jo, you're being crazy, I have to go into the offi—'

'And one more thing,' I interrupt. 'I am sick to death of waiting for your dribs and drabs of child support as and when it suits you. I spent the first three years after you abandoned us living on income support because you refused to pay anything other than the mortgage and the utility bills. And now another man is paying to raise your children while you drive round in your piece of shit penis extension and swan off to the Maldives every other month for a holiday. I want maintenance going into my account, from today, every single month. I am not the beaten-down pregnant housewife you once left. If that doesn't happen, I will put a claim in with child support. And you know what else, Mark? The only thing I pray that you've taught our children is to never conceive with dickheads, because the damage I've watched you cause them is absolutely soul-destroying.'

Mark couldn't look more bored if he tried so I turn round before I resort to hitting him with more than my words. As I walk towards the house, I do a quick check to make sure none of the kids are spying on me from the windows. When I'm confident they aren't, I hold up my left arm, as high as possible and give him my middle finger. I hear his horn beep as he speeds off, and I'm unsure whether it's to gain my attention so he can argue back with a better hand gesture or whether he's just letting me know he's seen my middle finger. I keep walking into the house with my arm held in the air and my finger on display the entire time.

Then I slam the front door behind me. As I lean against it, I find myself sliding downwards into a heap on the floor, my knees pulled up to my chest and my heart beating so hard it's like it's about to burst out of my chest. I was right about the sky. I hear the rain beat hard and heavy on the windows of the house.

I can see myself back there now, as I write this, and it puts a lump in my throat all over again. I felt drained, so drained, that the sobs came within seconds. Sobs of frustration, hurt and anger for my babies, for me, the sobs of guilt that there is nothing I can do to protect them or make this situation any better, and the sobs of disappointment in myself because I reacted to him when I knew it was just so, so pointless.

*You should have bitten your tongue, Jo.*

So.

A journal.

It was my therapist Myrah's suggestion. Well, her plan B. At first, we discussed me writing letters – to all the people I wanted to say things to – but never sending them. She told me this is what a lot of people in therapy do to help get their thoughts and feelings out. However, I have so many people I'm trying to mentally deal with that I feel like the content of my letters would constantly change, because some days feel like I'm OK with things, and how I feel, and then other days, I have so many unanswered questions, I drown in it all.

So, we decided on this. This book: my diary, journal, memoir – Myrah said I can call it what I want, and I can write what I want. Anything and everything to help me process my thoughts and feelings; something I can read back when I need to – if I need to. I also know that we forget so much. We forget how deep we were in the trenches; we forget the funny stuff that made us laugh until we were in physical pain. So this is where I will write all of that – the positives and the negatives and all the bits in-between that make up my life.

And writing so far has really helped me. And reading it back makes me feel the things Myrah tells me I lock away – and I've decided I don't want to lock anything away any more because that doesn't get me anywhere. Instead, I want to write about it – whenever I get time or feel it's necessary.

So, here goes …

# CHAPTER ONE

## HOW I GOT INTO THIS MESS

My name is Jo. Born Josephine, weirdly, because my elder brother was named Joseph a few years before my arrival, hence why I have always been 'Jo' and he has always been 'Joseph'. We don't use my full name and we don't shorten his, otherwise we would have the exact same name, which would be even weirder. My full name, right now, is Jo Cassidy, I say right now as this is 'his' name, my ex-husband – before that my maiden name was Smith, which is why I haven't reverted back, because I didn't enjoy having the same name as so many other people, as well as not feeling ready just yet to have a different surname to my children. It seems so unfair to me that even though I was the loyal, devoted wife and now I am the only one raising our children they carry someone else's name ... and my third name, the one I was born with and kept for the first two years of my life, is Addison, which ironically is my favourite name out of all three – we will get to that part shortly.

I'm thirty-four. I am a mother to Belle, fifteen, Arthur (who we call Art), eleven, and Rex, who is almost five.

As you now know, I have a twat of an ex-husband named Mark. I also have an amazing partner called Jamie who I've been with for the past two years.

I suppose for this to make any sense to you, and to me when I'm old and I forget myself, I should go back to where it all began. I want to do that – to write down what I remember, to tell my story. And, kids, if you are reading this when I'm gone, I wrote this so that you guys have as much detail as possible about who your mummy was. Maybe you won't want to read this, but I know what it's like to be an adult with so many questions about childhood and no one to answer them; in case you feel that I got things really wrong with you, I hope this journal will help you to see that I was only ever trying to get them right. Perfect, even. A girl can dream.

I was the third child born to my parents who, according to the few people I have ever spoken to about them, should never have had children – my father, not at all; and my mother, not with him. I have a sister called Kitty who is thirteen months older than me, and of course my brother, Joseph, who is three years older.

I have no memory of my parents and I have never met them as an adult. My siblings and I were removed from their care when I was fifteen months old and we were adopted after being in foster care for a short time. My brother has never spoken of memories he has, and maybe that's because he doesn't have any. I don't know.

We had a happy childhood after we were taken away from our biological parents. Our adopted parents gave us a good life. My dad owned a timber business with depots across Central London and he worked hard. My mum couldn't have her own children so when she got the three of us, she told us all her dreams had come true at once. She lived for us, for being our mum.

She spent her days in an apron and would teach us all how to cook and bake. In the summer she would potter in the garden and show me and my sister how to dead-head flowers and teach us the importance of watering them every evening so the heat didn't make them bloom too soon. She was amazing at interiors and would make bedspreads and cushions, and every year she would strip and put fresh wallpaper in the lounge, changing the entire theme. My dad would pretend to be annoyed and moan, but secretly he loved it. He loved her – so much. She was an amazing mum, and she wanted what was best for all three of us. She supported our dreams and hopes, and I felt lucky, so very lucky.

Mum died of breast cancer when I was seventeen. It came out of nowhere and by the time we got the news it had already spread throughout her entire body and was in her bones. She had to make the decision to either have chemotherapy to try to extend the little time she had left or just roll with how she was. She had one round of chemo, but the side effects were truly gruesome; I remember her sleeping on the bathroom floor because she was so sick. My dad would lie next to her on a blanket and rub her back while she just hung her head in the toilet, vomiting and retching constantly. She made the choice to stop the chemo then and try to live for as long as she could without her body being pumped full of drugs. The cancer took her life in just under nine months. She was forty-nine years old when she died – three months away from celebrating her fiftieth birthday, and seven months away from her and Dad celebrating their silver wedding anniversary.

After Mum died, Dad continued to work, only harder and longer hours. He didn't retire early like they had planned. When Mum died it felt like everything went with her. My dad no longer smiled or laughed, and my siblings left home pretty much immediately and rarely ever came back. Overnight our whole worlds turned upside down; we had gone from being a solid, happy family unit to all living independently – like strangers.

I remember after her funeral I overheard one of Mum's friends in the kitchen say to my dad, 'You need to make a choice. You either die with her or you fight hard and continue to live. These kids need you to live.' Not even those words made him change. Our family had been totally destroyed by Mum's illness and, if she could have seen what happened after she'd gone, it would have devastated her more than the day she received her diagnosis. I knew that life would never, ever be the same again.

The house was so quiet after Kitty and Joseph moved out, and being there alone made me feel so down. I don't think I was depressed when I look back on that time – I was just sad. I was a teenage girl, grieving for my mum, with no one to talk to, and everywhere I looked there were reminders of her. I'd always known I wanted to do something to help others. After watching my mum go through the ordeal of breast cancer, after seeing the compassion and empathy nurses had shown us and the fact that they had made such a devastating, life-changing part of our worlds that little bit better by being so caring and kind, I decided that after college I wanted to go into nursing. Specifically, I wanted to be a children's nurse.

A fresh start in a new area was just what I needed and I applied to Dundee University in Scotland – far away from everything that, at that time, was so bad. My dad drove me and my belongings all the way to Scotland and the journey there was so painful. He tried to make conversation but it was as if it hurt him to actually have to talk to me – as though any time I spoke about anything it triggered some kind of reminder about Mum, what we'd once had, what we had lost … I remember wondering if he was proud of me for getting accepted into uni, if he would miss me not being at home with him, or if it was a relief that he now had none of us there. I genuinely didn't know any more.

We arrived and he helped me unload my stuff into halls. He gave me an envelope stuffed with cash and said he was at the other end of the phone if I needed anything. I watched through the huge window in the corridor as he sloped back to his car, my heart physically ached for his sadness and loss. His heart had been broken and he had shut himself off from his family. He would spend his days alone in our home, surrounded by reminders of what he would never have again. I remembered wondering so often if he would die of a broken heart.

The following morning, I began my nursing degree.

It was draining, and relentlessly hard work, but I powered through my first year and remained just as dedicated as I went into my second.

I didn't go home during the holidays. I rarely spoke to my dad. Each time I called him, our conversation seemed to be even more strained and difficult than the time before. And Kitty and Joseph had moved on with their own lives too. Kitty had moved to Hong Kong to teach English and, although at first I missed her like crazy, I soon adapted once the uni work began flooding in. My brother had got married and joined the army, and he and his wife were now expecting their first baby. No one had been invited to their wedding, which hurt, because I knew things would have been so very different if Mum had still been alive. So many things would have been different. I imagine I wouldn't now be sat here, writing this.

Our entire family dynamic had changed since Mum had gone, and rather than try to cope together, each one of us just battled it alone. Today, looking back, I wish we had done it differently – I wish we had ambushed Dad into getting help, I wish we had all stayed living at home, together – but Mum had been the leader of our pack, and none of us had a clue how to do things without her, how to make things better, and so we all decided it would be easier to look after ourselves than each other. I know that's shit, because it's not what family is about, and I'd be devastated to think of my kids losing contact with each other if anything ever happened to me.

The contact with my dad had by now totally stopped – it was too painful to try to make conversation when he had become someone I no longer knew – and without his financial support I needed another way of getting an income. I had no choice but to get a job, and when I saw a sign on the window of a bar in town, I jumped at the chance.

The pub was busy and, although it was mainly men who drank in there while watching Premier League football matches throughout the week, I enjoyed it. I loved just being out of my bedroom, socialising and talking to other humans for a few nights each week for the first time in a long time.

I got to know a lot of the locals; there was a total range of guys who came in – some were divorced who didn't want to sit in their bachelor pads alone; others were young lads from uni who came in after the gym to watch the football.

Then there were older men in suits, tapping away on their laptops while keeping their eye on the score. It was quite an odd bunch, but they were nice and they always chatted to me when I was on shift.

One night there was a new guy at the bar and I remember thinking how good-looking he was, but in a kind of bad-boy way. He had a lovely smile and a huge, cute dimple in his left cheek. We were introduced just before I finished my shift and I learned he was called Mark. I noticed immediately that he had a strong London accent, and there was something about him that seemed really cheeky, but nice. He asked me if I wanted to go grab some food with him when I finished and I smiled and rolled my eyes, trying to act cool as if it was just a 'bite to eat', but in reality my hands were clammy with sweat and my heart was beating through my chest. Going out with a total stranger wasn't something I had ever done before.

It was the end of November; I remember it being so cold, and it was raining, which made the droplets of water feel freezing as they hit the back of my neck and hands. Mark told me his car was parked up just by the pub so we walked to get in it so we could eat our takeout food in the warm. I felt at ease with him; it wasn't cringy or awkward, and I didn't feel any type of pressure from him – that would all come much later.

We walked up the hill and I saw the lights flash on a huge, white, gleaming 4x4 Range Rover. Mark opened the driver's door and got in and I was glad he hadn't walked to my side to open the passenger door for me first. My mum had always made a point of my dad and brother opening and holding doors for women, and it was another painful reminder of her whenever any man did it for me. I clambered up onto the black matte leather seat, which was piped with red stitching.

The car looked brand new – smelt brand new too – I remembered that new-car smell from my dad – I recall asking him if he was test driving it or if it was a courtesy car while his battered old Nissan Micra was in for a repair. He'd laughed, said no and told me it was his. I was secretly impressed that a twenty-five-year-old could afford a car like this. I had thought that he must come from a wealthy family, a close-knit family who supported him. A family so unlike mine since Mum had gone … but rather than feel jealous of what he had, I had immediately felt a sense of contentment, and of wanting to belong beside this man.

We drove until we found a late-night café. We went in and grabbed a window seat, I got a hot chocolate and he ordered himself a coffee and as the rain smashed down on the window we sat there and talked for over three hours, about everything and nothing. Mark told me he worked in Central London and was in Scotland for three days on business. His job in sales meant he travelled a lot with work, and he made it sound like he was good at what he did without boasting about it. He seemed to be in complete control of his life –

secure, with his future mapped out – which was so different to my struggling student life.

At around 3am, he drove me the five-minute journey home to a flat I shared with two housemates. As we pulled up, he took my number and put it into his mobile phone before leaning over and kissing my cheek. He didn't do anything gross like you see in the movies, like hold my face or gaze into my eyes or ask to 'come in for a coffee', and I liked that. I liked that he didn't make me feel any horrible kind of pressure because all of this was so new to me.

As I got to my bedroom, I quietly shut the door behind me and heard my message tone beep on my tiny Nokia mobile phone. Mark had already texted me and I've remembered the wording from that text, all these years later:

*'Hey, thanks for a good night. So now you have my number – if you want to meet up again just let me know and we can make plans for when I'm back soon. Goodnight xx'*

I felt an excited fluttery nervous sick – a feeling I'd never felt before.

Despite me always being cool with being alone, and independent, things moved quickly with Mark. He seemed to be in Scotland every other week for business, and when he wasn't, he would pay for me to fly to his apartment on the outskirts of London for the weekends and holidays. His apartment was stunning, decorated in a plain modern theme with thick cream carpets throughout. It was the opposite to what I'd grown up with and it was obvious to me that in order to live here you had to have money. A lot of fucking money.

Everything was immaculate – and new. It looked like a show home and I was worried about where I should put my bag as it was the only thing that looked out of place. Mark put me on the insurance of his Range Rover and there was always a wad of cash in the top drawer of his gloss white kitchen, which he repeatedly told me to 'help myself to' if I needed it. I never did, but I felt looked after. Safe, and wanted. It was a nice feeling. I imagine it was how Mum and Dad made me feel when I got to them as a baby after the life we had been living with our biological parents.

Mark loved to travel and we also went away a lot for weekends. I remember the first time he surprised me and told me we were flying to Milan that Friday. And when I told Mark I didn't have a passport, he simply drove me to Wales to get one. I remember nothing ever being too much trouble or too stressful for him. He was so laid-back about everything.

Soon this way of life became normal for me. I was looked after, money was no object, and we could pack up and jet off all over the world at a moment's notice. But my studies suffered. Suddenly becoming a nurse didn't seem as important any more, and all that mattered was being with Mark. I'd never been in love before, or even in a relationship, and when Mark gave me life experiences I had never had, it was nice. More than nice. It made me feel less alone.

I remember one weekend, not that long into our relationship, Mark asked about my family. I explained a little more about my mum dying and not seeing my dad, and he picked up the car keys and said, 'Come on – let's go and visit him.' I was really hesitant as I hadn't spoken to my dad for over a year by this point and wasn't sure what the situation was at home. I felt so unwell at the thought of just turning up unannounced, but also remember feeling as though I had no choice. Mark had decided and that's what would happen, regardless of how I felt about it all.

Back then I believed he made all these decisions out of love, but now I see it for exactly what it was ... control.

It was odd when we arrived. I could see Dad's Audi estate parked on the drive, and noticed how unclean it was. In the past, Dad had always kept his cars immaculate, but, like everything else, since Mum had gone he'd lost interest, and like everything else in his life, it sat unloved and ignored. The huge oak tree that we'd climbed as kids had died, and that made me feel even more sad. It had once held so many memories for the three of us as kids and I wondered if it had died because, like Dad, it was also broken-hearted.

Dad took a while to answer the door, and when it opened, he looked surprised, and not happy surprised. He said, ''Ello Jo', in his thick cockney accent and then turned round and walked back into the hall. He didn't acknowledge Mark, which was beyond awkward, and I suddenly felt so, so sick.

There was no hug or kiss, which hurt, because growing up my father had smothered me and my siblings and our mum with affection. As we walked behind him into the kitchen, I noticed the house was still exactly as it had been before Mum died. All our pictures hung on the walls, the dried flowers were still in their vases, and the cross-stitch Mum had made when she was well was still on display. Everything looked just the same. It had a different smell now, though; it wasn't a horrid smell, just one I didn't recognise. It no longer smelled of our family.

I flicked the kettle on and introduced Mark. He instantly began talking to Dad; his accent seemed thicker than normal and I remember cringing at how he sounded, or how my dad would perceive him. He was asking my dad about business and what he does with his spare time.

Dad gave one-word answers, asked Mark nothing about himself and made it clear this visit was not something he was happy about. I wanted the ground to swallow me up. As I reached for the tea bags in the cupboard, I noticed how the handles felt greasy. Nothing in this house was 'looked after' or 'gleaming' any more. The entire visit was strained, awkward and actually, as I look back on it now, heartbreaking.

We left with Mark walking ahead, unlocking the car and getting in without saying goodbye. I still remember my dad's parting words as I forced him into an awkward hug: 'He could sell snow to an Eskimo that one, Jo. Just be careful.'

I couldn't work out if Dad still loved me and was trying to protect me, or if he was just so unhappy with his life he was trying to find fault with every other human in the world. Either way I thought he was wrong, and when I mentioned it to Mark over lunch shortly after, he called my dad to tell him some 'home truths'. I wasn't privy to the phone call. He told me to sit in the car while he paced the restaurant car park, but I could tell he was livid, swapping the phone from one ear to the other while throwing his arms around erratically. When he ended the call, he jumped in the car, squeezed my leg, smiled so I caught a glimpse of his dimple – and said, 'Well, that's that. It's the last time we will be speaking to that miserable wanker.'

I remember feeling so ashamed and riddled with guilt that my dad would know I had repeated his words to a man I had only recently met. I also knew deep down that he wasn't a miserable wanker; he was just broken. But Mark was right; to this day I have never spoken to him again.

Mark and I carried on for the next few months as we were – happy, carefree and in love, still living between Scotland and London. And then I fell pregnant. I found out in the May of my second year, in the middle of my exams, that I was seven weeks gone. I was devastated and worried. This wasn't what I had planned, and it didn't fit in with what I wanted out of life.

I dreaded telling Mark and had no idea how he would react. I wasn't on the pill but we were always careful. We had never discussed having kids and the reality was we had known each other for just six months. I wondered whether I should book a termination in secret, but then I panicked that if I DID spend the rest of my life with this man, like I wanted to, and one day we had a child, would it come out then, in my notes or at the hospital? And what would he think? I decided to just be honest and tell him.

But his reaction made me feel even more confused. He was happy – genuinely happy – and excited and, as usual, totally relaxed about the whole thing. When I started off-loading and worrying about the negatives of us having a baby so young, he batted them all away, assuring me that this was the best thing to happen to us.

We agreed to keep the baby and I battled through my exams, passing them all. I was so happy because it was the first year that I had focused on children's nursing and it felt good to have done so well, but I was also sad because the baby was due at the beginning of January, which meant I wouldn't be able to finish my studies or graduate. Mark kept telling me not to worry, that financially we were secure, and I could go back and finish at a later date, but I ignored him and started another year of uni, determined to be a nurse.

It immediately became clear that the workload was much heavier than in the previous two years. I was six months pregnant and studying far away from Mark. It was hard. I was lonely in Scotland without him, and I struggled. He was right. I would have to give up my nursing dream to have the baby but the reality was that I was devastated, and disappointed in myself. Determined to prove that I hadn't made a huge mistake, I ignored those thoughts and feelings that I was fucking up my entire future by jacking in uni to have a baby that wasn't planned.

I loved Mark, he made me happy, he was good to me and he wanted this baby, so I packed up my belongings into the back of his car, said goodbye to my housemates, made the eight-hour drive to our beautiful new family home that he had bought for us in Canterbury, and I began planning to become a mum at the age of nineteen ...

# CHAPTER TWO

## THE 'HAPPY' FAMILY/
## THE TURNING POINT/
## DAD WAS RIGHT

Our baby girl, Belle, arrived on a cold January day, weighing 6lb 13oz, and with a mop of jet-black hair. She was perfect in every way, but after she arrived, my immediate thoughts on that day turned towards my own birth mother. I'd rarely thought about the woman who had given birth to me, who had brought me into this world, but once I held my own child in my arms, it made me question so much about my own adoption. I wondered again what my birth mum's situation was to have had three babies in such quick succession and then have given us all away to a stranger. I was in love with Belle immediately, and it felt like she had come along to fix all the parts of me I didn't know were broken. I knew I could never part with her.

But motherhood was hard. It was harder than hard. Some days it was impossible. And it was so lonely. No one ever warns you about the loneliness and yet it was almost overwhelming at times. And it especially made me miss my own lovely mum even more. When things got really tough with Belle, all I wanted to do was pick up the phone and ask my mum for help. Or when Belle cried and I had no idea how to placate her, I longed to ask my mum for her advice. Becoming a mum made the pain of losing her even worse and in a whole new way.

But I carried on plodding with Belle; I met some other mum friends and I got used to being a stay-at-home mum, having Mark's dinner ready every night for when he got in from work, and keeping our new house immaculate.

I always felt grateful for the life Mark provided us with; we had a beautiful home, new cars every year, and I had a credit card to use as and when I wanted. I knew I led a privileged life because of him and I never took that for granted. To the outside world, our life seemed pretty perfect.

Four years after Belle came along, I gave birth to our second baby, a boy called Arthur. Again, the love I felt for this little baby was instant, and I knew I would do everything in my power to protect him, always. I'd never abandon him to strangers, like my own birth mother had done, and I would cherish him and love him every single day.

When almost six years after that I fell pregnant with our final son, Rex, I felt as though our family was now complete. Mark and I had been together for a decade, and he had desperately wanted the three children we made together – or so I had always thought. Because then, when I was seven months pregnant with Rex, the perfect family we had made together, the perfect life we had built, all fell apart in moments.

I found out in the cruellest way possible that my husband was shagging someone else. It had been a very normal Tuesday afternoon when I had left to do the school run. I'd needed to whizz to the supermarket on the way to grab some bits for dinner, but when I pulled up outside I realised I'd forgotten my purse. I shot home to grab it to find Mark's car already on the drive. I was surprised he was home; he was rarely ever home before 6pm and had told me he would be at the office in Central London all day. As I let myself into our home, I saw his laptop case and mobile phone on the bottom stair. I heard the shower running from our bedroom and as I bent down to grab my purse, I saw a message flash up on his phone from Sofia. It just read 'one new message from Sofia'. I was instantly curious, I had never heard him make mention of a Sofia.

I clicked on her message. She was missing him, she said – even though he had only left her apartment ten minutes earlier after fucking her so well for the whole afternoon. She was still missing him; she couldn't wait to see him on Friday afternoon, and had used the card he'd given her to buy some more of the dresses and heels that he liked for their next trip away.

That one message snapped my heart in two and tore our family apart.

I wanted to die. I just couldn't face the thought of living after reading that message. I knew our whole world had just changed, forever, no matter what came now I knew in that instant nothing would be the same again. I opened the front door and violently vomited on our driveway.

Mark, after he'd finished washing his dirty afternoon away in the shower, rushed down the stairs to play the doting husband – a role he had gotten quite good at. I remember the look of shock on his face as I handed him his phone with 'that' text message still open.

But, as always, he wasn't upset or panicked; looking back, I wonder whether in that moment he actually felt relieved. He just shook his head and said, 'Fuck, Jo. I'm sorry, Jo. Fuck.' He couldn't deny it; it was there in black and white.

It's funny, when your entire world falls apart, how quickly you notice things you were totally blind to before. Even within five minutes of reading that message I remember looking at Mark, stood there in front of me, watching him watch me, and realising how tanned his body was. It was March and we hadn't been on a sunny holiday for over five months. His chest was also different, his pecs looked more muscly, the tops of his arms more defined. I realised then that my husband had been using sunbeds and going to the gym and I hadn't even noticed. We'd stopped having sex for a while, because I had been so busy trying to keep him and our kids happy, grow another baby inside me while trying to keep our house immaculately clean and our meals tasting like the restaurant dinners he liked. And as soon as I noticed 'the obvious', the self-blame began to kick in – was he having an affair because I'd let myself go? Because I never make an effort with myself? Because I don't try it on with him any more? Had I allowed things to become boring?

My head was fucked and I spent the rest of the afternoon in bed, watching my belly move up and down where my unborn baby kicked away, and listening to Mark play the perfect father to Belle and Art, who were none the wiser that their entire childhoods had totally changed.

Being pregnant, hormonal and desperate to not destroy my kids' worlds, I put them to bed that evening, then sat on the opposite end of the sofa to Mark. I asked him to end his affair with Sofia and work on our marriage. I said we could get some marriage counselling, and after the baby was born, we would make time for 'us', and I would pay more attention to myself and him.

Desperate.

But he told me he'd fallen in love with Sofia, the twenty-year-old barista from the local coffee shop with the pert tits and perfect lips, and then he left us – his family – to go and be with her. He left me on our lounge floor, on my knees, begging. Begging so hard there were just tears but no noise, not a sound because I was in such a state. He went upstairs, packed two bags and walked straight past me to the lounge door, he didn't even look at me before he walked out of the front door of our family home and left us forever.

I can honestly say I have never felt pain or panic like it. Not when my mum died, not when my dad changed into someone I no longer recognised, and not when I lost touch with my two siblings who had once been my best friends. I had been abandoned and rejected just before I was due to give birth, with two small children to care for, and I wanted to die even more than I had six hours earlier when I'd found the message. A chest-crushing anxiety landed on me and I was about to learn it wasn't going to vacate for a really long time.

Mark and Sofia set up home together immediately, and her Facebook page documented the life I'd had ten years earlier, where she was jetted all over the world on fabulous holidays and had a wardrobe like Beyoncé. She was ridiculously beautiful and I obsessed over everything I could about her. Looking back now, if I had to give advice to anyone in my situation, then I would tell them not to look, not to read things or search out pictures that continue to break an already broken heart, yet here I was, constantly refreshing her page each day. Hundreds of times morning, noon and in the middle of the night when I was feeding, studying her, what her features were like, what friends and family commented on her pictures, her hobbies, likes and interests. She set all her social media accounts to public, I imagine for my benefit, and within six months (and before we were divorced), her relationship status on Facebook had changed from 'It's complicated' to 'Engaged', followed by a series of photos showing Mark proposing to her in Paris. The ring was the size of a rock, and to the outside world looking in, they seemed to be the perfect couple – just as we once had.

Mark didn't even make it to Rex's birth. He didn't answer his mobile when I began getting contractions. When I called his secretary to deliver the news, she told me he was uncontactable. I could hear from her tone she felt desperately sorry for me, even without her repeating the words 'I'm so, so sorry, Jo' as she tried to stop her voice from breaking. And so was I. So sorry. Sorry that my husband was out of the office with his new fiancée after destroying his entire family. Sorry for what my life had now become.

I gave birth to our third child at home in my marital bed. I had a midwife at my side as my other babies slept in the room next to me. This 7lb 7oz crying bundle was placed on my chest and I cried too. In fact, I sobbed just like I had with my other two births, only these tears were different. I wasn't overjoyed, happy, or in a love bubble. I was devastated, broken-hearted and in a pain I never knew existed until then. The divorce papers arrived the very next day.

I stayed on my own for the following three years; three desperately unhappy years where I tried my hardest to survive with my small brood of children. I had no job and only the odd maintenance payment when things were needed like uniforms, shoes or they grew out of most of their clothes. I had to point out what they were wearing was too small for them – because, as Mark repeatedly reminded me, he 'provided us with a roof over our heads for free and all our bills included'. As if he was a generous landlord, not a father who had made a promise and commitment to his children and wife. And I didn't have the energy to fight for anything any more, I was just trying to make it through each day. I look back now and I see I wasn't living, I was surviving – and barely. I budgeted what little money we had so that we could afford to eat, buy our necessities and put petrol in the car. If we were lucky we would be able to afford a trip to soft play once a month where Belle would play Mum to Rex, whizzing him down slides and hurling themselves over foam blocks, Art would go off and make new friends and I would bury my head in a book and avoid contact with any other humans for a few hours.

I reached out to my GP, who put me on a large dose of anti-depressants, anti-anxiety tablets and sleeping tablets, and referred me for therapy. The wait for me to be seen seemed to take forever and during that time the medication numbed me even more. I didn't find things funny like I had done before, I didn't beam with pride in school assemblies, and I didn't feel happy or sad, ever. I just felt nothing.

I realised I couldn't carry on any more. I wasn't me. I wasn't OK and the medication wasn't making me better. It wasn't helping me to live; it was just enabling me to keep surviving. I knew I needed help.

# CHAPTER THREE

## THE TURNING POINT/THE LIGHT IN THE DARKNESS

Myrah, my therapist, was an older lady. Her home smelled of incense, and she had a warm, welcoming manner. I could feel her empathy towards me from the moment we met and I liked her. I felt safe when I was around her and I liked that she didn't stay silent and 'take it all in' when I spoke to her about my problems. Instead she listened, and asked me what *I* thought about the things I had confided to her, and then she explained what she thought, including the things I was feeling, and she helped me make sense of it all. I remember how, after my second session, when I told her about parts of my life, she said, 'It seems like you haven't ever really come out of the trenches since your mum died when you were seventeen, and before that time you never really knew who you were or where you came from.'

The realisation of the reality of what I had deemed a 'happy' marriage was frightening. As I spent more time with Myrah each week, charting my life over the previous thirteen years, it hit me that I was never happily married. I was controlled. I was a servant to Mark, with no life other than raising his children and cleaning his house. In the time Mark and I were together, I had never done anything for myself, and I hadn't even noticed that. I had never had a night out. When the mums at toddler group were planning the Christmas party or meals out to celebrate birthdays, I'd always claim to be busy – Mark having the children so I could go out with friends was just something that never happened; he wouldn't have ever agreed and I came to accept that it was just the norm for me not to go anywhere. I had no clue about anything financial within our marriage, and had to check and ask permission before making any decisions. Although he gave me use of a credit card I never had 'free rein'. I never would have bought myself anything like clothes, shoes or perfume after Belle was born. There was an unwritten rule: it was there for a weekly food shop and petrol, and after the food shops he would frequently question my spending, especially in the last few years. I remember him often querying the price of a pack of bacon or a block of cheese, and I would try to justify this. I would always try to get the best offers and deals to make him happy. I would spend more money on the foods he ate, like steak and chicken, and cut back on cheap sausage rolls or ham for the children's packed lunches. And I look back and think I genuinely didn't even see an issue with it. I was made to feel nothing but grateful for the life he gave me as if I gave nothing back in return.

As the epiphany hit, I felt so many things. Shame, that I hadn't seen things for what they were. Devastation, that I had thrown away a career that would have given me a totally different life to the one I had today. And relief. Relief that my life was no longer controlled by one man who I now saw so clearly was a narcissistic fuck.

But I also felt proud of how I'd coped. In my head I felt that I had failed my kids by wallowing in misery, but the reality was they rarely saw this. They rarely saw my tears and heartache. I always waited until they were out of sight or asleep. I had still managed to be a mum. I had still functioned. I didn't fail my kids or let them down like I believed I had for so long, and it was a nice feeling to eventually see that I was their stability, their routine and their constant love. I was the only person ensuring that they were OK and making sure that my heartbreak didn't break their hearts. And the last thing I felt was excitement. For the first time in what felt like forever, I was excited again, about finding myself and finally being happy.

Before I started therapy, in those dark days when everything had seemed so raw and impossible, I'd messaged Mark each evening with a photo of the kids and details about their days. I'd even included his new son, Rex, who he chose to have no relationship with at all. Most days he would reply with just an 'X'. Nothing else. Some nights he wouldn't reply at all. He would hardly ever answer their

FaceTime calls and he stuck to seeing them once a week for dinner but nothing else.

I remember wondering how he could sleep at night, only seeing two of his children for four hours, once a week, after living with them for so many years, and not even knowing his third, but when Myrah broke it down in therapy it all became so apparent. Although he had once 'lived' with them, with us, that's all he'd done. He might have occasionally taken Art to his rugby game on a Sunday morning, and he smothered Belle with gifts from his work trips abroad, but it was *me* who parented them. I cooked their dinners, I made the volcanos and drew Tudor houses for their homework projects, I bathed them and took them to school, I was the one who answered their questions and listened to their opinions, and I was the one who put them to bed and kissed them goodnight.

Once the therapy began to work, it hit me like a bus, and I stopped calling and texting him. When the kids asked to FaceTime him, on the *very* rare occasions when he bothered to answer, I made excuses and left the room. Instead of fighting to make him want to be a good dad and love his babies, I gave up. They soon got fed up of the 'unavailable' message popping up and gave up trying too. Part of me was pleased to not have to deal with the calls any more, but a bigger part was crushed to know that he'd destroyed something in them – their pure, loving, hopeful natures – and I was worried about the long-term damage he'd done by not letting them feel loved enough. Before long, they barely spoke about him at all. I realised that, actually, Myrah was right: they would be far better off with one stable, loving parent who would focus on their needs without the other one causing them even more damage.

Feeling better every day, I started to make more of an effort with myself. I no longer lived in faded leggings, nursing bras, worn vest tops and an oversized cardie, trying to make myself as invisible as possible. I climbed up into the loft and pulled out my old designer clothes that I had stored in bags years earlier, which I could now fit into again. Most were barely worn and still fitted me and those that didn't, along with all the kids' designer clothes from when they were babies went on eBay – I made to me what was a fortune selling our bad memories online. I began tousling my hair with curlers instead of scraping it back, and I put on some lipstick and applied a bit of mascara once again. All the little things that I hadn't done for such a long time. Mums on the school run would comment that I looked amazing and when I started uploading photos to Facebook again after years of being silent, people I hadn't seen since uni or school would write under pictures of me and the kids how happy and well I looked, how beautiful my babies were. And it felt good. I felt good for the first time in such a long time.

Within a short time of Mark seeing all of this, he then let it be known that he missed me. He would make comments to try to fuck with my head, and he'd brush past me in the kitchen as he'd reach for the milk to make Rex his bedtime bottle – something he had never done before – and he would often call me when the kids were at school and nursery to see if he could 'pop round' for a cuppa.

In weaker moments, I almost cracked. It would have been so easy for me to slip and to have allowed him back in, but he had ripped out the hearts of two of my children, disowned a third, and the reality was I knew he would do it again. His performance as the 'perfect dad', acting like he cared, would have soon stopped. If I caved and accepted him back, he would have soon got bored of family life again, and the next time a young pretty girl was impressed with his flash car or expensive suit, that would have been it.

I didn't want that life. I didn't want to walk on eggshells because I'd spent too much money on a block of cheddar, waiting for him to leave us again. I didn't want that for me, or my kids. I decided I'd rather be alone and safe than open us up to getting hurt again by the one man who should have done nothing but love and protect us. We were worth more.

# CHAPTER FOUR

* * * * * * * * * * * * * * * * * * * * * * * * *

# A SWIPE IN THE RIGHT
# DIRECTION

The following year, with the very few remaining friends I had still blissful in their happy marriages, and with me having no family support and still dealing with Mark popping in and out when he fancied, I realised I was as lonely as fuck. Mark was a wanker, but I knew I had to stop thinking that all men were the same, so I joined a dating site called Love Finder. I had to pay a fee, but I'd read some grim tales online about the kind of men who signed up to dating sites and apps for free and just spent their weekends spreading the love – and STDs – to various vulnerable women. If a man was serious about finding love then maybe he'd pay a subscription fee ... then again he may just be another rich twat like Mark, but all the same I just felt a bit better about it.

After a couple of disastrous dates where I had to text my friend Janey from playgroup and get her to fake-call a child emergency so I could urgently leave, I met Jamie. He had only joined the dating site the day before we began speaking, and he seemed reasonably decent. His picture showed a kind face with sparkling blue eyes and an endearingly self-conscious smile. His profile's opening line – an observation about how he wasn't sure if he was doing this properly since, as a law-abiding citizen, he wasn't actually looking for 'a partner in crime' – actually made me snort when I read it, so I messaged him immediately. He wasn't sleazy or pushy like the others, and he didn't make any jokes that made me cringe so much I wanted to eat my own foot.

We met at a pizza restaurant in town. I knew it would be busy, so it wouldn't be obvious to the world that we were strangers from an internet dating site, on a first date. When I saw him waiting outside, I got butterflies in my tummy and a fizz in my throat. He was really pretty; I don't know if that's the right word to use for a man, but that's how I best describe him – his features were just pretty to look at. He was tall with dark hair that had a slight wave to it. He had little lines at the sides of his eyes, from his age, I imagine, but I remember them being visible because they were lighter than the rest of his face which had a lovely olive tan – and I liked that instantly because the lines were there when he smiled, such a beautiful genuine smile. He also had the most piercing blue eyes, like little twinkling crystals – his profile picture hadn't even nearly done him justice.

He leant in to peck me on the cheek and he had that just-showered freshness to him. He'd dressed up but not too much, and he looked cool and casual in dark jeans, a khaki shirt with the sleeves rolled halfway up his toned forearms, and a pair of brown suede Adidas trainers. Trying to make conversation, I awkwardly commented on how nice his unusual shoes were and he gave me a cheeky smirk and said, 'Limited edition Specials. I am a bit of a trainer freak,' which made me giggle. I was relieved that I'd pitched it right in a denim dress and old-school Vans. Jamie's first impression said 'I take care of myself and I'm a grown-up, but I don't take myself too seriously'. I liked that. I *really* liked that.

It was a warm summer evening so we'd sat outside at one of the pavement tables and immediately settled into a rhythm of easy conversation. He was charming without even a hint of arrogance, and funny, seemingly without trying to be. To my surprise, so was I. I made him laugh repeatedly and I found that I had things to say that weren't about the school's latest SATs scores or today's episode of *Hey Duggee*. I realised that not only did I like him, I liked me too.

The waitress had to come to our table three times before we'd stopped talking for long enough to decide what we wanted to eat. The way he bit his lip in concentration when perusing the menu made me melt and I considered sending her away yet again. By the time the pizza arrived I'd found out all about his younger days living in Canterbury, his favourite football team (Arsenal, which was a shame but I guess it's good to know the flaws early on) and his boring-but-pays-the-bills job.

We spoke about our kids, too, of course (he had two of his own, Ruby – who is a year older than Rex, and Will, who is the same age as Art), but he was genuinely interested in me – in my thoughts and opinions, what I wanted from the world, without being over the top. It made me see that it had been years since anyone had paid any attention to me. Mark never asked me how I was, or what I wanted. And to be honest, I didn't even know what I wanted out of life any more. Once upon a time I'd had a passion, a dream, but now, it was clear, I had totally forgotten who I was or what my hopes and ambitions were. It was a question that when Jamie asked, not even I could answer – and it was the first time I felt really sad about that.

I remembered that I went to the toilet then to give myself a pep talk and avoid the date turning downbeat. When I got back, we'd both had the chance to realise that now it was dark it was cold too. I thought I'd messed it up – perhaps I'd been even more miserable than I'd realised – and was convinced that he was going to use the cold as an excuse to wrap things up there and then, but he turned to me and said in his lovely Kent accent, 'Do you fancy heading inside to split a tiramisu and have a negroni for the road?' which immediately gave me a flutter of butterflies in my belly.

The night ended with another kiss on the cheek – although this time he lingered slightly and aimed it close enough to the corner of my mouth to make my stomach flip again – and a flood of relief that the date had been worth selling half my wardrobe on eBay to pay for a sitter for the night. I remember that it only dawned on me on my way home that I hadn't even noticed, let alone minded, that he'd held the door to the pizza place open for me as we'd left. I was just concentrating on making sure that we planned a second date. That made me feel good, that being with him had stopped me thinking of shit things.

The feelings I had for Jamie worried me. They came so quickly, and they were fierce – as soon as I left him that night, I missed him and I didn't like it. Being alone again gave me time to overthink things and I was adamant that I wasn't ever going to put myself in a position again where I could get damaged or hurt. Where someone could make me suffer again, which in turn would mean my babies would suffer.

I spent the next few weeks being a total moron, waiting days before I returned his texts or calls, cancelling dates at the last minute and then repeatedly trying to call it all off because I'd convinced myself it was too good to be true. But Jamie kept coming back. It took me a while to realise that actually I wasn't 'jumping in' like I'd convinced myself; I had in fact spent a shitload of money that I didn't have on therapy to get here, and so I decided life was too short. Jamie made me feel things I'd never felt before – not even when I first met Mark – so I decided to give him a chance, and he hasn't let me down yet.

As we got to know each other more and more, Jamie opened up about his situation with his ex, Laura. I could tell that it was hard for him to talk about and it felt like an important step for us. They'd also split up when Laura was pregnant with Ruby, but, unlike Mark, Jamie didn't abandon them, and he doesn't ever speak badly of her.

He told me Laura had struggled to be a mum after having their first baby, Will, and her family lived miles away in Cornwall. I understood immediately how lonely she must have felt, being a young mum with no family nearby. But she became really unwell a few years after Will was born, to the point that her mental health went into crisis. She was hospitalised and put on a cocktail of prescribed medication, which she was still taking when she fell pregnant with Ruby.

Laura became even more anxious about her health with the new baby arriving and wanted to return to her family in Cornwall. Jamie resisted – he'd begun to see that there was more wrong with their relationship than its location – and after weeks of talking it over, they realised it would be the hardest but best thing for everyone if they split. They just weren't in love any more.

Jamie is an amazing dad, and when Will and Ruby are with us it's easy to see how torn they are when it comes to the time to leave; keen to get back to their mum but reluctant to leave their dad behind. They idolise him so much. The long drive to meet Laura's parents halfway is always difficult as we prepare ourselves for the goodbyes. More often than not, Jamie has to talk them round in the car park of the motorway services and remind them how much their mummy will have missed them and how excited she will be to see them. It's devastating to watch and I always try to put myself in Jamie's shoes and imagine how I'd feel if this was the set-up me and Mark had agreed upon. Mark's unbearably difficult, but at least I get to see my children every day. During these moments, I wish that I could do something to make things easier on them all.

Speaking of exes and difficult relationships, not long after mine and Jamie's pizza date, it started to become clear that Mark was unhappy with Sofia. I found it weird that despite them getting engaged within months of meeting there was never a mention of a wedding. Then, after another couple of months, when Jamie and I were becoming more serious, I eventually plucked up the courage and told Mark that I had met someone else. He broke. He begged me to try again with him. He promised he would be faithful, asked me to go to marriage counselling and said we shouldn't give up on our relationship and destroy our kids' worlds. He told me he had never been happy with Sofia, not 'properly' and that she was never going to be me. The irony of his speech left me flabbergasted as he'd sat on the sofa, covered in snot, begging and sobbing for me to give our marriage another chance.

It took me straight back to that dreadful evening when I had sat on that exact same spot on that exact same sofa and said those exact same words to him. Only he had walked out, abandoning me when I'd been heavily pregnant and broken-hearted. And he hadn't given a fuck about my pain – or our children's.

As much as I want to be able to say I took pleasure in turning down his offer, I just didn't. I felt genuinely sad that he had thrown away his entire family to spend his afternoons fucking a woman he didn't even love.

It made me realise that in life some people will never settle down; they will never be happy with what they have. No matter how good things are, they don't feel content. They always chase something bigger, better. They are always looking for something else, something more, only in reality that just isn't there, because any relationship faces problems. And some people, like Mark, don't fight to get back what they once had – instead they give up, they move on, looking for something different, something new and exciting, leaving a trail of destruction behind them. And ultimately, the person they hurt the most is themselves.

Mark didn't make things easy after I told him about Jamie. He began demanding to see the kids more, requesting overnight stays, which he hadn't ever wanted to do previously, only to let them down at the last minute as they were excitedly sat in the lounge window with their coats on. I'd get letters from the mortgage company saying we had defaulted on payments. He would harass me constantly about pointless things and whenever I tried to fight my corner, I would receive a barrage of abuse where I was reminded that I lived in 'his house'.

Jamie always told me not to react, to 'bite my tongue' to the point that those three words have become a bit of a standing joke between the two of us, mainly because I am so shit at doing it. Ultimately, we both knew Mark was after a reaction from me and I had to ignore it as much as I could. So, I stopped giving him the attention he craved. I ignored his relentless, demanding voicemails and texts, and I didn't react when he cancelled on the kids or dropped them back a day early pretending he'd been 'called into the office'. But as things with me and Jamie got ever more serious, and I saw what a healthy relationship looked like, I was just sick of Mark's constant game-playing and manipulation. I'd had enough and something had to change …

One Sunday after we had dropped Jamie's kids back to the Bristol services then made the long journey back home, I realised that Jamie was broken too. He had his head slightly turned towards the driver's side window to try to hide the tears running down his cheeks, and I had to try to do something.

'Jamie, listen. I know it's hard, I can't imagine, but the next visit will come round before you know it and—'

He quietened me with a flash of his brave face and a gentle squeeze of my thigh. 'I know, Jo, I know. I just don't understand why this isn't getting easier. I'm missing so much and I … ' he trailed off as tears threatened again.

'It will. You're still finding your way and it was always going to be difficult, shifting your life from what you thought it would be to what it is. It's hard when things are taken out of your control, time heals and … ' I quietened myself that time; my platitudes wouldn't help.

We settled back into silence and I stared out of the window as we drove past town after town, and I began to think about the people who called these places home and then about how home was actually more than just a place, it was people.

Canterbury was only my home because that was where Mark had wanted us to be; now my home was where my children, and Jamie, and his children were. By that measure, Jamie was never really 'at home', with his children living hundreds of miles away. And really, Canterbury itself held nothing for either of us any more. Granted, Jamie's mum, Pat, was there, and we loved her and relied on her a lot – not least for sleepovers for my three when Jamie and I made the journey halfway to Cornwall to take his kids home – but she hated seeing him wrenched from his children as much as I did, and I knew she'd have given anything for him to see them more.

An idea started to form.

As we hit the Surrey hills, I began to search for available jobs for Jamie and for houses close to where his kids lived that we could rent together – we were more than ready to live together and would have been by now if it wasn't for Mark. It was doable, totally. I bookmarked everything and tried to put a lid on my excitement until we got back 'home'; this wasn't a conversation to have while driving seventy miles per hour down the M25 while trying not to cry.

We got home and he was really withdrawn, pretending he was OK. I suggested getting a takeaway, but he said he was happy to cook us something. I assumed he was looking for something to keep him busy so I replied to him saying we had loads to do so it would be easier to order a curry. I saw his face look instantly confused by my 'loads to do' comment and when he asked what, I told him I wanted him to look at some properties I had favourited, give me the OK on the Airbnb I had chosen for the following weekend so we could view the houses, and sign himself up to Indeed for job alerts.

He looked totally confused by then and when he asked what I was talking about, I burst with excitement and practically screamed, 'We're moving, to Cornwall. There is nothing here for us any more, and I prefer you when you're hanging out with your kids.' After a mild flashback of Mark simply *telling* me where we were going to be living, I tempered my earlier statement with, 'If you want to, that is. We should definitely talk about it as a possibility at least, and a weekend away next weekend to think it all through and weigh up our options would be no bad thing. I could do with some sea air.' I giggled nervously at my last comment and met Jamie's eyes to try to gauge his reaction.

He still looked confused. So I blathered on and took my phone out to show him the available properties (including the one we have just paid a deposit on!), and the job vacancies that were similar to what he was already doing. I think that was the moment he knew I was serious. I think it was the moment I really knew I was too – I was never this decisive and I'd surprised myself.

His confused face turned interested, then hopeful, before breaking out into full-blown excitement. He needed to be with his children. He had a little cry, which he tried to hide again, but this time it was a happy cry, where he affectionately pushed his forehead into mine and just repeated the words 'Thank you, baby' over and over again.

That night, we ordered curry and revelled in our own private excitement. Since Belle was staying over with a friend, and Art and Rex were at Pat's for the night, we had time to think it through before broaching the subject with them the next day. I'd prepared a whole speech. For me there was no downside, I didn't really have any proper friends, not ride or die friends, I had no job to worry about. The only thing that concerned me was Belle's reaction and the impact the move would have on her – she's fifteen and I was planning on uprooting her whole life right before her GCSEs – but we talked it all through and we all felt good about the outcome. She loves Will and Ruby and she loves Jamie, and I'd never been more proud of her than when I saw her taking in his hopeful face and declaring herself on board. Later, I overheard her telling her best friend Suze about the hot Cornish surfers she'd be hanging out with and I realised her decision wasn't entirely selfless.

It was agreed. We are taking the leap and moving to Cornwall to be closer to his kids, and embracing the fresh start we both craved. We are swapping city life for the seaside, our crazy-busy for quiet and relaxation (well, maybe not 'quiet' with five children in and out on different days, but this is my book, I can dream). I'm scared but excited and I think it will be the making of us going forward ... as a family.

So now, we're leaving our leafy townhouse in Canterbury – Jamie packed up his flat and moved out a few weeks early, in with us, to facilitate a quick sale above asking price – and renting for six months to begin with, to get a feel for the area.

We've found a huge house to rent right by the beach, with five bedrooms, a conservatory and a summer house. It's a stunning home and I know it will be perfect for us. The terms of my divorce from Mark stated that when we did sell, or if he decided to buy me out, I would receive half of the equity from the sale. Along with the profits from Jamie's flat, we had a decent pot of cash to start our new lives with. Jamie's new company were very keen to have him on board so the salary ended up being more than we'd dared hope for, but even so, the monthly rent payments still felt like a bit of a splurge. It wasn't long ago that I couldn't afford school meals for my children so I was uneasy, but Jamie reasoned that it was just for six months, and we wanted to make sure that the transition was as smooth as possible for all the children. Having space felt like a key part of that, especially for the older ones.

\*

Fast-forward eight weeks and I'm sat in the passenger seat as Jamie drives the five of us down the motorway in convoy with the removal vans. We have just said a tearful goodbye to Jamie's mum, who, it turns out, has a brave face the exact same as Jamie's, and I can tell that we're all dealing with a multitude of emotions as we head towards our new life.

In the end, the plans for the move came together very quickly. Pat displayed nothing but enthusiasm for us, despite what we knew she was feeling inside, Laura was all for it, and Mark, of course, was dead against it. Despite that, the practicalities actually went so smoothly that I couldn't help but take it as a sign that we were making the right decision.

'Mum?' Art calls from his position squished between his brother and sister. 'Are we going to the beach when we get there? I don't know where my trunks are.'

'We might have a few things to do first off, sweetheart, but we'll see what we can do tomorrow.'

'Urgh, Art.' Belle rolls her eyes, trying to play the grown-up. 'We've got a million things to do; we're *not* going to be able to go to the beach for weeks. It's not even summer yet!'

His face drops, never getting used to his big sister's knack of cutting him down, but I twist round and shoot him a wink that puts the smile back on his face. I tell Belle that although it's only April it's always summer in Cornwall and will be boiling hot on our arrival and she pipes up 'Really?'. I giggle and say 'No' and she immediately realises I'm winding her up as payback on behalf of Art.

'Anyway, Art,' Jamie chimes in, 'first things first: we have to hold the race for the bedrooms. Remember there's seven of us but only five bedrooms. Me and your mum have agreed to share but that still means that one of you is outside. I can't wait to see who it will be!'

Even Belle laughs, despite herself, while Art runs with the thought and starts imagining the various ways that such a scene might play out – he's convinced that it'll be Ruby in the garden. Belle looks up from her phone, where she's no doubt been constantly texting her friends since their goodbye last night, and ventures that Rex will be the one, and Rex, for no reason other than that she's given his name, becomes adamant that Belle will be outside. The reality is no one is outside as the attic has been converted, meaning we have a sixth bedroom, but Jamie loves to wind them up and Belle loves playing along.

I sit back and listen to the three of them talk about life with their new brother and sister, in their new home, going to their new schools and I'm thrilled that excitement has become the overriding emotion.

Now, we can concentrate on the seven of us becoming a blended family under one roof. And, as exciting as that seems, I am also shitting bricks about it.

# CHAPTER FIVE

......................

# FINDING OUR FEET

*Monday*

They say moving house is one of the most stressful things alongside death and divorce. They're right, whoever 'they' are.

We've been in the house eighteen days.

Jesus, it's hard enough moving towns let alone halfway across the country. Despite the light-hearted joking in the car, the boys actually ended up in a full-blown punch-up when we were picking bedrooms, and Belle – who has always moaned that we don't live near to the sea – has decided, now that it's on our doorstep, she 'hates the beach' because the sand grains getting everywhere send her over the edge. Brilliant.

While Belle and Art continue to bicker over something and nothing, I take a moment to let this new life and home sink in. The house is bigger than I remembered it from our visit that weekend a couple of months ago. It's beautiful and sits on a private lane off a main street, which leads down to a huge beach with golden sand. It's the biggest beach in our town and it has kayaks and pedalos and deckchairs for hire in the summer. The front is lined with beach huts with pastel-coloured doors, and there are seasonal huts that sell fast food and ice cream. It's not tacky like some beach resorts I went to as a kid, but tourists obviously play a big part in the industry here. As you walk down the hill, before you turn left to the beach or right into town, there's a row of shops that overlook the beach, with a café, a little hairdressers and a small shop that sells essentials. It's a pretty place; there are flowerbeds dotted around the streets that are maintained by local volunteers and the shops have huge, trailing, colourful hanging baskets outside of them.

The last people to live in this house before us were the original owners and you can see they loved this home so much. The landlord told Jamie they bought it over forty-two years ago and raised their own children here. It's a Victorian property with huge high ceilings and tall sash windows. There's the large attic room, four doubles on the main floor and one bedroom with an en-suite on the ground floor, which I imagine has been added on since the house was built. There's the summer house in the garden, which is currently storing all my furniture and bits and bobs. It has an en-suite and will be perfect for guests once we get it sorted. There are fitted solid oak floors downstairs and the carpets are new throughout the upstairs, cream and thick – the same as the ones Mark had in his first apartment, which makes me roll my eyes. The walls have been painted a sandstone colour throughout. Everything you look at is the best quality possible – from the door handles to the white goods. I worried it may be dated or shabby due to it being in the same family for so long but it's clear they've always spent money on it and kept it modern. I panicked about renting because it's not something I've ever done with the children, but it feels like home, a beautiful home. Our family home, together.

I feel so lucky and so happy, but a part of me, buried deep inside, can't help thinking, What if it all goes wrong?

I push the thought away, determined not to let any of my old anxieties cloud our new life here. I watch the way Jamie is with my kids and I know he genuinely loves them and enjoys their company. He makes the effort to spend time individually with all three, talking about their interests, helping them do stuff or just sitting on the sofa, snuggled up to them, watching what they want to watch on the telly. They haven't ever had that; even when Mark lived with us, it was always me that they wanted, and they never sought their dad out to ask him a question or spend time with him. The more I watch Jamie so naturally enjoying playing a parenting role, with such ease, it makes me wonder if being a dad was something Mark always knew deep down he didn't want. Still, it's made me grateful for now – for what we have and who we are, and that's something I don't ever want to change.

The majority of our lives are now unpacked and out of boxes. Jamie is well settled in his new job and he seems to like it a lot. The two eldest have started school; Art is finishing his last few months of primary at the local school just round the corner – it's a lot smaller than his last school but it's nice and there doesn't seem to be that 'cliquey playground vibe' I experienced in Canterbury.

Rex has been accepted to start there in September in reception, theoretically he could have started last year but I held him back so rather than him being one of the youngest he would be one of the eldest. People often ask me why I decided to do that and the real answer is I'm not sure, but mainly I think, it's because I know he's my last and I wanted to hold on to him that little bit longer. Belle has begun at the comprehensive school, which is a fifteen-minute bus ride away. They both seem to have enjoyed the first week. Belle has spent her evenings on FaceTime to her friends back home, which has left me riddled with guilt that I've ruined her teenage years, but she assures me she's OK and is still happy we moved. I'm so proud of her for being the way she is. It's possibly the worst age for a child to be uprooted – and we did talk about waiting another year and getting her GCSEs out of the way – but her teachers assured me she will get good grades and the reality is I think she would have been more damaged staying around her dad for a longer period of time.

All the kids seem happy, to be fair, and they also seem a lot closer since we moved. I feel less stressed too. We have a laugh before we go to school in the mornings, and I've noticed how quickly they're growing up by the things they come out with. This morning I called the doctors to make an appointment and, when I ended the call, I remarked about how miserable the receptionist was. Belle said I shouldn't be so harsh and maybe she was just having a bad day. I told her I had spoken to her three times now and she was miserable on every call and then Art came out with, 'Maybe every time you call up its her time of the month. I've learned that can do funny things to girls and ladies.' Belle told him to shut up and he said, 'It does to you, Belle. I always know when it's your time because you scream at everyone and eat all the chocolate.' We all cried with laughter, Belle included – and it reminded me that these babies of mine are no longer babies.

Mark hasn't called or texted them – not once – and the kids haven't mentioned him. I haven't bothered getting them to attempt to contact him either. When we decided to make the move down here, I knew I had to tell Mark, and I arranged to meet him in a pub close to the house. He walked in with a huge bouquet of yellow roses, beautifully wrapped. I could tell they were expensive – like the flowers he used to present me with weekly at the start, the flowers I imagine he presented Sofia with when I was carrying his child and he was seeing her, flowers once upon a time I felt so lucky to be given, but flowers now that when he walked into the pub carrying them they made me want to vomit. I genuinely believe that he thought I was going to say I wanted us to try again. When I told him we were moving away to give the kids a fresh start, he burst into tears and my heart genuinely hurt for him ... until he stormed out of the pub just minutes later (taking his expensive flowers with him) and told me, loud enough for the rest of the establishment to hear, that I could 'go fuck myself'.

I tried to call him the next day but he didn't answer. I informed the kids' schools that I wanted to move them and they contacted him to gain consent, which weirdly he gave, yet he never had a conversation with me about it after that night when he stormed out of the pub. I'd tried to talk to him like an adult, and as the other parent to the children we shared, but I was done with his game-playing and I was done chasing him. He had been the one to destroy our family in the first place and this move was the first step in putting us all back together.

I met a lady the other day when I popped into the café down the road. Rex and I often call into it on the way back from the school run in the morning and it's a really beautiful place, only small but done out in a nautical theme with a mix of blues, reds and whites and little sailboat ornaments dotted about the place.

Outside they have a stand, which sells buckets, spades, crabbing lines and bait. Inside it smells of fresh bread and hot coffee, and they serve the best home-made carrot cake. They have a play corner where Rex spends his time chalking on the blackboard on the wall, building tall towers out of the blocks or cooking up a storm with the wooden food in the play kitchen while I sit, sipping coffee and watching the world go by through the window for half an hour.

The lady was already there when I walked in, stood at the counter, chatting to the girl making her coffee, and I recognised her from the playground at Art's school. Her jacket was hung over a chair at one of the small tables, and I thought how nice it would be to have a new friend to go with my new life, so, as Rex headed to the play corner, I bit the bullet and sat at the empty table next to where her coat was reserving her space.

I heard her ask the girl where Lou was, who I assumed was the owner. The young girl serving explained that Lou had fallen and fractured her wrist so was unable to drive in, or do much at all really, and she would be covering most shifts until Lou was back. The lady's little boy, who looked slightly younger than Rex, walked over to play with him in the corner, she followed, saw me sat smiling at the boys and said, 'Hi, is he yours? He's adorable,' before introducing herself as Jen, a midwife with three sons of her own, and sitting down at her table. Jen was instantly warm and friendly and I liked her immediately. Her little boy Jack had just turned four.

'A job as a midwife and three sons? You must be exhausted!' I said to her, with what I hoped came across as admiration.

'Oh, absolutely! I can barely remember what it's like to be asleep, and I haven't been more than three feet away from a child at any point in the last five years, but—' at this point her little one ran over and squished the half-eaten soggy biscuit he'd been munching on into her hand before dashing away again. Jen rolled her eyes and, gesturing towards her hand, said, 'It's worth it for these perks, though, right?'

We giggled like old friends and, as we chatted more, I found out that she was six years younger than me, and when I looked at her I felt a bit shit about myself. She seemed so young and cool, with highlighted hair with a pastel-pink shade running through it, and was wearing a dungaree dress with Converse boots. She had accessorised her look with bangles and matched a smear of red lipstick to a scarlet head scarf she had tied in a funky knot. I felt a bit envious of her look; it was one of those where it appeared to be thrown together, but it worked well and she had the confidence to pull it off.

It made me realise how bad I looked. I hadn't even changed out of the vest top I had slept in the night before, and rather than bothering to put a bra on, I'd just thrown a jumper over me instead, which I now noticed had a dodgy orange stain on the front. Probably Bolognese, which I hadn't cooked for over a fortnight, which meant my jumper hadn't been washed since then – ideal. My hair was stacked on top of my head in a crocodile clip and I was pretty sure my leggings were so old they were now see-through from the back.

I wondered right then if Jamie ever noticed other women, other mums, who seemed to just have it together way more than I did. I then felt that pain, the quick stab of 'what if?' and the panic that hits your chest. What if he did notice other women? What if one made a pass at him? What if he declined her advances but then came home and I looked like shit? What if he then ended up having a full-blown affair and ripping my heart out just like Mark did . . . ?

I pulled myself back to reality and felt a quick surge of hatred for Mark for making me question everything and everyone because of what he'd done. I was dressed like this because we'd moved house, we were unpacking and constantly busy – it would be pointless me dressing up with a full face of make-up. And actually, when Jamie got in from work, he would wrap his arms around my waist, pick me up and kiss me a hundred times no matter how I looked or what I was wearing. He saw me, as a whole – not just the Bolognese stain.

I brushed aside my anxieties and carried on chatting to Jen. She told me her two youngest sons are from her current marriage but that she has an older son who is twelve who she had with her previous partner. She told me their separation was like a scene from *EastEnders* and, before I could join in and top her story with mine, she told me he'd left home as normal one Wednesday morning to go to work – kissing her and their son goodbye – and he'd never returned. She'd called the police and reported him as a missing person and his friends and family had all gone out looking for him in a frantic state. It turned out he'd been shagging a neighbour and had moved in with her a few streets away.

'He *never* came back to the house, not to collect over a decade's worth of belongings, and not to wish his son a happy birthday when he turned three a few days later. It very nearly destroyed me completely, but I picked myself up, and two years later I met the man who would become my husband. My ex then agreed to me changing our son's surname, if I'd relieve him of all his parental responsibilities. Oh god, am I oversharing? We've only just met, sorry if it's TMI!'

'Not at all! What a bastard!' was my response. 'I'm going through similar with my ex and it's soul-destroying that when you look at your babies and see all their qualities, and you feel that love, that they don't feel it too. That they've just given it all up.'

'I don't see it like that,' she told me. Although her ex was a total fuckwit, she felt that it was for the best that at least he could hold his hands up and admit he didn't want to be a father or have any involvement in their son's life. And because of that, her new husband has taken on the role of dad and everyone was fine and happy with that.

I realised that, actually, if Mark had just done the same and admitted that he didn't want that involvement, and had just been honest about the fact he no longer wanted to be a father to our children, things would have been far easier. Yes, it would have been devastating at first, but not as devastating as him continually coming in and out of their lives – appearing too much one minute then not at all the next. It's like a wound on your knuckle that keeps opening up – one that can't heal because every time it starts to get better, you bend your finger and it breaks open all over again.

After chatting with Jen, Rex and I began dawdling up the hill towards home and he asked me what a bastard was. I almost choked on fresh air and he said, 'I heard you say bastard to Jack's mummy.' Brilliant. I told him it was an 'adult word' and that he couldn't use it until he was older. Hopefully that would put him off.

After the chat I'd had with Jen, I decided that I really felt different about my reasons for not encouraging the children to call Mark; they had enough love in their lives to not be missing out on what Mark could offer, and let's face it, they were worth more than that. I also decided to go and see a local solicitor about the house sale. Mark had decided that he couldn't in fact afford to buy me out so he put the house on the market and said I would receive £150,000 once it sold. But then I'd seen it for sale at a price that was much higher than I'd expected, going off my share, even taking into consideration the deductions, and I decided that, actually, we weren't going to settle for any less than what we were entitled to, even if it did mean dragging it all out for longer. My name was still on the deeds and Mark hadn't paid me a penny yet and wouldn't until the house sale went through. I might have agreed to accept his previous offer, but it wasn't in any way fair.

I had given a third of my life to turning that house into a home, after giving up my career to dedicate myself to my husband, who thought it was acceptable to shit all over me then try to rip me off. Fuck that, fuck him. The solicitor said I was entitled to at least half, being around £270,000 rather than £150,000. Part of me felt guilty – like it wasn't my money as I hadn't earned it – but then reality struck, and it dawned on me that I couldn't have earned anything because I was so busy raising the children that Mark had desperately wanted. And every time I'd mentioned going back to uni to complete my nursing training and qualify, he had kiboshed the idea, making me feel like I was stupid for even bringing it up.

What I had done was work twenty-four hours a day for him and our children. I had cooked, cleaned and driven myself into the ground to keep everyone else happy.

This money was what I was entitled to – this was what was fair.

And Mark could fucking well learn to deal with it.

# CHAPTER SIX

## SECOND CHANCES

*Friday*

Jamie's children are coming over to stay with us for the first time this coming weekend. Belle and Ruby have their own rooms but Belle has a double bed and Ruby has asked to sleep in with her for the first night. Belle was fine with the idea – she adores Ruby and always refers to her and Will as her brother and sister, exactly the same way she would about Art and Rex, which is such a relief for me and Jamie. Will is up in the attic with Art, and the boys are excited about sharing a room. They're the same age, and they get on so well. Rex has his own room. Theoretically they could all have their own rooms but the boys like sharing and I'm happy they do.

I've bought both Will and Ruby clothes to keep here; when we were in Canterbury Laura would send their clothes up for weekends but I'm hoping we'll be having them a lot more now we're closer to them and I want them to feel like this is their home rather than that they're just 'staying at Dad's'.

I've spent this week trying to personalise the rooms too with cute signs with their names on their bedroom doors.

I can't bear the idea of them walking into a house that feels like my kids' home more than theirs and I'm trying my best to make it feel like a home they can relax in.

I can tell Jamie thinks I overthink it all. Every time I try to speak to him, he just kisses my forehead and says, 'Babe, it will be fine.' But I don't think men think about stuff like that; they don't view it from a child's perspective – they see it so black and white and think their kids will too ... anyway, I have tried to make it feel like their home, and I hope that they like it here. Being a stepmum, I've decided, is one of the toughest jobs in the world.

It's amazing now that Jamie has weekends off work. When we lived in Canterbury his job would get so busy at times he would have no option but to go into the office on weekends, but he's been assured by his bosses here that the weekend is for family time and that's something I know he's really pleased with. It will be lush to spend some time together, the seven of us, exploring the area.

I feel so happy that we've moved – like a weight's been lifted – and I'm excited for what's to come in our future.

Will and Ruby arrived at 5pm. Jamie wasn't back from work and when I answered the door and saw Laura there, I didn't really know what to do. Although I've heard so much about Jamie's ex, I haven't ever really spoken to her before, beyond saying a quick hello or a wave at the service station. Now was my chance for a proper chat, I guess.

'Hi guys!' I said to Will and Ruby. 'And Laura, it's so good to see you. How are you? Do you want to come in? Jamie isn't back yet but the kettle has just boiled if you fancy a coffee.'

'No, thanks,' Laura spat back at me, in front of the kids, as she looked me up and down in disgust.

This was not the reaction I had been expecting.

'Have a good weekend, kids. Hopefully your dad will be back at some point to actually spend a bit of time with you.'

I felt sick. Immediately sick. Both the kids fled into the house with their heads bowed and, as they got inside, they stood awkwardly behind the front door awaiting my instruction on what they should do next. This wasn't what I'd expected either, and it wasn't how I'd wanted their first day in our new home to be.

When we got inside, I bent down and removed Ruby's coat. Belle came down the stairs and immediately grabbed her and swung her round, kissing her neck and making her squeal. She then took her hand and ran up the stairs to show her the bedrooms. I felt really lucky, so lucky, that I have a teenage daughter who was there to make everything better without even knowing that's what she was doing. I told Will to help himself to any food and drink that he wanted, that this was his home.

As he walked up the stairs, he turned round and said, 'Sorry about Mum.'

I felt a lump in my throat. He was embarrassed, and upset – and I was gutted that at the age of eleven he was carrying that weight around where he was apologising for his mother's actions. I shrugged it off like I hadn't noticed and he gave me a smile before he ran upstairs. Within minutes I heard him and Art in a fit of laughter and despite Laura making me feel like crap, my heart soon felt full again. I had a feeling we were going to be OK.

Jamie got back from work with three carrier bags full of fish and chips and two bottles of red wine. I could tell he was buzzing. Seeing him so excited about spending the weekend with us all made me feel really happy. I didn't want to kill his mood but I had to tell him about how Laura had been. He didn't look surprised. He asked if I wanted him to speak to her, but I didn't. My anxiety couldn't cope with having to do another tense handover if Laura thought I was trying to cause issues. Jamie said he would speak to Will and Ruby and check they were both OK, and with that we got on with planning our amazing weekend together.

I had thought that Laura was cool with us moving nearby so I was a bit thrown by her reaction today. Maybe it was proving more difficult in reality. It wouldn't be easy for anyone to see their ex happily living with someone else and building a home together.

Perhaps it would just take her some time.

*

## Sunday

Jamie and Laura have had words. I went out this morning to get the umbrella out of the car and found a bag on the front doorstep full of Will and Ruby's school uniforms.

Jamie called her to find out what was going on and she told him that she'd made plans so he couldn't return the kids at 5pm as planned; instead he could take them to school in the morning – she had apparently emailed them to say Jamie and I would be doing more school runs now.

He explained he started work at 8am and I had to get Art to school then Rex to pre-school fifteen minutes later.

She responded with 'It's called being a father, Jamie – something you have apparently decided you now want' and hung the phone up on him.

I reassured him it was fine. We would manage. I had no idea how, but I would figure it out. Will and Ruby were chuffed to bits that they were sleeping over again, and as much as it would make things a bit more stressful in the morning, we had moved here to spend more time with them and an en masse school run, complete with hastily eaten bowls of cornflakes and missing reading books, could only help them to feel that we were all one big family. I never want them to feel they are a burden when they are here.

I could see Jamie was angry and upset. He kept apologising to me for the way Laura was being, and I kept reassuring him that it was fine. He had taken my three kids on full-time; the least I could do was take his to school one morning!

But despite my reassurances to Jamie, it made me realise how hard it was going to be raising all these kids together as a blended family. Questioning and panicking and overthinking every decision or choice we make as parents. If these were all our kids together, we would just get on with it. But they aren't and so we have to try our hardest to make sure they grow up having the best childhoods possible. That they feel loved and included – no matter what is going on behind the scenes.

*

## Monday

Fuck me – that was a stressful morning. I decided that in order to get everyone to school on time, I needed to pull up outside Art's school at 8.45am. Theoretically he doesn't start until 8.55am but he said he would jump out and read his book in the playground. I felt a stab of parental guilt at leaving him, but Ruby and Will need to be at their school at 8.55, which is a ten-minute drive away, and then I'd have to circle back to Art's school to drop Rex off for pre-school, which starts at 9.10am. I got stuck in the school-run traffic so got them there at 8.57. Parking was an absolute twat, and while Will jumped out and ran ahead, by the time we pulled up, got out and I'd walked Ruby into class while attempting to restrain Rex, who was losing his mind because he wanted to get to his pre-school, it had just gone 9am.

Ruby's class teacher said I had just made it but if we were going to be 'late like this again' I would need to sign her in at reception. Another stab of parental guilt – and then the panic hit me that the teachers would be sat in the staff room at lunchtime slagging off the 'new disorganised stepmum'. I wondered if they knew Laura and if they'd tell her I was late today. My head was swimming with the 'what ifs?', and I was turning such stupid minor things into first-world problems.

I went to give Ruby a kiss goodbye and she got really teary, telling me she didn't want me to go and gripping me round the neck. I didn't know that she had issues with being left at school so I didn't know what to do. I had that immediate feeling of upset watching her big eyes well up.

Her teacher looked surprised, though, and asked Ruby if she was OK – it turns out that this wasn't normal for her – and after a while of unsuccessfully trying to distract her, she mouthed the words 'I think you'd better just go' while she held her so she couldn't run after me. The majority of me felt nothing but guilt that she was in this state, but there was a small part of me that felt relieved, and honoured, that she loved me enough to want to be with me, and then I felt guilty for feeling that.

I then had the issue of removing Rex, who by this point had helpfully pulled up a chair at one of the tables in Ruby's class and was practising letters with his new mates. As I tried to hold his hand to leave, he decided to begin wailing at the same pitch as Ruby. This is totally unlike Rex, he rarely has tantrums – let alone ones to this extreme – so I was totally out of my comfort zone. He began screaming the words 'NO MUMMY, NO MUMMY', like I was surgically removing a tooth without anaesthetic. I had no choice but to do a double-armed restraint to remove him from the classroom, while the teacher was doing the same to Ruby who was now crying so hard that there were full choking sobs. I now had the added guilt that holding him back a school year would cause him lifelong issues.

I could feel a lump forming in my throat, I was stress sweating and wondering how the fuck things were this bad before 9.15 in the morning.

As soon as I got to the car, Rex changed his entire personality, asked me to pass him his toy dinosaur, and announced he didn't actually want to go to pre-school now. But in we went, twenty-seven minutes late, Rex crying that he didn't want to be there, and right now I'm sat writing this in my new favourite café, alone, gorging on carrot cake, sipping a latte and using this book as some kind of therapy.

Despite the hectic school run today, all in all we've had the best weekend. On Saturday we went to the beach. It was really windy and still quite nippy, but we took buckets and caught baby crabs. I used to do it when we went on holiday down here when I was young. The trick is to find the huge rocks that are almost impossible to lift because of their weight, because they're wedged in the sand. As soon as you flip it over, there are baby crabs, tiny ones dancing about. Sometimes there are big ones, but the kids didn't like them.

I could tell Jamie had been quite impressed by my crab-catching skills, and I noticed how he does the same thing I do: that every now and then I could see he was just taking it all in. Us, being together, our kids getting on, and being in such a beautiful place – and I could see that he was happy. Maybe that's why we get these second chances, to appreciate everything that we once took for granted.

# CHAPTER SEVEN

## THE OTHER EX

### Tuesday

I called into the café this morning after a more prompt school run. There was a beautiful woman with wild red hair behind the counter today who I hadn't seen working there before. Just as I was about to go up and order, Jen walked in with Jack and offered to get me a coffee. She walked up to the counter as the pretty lady walked round to greet her. They embraced and she showed Jen her wrist, which I hadn't noticed until now was in plaster. The woman looked like she was pretending to be OK – I know from my own experience exactly what that looks like – and she was smiling and saying she could manage while Jen was telling her she should close the café if she couldn't get any staff to work. I gathered this must be Lou, the owner.

Jen said she would make our coffees and they started joking about how she would mess it up, and I felt like I was being a total pain, so I went over and said I was happy to just have a glass of water to save any hassle.

Jen introduced us and as I took in Lou's features more closely, I realised that she was absolutely beautiful. Her nose and cheeks were covered in soft freckles and she had the brightest blue eyes. They stood out against her skin, which was so pale it made her look like a china doll. She had no make-up on but her cheeks had a rosy pink flush like she had just come inside from a cold walk. She wore a long-sleeve white T-shirt, cropped navy chinos and gleaming white Converse boots. Here was another woman who looked like she'd thrown an outfit together with minimal effort but still looked amazing.

I noticed she was different to Jen, much quieter, and although she asked me question after question about me, she didn't freely offer up much information about herself.

Jen walked behind the counter and made a pot of tea for the three of us, which we shared over a freshly baked coffee and walnut cake that Lou told us had taken twice as long as usual to make.

Lou said the young girl who had been helping was sick, so she had to come in to cover for the day. It was clear she was struggling to do most things and she had another four weeks at least of being in plaster.

Jen and I cleared our cups and plates into the dishwasher, and Jen told Lou she would pop back in after the afternoon school run to help for an hour. Lou looked so relieved and thanked her for the offer.

Jen and I left the café together and sat on the wall overlooking the beach, while Jack ran round the beach, rolling in the sand and getting a bit too close to the waves.

I asked her what Lou's situation was and she told me that she was married to a local guy called David who seemed really nice, although she didn't know him that well. He owned a chain of solicitors and his firm specialised in family law. They had two boys: Harry, who was fourteen, and George, who was nine. They sounded like a perfect family.

Jen asked me what I did workwise, and I felt embarrassed suddenly. My dream, once upon a time, was to have a career just like hers – and I'd so nearly made it. I didn't tell her that though – I just said due to having Belle when I was young, I'd been a stay-at-home mum. I was bored now, though – with Rex being in pre-school and starting properly in September I do often wonder how I'm going to fill my days. It feels quite frightening to know that soon – for the first time in fifteen years – I won't have a sidekick around me, and I'm worried I'll be lonely. Then I worry what that says about me as a person, that I need my kids around me because I have nothing else in my life ...

I like Jen. She's fun. Her sense of humour is dry, and she makes me cry with laughter with her one-liners about the funniest things, and she giggles at herself. I love that about her. We've exchanged numbers and she said she would message me to meet up. I like feeling that I have a friend; it's something I'm not used to, but maybe now is the perfect time to start getting used to the idea.

\*

## *Thursday*

I got a job! My first job in over fifteen years!

I called into the café again this morning and Jen was behind the counter with Lou. I could see she had a stupid smile on her face, and when I said 'Whattttt?', with a bit of anxiety in my throat, she told me she had come up with a genius plan: Lou needs help in the mornings; she can be there to oversee and guide someone but due to her injury can't actually do a lot physically in the café, whereas I can.

I felt sick saying yes – I think it was a happy sick, a kind of nervous sick, but not a bad sick. With the kids now at school this is the perfect opportunity for me to do something for myself and I'm really looking forward to it! This has made me see that as much as I don't have the qualifications to work a demanding career, I can get a little job to tide me over, give me some spending money and a bit of independence – something I haven't had for such a long time.

\*

## *Friday*

Today was shit.

Jamie was home when Laura dropped the kids off, but in hindsight I'm not sure if it was worse that he was here. For some reason she seemed to be in a furious mood and she told him he was a shit father, in front of the kids on the doorstep. I was listening from the kitchen and my stomach was doing flips. She then said to Will, 'Why don't you ask your dad why he couldn't move here for us six years ago, yet now he's done it for three kids that aren't his?'

I saw Will bow his head and then I heard Jamie snap back at her, telling her she was being unfair and that it was uncalled for saying that to Will. Laura began shouting louder, saying he was a useless twat, and I could see both kids stood in the driveway, holding their bags like little rabbits in headlights. I felt so sick. I hated confrontation – it wasn't something I had ever been good at – but I couldn't let the kids listen to her spew any more hatred, so I opened the front door, acting like I was walking out to a scene from *The Waltons* and beamed, 'Hey kids, come in. Dinner's almost ready.'

Laura really lost it then. 'Oh, here she is, Little Miss Perfect. Parading around like she's got the perfect life when in reality she's nothing but a whore!'

I ignored her, as hard as it was not to scream back telling her to stop being a nasty bitch. Instead I ushered the kids inside and closed the door on the two other adults. I could feel tears stinging my eyes and a lump in my throat, and I could see Will and Ruby looking up at me for a reaction, any kind of reaction.

I smiled at them and shouted to Belle and Art to come down the stairs, and told them to take Ruby and Will up to play.

Belle saw my face and said, 'You OK, Mum? What's happened?'

I told her I was fine, but she wouldn't leave it and carried on saying, 'You're not. You're crying. What's happened?' Ruby was stood next to her, biting her lip and looking down at the kitchen tiles. I was feeling every emotion possible and I could feel my neck and chest burning where patches of my skin had turned scarlet, which they always did when I was anxious or upset.

My heart just ached that two innocent kids had witnessed something they shouldn't have. I was seething that their mother thought she could turn up at my home and abuse me, and I was so devastated that this was how it now was – conflict and hatred between us. We were adults who should be focusing on the children's needs, not dragging up old baggage and making relationship problems seem simpler than they were.

I almost begged Belle to take Ruby upstairs in my firmest voice as the row outside the house between Jamie and Laura was continuing and the vile language pouring out of Laura's mouth was worsening.

I was conscious Will's room overlooked the drive and he would no doubt hear what was being said, but I also realised that this wasn't OK and I snapped. I opened the front door, and calmly said, 'Jamie, inside'. He looked at me like he was in actual pain at what was happening. By now Laura was in a total state. She was crying so hard she was choking on her tears, and she kept saying 'Don't Jamie. Don't walk away from me!'

Part of me wanted to bring her in for a cup of tea to calm her down and the other part wanted to scream at her to never come near us again.

As Jamie was walking up the drive towards the house, she started screaming, a high-pitched, out of control scream. She then started hitting herself on the sides of her head. Slapping one minute and with a clenched fist the next.

Jamie turned around to go back to her, and I repeated, 'Jamie. In. Now.' I had no fucking clue what was going on. I know she's had problems in the past but I had no idea that her mental health was still so bad.

He came into the house and just shook his head repeatedly, like he was in shock. Meanwhile Laura was now holding her hand on her car horn while shouting all sorts of obscenities. Belle came to the top of the stairs and shouted, 'Mum. What the fuck is going on?', and I shouted at her to mind her language. The irony. She went back to her room and began blasting Little Mix and I heard thuds from dancing come through the ceiling where she was clearly trying her best to stop Ruby hearing her mum having a full breakdown on our drive.

'She's doing it again, on our driveway, in front of the kids,' I heard Jamie on the phone, but I had no idea who he was talking to. I was worried it was the police; even though Laura was behaving badly, I didn't want to get her into trouble.

'Pete, please just come over or I'll have to call the police and I really don't want the kids to see that,' Jamie said firmly, and I knew then who he was talking to. Pete was Laura's dad.

I feel devastated.

I didn't go to bed until 3am.

By the time Laura's dad came over to get her, she had already left, and so he came in and spoke with Jamie and me for over an hour. It turns out that they cover most of the childcare for Laura now and have done for quite some time. Until we moved here, the kids stayed with them most of the time rather than at Laura's, and Laura 'flits in and out' when it suits. Pete's mum died last year, she had a huge estate and left it to Pete, his wife and Laura and her sister. He thinks Laura inheriting so much money was the issue because she quit her job as a sales manager and suddenly had her days free to fill – which she ended up doing with bad decisions. I can't believe we didn't know about this before now and I find myself re-running conversations with Will and Ruby for clues that all wasn't as it seemed. I come up with nothing.

I can tell Pete is far from happy about the situation. He's worked hard all his life and at a time when he should be enjoying his retirement, he and his wife are practically raising their two grandchildren. After listening to everything Pete said, Jamie and I decided that the kids would be staying with us for now. Jamie explained that he wished for things to remain amicable but he was their dad and we had a home for them now where they would be a part of our family.

I think from Pete's reaction he was torn between being worried about delivering the news to his wife and daughter but also relieved – because raising two children is hard work for anyone, but especially retired grandparents in their late seventies.

When he left, Jamie broke down and kept apologising, but I told him he had nothing to be sorry about. He had taken on my children without question and it was now my turn to do the same. They were Jamie's children and they needed him, they needed us, and we are going to do all we can to make sure this is going to be OK.

*

### Saturday

Ruby woke up before all the others this morning. I snuggled her on the sofa with a blanket and made us a pot of tea to share. I gave her Belle's old cup and we sat on the sofa, cuddled up, dipping rich tea biscuits into our mugs. It took me back to the days after Mark left where I felt like I was drowning, and every morning Belle and I would sit under a blanket on this same sofa, drinking tea out of these matching mummy and baby cups, and I would look at her tiny hands clasped around the mug. I would study her perfect turned-up nose and her blonde ringlets that fell upon her face and just wonder if one day we'd be OK.

It made me wonder what was going on in Ruby's head, and so I asked if she was OK after last night. She told me she was, and that her mummy is busy most of the time so she stays with Grampy and Granny a lot. I asked if she likes sleeping there and she replied with the words 'Yes, but I like it here more'. And I knew then that we were going to be OK, no matter what. The kids feel safe here and that's really all that matters to me and Jamie.

I never anticipated how hard and heartbreaking being a step-family would be at times. I don't want 'yours and mine' or 'them and us' but you're just thrown together and really no one's got a clue how to do it right – you're just trying your best to get through while giving them the best upbringing with as few issues as possible.

I don't know what happens with the kids on Monday, or how I'm going to fit my new job in around them all, but I know that together we will make this work. Our little family is all that matters.

# CHAPTER EIGHT

## A DAY OF HIGHS AND LOWS

*Monday*
Well – I DID IT!!!!!! I worked my first day at the café and I bloody loved it ...

However, the day started out beyond shit. With my new job at the coffee shop imminent, I'd managed to arrange for Rex to start breakfast club, which, given Laura's breakdown on Friday, turned out to be one of the best decisions I've ever made.

But when we got to breakfast club, Rex went on full meltdown that he didn't want to stay there, and Art totally took control, showing him the crayons and telling him he would teach him noughts and crosses. Rex stopped crying and, as I watched them walk across the school hall together hand in hand, I felt a lump in my throat for Art. I was so proud of him; he had endured so much these last few years and he always tried to do everything to make things as good as they could be for me. Sending them to breakfast club also makes it far easier for me, because Art needs to start at 8.55am and pre-school doesn't open until 9.10am, which is why I have to drive all over getting them to various places. I remember it being the same when Belle and Art started school in Canterbury – we would have a fifteen-minute wait after big school drop off until pre-school opened. I suppose to the schools it's just a fifteen-minute wait and it also means all the children aren't rushing in together at once, but I used to watch the parents who didn't have a car wait outside the pre-school entrance after dropping an elder child, standing in the rain, or desperate for the doors to open so they could rush off to work. I used to feel so lucky while thinking that fifteen minutes is just so painful for 'some' parents, and now I am one of them, rushing to get various children to schools and then getting to work on time.

I got Ruby and Will to school on time without any fuss, and it was all going smoothly until I took Ruby into class and I felt her little palm turn sweaty and lock onto mine. And then the tears came. Her teacher came over and bent down, talking to her in a kind, reassuring voice, but the closer she got, the tighter Ruby's grip became.

I couldn't work out why this was happening again, why Ruby was so upset about being at school, and I worried that all this turmoil with us parents had affected the kids more than we realised.

In the end I couldn't find a way of getting her off me, so the teaching assistant came and prised her away. Ruby screamed as though she was panicking about me leaving her, and my heart ached for her. The lump in my throat returned and as I walked out of class and tried to swallow it away, I knew that tears weren't far behind.

'Excuse me?' I looked back and saw Ruby's teacher following me across the playground.

Brilliant.

I started apologising profusely, making ridiculous excuses about anything and everything to justify my tears, which now weren't stopping and the more I tried to talk the worse state I was getting into.

I was also aware I was meant to be starting a new job in seventeen minutes and I had no make-up with me to cover up my red, blotchy, tear-stained face.

The teacher was so sweet. Which made me cry even more, if that was possible. She asked if everything was OK at home as she had noticed Ruby had become really quiet recently and that her grandparents had taken to doing most of the school runs.

I didn't know what to say ... I worried if I told her about Laura's breakdown on Friday, she may get the authorities involved, but I also felt like a kettle whistling away on a stove, ready to blow. I have no one to talk to. I have no friends around here, only Jen – but it's too early to be offloading all my worries onto her.

So I told her that I didn't know what was actually happening. I explained how Laura had been difficult on Friday when she'd dropped the kids off and how I was worried that Will and Ruby were at risk of being seriously affected, if they weren't already, by their mum's behaviour. I told her that they would now be living with us for the foreseeable future, and that I wasn't sure how we were going to cope, and that it was all totally shit. I actually used those words 'totally shit'. Great.

She rubbed the top of my arm the whole time I was ranting, which made me cry more. Why do people insist on hugging or touching you when you're crying? It's the worst thing that can possibly happen because it turns your tear ducts into an actual tap that's on full blast. I noticed she had her head tilted to the side and although she was studying me, I felt she was sympathising with me. Her face looked like she could tell this was a situation out of my control, and it really was 'totally shit'. I was not exaggerating that point.

She reassured me that she would keep an extra eye on Ruby, and that she would meet with both Will's teacher and the head of their pastoral care team so they could make sure the kids were doing OK. She advised me to speak to Jamie again – to voice my concerns like I had to her, and make him see that we needed to find a way to manage this situation better. I felt like she was on our side and – although she didn't say anything negative about Laura – it was like she knew things needed to change, and she was relieved we had spoken about it.

I got in the car and laughed. A cry-laugh you do through tears at the state of yourself; the fact the entire morning had turned into a total fuck up and it was only just 9am. The tears stopped and I just laughed to myself – surely it couldn't get any worse than this.

I walked into the café and Lou instantly noticed my blotchy face. She was just so kind and made me a coffee and told me to sit down. There was no one else in yet and she asked me what was wrong. I felt so stupid, and I was worried Lou would think badly of me, almost like I was a total wreck and not want me working in her café, but I explained it all to her. She told me that she had 'heard' of Laura – even though she lived in the next town, which is a fifteen-minute drive away, the area is still small enough for people to know other people's business.

It was clear Lou felt uneasy discussing it, and she was so kind and I knew that she would never want to bad-mouth anyone, but from her response I could tell that I was dealing with something else here. That there was more to Laura's story. I wondered if Jamie even knew what she was truly like now.

Lou was so lovely to me and, even though her life is the opposite of mine, she didn't judge. In fact, she reminded me of everything Jamie and I did have. We love each other so much. He idolises my kids and I idolise his. We have a beautiful home and our health, and speaking to her made me realise I needed to talk to Jamie about this and sort things out to get things right for *our* babies and *our* family, because I wasn't going to let this go wrong.

Later that day, I got a text off Lou that just said 'You can do this, Mama. Lots of love'. That made me sob. It's been so long since I've had a female friend text me nice things and I realised how lonely I had been for so long. It actually made me think that having people care for you is a pretty special feeling.

Jamie didn't get home until gone eight tonight and when he walked in I felt so emotional. I knew we needed to talk, but as soon as he appeared at the lounge door I walked over and buried my face into his neck. He held me so tight with one arm round my back and held my neck in his other hand in a grip that made me feel nothing but loved and secure. His smell immediately makes me feel safe, he has a beautiful smell, always – no matter if he's worked all day or just woke up in the morning – he always smells good. He kissed the top of my forehead while saying 'I love you so much'.

I could tell he felt as crap as I did, and I promised in my head that we would make things OK for us all.

# CHAPTER NINE

## WOMAN'S BEST FRIEND

*Thursday*

The kids are desperate for a dog. Mine have always wanted one but Mark hated dogs, so it was never an option, but now things are different, and we have agreed that the time is right for us to get one. Maybe we're completely mad doing it now with all the stress going on, but we've never been ones to make life easy! We haven't told the kids, but we've been researching the best dogs (for busy chaotic families, and a woman who will be in charge of training it who doesn't have a bastard clue) and decided upon a Golden Labrador puppy. We went and looked at it yesterday while the kids were at school, and we immediately fell in love with the same one. Jamie is finishing early tomorrow so he can collect Will and Ruby from school, then we are going to surprise them all.

I feel so happy. I'm loving work and I feel like I've made a real friend in Lou – and Jen. She comes into the café most days for a coffee and the three of us put the world to rights together. We also have a WhatsApp group, which we speak to each other on in the evenings, and I feel like I have a proper friendship group for the first time in forever, which is lovely. We've become quite close in just a couple of weeks and it's made me realise how important and necessary female friendships are. It's made me see that I've missed out on so, so much over the last fifteen years by not having other women in my life to confide in.

And as a family, we're all getting on really well too, and I think the stress of the house move has finally disappeared and we're now settling in as a family unit.

Belle has begun a dance class on a Thursday evening, and she's got a really nice group of girlfriends who she brings home most evenings to spend time with in her room. Both the boys seem happy, and Art's teacher Miss Gilmore is now doing one-to-one work with him twice a week, which she believes is massively helping him settle in better at school.

What Jamie and I know we need to sort is Ruby and Will. The situation is still shit; they're living with us, which is great, but haven't seen their mum since her outburst, which is only making things weirder for them.

Jamie has promised to organise a meeting with the school in the next week so we can see how they're getting on and whether what's happening with Laura is having any impact on them at all.

I can't help feeling that things are going to get worse before they get better but I have to remember the life Jamie has given my babies – and his children are just as precious to me. It's our duty to ensure that they grow into well-adjusted adults who don't have to recover from their childhoods. The five of them need us to be totally dedicated to giving them all the love they need, and when we need a bit of back-up, we'll have the dog to help.

\*

## Friday

I finished slightly earlier today as the café was dead and I wanted to pop to the pet shop and grab some bits for the new addition. That was hell. I'd have rather sold a kidney than go through the stress of figuring out what to buy the puppy in terms of food, teething toys, leads, collars, beds and bowls. Jeeeez, I think planning for a newborn baby would have been less stressful. I also decided on the way to call Mark (because I clearly love creating shitloads of stress for myself).

I *thought* I could try to see what he wants to do about seeing the kids now that it's been over a month since we've been here and he has made no attempt to contact them. It's the beginning of May, they have a week's half term soon and I did think he may want to come and spend some time with them. He answered the phone and as much as I wanted to bite my handset in anger when I first heard him answer with the word 'Yes?' in his irritated, arrogant tone, I stayed calm and asked him if he was planning on contacting his children any time soon. I then received a barrage of abuse.

The entire call turned into a shitshow about nothing else but the money from the sale of the house. He was obviously still furious about having to give me more than he'd planned. He made no mention of the kids or how they were getting on with their new lives down here, and all he did was shout about me being a money-grabbing bitch.

I kept trying to interrupt, to explain that this money was for his children, to buy them a home and one day they would eventually inherit it – but I couldn't get a word in. He ended the call after screaming, 'You are an evil slut and I fucking hate you for what you've done to me!'

Every single part of my body trembled with a rage that left me feeling freezing cold. I was overcome with a physical shake and if someone had been standing next to me, they would have easily seen it. Everything in me wanted to call him back and remind him what an absolute bastard he was. I wanted to tell him how he had destroyed his children's worlds with his actions, but then I remembered my mantra – 'Bite your tongue, Jo' – and so I did. I bit my tongue and decided that would be the last time I would contact him; I was done. From now on, I would solely focus on my children. Instead of calling him back and attempting to scream the truth, I composed an email to my solicitor, with my fingers still shaking, my heart pumping and my left leg still trembling with adrenaline, asking her what we could do to speed up the sale of the house.

I cut the pet shop visit short and called Jen, who was at home. I started to tell her about Mark, and how shit I felt, and she invited me over. When I arrived, she poured us both a glass of Prosecco even though it wasn't even 2pm! But we sat in her garden and put the world to rights for an hour before the school run. Just that sixty minutes of sipping a small glass of fizz, nibbling on olives and laughing until my sides hurt did me the world of good. Having friends that are 'just there', I've decided, is the most amazing feeling in the world.

On a happier note, the kids think Jamie and I are the best parents ever. He came home early and we collected the dog tonight after school. The kids repeatedly asked what we were doing and where we were going, and when we walked into the breeder's house, they still didn't get it even when they saw a dog bed full of puppies! When I told them we had bought one, they began screaming and jumping up and down. We picked up our chunky twelve-week-old boy and as we were driving home in our trusty 'big family' people carrier, picking names, I looked in the mirror at Belle's reaction and saw that she was crying and she had her head buried into our new dog and it made my heart hurt for the love I knew she had to give it.

We decided on the name Stanley. Stanley the Golden Lab. Who not only got car sick on the way home but also took a shit, which smelt like death in his new blanket. Brilliant.

\*

### Sunday

Whose idea was it to buy a fucking dog?

I genuinely haven't had more than three hours' sleep. All night. I searched everywhere and spoke to the vet about how best to settle him. I repeatedly see 'DO NOT let the puppy sleep in your bed as it will not ever be able to self-settle'. DO NOT go into him when he whimpers and set your alarm every 2–3 hours so he can go to the toilet. The best way is to put him in a crate with something that smells of his mum, a hot water bottle for warmth like he got off mum, a blanket over the crate so it's like a den. We brought home a T-shirt that the breeder gave us that smells of mum and popped him in his crate, we snuggled a hot water bottle under his blanket. He whimpered the minute I shut the kitchen door at 11pm … within half an hour that whimper turned into a howl that sounds like it's being tortured. I re-googled, reading that this would last 'a few nights' until they got used to it but of course I had the puppy mum guilt that he was frightened, lonely, panicking and scared and by 4am when I was going down to let him out for his third toilet break Jamie woke and asked if I thought we should call the breeder and check whether this was 'normal'. He then went on to tell me he doesn't ever remember his dogs crying like this when he was a kid, but as I found out this morning our kids won't remember him crying because none of them heard a sound and they all had a blissful night's sleep. Anyway I threw the towel in at 5am and carried him up to bed with me. As Jamie started whispering how I was 'making a rod for my own back' and 'creating a monster' Stanley fell into a deep sleep and as I snuggled into him and sniffed his little warm paws that smelt of biscuits and saw how much he just wanted to be loved I decided this, for now, was an OK mistake to make – and we all get a better night's sleep.

Other than that, we've had a great weekend, all of us, together.

Jen and the kids came over this afternoon. She rocked up with big bags of sweets and crisps for the kids and a bottle of Prosecco for us. It was quite windy, but the sun was still out, so the kids played in the garden and we sat in the conservatory. We managed to finish the bottle of Prosecco and talk the afternoon away again.

After she left, I sat there for an hour after watching Jamie and the kids play while the spag Bol stewed in the slow cooker and I thought back to how I'd got to this point in my life ...

It's funny how you just 'think' you're happy. You believe you are, you get married, have kids and you just plod along, thinking this is the way everyone else feels – you have no concerns or worries until one day the whole thing crashes around you and your marriage falls apart.

When I think back to that day with Mark, I still get a moment where I physically feel those feelings, that chest-crushing anxiety, and the bile rises in my throat. When people tell you about something and use the term 'my head spins' and you're never sure what they mean, until you feel it – because your head actually does spin, out of control like when you were a kid and your friends push you on a roundabout and they won't stop, or when you've had too much to drink and you're trying to go to sleep – it's that exact feeling, where everything is spinning and you have no control over how to make it stop.

During a marriage you believe is happy, you watch a programme where you see someone say they're 'heartbroken' and you feel sorry for them, you think you understand how that might feel, but you don't – not until it happens to you – only then do you really understand. Because your heart actually feels broken. Like it's been hit with a bat or shot at with a gun. It is a physical ache that hurts, a genuine pain, that doesn't go away with paracetamol or a bandage …

And for a while you don't ever think those feelings will fade and you don't think you will ever be happy again, not like you were with that person who's now caused you such devastation.

Only you do heal, you do get better, and some days you don't even see that's what is happening. You just wake one morning and realise you feel better than the day before, or you cook your ex-husband's favourite dinner and only realise when you bite into the last mouthful, and all the things that once felt like they were killing you slowly start to disappear and normality resumes.

You find your smile returning when you see your kids laughing together – and that's not because 'he' is missing from the family unit; it's because you realise how lucky

YOU are ... and then you eventually go on to meet someone who treats you so much better. They make you see that you actually weren't happy like you thought you once were – you were coasting, plodding, because you didn't know any better. And now they're here, to show you actual happiness, and it blows your mind at what you thought happiness was, once upon a time.

And although you still get pangs of those horrid feelings you once felt, just for a second or two, when you think back to 'that time' it makes you grateful. It makes you realise what you have right now is even more special, that this is actual happiness – this is really what it feels like.

I imagine most people live their lives believing they have it all, thinking they're truly happy, maybe with their first love – probably looking at step-families like mine and feeling thankful they're not us. They watch our kids on the beach trying to fathom out who belongs to who and when they hear Jamie or I being shouted at by one of the kids by our Christian names they nod to themselves, a nod to confirm they were right, that they're not 'all ours together', but actually I've come to realise that I'm the lucky one because I've been given a second chance, and although two of the children I now help raise didn't grow inside of me or call me Mum, it doesn't matter, because I've found out what true happiness is and that makes me work so much harder on getting it right now, for Jamie, our babies, and for me, together.

# CHAPTER TEN

. . . . . . . . . . . . . . . . . . . . . . . . .

# THE TRUTH ABOUT LAURA

*Monday*

Jamie arranged to work from home today so he could take Will and Ruby to school this morning. And Ruby lost it again. He couldn't prise her off him and when the teaching assistants arrived and attempted to do a two-person restraint, she ended up getting herself in such a state she was sick. The times I had left her it had made my heart hurt but this was him, watching his baby girl, and I could just feel his pain when he relayed what had happened back to me. Was it worse today because they were going back to their other home after school tonight? Of course we didn't want them to but we knew we needed to be reasonable and Laura had called Jamie on Saturday to apologise for how she's been, saying she has stuff going on and her mental health hasn't been the greatest. I was shopping when she called him so I didn't hear the conversation, I asked him if he had spoken to her about her dad telling us they're practically raising the kids, he hadn't. I was annoyed, but I have to remember this is all new to him, he hates conflict and ultimately he just wants everyone to get on and for her to be OK for Will and Ruby so I think he's just hoping for the best.

The teacher had asked if she could speak to Jamie alone when he arrived and she explained that Ruby had not been herself for some time. She had also checked in with pastoral care last Friday and been told that Will seemed to be withdrawing at school more and more. He no longer participated in class discussions, he looked like he was a million miles away all the time and had no interest in his friendship group at lunch and break-times, choosing instead to play keepy-uppys with a football on the field, alone.

Apparently, they had tried to contact Laura but never got a response to the emails sent or voicemails they had left and Jamie asked why he hadn't been contacted. They then told him that Laura had requested to remove him off the database, which really pissed me off because when I started my kids at their new schools, I was told Mark's details HAD to be on their systems as he had parental responsibility – even though he was an absent father who was incapable of answering his phone and lived a six-hour drive away.

Jamie was devastated and when he tried to call Laura, her phone rang out so he called her dad instead. Pete sounded done in and although initially he was quite defensive, saying that the kids were fine, and everything was 'in hand' now that they were going back to them, once Jamie explained that the school had raised concerns, Pete told him what was really going on.

Even before they had moved in with us, Laura wasn't seeing the children much, at all. Pete believed she had begun a new relationship, which had taken priority over Will and Ruby. He said both his wife and him, and Laura's sister had all tried to speak to her, offer to pay privately for her to get help but she refused, either becoming aggressive with them in her response, or absent. Maybe her mental health issues were stopping her from seeing things clearly, but either way, it was evident from just listening to him that he was upset and unsure how to make things better. I thought how confused the kids must be in all this. I could also tell Jamie had no clue how to change things, or make things better for them, but we agreed that we needed some professional help and first thing tomorrow we are going to take steps to put this whole situation straight.

*

## Tuesday

Jamie and I had managed to get an urgent appointment at the solicitors this afternoon.

I wasn't sure who we were seeing; Jamie had called and made the appointment and they had got us in really quickly.

We were greeted by a tall man, mid-forties, with a golden tan and sandy-coloured hair, which flopped to one side. He was wearing a Hugo Boss navy suit; the leg fit was slim, which made him look taller, and he had pointed, laced-up leather shoes on which were two tones of brown, again expensive. He greeted us with 'Mr and Mrs Adams, my name is David Metcalfe.'

Lou's husband.

Mr and Mrs Adams – this is the first time anyone's ever called us that, I mean we're not – we aren't even engaged, let alone married – but neither of us corrected him. 'Jo Adams.' It was the first time I practised that name in my head. I quite liked it.

David seemed like a genuinely decent guy and he certainly knew his stuff – how the family court process worked and what we could and couldn't expect if we decided to proceed. He asked what we wanted from this – did we want the reassurance from professional reports that the children's needs were being met when they were in Laura's care? Did we want the court to look into Laura's medical records, have a psychiatric report done, alcohol and drug tests? Or did we want them to reside with us full-time?

All of the options he mentioned were expensive and took time and if the outcome was that Laura was ultimately deemed a fit mother, it would be a total waste of time as we would continue to get the access we get now and we'd also be tens of thousands of pounds down, maybe more.

My head was blown. I didn't know what to do but ultimately I knew things weren't OK, Jamie knew things weren't OK, the school knew things weren't OK, Laura's parents definitely knew things weren't OK, yet I had no idea what Laura was thinking.

David suggested mediation between Laura and Jamie, which Jamie immediately ruled out. They'd tried this before, right at the beginning of their relationship breakdown, and Laura was incapable of speaking with Jamie and it would just be a waste of time and money.

We went away to think about things and realised we didn't really know what to do next for the best. What I did know is we both had real concerns about what was going on with the kids when they were in Laura's care ... *if* they were in her care and not her parents', because that looked to be more and more what was really going on.

We went for a walk down to the harbour before we collected the kids, we spoke about the meeting with David and I asked Jamie what he wanted to do. He didn't know. He replied saying, 'I just want her to get better and be a mum to the kids.' That is genuinely all he wanted. In the time I had known him, he didn't argue or fight with anyone, he hated drama or conflict, but more than anything he just wanted his kids to grow up not having to recover from their childhoods.

Despite the situation, the walk we had was lovely, just the two of us strolling about where we now lived, taking it all in, holding hands and telling each other we *would* be OK.

\*

### Wednesday

I ran the café alone today for the first time after Lou texted me to say she couldn't come in as she was feeling unwell. I was slightly nervous about the responsibility, but also really happy that she trusts me to do it already. It was quite busy today, mostly with regulars and I coped OK. I know more of the mums from school now, too, which has helped. I never walk into the playground with that flustered feeling I got when I lived in Canterbury. The mums here seem far less judgemental, and are friendlier and chatty.

My solicitor also called to tell me there has been an offer on the house for full asking price. She told me the viewers had fallen in love with the decor of the house and the 'family feel' of the property because of the way it had been decorated and cared for, perfect for raising their young children, they said, and it made my tummy do a little flip. I remembered back to how I had once thought that too after I had spent so long making it 'ours'. I thought back to all the work I had done making that house into a home and I just hoped that this time it got the happy family it deserved.

I asked her if Mark's solicitor had been difficult about splitting the money and she had laughed and said, 'They tried to stamp their feet but soon realised it would be pointless.' It made me feel a tinge of sadness, that Mark was so wealthy he could have bought me out when I first left for Cornwall without waiting for the house to sell but he wanted to make things difficult and drawn out. And now, he still didn't want to hand over enough money to ensure his children are taken care of. It also, for me, felt a bit surreal. Jamie earned a good wage; he was happy to pay for the things we needed over the past few years – shopping, when we ate out or got takeaway – but it never sat comfortably with me. I had been 'kept' by Mark for so long, then when he left so did any access to money, and I lived hand to mouth most weeks. Despite looking to everyone like he allowed me to still keep the lifestyle he had 'given me', the reality was I was surviving off income support – and I promised never to allow anyone to financially take care of me again. When Jamie and I got together, it felt different, it was a decision we made together, but I was so happy to be contributing now.

For so long I had penny-pinched, bought clothes for the kids off eBay or from charity shops, and learned how to cook meals on a budget – so now, to know that I will have this amount of money coming to me is crazy – because it is enough to ensure we're OK, and being OK is something that we weren't for so many years after Mark left.

After work, we took Stanley for his second lot of jabs so he can now be walked in public. I thought it would be nice to do it 'all together' as a family, but it needed doing asap so we went without Will and Ruby. It was hell. The three of them fought over who held the lead, and he sat on his back legs being dragged along, refusing to walk anywhere. Every time I end up trying something new with this dog, I end up sitting on Google for half an hour as I have absolutely no idea what I'm doing. Today I was stood at a crossing, waiting for the green man to appear, trying not to scream at my kids for having a full-blown punch up over walking a dog that was refusing to be walked, and at the same time I'm on my phone googling, 'Why won't my dog walk?'. Fuck my life . . . .

## Friday

Laura's dad dropped the kids back tonight. Jamie wasn't home from work, and as I answered the door, I noticed he looked tired. He was very sweet and told me to call if I needed anything and I couldn't help but feel sorry for him.

Will and Ruby were quiet at first but after ten minutes of Belle pretending she was Anna from *Frozen* and allowing Ruby to be Elsa, and Will and Art kicking the ball at the back fence then rolling around on the trampoline, they were fine. I didn't ask them any questions about their week and when Jamie rolled in with our usual Friday night fish and chips takeaway, the house turned crazy, busy – and happy. We played Twister and Junior Monopoly, which was chaos because Ruby and Rex didn't get the rules and kept losing their shit, but Twister was fun after Jamie and I had finished a bottle of wine. I thought we would be spending the evening pretending everything was fine and dandy – but actually it felt pretty fine and dandy.

\*

## Saturday

I'm fucking livid. With Belle, and myself.

Belle asked to sleep at her friend Gracie's tonight. I've met Gracie many times and she's sweet and chatty, and as

I've met Gracie's mum numerous times, I had no problem agreeing.

But Belle wasn't staying at Gracie's like she had told me. And Gracie wasn't staying at ours like she had told her mum.

Instead they were camping in a field with another load of girls – and boys – where they all got shit-faced on alcohol they'd stolen out of their parents' cupboards.

I got a call just after 10pm from a wailing Belle to tell me Gracie was dying. I could tell instantly she was pissed, and the panic kicked in. They were in the field next to the beach and Gracie was out cold. I didn't have Gracie's mum's number and Belle started shouting about police and ambulances and uncontrollably crying, as I started putting my shoes on.

'Stay there, I'll go,' Jamie said, as by this point I was wailing and crying more than Belle, while shouting things like 'Hold on, baby' as if she was saying her last goodbye in a zombie apocalypse.

I kept Belle on the phone as Jamie drove down to her, and as we spoke I could hear sirens in the background. By this point, she was a drunken hysterical mess that couldn't get her words out and I could hear the paramedics shouting that he needed them all to move back. Belle was sobbing, saying, 'I'm sorry, this is all my fault,' and I wanted to physically hurt her for being so stupid as much as I wanted to hug her and tell her everything was going to be OK. But more than anything I wanted to know her friend was OK.

Jamie came on the phone and told me he'd got her and that everything was OK, and that he was bringing her back. Gracie's mum had somehow since been notified too and was getting in the ambulance to go to hospital with Gracie, who was unconscious.

Now that we know that Gracie is OK, I can see a way to imagining that this will actually be quite amusing to look back on in the future – Jamie carrying Belle through the front door in a fireman's lift while she was singing 'Umbrella' by Rihanna then lying on the sofa over a sick bucket, shouting 'I just love you all. All of you' to no one. The room was empty – not even Stanley (who doesn't ever leave her side) wanted to keep her company tonight.

It's now 2.20am and I'm sat with her chatting away as I write this, like a little old drunken sailor, making no sense. She has repeatedly vomited a concoction of Jack Daniels and gin by the smell of it.

Jamie, unlike me, is far more laid-back with this sort of stuff. 'Remember what you were doing at fifteen?' Only I wasn't doing this. I never did anything like this, but then I also remembered throughout life I had missed out on so much fun and so many experiences and perhaps this was 'normal'. Perhaps I should have done this. Perhaps if I'd have done this I wouldn't have walked into the trap with Mark. Either way, it made me see how hard it is parenting a teenager.

I thought back to when she was born and I had a huge selection of books all about getting her to sleep, weaning and teething. Now what? There is no manual that I can order from Amazon that teaches me that when I trust my teenage daughter is staying at a friend's and doing coursework, she's actually in a field, downing spirits, getting shit-faced and getting up to god knows what. There is no 'mums of teenagers' group I can sit at on a Wednesday morning and instead of discussing baby-led weaning or whether your toddler could be allergic to dairy with other mums we talk about the best ways to understand our children and just somehow know when they begin lying, drinking alcohol or becoming sexually active. I don't know how to manage or discipline this stuff or how to prepare for the 'next stage' when I have absolutely no fucking clue what the 'next stage' could be.

God help me.

# CHAPTER ELEVEN

# GEARING UP FOR
# A FIGHT

## Monday

Belle spent yesterday in bed hungover and left for the school bus this morning without saying good morning or goodbye. I am going to speak to her properly tonight once the boys are in bed. When she walked out the door, Jamie gave me a smile and a head shake, as if to remind me things aren't as bad as my head is telling me. He spent all day yesterday singing 'Umbrella' – Belle didn't get the joke, but he found himself hilarious.

Jamie did the school run again today, and although Art and Rex went into breakfast club fine, he had the same issue with Ruby when he took her into her class. Her teacher said that they had received a social services referral and although she was unable to discuss the details, she was aware that Jamie had parental responsibility, so urged him to contact them as she had concerns over the children's welfare. He called Laura's dad but there was no answer.

He came into the café to tell me and it was the first time I realised how exhausted he looked. His face was pale, his eyes sunken and he just looked physically drained. We talked for a bit and he told me he was going to collect Will and Ruby from school that afternoon and take them out for dinner so he could speak to them about things before he dropped them back to Laura's parents.

I felt a bit excluded when he told me this, but then almost instantly felt guilty. I was so lucky to have a partner like Jamie who cared so much about his kids that he wanted to spend time with them to check they were OK, and that he cared so much about my kids that he didn't do it in their home – where they might overhear and get upset or worried. And he cared that much about me that he'd wanted to get my take on it all before he actually did any of it. As shit as this situation was, I realised how lucky I was to have him. He cared about all of us. All six of us.

He came home just before 7pm, with both kids in tow. It was clear from Will's tear-stained face that he had been crying and from Jamie's false, happy, high-pitched voice telling Will to go jump in the shower and get in his jammies and telling Ruby to pop up and see Belle before he ran her bath, that he had brought the kids back to our house to sleep, rather than take them home as planned and that things were not OK.

In fact, things were much, much worse than we thought.

It turns out that Laura has been drinking – a lot. Will said that when they were staying with Laura, he was finding her asleep on the sofa most mornings with empty bottles of alcohol surrounding her and that she was getting the neighbour's teenage daughter to babysit most nights. Then one day Laura's parents had turned up unannounced and there had been a huge row, which is when they had started staying with their grandparents. Will had told Jamie about how bad it had all got, all while being in floods of tears because he was frightened about telling him because he didn't want everyone fighting and falling out. What I found most distressing with it all is that all Will seemed worried about was upsetting everyone. He was desperate not to cause arguments by explaining his feelings and it made me wonder how many children there are right now, out there, carrying the weight and burden of adult issues on their shoulders – keeping secrets for Mum or Dad so they didn't cause fights, but ultimately to keep themselves safe so they didn't get into trouble or have to carry the responsibility of upsetting anyone. Heartbreaking.

Jamie called Pete and said that Will had told him what had been going on and that the children would now be staying with us permanently until Laura sorted herself out. We were disappointed that Pete hadn't told us the full extent of it when we'd spoken before, but I guess he was hoping she'd get better and things would get back on track.

I don't know where we go from here. Jamie is going to take the kids in to school tomorrow and speak to the teachers. He is going to call David Metcalfe and discuss beginning court proceedings. I don't know how much stress this will put on us or what it will entail and I have no clue what it will cost financially. We have the equity in the bank from Jamie's house sale. I haven't heard back from my solicitor since last week about the sale of my house but I worry this court case could go into the tens of thousands – and we didn't know yet how much Laura would fight.

But it's clear to all of us that Ruby and Will can no longer stay around Laura. She needs time to get herself sorted out, but who knows how long that will take?

I also have no idea how we will manage five children at three different schools full-time from September. I'm now working during school hours and I wonder where I will fit in keeping on top of the house, washing, cooking and looking after Stanley, who has decided he enjoys taking a morning piss on a random bed and chewing only my shoes, and no one else's. I also worry about giving the kids the time they all need.

I feel like things are so stressful right now and that we are losing control. I love having all seven of us here but in these stressful moments it can feel a bit out of control, and I look at other families, like Lou's, and wonder why my life can't be that simple.

I can see Jamie is feeling exactly the same as I am yet we're both here, pretending to be positive, like it's all OK and we can manage it, both walking around using those fake, high-pitched happy voices in front the kids. I can see from the looks Belle keeps shooting us across the room that we're fooling no one.

It's only Monday but I need a glass of wine. A large one.

# CHAPTER TWELVE

* * * * * * * * * * * * * * * * * * * * * * * *

# LAWYER UP

*Friday*

What a week . . .

I had a really long chat with Belle about the drinking episode. She was really embarrassed, and had been terrified for Gracie, but I feel like she was also honest with me. She said she had wanted to try alcohol and so had been siphoning off measures of gin from the bottles in the cupboard. A bellyful of spirits, as your first drink – now if that wasn't enough to put you off in future . . .

We walked along the beach – because I've learnt it's impossible to have a private conversation in our house – and as the sun began to set, we moved on to talking about other things that were worrying her too. It felt really good to just spend some time with my biggest girl. She told me most girls in her year had done 'sex stuff' with boys and that the girls had asked her if she had done stuff with boys back in Canterbury and, although she'd told the truth and said no, she worried they would take the mickey because she hadn't. I realised that teenagers growing up now live in such difficult times. The pressure upon them to do things that they're not ready for, or worse still, don't want to do, is so strong, and the stuff flying round on social media is utterly crazy – then there's the bullying they endure if they remain strong enough to go against the grain and not do what everyone else is doing. They're damned if they do and damned if they don't. Such an awful world we live in at times.

I explained to Belle that I was upset that she had lied to me. That I was worried about her drinking at such a young age, but that the outcome could have been far worse, which scared me.

I realise she's growing up; she is going to try things and make mistakes and me trying to stop her or tell her she isn't allowed is only going to cause more Saturday nights where she lies and puts herself at further risk. We agreed that if she is honest with me, she won't get into trouble. I feel very lucky that I can have a calm and rational conversation with her about things and that we can get to an outcome where we both agree rather than one of us being annoyed or angry, and I can only hope she keeps to her promise where she tells me her plans, good or bad, and I can support her and offer advice. It's all we can do.

We actually ended up having a real giggle, and she told me several stories about different things people were getting up to in her school – one kid was so embarrassed that the stubble that was kicking in on his face was so pale and patchy that he'd pinched a mascara from his mum and lightly coloured it in. He'd somehow managed to get away with it, right up until PE at the end of the day, when it started melting down from his top lip in the middle of the hockey pitch. Not all of the examples were so endearingly naïve though; some were downright terrifying, and I thanked my lucky stars that I had only had to cope with my daughter getting shit-faced in a field. I felt quite privileged she trusted me enough to confide in me with stories that I would have never been able to talk about with my mum.

Jamie took the kids into school on Tuesday morning this week and met with the head of their pastoral care, Mr James, to explain the situation. He told Jamie that until a court order was in place, both parents had parental responsibility and could collect and drop off the children at any time, and the school would not be getting involved. Knob. Jamie tried to explain he wasn't asking them to get involved but was simply informing them so they could ensure the children could be safely monitored at school.

But Mr James was really off throughout the meeting, repeatedly telling Jamie this was a civil matter for the family court and that there were to be no incidents between him and Laura in the school playground, should they turn up to collect the children at the same time – as if he was some kind of yob who was about to go to war with his ex-partner in front of a playground full of people. I could tell Jamie felt defeated and upset when he was just trying to do right by his children and protect them as best he could right now.

He then went to see David Metcalfe to begin preparations for family court. He also had to go and get a certificate from a mediation company to say that mediation was unsuitable for him and Laura so that it could go to family court. The application was just over £250. With David's fees and the mediation certificate, we were over £1000 down already.

David said for now he would send Laura a letter stating that the children would be residing with us due to what they had disclosed and in response to their wishes and feelings. He said he would make the letter detailed enough that she would hopefully agree for us to keep the children and concentrate on getting herself better.

Then Jamie spoke to his boss this afternoon who agreed he could spend the next two weeks working from home three days a week, which meant he would be able to do all the school runs for Will and Ruby. In fairness, his workplace was being good and flexible about things, and they were really family focused, which helps us massively.

I am worried that if I attempt to collect the children from school and Laura also turned up to collect them, then they would legally be allowed to leave with her over me as I have no parental rights. My anxiety was in overdrive just thinking about her rocking up to the playground and kicking off, and the effect on Will and Ruby would have been devastating.

But despite all this tension and anxiety for Jamie and me, the weirdest thing right now is that the kids seem really calm and happy. Neither of them have asked any questions about why they are here every night and what's happening, and that fills me with a little bit of hope that everything is going to be OK.

When I got into work, Lou looked really down. I asked her what was wrong and she told me that David had booked a week's holiday for them at the end of the month for the May half term. She was stressed because she had no cover for the café during one of its busiest times. The tourists come for their holidays from May through until August, so I understood why Lou didn't want to close for the week.

'I'll do it!' I said. I had no fucking clue how. I had five kids and a dog to care for and I hadn't even discussed with Jamie if he was taking any time off work. Lou asked how I would manage and I said Belle could help out making coffees and washing up. She and I would sort it between us. Lou deserves a nice week away and I needed some space for myself while things were difficult at home. I loved working in the café and it gave me precious moments to step away from being a mum and just be me.

When I got home, I asked Belle if she would help me at the café and she was so sweet. Just instantly agreed, didn't even ask about getting paid or moan she wouldn't be able to see her friends or do the stuff she'd planned. I feel so lucky at times for the way she is, paralleled with a panic about what if she changes and becomes one of the teenage girls I read about or see in BBC sitcoms – the ones who can't stand their parents, are mean to other kids, steal cigarettes and hate the world ...

# CHAPTER THIRTEEN

* * * * * * * * * * * * * * * * * * * * * * * *

# FINDING MEANING IN THE MADNESS

*Monday*

It's almost midnight.

Today has been rubbish.

We found out from Ruby's teacher that Laura had left several voicemails on the school answerphone over the weekend, where she sounds either medicated or intoxicated. Or both. They're not entirely sure. She has made several allegations about Jamie and me (although they won't say what) and asked the school to contact her to inform her of what they are doing to protect her kids.

I wanted to vomit. I can just picture all the teachers in the staff room slagging us all off and pitying the kids like we're all 'as much to blame'. Jamie tells me it's not like that and they deal with families who have far worse issues than ours, but I don't want to be a family with issues in the first place! We shouldn't be labelled as having 'issues'. I don't want my children or step-children on some kind of register where the teachers just see you as 'that' problem family whose kids need extra support because along the way you haven't done your jobs right. And that's shit, and unfair, because since I gave birth all I have done is dedicate my life to trying to make sure my kids aren't fucked up or labelled, and since I've known the true extent about who Laura is, I'm now dedicating it to making sure her children are OK too, and I'm exhausted.

I'd like to revise my opening: it's not been rubbish, it's been a truly shit day – bouncing from solicitor emails, guilt from the school, ruminating on all the past wrongs, and feeling bitter about Laura's behaviour.

Jamie and I have five kids between us and both our exes are idiots. I am trying to get enough money out of our house sale to set us up for the future while knowing we are likely to enter into an expensive family court battle to protect Jamie's kids. We rent our home and I have no idea if and when we will be able to buy our own, and drama seems to constantly surround us despite the fact, and I truly believe this, that neither of us ask for it.

But even right now, with the shit we've got going on, I would still choose Jamie and this life over what I had with Mark. I would still choose the steps and halves, I'd pick the rented accommodation over the big owned house, the battles with exes and the fights to make things right for children we didn't biologically produce. It is odd because all we ever want in life is to find 'the one' and the dream is to have your children together, to do all your 'firsts' with this one person that is your happy ever after – but the reality sometimes works out so differently.

I am happy, right here and now, with what I have – all this crazy chaos is just fine by me to love like I do and feel as loved as I am.

*

## Wednesday

The house has sold.

Properly sold.

My solicitor called to inform me that Mark has agreed to pay me £237,000. Wow.

I felt a wave of sadness, that that was it. Not sadness for him, or us. I mean it's been a long time now since my marriage was over, and after that ended, our home had just turned into an empty lonely house where I was often at my very worst and loneliest. It was a house I had come to feel trapped in, but before all of that, it had once been my home, where I'd birthed all my babies, and where I had once upon a time felt happy.

I wondered if I should mention the house being sold to the kids but since we had moved they hadn't asked; the boys had no clue of the difference between renting and owning, and Belle had accepted that it was in the past and our lives were here now, with Jamie and the kids, next to the sea in this beautiful beach house.

I decided not to mention it, and when I looked at them all across the dinner table tonight, I knew that we are doing OK. We are luckier than most. Parental guilt has a way of storming into your life and making you question any decision or choice you've made, but we're doing OK, we're really doing OK here, despite everything, and I'm determined to only look ahead from now on.

*

## Saturday

Belle started work at the café today. Lou has taken her on to do Saturdays with another two girls who are in their early twenties. It means she gets a bit of her own pocket money and also builds up her confidence. Jamie was working today too, so I took the other four kids down to the beach for some fresh air. It was so good to see Ruby looking carefree as she chased her brothers across the sand and splashed about in the shallow waves.

Not long after we arrived, Rex spotted his friend Roman and ran over to play with him. Roman's mum is Megan, a lady who I'd seen in the café from time to time with her kids. A few weeks ago, we had all been devastated to learn that Megan had lost a baby at full term. It had made me feel sick, and I'd hugged each of the kids just a little bit harder when I'd got home that night.

I watched her now sitting with her children on her own and noticed she still had a very slight baby bump, her body trying to recover from the devastation of delivering a full-term baby, born sleeping, almost three weeks ago. I felt knots of anxiety in my tummy when I saw her. She was sat on a blanket on the sand with her elder daughter and I decided to follow Rex over and say hello. She had huge sunglasses covering her face, and perhaps her tears, and a huge shawl covering her shoulders. She was really sweet and welcomed us to sit with them as the boys dug out the sand with their spades. Will and Art were now kicking a ball at the other end of the beach and her daughter, Edith, was just four months older than Ruby, so they took their dolls for a paddle in the freezing cold sea.

We sipped steaming hot tea from a flask Megan had brought with her and we chatted to one another while avoiding the elephant in the room. I then gently told her that I knew about the baby she'd lost and, now that her sunglasses were perched on top of her head, there was no hiding the tears that filled her eyes. This poor woman was only a few weeks post birth, with a body full of crazy hormones, no baby and her boobs the size of melons. I just knew that if I'd been in her situation I would want as much support as I could get. And I'm so glad I told her I knew because she slowly began to open up to me.

As our children played close by, Megan told me how she'd had a normal birth with Edith seven years ago, but that Roman had been breach with only a little amniotic fluid surrounding him and the cord wrapped around his neck so she was advised to have a planned C-section. When she got pregnant with her last baby, another boy who they named Wilf, she was offered the choice of a C-section or vaginal birth. She chose a vaginal birth based on her two previous experiences as she knew the healing process was a lot quicker so things might be easier.

'The irony,' she told me in a small, unsteady voice, 'is that if I'd had a C-section, I'd have been in five days earlier and he would probably have been born healthy. But I did the wrong thing.'

I offered her a tissue from the crumpled packet in my pocket and thought, what a cruel world we live in. That decision is something she will live with and blame herself for, for a very long time.

It didn't matter how many times I told her she 'wasn't to know' and that there were no guarantees; she has heard those words from every person around her, from her consultant to her husband. The fact is she *knows*, she knows that she was feeling her baby move on the day she would have had that C-section, and the day after that, so in her mind it's now her fault, and as she choked into her tea while she said those words, my entire throat and chest throbbed with pain as I held in my tears for her tears. I had spoken to this woman for only an hour of my life but the pain I could feel she was in was just unbearable. Here she was trying to get through life while in the absolute trenches, but with minimal people to support her because it still isn't OK to tell people 'I lost my baby'. How utterly devastating is that?

Later Megan and the kids came back to our house. The kids got on so well and we sat at the kitchen table and chatted over more tea and biscuits. She asked me all about Jamie and the kids and I just offloaded, at first I felt bad for doing so but I could see by her listening to my problems it was taking her mind off her own, and she was so supportive and sweet. Turns out her husband has a fifteen-year-old son, Jacob, from a previous relationship, who lives with them half the time and she had similar issues with his mum when they got together. It was good to hear they'd come through it.

She invited us all over for a BBQ in the half term. I liked that idea. I liked her, my kids liked hers and I was sure after speaking so much about her husband and Jamie they would get on too. Jamie and I had never had any 'couple friends' before, and it's only since moving here and surrounding myself with others that I've learned the world is a lot better when you are around decent, kind people.

Later, when Jamie walked through the door, I hugged him so tight and hard, and I gave our babies extra kisses when I tucked them in bed. Sometimes, just one conversation with someone else makes you realise you never know what's around the corner and you should feel grateful for what you have right now.

# CHAPTER FOURTEEN

* * * * * * * * * * * * * * * * * * * * * * * * * *

# SUPERMUM (IN LAW)

*Monday*

Jamie received a call at 5am from the police. They wanted to check whose care Will and Ruby were in. He told them they were in our care and asked what the call was regarding. The police informed him that they had Laura in custody but that they couldn't disclose why. He immediately asked if she was OK and I was filled with love for him again, that he still cared about her well-being. She was the kids' mum, after all, and I know if he could have one wish, it would be for her to get well so that she could be their mum again.

The police said they had made a referral to social services and Jamie would need to speak to them. He called all day but no one was available to speak to him, and no one called us back. When he went in to pick the kids up from school this afternoon, he asked the teachers if they knew anything. They said they didn't, but when the local newspaper headline flashed up on my phone later that afternoon, we quickly discovered what had happened.

'Thirty-four-year-old mother survives suicide attempt at local cliff spot' screamed the headline; and the article went on to state that the lady was found by a dog walker, injured, who called for help. Her injuries weren't mentioned but she was said to be in a stable condition at hospital.

In shock, Jamie went through all the 'What ifs?'. I waited all day for more news, which I imagined there now wouldn't be.

Jamie called Pete who told him that Laura was not in a good place and was in no fit state to see the children. She would write Jamie a letter via their family solicitor as soon as she was better, but he did say that as a family, alongside the authorities, they were all in agreement – Laura included – that the kids were to reside with us for the foreseeable future. I felt so sad for Laura that things in her head had gotten this bad, but also relieved that she would now get the help that it was clear she desperately needed, and ultimately that can only be a good thing – for her, for Will and for Ruby.

I called Jamie's mum to tell her what was happening because she had been worried about Jamie and the kids too. I speak to Pat every day via WhatsApp, send pictures of the kids and the dog, and she loves to send me a selfie from the garden sipping her gin, or a picture of the tray of brownies she's baked for the women at bridge.

When she answered the phone and I heard her voice, I realised how much I miss her.

Jamie's mum doesn't judge, or bad-mouth people. She seems to see the good in everyone, even when they do bad things; and, although she knows Laura has done some pretty awful stuff, things she tells me happened before I came along too, she refers to her as 'damaged, wounded and broken', never anything nasty.

I felt like I whinged for the entire phone call; I tried not to, but the reality is that, right now, things feel hard. The house is just a battle to keep on top of every day, with laundry and cleaning, and with me working part-time, trying to keep the house clean just feels like mega hard work. I then worry about how affected Will and Ruby actually are by what's going on with their mum. And then I worry that I'm not giving my own children enough time and attention. So, I basically spend most of my days worrying about things I have no choice about or control over and it's got to the point where Jamie and I have stopped talking about it because we're both shit scared of what each other is thinking.

And I don't want to be 'that' mum – the one who is super stressed because the house isn't immaculate or there is a basket of dirty laundry. I can't physically be 'that mum' anymore because I cannot keep on top of everything like I once did. I have gained two extra children, a bigger home, a job and an untrained puppy – I am going to have to learn to live with a little bit of mess and chaos.

After I had spent twenty minutes bitching, Pat said, 'If it would be helpful, and I don't want to impose or be in the way, I could come down for a few weeks and help out. Just until you're all feeling a bit more on top of the situation with Laura.' I grabbed hold of that life raft like I'd just fled the Titanic.

I didn't hesitate or say no, and almost shouted, 'Yes! Do come! Thank you, thank you, thank you! We would all *love* that!'

She said she'd book a train first thing in the morning for her and her border terrier, Digby, and come down to help for a few weeks. I wondered briefly how life would be with two dogs, one well-behaved terrier who could walk to heel without a lead, and one Labrador who is incapable of listening to any instruction that comes out of anyone's mouth. But despite me wanting to rehome this silly shit-head dog multiple times a day, he is also the sweetest, cuddliest puppy and our kids are absolutely obsessed with him, as he is with them.

I really need her here. We all need her right now to come and look after us and help stitch us back together. I feel totally relieved that she will be here tomorrow and luckily Jamie cleared out most of the summer house last weekend. We moved the extra furniture into storage so we can make use of it rather than having it as a store room when it's so beautiful. I'll force myself to find time to give it a good clean in the morning so at least while Pat is here, she will have her own space to get a break from us all in when she needs it – and I imagine she'll definitely need it.

\*

## Tuesday

Jamie's mum and Digby arrived at 3pm today. I didn't tell the kids they were coming and when we walked in from school, they went crazy. All five of them – and Stanley! They've been here a matter of hours and Digby has gladly been put in the summer house away from Stanley, who is constantly pawing him, barking at him and shagging his backside, which the kids find highly amusing ... so everyone is happy, apart from Digby – who, I imagine, can't wait to get back on the train home.

Pat made herself busy within the first hour of her arrival, loading the washing machine and emptying the dryer. As much as I kept telling her I would do it all, secretly I felt the relief escape my entire body and as the kids ran to raid the fridge and cupboards, she hugged me to her so tightly I could smell the sweet scent of the Jo Malone perfume on her scarf. She is so glamorous and, although she is in her early seventies, she always has perfectly shaped nails painted scarlet red, a smear of pink lipstick and not a highlighted hair out of place.

I sobbed into her neck. Not big sobs, but sobs that she heard, and she held my face in her hands, wiped away my tears and said, 'It's OK, my darling girl, these times are sent to test us, that's all. It's just temporary'. With that Belle walked into the room and declared, 'Thank God you've arrived to sort her out, Grandma; she's been like this for weeks.' The three of us really giggled and Pat invited Belle into what was now a group hug.

Jamie didn't know his mum was coming either and when he walked in from work to see her, he was made up. I loved how he loved her and I hoped our three boys would be like that with me when they grew up. 'Our three boys.' I just wrote that without thinking. But I do see Will as mine. I know he didn't come from me, and he has his own mummy, and I didn't get to love him straight away, but I am head over heels in love with his daddy, and him and his sister are tiny extensions of Jamie, who both deserve and need a mother's love, which right now they don't have – so that's what I will give, always, no matter how tough things get.

Tonight was a good night – over-excited kids, an over-excited Golden Lab humping a pissed-off border terrier and three adults sipping wine in the garden and chatting about everything and nothing until the sun went down. Perfect.

*

## Wednesday

Jamie leaves for work just after 6am now. Usually I have always got up with him so I have the time to get the house organised before the kids wake, but recently, like today, I end up hitting snooze repeatedly then getting up at 7. This morning, when I woke up, I could smell cooked food and I came downstairs to see Pat showered and dressed, as glamorous as ever, frying pancakes for the kids who were also up and getting ready. There was a pot of tea brewing and she greeted me as I walked into the kitchen with 'Good morning, my darling', and passed me a bottle of maple syrup and bowl of fresh berries for the kids' breakfast.

She told me she had hired a small car as a run around, so she could get about and help with the school runs and stuff. I always used to think that seventy sounded really old, but knowing Pat and some of her friends, I've revised that opinion enormously and am now dreaming of later-in-life worldwide trips and the spontaneous weekends away that we're not getting in our thirties. My mum died more than twenty years younger than what Pat is now but before her death, before she got unwell, I don't remember her having as much positive energy as Pat does now. She blows me away with how techy she is. Nothing seems to faze her and she is just a bundle of happiness without ever getting in the way or becoming 'too much'. Even when she gets things wrong – like this morning when she said to Belle, 'I think I might open a social media account now it's all the rage and join this Facewall,' and we all just fell about laughing – she laughs at herself too. I feel so relieved she's here.

I dropped her off at the car rental place after we had taken the kids to school so she knew where they all went and they were so chuffed that she took them all in and they could show her off to their teachers.

Ruby has been calmer going into class since she's been living with us, and Jamie has explained to both her and Will that they're staying with us full-time for the time being as their mum is poorly. Something switched almost immediately and since then they both seem much more settled and happier. All in all, today has been an excellent day.

*

## Thursday

Our house is immaculate. I have never seen it so clean. I mean it's always clean because I like clean but the little things that I often ignore have been done.

There are no cobwebs hanging from the high Victorian ceilings in the lounge any more. The salt and pepper grains are no longer scattered on the cupboard shelves as they've been wiped clean. The fridge is gleaming with all the contents in an order and the overflowing odd sock basket is finally empty. Cushions are plumped and scattered lovingly and throws and blankets are folded neatly and smell of fabric conditioner.

When I lived with Mark, our home was pristine. Fresh flowers in every room, not a fingertip of dust visible anywhere and the smell of our home was always divine, with candles burning from the White Company and reed diffusers from Jo Malone in the hallways. I remember telling Pat this when she first came round to my home in Canterbury, as if trying to explain that it wasn't to the standard it had been when Mark and I were married.

'It's like shovelling snow when it's still snowing,' was Pat's answer to this, and I knew she was right. Trying to keep a house that clean while raising tiny children was utterly pointless, and I often got a pang of guilt after Mark left at how often I missed out on a toddler group or a reading session at the library so I could clean the inside of the windows or wipe the dust off the skirtings to keep him happy yet I don't think he even noticed.

I'm so thankful that Jamie is the total opposite of Mark in terms of how he feels about how the house looks, but also that he pulls his weight equally. It doesn't matter that he goes to work full-time, he recognises that me being home with the kids and working in the café part-time is hard work, so he comes in and cooks everyone's tea or gives the bathroom a good clean. It started off with me panicking that he was doing it to 'have a dig' because the house wasn't clean, but I came to realise that actually, he does it because he has total respect for me; our roles are equal and if he sees something that needs doing he will just do it. It's refreshing, and it makes me love him so much when I see him bringing the washing in off the line while chatting away to Rex, or sweeping down the front steps, pulling the weeds out of the flower bed – mainly jobs that I didn't even see needed doing until I saw him doing them. I just get a pang in my chest where I think, God, I love you so much, and it's a good feeling.

For now, though, he doesn't have to do any of that because Pat has it all covered – and not in an annoying, irritating, interfering way, or because she's some kind of martyr. She enjoys helping and she just makes it so easy.

I got home to find a lasagne sat on top of the hob.

'Just needs forty minutes in the oven, darling,' she called as I entered the kitchen, 'and there's garlic ciabatta and side salad are in the fridge.'

What it meant was Jamie and I had the time to do the stuff we had been neglecting with the kids. Their homework. Usually this was down to Belle to help and monitor the younger children while we did baths, packed lunches, sort uniforms for the next day. Now, because Pat was there to cover all the mundane stuff that took up our evenings, we could spend more time than usual, reading bedtime stories with the children, and actually enjoying it as quality time rather than just being another job to tick off before we could sit back with a glass of Malbec and prepare ourselves to do it all again the next day. I had the time to lie on Belle's bed and listen to her tell me about everything that consumed her life right now, or just play with her hair while she scrolled through online stores repeatedly saying 'Do you like that?' ... and it made me realise that, for her, it is SO important that I'm there to sit and talk to her about everything and nothing.

She told me about a girl in her year, Molly, who is being bullied and harassed because she got drunk and slept with a lad after a party and then texted her other friend asking if she could get her mum to get her the morning-after pill because she couldn't tell her own mum. Rather than this girl being a good friend, she screenshot the text and smeared it over social media, so this fifteen-year-old girl is now taking time off school pretending to be unwell because she's been branded a slag and a slut by everyone, including her so-called friends.

Belle showed me some of the things people had written about Molly across social media and it made me feel physically sick. She was being called words that I didn't even understand – a 'sket'. The 'c' word. Dirty. It was horrific and I suggested that Belle contact her – to offer her some love and support. The stuff you see nowadays in the news about the damage social media causes to teenagers and the devastating actions they take because of it made my blood run cold and I had no understanding how, despite this being in the media constantly, teenagers were still bullying each other.

Belle told me she didn't really know her and was worried Molly might think she was making fun of her or just being nosey by texting. I asked Belle to pretend she was Molly for just for a minute. To imagine a few hundred people were sending messages slagging her off, name-calling and being vile because she had made a mistake while drunk. I asked her to imagine that she then had the added stress at home of her mum finding out plus the thought of returning to school and facing people, and Belle soon decided to send her a message.

I continued to feel sick after speaking to Belle about how hard teenagers have it now, growing up in a world where they're fixated on likes and comments on an Instagram post or seeing what's being sent around on Snapchat. I felt grateful that Belle was honest with me about what was going on; I told her I always wanted us to be like this and I reminded her of our conversation on the beach that day. No matter what's going on in her head, what she has done or is thinking of doing, or if she had made any mistakes or decisions she's ashamed of, I just want her to be honest with me. If she can promise that, then I can promise I will always help her with any situation.

When you are in those last few years of secondary school, it's funny how it feels like forever. You don't see life past spending your days at school and your weekends with the same friendship groups when the reality is those years are such a small insignificant part of your entire being. In years to come, the people sending texts about Molly having unprotected sex will pass her in the street and not recognise her ... everybody grows and moves on.

Some will go on to uni, move away, get jobs, and have a family. As an adult, those last few years of secondary school are something you rarely think of; yet, when you're in it, like Belle is now, you can't see past it, and I think it's so important to educate our children about that so they don't get overwhelmed with the here and now.

\*

### Sunday

Jamie and I stayed in a hotel in Devon last night. It was amazing!!

Pat ordered us to have a night away together and we had the most incredible time. We've just never done that – like dated; like a couple. When we met, I had the kids and Jamie had to get to know me while I was being a mum, but at least if he could fall in love with me while he was watching me be that then we've got it better than most.

The hotel was in Exeter, in the city centre, and was converted from an old hospital. The view from the room overlooked all the shops and busy roads and it was funny to stand and watch how life carries on, so busy and fast, despite what anyone else is doing.

When we arrived, it looked really contemporary – the reception was just a huge round table made from driftwood and glass. There were young trendy staff stood waiting to greet us wearing crisp white shirts and Converse boots. There was a spa and the food in the restaurant was to die for. We had a walk round the shops and cathedral in the day and sat outside a couple of pubs and basked in the sun, sipping on gin and tonics full of berries and ice. It was a glorious day – bright sunshine with no wind at all.

Today Jamie had booked me a full body massage in the spa and we had a swim before we left for home. On the way we stopped off at a small town called Topsham and wandered round lots of shabby chic shops: my idea of heaven. We had lunch in a pub on the river this afternoon before driving back.

We spoke about everything and nothing. What staying there showed me is that Jamie doesn't do anything for himself, to make him happy, and I want to make sure that when things calm down, we find time to be Jamie and Jo, not just Mum and Dad. I think because we're just so busy day to day and always feel like there must be something we haven't told the other, we spent the majority of the time talking about the kids. It's what all parents say, though, isn't it? That's what happens when you have babies – you crave time away from them but as soon as you get it, all you do is miss them, talk about them and stalk your camera roll for pictures of them! We have definitely enjoyed the time to reflect, though, on how we have got something a lot of people dream of. Despite biologically not having our children together, they all now live under one roof as siblings, and we get to watch them grow each day – and it kind of feels that this situation is a blessing. We're happy. Happy and healthy and luckier than most.

We came home to an 'incident' where I found Pat in the lounge with Marigolds on up to her elbows, hunched over a bucket, scrubbing brush in hand. My first thoughts were that Stanley had shit or pissed – or that Belle had got drunk again – but no. No, what had happened is that Ruby had spent her 50p toast money at school on Friday buying a pot of homemade slime off her friend. A pot of luminous pink slime that was now engrained in the cream shagpile overpriced rug and the arm of the sofa. I could see Pat had lost the will to live by now, and when she looked up, shook her head and said, 'I hope you like pink,' I knew that it wasn't coming out.

I went to the supermarket and bought every stain remover and carpet cleaner I could see but … it's fucked. We now have an entire pot of pink slime scattered through the lounge; there's even a blob on the ceiling. Fuck knows what she was doing with it. Of course she doesn't know how it happened, and after being away for two days I didn't want to come in and lose my shit, so I was super positive about it all, singing away about how 'accidents happen' while wanting to hunt down the person who first put the slime recipe on YouTube and cause them a considerable amount of harm.

Meanwhile Belle stood gawping at me, open-mouthed, reminding me how I lost the plot last week when she spilt a splodge of chocolate milkshake on her bed sheets that can be easily washed, banning her from eating and drinking in her room!

Honestly, I've come to the conclusion that it's pointless trying to have a nice home while raising happy kids. It's one or the other, and I think I'll take the happy kids.

# CHAPTER FIFTEEN

. . . . . . . . . . . . . . . . . . . . . . . . .

# THE PROPER FAMILY

### Monday

Pat has taken over the morning school run. I did try to protest but the kids love her taking them and it means I can just walk from home down to the café without taking the car and my mornings are less stressful – and actually, so are the kids.

Pat has her shit together so well that she stops at the field on the way so they can walk Digby. I mean, I struggle to get them to school on time while they're scoffing a chocolate brioche in the back of the car, and I'm licking a manky tissue I found in the pocket of the car door to wipe the toothpaste off their faces as they run in as the bell sounds. Pat manages to get them all fed, clear up and then walk the bloody dog. It's like a scene from *The Brady Bunch* watching them all take a leisurely stroll out to the car, calm as cucumbers. And instead of knowing that I'll be coming home to Weetabix-cement-encrusted cereal bowls stacked in the sink or the mounting pile of dirty laundry, now I stroll out the door with the peace of mind that the dishes are dried and put away, and the washing is out hanging on the line or in the dryer.

When I arrive at the café, Lou still seems really stressed about going away on holiday. She assures me it's not because she's leaving me in charge, but I can't help think that she isn't completely OK with not being around. Now Pat is here, things will be easier next week; she often pops into the café during the day as she walks Digby down to the beach and ends up pottering about clearing tables and running a dishcloth around.

I can tell Lou really likes Pat – it's impossible not to. She has so much wisdom about everything and her opinions come from a place of knowledge and love. I find I learn so much from the talks we have; whether she's educating me on things I didn't know about or showing me how to look at things differently – and I suppose that's because she's had many years' more life experience than I have. It makes me see we are never too old to learn or teach.

Pat told me she has concerns about Lou. She doesn't say why she has concerns, and I imagine she thinks she's maybe lonely. It's true that Lou doesn't do a lot besides run the café and tend to the boys and her home, but when she left the café that day, Pat took my hand in hers and whispered to me to 'be her friend, always – and if you can, make her a part of our family'.

When we got home later that day, Belle had bought her new friend Molly home from school. I instantly felt a little panic when she introduced us, then I felt guilt. The panic was because I immediately worried about what type of girl she was, what influence she would have over my daughter and what they would get up to, then the guilt that followed was because I realised how judgemental I was being, and hypocritical since I was the one who had actually encouraged Belle to reach out to her and be a friend.

Molly wasn't a slag or a slut, and in the four hours that I spent in her company this evening, I realised she was a really intelligent, kind girl. In my mind, before meeting her, I had decided she came from parents with 'issues'. Maybe drugs or alcohol, maybe they lived in poverty. I realised how wrong and judgemental I had been, and who was I to talk anyway? Molly's mum was a solicitor in a firm across town and she didn't have a dad. When I asked if her parents had split up, she just answered really casually that she had never had a dad and didn't know who he was.

It was clear that Molly didn't want to ask her mum for the morning-after pill, but that wasn't because she would get beaten by the drunken father I had pictured or spat at by her alcoholic mum – it was because she had absolutely no relationship with her mother because she had been raised by a series of nannies.

It made me realise that any child can choose the wrong path. It doesn't matter what upbringing they have, whether they're raised in extreme wealth or desperate poverty. All our kids are at risk of being one decision away from destroying their lives, and it made me more determined than ever to keep my promise to Belle and build an open and honest environment at home for all of the kids. They needed to know how much Jamie and I loved and supported them. I can't bear the thought of any of them going to a friend's parent for support because they can't speak to us.

As I walked up the stairs to put Belle's clean washing in her room, I heard Molly say, 'I wish I had your mum and dad. They're so nice. You're so lucky you all get to eat together round the table as a family and that they want to talk to you.'

I had never even thought of that; in fact, most nights I dreaded mealtimes. The half hour spent eating dinner together round a table where Rex would be so tired Jamie would ask why I was spoon-feeding him when he was 'capable of feeding himself' and I would bitch it's 'just easier AND he's tired out'. Belle would either be in a silent hormonal rage or over-the-top happy – and be loud to the point she usually then made the others hyper. Art and Will would argue over who has the best team on FIFA, and Ruby would cry that she hated whatever meal was served.

Jamie and I would play referee between all the kids where we would usually stick together and be united, but I spent some evenings wishing family meals were quickly over. Sometimes, though, like tonight, someone would tell a tale about something that had happened at school or ask a question that would make us all debate, and we would have a family meal where I would catch Jamie's eye and we would hold each other's stare and I knew he was sat at that table thinking the same as me – that we were so lucky to have this. This crazy chaos full of love and laughter ... and when I heard a fifteen-year-old girl, who had only spent a few hours in our home, pointing that out to my daughter, it made me feel really quite proud at what we've created and it was sad that she didn't have that.

No, Molly wasn't a slag or a slut; she wasn't a sket (whatever that is) or the 'c' word. She was a beautiful teenage girl whose father was absent and whose mother had never taken the time to educate her on self-worth, safe sex or choosing your friendship groups more carefully. She was desperate to be part of a family and be loved.

When she left, I told Belle I had concerns over Molly. I didn't tell her why; I just said, 'Be her friend, always and if you can, make her a part of our family.' Thanks Pat, once again, for passing down your knowledge and guiding me through the universe without even knowing that that's what you're doing.

*

## Tuesday

Pat and I took the kids out after school today. And the dogs. Why the fuck I thought taking Stanley out with five kids and another (perfectly well-behaved) dog was a good idea is beyond me. Every time I'm bordering on desperation with this bloody puppy, I re-google 'Labrador dog help' and I see it flash up that they are 'easy to train'. I can't work out if I am just an incapable dog trainer or if I ended up with the only Labrador puppy that cannot be trained.

When Jamie comes on the walks, he says it's me that's the issue – not the dog. He mutters things like 'Do NOT start being neurotic' when he sees me spot a dog in the distance and reach for Stanley's lead. I wonder if it is partly me – panicking about how he will behave and worrying about other dog owner's reactions so that I end up making him worse. Probably. Probably not. I don't even know. Either way right now it's utterly painful – but the kids are still as obsessed as ever and seeing the way they constantly throw him balls, chase him round, or lay with him on the rug in front of the TV when he finally crashes and burns, makes my heart happy.

Jamie sent a message to Laura today. We spoke about it first and I said I thought it was a good idea because it may help her see we're not her enemies, plus Will and Ruby are her children and hopefully by hearing about them it may keep her focused to get well.

He sent a picture of them together from the garden last weekend. They're beautiful children, they have Jamie's olive skin and both have dark hair – Will's is coarse and thick making it easy to style and Ruby has a real curl in hers that bounces up tight and short when her hair has just been washed. He wrote alongside the picture that both kids are well, happy, doing OK at school and they're both missing their mum; he then ended it by saying he hopes she is OK and gets well soon. Weirdly the kids haven't mentioned her, which I find odd, but their days are busy and Jamie is hands on so I think they've just adjusted – we regularly tell them Mummy loves them and misses them, just so they know it's OK to say it too and they don't pick up on any bad feeling.

Truth is, Laura makes my head tick so often; she makes me wonder about my biological mum more than I ever have before. When my adoptive mum was alive, I rarely thought about my bio-mum. My mum always just told me that my biological mum was too unwell to keep us and she couldn't put our needs above her own. And I suppose since I've ended up taking Will and Ruby on full-time, it's made me question how some mothers struggle to care for their children even more.

I feel annoyed that these things that are happening to us now make me think about things that for the past thirty years haven't ever really been in my head. Like other people's actions make me question and go over my own life and people that are or once were in it. I feel like I should be happy for the here and now and grateful for what I have rather than looking backwards, but maybe looking backwards and learning about what happened to me and my own biological parents may somehow teach me things about moving forwards?

Anyway, Pat and I had a lovely afternoon. I love seeing her with the kids, too; she has all the time in the world to teach them things and explain the unexplainable to them, and she is calm and patient. They love listening to her stories about when 'she was a girl', and they ask her all sorts of questions that make me smile. Questions about things I didn't even know they knew about, like the Fire of London or the Plague. Of course they're asking because they believe their Grandma was around when these things happened and she knows all the answers from her own experiences; I love watching them listen intensely to her answers. Having her here has filled a hole that I didn't even know was there.

*

## Wednesday

Laura replied to Jamie late last night, but we didn't see it until this morning. She wrote 'Thanks to you and Jo for taking such good care of them, please tell them I love them'. It wasn't much of a reply, but it was a reply, and not a negative one, so it can only be a good thing.

I thought about my dad today, a lot. I've realised of late I have always thought about my dad. Even when I haven't realised that's what I'm doing.

I wrote an email to Kitty and Joseph, but I haven't spoken to either of them now in such a long time that I didn't really know what to write. When I see pictures of Joseph's two boys on Facebook, it makes me sad that I'm not a proper auntie to them. Yes, I send them both a gift and card at Christmas and birthdays, but what's that in real life? They don't know who I am – and my kids don't know who Joseph is really . . . and that's such a shame because if you'd have said that to any of us while we were growing up, I don't think we would have ever believed it.

Once upon a time, we were all so fiercely close, and Mum would be devastated to see how we have drifted apart. I will finish the email though, and I will send it. See how they are, see if they've spoken to Dad. See if there is a chance of the three of us getting together to catch up. I don't know whether to just ring Dad. I haven't discussed it with Jamie – I feel embarrassed and worried if Jamie asks why we stopped talking that I will have to tell him, and I'm ashamed of how I acted at that time, so I have always just told him that after Mum died he never recovered and it was easier for us to walk away – which is kind of true, and kind of shit.

I suppose since then I have just buried it away, but with Pat being here it reminds me of how my parents once were, and how I was, and despite my dad now being the opposite of what he once was, I know that he used to be a really good guy, and that he loved us. I wonder if I should perhaps just go and see him, alone, and try to speak to him properly before it's too late. I hate to think of him rattling around the house alone, with no one to look after him – or him even having no one to speak to. He must just drown in loneliness and it makes me wonder why life is so unexplainably cruel at times.

The whole time I have been writing tonight, Stanley has been curled up in between my legs. He has to sleep on you, not next to you or near to you; he has to lie his bodyweight on yours and, despite him driving me crazy, he really is the most loving pup – although he covers the conservatory windows in dog slobber where he tries to catch the flies with his mouth, although he's been stung twice by bees, whenever anyone in the family sits down he sits with you, on you. It's almost a relief to him that he can just stop, chill out and have cuddles – and isn't that what we all want at the end of the day?

\*

## Friday

I took Will for a haircut after school this evening. Pat watched the other three and Belle went to Molly's to get her overnight stuff as Molly's staying at ours tonight. She came for tea last night too. Her mum doesn't get back from the office until late, and her housekeeper clocks off after she's made her dinner at 5.30pm, so she's in the house alone most evenings. I couldn't bear to think of Belle home alone each night with no one to speak to. I worry about not having enough time for Belle in our crowded home, but no one has time for Molly in hers and it's empty. I can't help but feel like she's neglected – yet as a society, we always think neglected children are the ones that come from families living in poverty – not career-driven, wealthy people. It's funny how we all parent so differently.

I realised tonight that when I was driving across town to the barbers, I have never been alone with Will before. Not once. I have never ever been in his company without one of his siblings or Jamie with us. There has never been a time where it's just been him and me. It seemed odd. But a really nice odd. He was so inquisitive about things; he asked me questions and my opinion on various topics, and he wanted to know things about my childhood and family. It made me see there is still so much for us all to learn about one another – and that the children act so differently when you are one-to-one with them than they do when they're together.

After his haircut we walked along the seafront together and sat outside an American diner. Will ordered an Oreo milkshake while I sipped a latte. I told him if he ever needed to speak to me about anything regarding his mum or anything else at all, I was there for him. I tried not to get emotional, but when I told him I loved him very much and how proud I am of everything he's come through, and the fact he's looked after and protected his baby sister so well – a job and responsibility that was never his – I'm afraid I did shed some tears.

He looked embarrassed, probably because he could see I was trying not to get upset, but he said thanks and then he finished it with the sentence, 'Thanks for making us a proper family, Jo,' and my heart almost broke in two.

I knew that's what we were. It really didn't matter that we weren't all related by blood in one way or another. It didn't matter that we had various surnames. We love and care for one another, we argue and shout and fight and we giggle, make jokes and laugh under one roof.

We are a proper family.

# CHAPTER SIXTEEN

. . . . . . . . . . . . . . . . . . . . . . . . . .

# DOING NOTHING BY
# HALVES

## *Monday*

Lou left for her holiday yesterday and I am now running the café until Saturday when the girls and Belle take over and cover.

Surprisingly I don't feel nervous. Belle is in the café helping me this week too as it's half term and we were really busy today; the joy of living in a seaside town in school holidays – I can't believe how crazy it gets with tourists.

Belle's so good; she's really quick and ran rings round the other girl who has been there for the last few months and is a few years older. I watched her as she was wiping and clearing tables and scooping ice creams onto kids' cones, and my heart swelled.

She speaks to people – all types of people. Little old ladies and babies in prams. Families on holidays and the delivery driver.

We have a little old man called Oscar who comes in every Monday when he comes into town to collect his pension. He is eighty-two years old and his wife died three years ago after they'd been married for fifty-one years. They lost their daughter in a car accident when she was just twenty-two and their son emigrated to Australia when he was in his early thirties, leaving Oscar all alone.

Whenever he comes into the café, he finds an unsuspecting customer and tells the exact same story every time. He makes my heart hurt. It's obvious he has learned to live with a broken heart – and I wonder whether he is living, or just surviving.

Today it's a young couple, one of them wearing their baby in a sling. 'Ah, what a bobby dazzler,' Oscar says with a huge smile. 'I remember when my lad was small like that, but to look at him now you'd never believe he had been. This one will grow up before you know it and be running around having his own adventures. My youngest used to write notes and pop them into bottles and drop them into the stream at the bottom of our garden. My boy would chase them down the lane and fish them out in one of our neighbours' gardens to see what she had written, cheeky boy!

His life sounded like once upon a time, it was idyllic. He carries on chatting to the couple but moves on to the delicious bakes his wife would create and their weekends spent on the moors in Devon, frying sausages on a camping stove and feeding apples to wild ponies. When he tells me the stories it reminds me of my parents, and our family, and the hurt I see in Oscar makes me feel so sad for my dad, and men in general. Good men who love their wives are left to somehow cope when they pass away.

I watch Oscar get up from his table and bump into Belle, stopping altogether to tell his story to her, and I can see her face taking it all in as she asks him question after question, which I know he loves. Afterwards she comes into the kitchen with a tray of dirty dishes and bursts into tears. When I hug her and ask her what's wrong, she explains that she hates the thought of him living alone and she genuinely can't fathom why he doesn't have anyone.

My heart hurts at her's breaking and I think about how our babies learn most about life – and the stuff that goes on in it – through other people's stories and experiences. They learn about the good and bad in the world by sitting in a local café and speaking to a man in his eighties about his life, and that's how they understand what goes on, and that's what gives them the empathy and feelings to turn them into better people who can hopefully go on to help others.

Despite being left sad after speaking to Oscar, Belle continues to speak with genuine interest to anyone and everyone about what they're doing – if they're having a good day, if they enjoyed their food – but I've also noticed that she also speaks with pride to total strangers about our family. She tells anyone who asks her that she has 'three brothers and a little sister'; she doesn't add the prefix 'step'. She refers to Jamie as her dad and Pat as her gran, and when she speaks of our lives and what she gets up to, she seems genuinely happy and settled, but more than anything, she seems proud of our little family unit.

As we wander home together later that day, I tell her she doesn't have to tell people we're something we're not. She can be honest if she wants to say that Jamie is my partner and his children live with us; she doesn't have to make out we're the 'perfect family'. She responds by saying, 'We are, Mum. We're perfect compared to a lot of my friends and we're perfect compared to what we had with Mark.'

Mark.

How devastating that this was how she sees her own dad. I try to remember the last time she spoke of him at all, but can't. Part of me feels crushed at how things are but part of me wonders if it's a good thing that she sees it like this and is protecting herself from him causing her any more damage.

One thing I need to always remember, as hard as it feels at times, is that I am not responsible for the actions of Mark, and Jamie isn't responsible for the actions of Laura.

We are two parents out of four, just trying to hold it all together.

*

## Wednesday

The café has been crazy for the past two days. Usually that would be fine as all the customers are regular, but with it being the holidays it's heaving and the tourists don't take it as well as locals when there's a longer wait on food or you serve them a latte instead of a cappuccino because your head is exploding with too many orders.

The locals still come in each day, though. I am lucky to know so many people around here now, and it's shown me what a 'home' feels like in a town, rather than it just being a town (which, it's clear to me now, is what I had in Canterbury).

I am so thankful Belle has been there to help as I have had to order in loads more stock than normal as we have just been inundated with customers. I love the café, and everything about it. I would love, one day, for us as a family to have something similar. I realise now how much I love speaking to people and hearing about people's days, where they're from and what they're up to – and I like people asking me about me.

When Jamie and I first got together I almost felt embarrassed – perhaps even ashamed – of our family unit. Explaining we had five children, but they weren't 'all mine', then watching people trying to figure out the dynamics and who stays where with which parent how often, but now that's stopped. We have five children, my 'partner and I'. When I get remarks such as 'Is there no TV in your house?' or 'You don't look old enough', I laugh it off. I don't explain some aren't biologically mine or that mine don't see their dad. I take my lead from Belle – we are a family, there are no steps or halves, Jamie and I have five children who all live together, under one roof.

One family, that's all people need to know – and now, when I talk about 'us', I burst with pride at what we have created.

\*

## Friday

I am SO glad the week at the café is over. As much as it was fun to run the show full-time and I enjoy being there, I am exhausted.

I asked Pat to help me write a letter to my dad tonight. After hearing the way Belle spoke in the café last week about our family situation it made me see how important it is to have a dad around. As we started, it was like turning a tap on. There was so much I wanted to ask, so much grief there for my mum, and him, that I realised I'd just locked everything away in a box. Even with all the therapy after Mark left me, I had never dredged this up. Pat asked why I didn't just go and see him, why I didn't just knock on his door and see how he was? After all, he was never a nasty man, just broken-hearted and distant.

If I sent a letter, she said, I was making it too easy for him to ignore me; if I rocked up in person, he wouldn't have that option.

I gave up on the letter and agreed to try that. It had been almost sixteen years since I last spoke to him and I felt such a pang of guilt for that. I started thinking about what I would say if I did ring that bell, and he answered the door.

The thought made me feel sick to the pit of my stomach ...

## Sunday

Jamie and I had a fight this morning.

It started when we went downstairs for breakfast and Jamie just started nagging at the kids. I know everyone nags at their kids but it pissed me off because I felt like he was picking faults simply because he was tired and miserable.

He started off telling Belle she should eat some fruit, and when she rolled her eyes in annoyance, he just went off on one about them all constantly eating too much crap and not enough fruit and veg. It sounds so pathetic even when I write it down but I got so annoyed with him because it was the first morning in ages that he had sat and eaten breakfast with us, and it should have been enjoyable, yet having him here just felt like hell.

I know in hindsight I overreacted, and I know I should have spoken to him away from the kids and his mum, but with everything that's been going on just lately, with Laura (who's still scarily deadly silent), the worry over Ruby and Will, and my issues about my own dad, I just lost my shit and told him he was being an arsehole. I saw Will look up from his cereal bowl in shock and Pat began scurrying around talking to the children extra loudly in a high-pitched voice to try to drown out my rant.

Now, I keep cringing every time I think about it. But it felt like he was having a dig at me; like I don't feed the kids well enough when actually they all eat really well, and then I just felt really defensive towards the kids and I just lost it.

At the beginning he was trying to defend himself, telling me (calmly but firmly) that he's out earning a wage and trying to be there for us all as much as possible, but by the end he was silent (like the kids, and his mum) while I continued to lose my shit (now with the entire family) about how fucking hard it all is and how the only person that helps and supports me is Pat. I ended it with 'so when she goes home – we're all fucked'. Even Belle stayed silent when she is always usually the voice of reason.

I came upstairs and sobbed into my pillow, those heavy sobs, like a toddler would make when not allowed another Jaffa cake before dinner. The sobs where you still miss a breath half an hour after you've finished crying and your eyes are puffy and sore for a good day after. Stanley lay beside me, as if he knew I wasn't OK. It's funny how a dog loves you no matter how much of an arsehole you've been.

Pat came up after a while, laden down with a tray bearing a cup of tea and a warm croissant with a slab of salted butter and dollop of her home-made jam. As soon as I saw her, I started crying again. I felt so ashamed of my behaviour. I told her I was sorry and that her son was a good man and I didn't know why I had behaved like that. I promised her I have never spoken to him like that before, and I can't bear the thought of her thinking that's normal for us. I was trying to talk but was now in such a state I couldn't get my words out and was heaving with sobs.

Pat sat on the bed, pulled me into her scarf, which again smelt of the most sweet, expensive perfume possible, and repeatedly whispered, 'It's just too much right now, darling, it's all too much,' while stroking my hair.

And she's right.

Right now, five children, running a home, the ongoing issues with Laura, a house sale and holding down a job just feels too much.

# CHAPTER SEVENTEEN

* * * * * * * * * * * * * * * * * * * * * * * * * *

# LAUGHTER IS THE BEST MEDICINE

*Monday*

Sertraline.

That's the anti-depressant I was prescribed today after I went to see the GP. I explained how I was feeling, and I tried to explain the reasons I was feeling like it. I wanted nothing more but for the doctor to reassure me, and tell me everything would be OK – but he didn't. Instead he gave me a leaflet to refer myself to the depression and anxiety service (with the words 'There was a considerable waiting list when I last checked'. Reassuring). And a prescription for medication (with the words 'If you don't feel it's getting any better after a couple of weeks, pop back and I will up the dosage'. Even more reassuring).

I don't think I'm depressed. I don't want to be depressed. I know I am so lucky compared to other people.

I felt awful telling Lou – she's just had a week's holiday where I promised I'd hold the fort and the day she returns I rock into work an hour late, which in hindsight I think has made me feel worse.

I was really honest with her and she was so kind to me, so reassuring ... but I could tell she almost didn't get it, and why would she? She is happily married, she and her husband both have careers they love, and they have two beautiful kids together. Ultimately, they don't have the challenges that come with ex-partners and trying to be a blended family ... life for them is like mine was years ago – easier. Easier in terms of just being a family, with nothing but a few family issues, that you work through together, because you're all on the same page. But on days like this I need to remember that even though my life back then was 'easier' in some ways, I never got the pangs of happiness and contentment I get these days ... it's hard to remember that sometimes.

*

### Tuesday

I am not going to collect my prescription.

I'm not depressed.

I'm stressed – there's a difference. Pat agrees I'm not depressed, and that I shouldn't start the tablets, and that made me feel better.

I spoke to Jamie before he left for work this morning, both of us were tossing and turning all night, pretending to be asleep when we both knew the other one was also wide awake. It feels awful when we argue, a hideous worried feeling in the pit of my stomach. I told him there was no excuse for how I was, it shouldn't have happened. As usual he made everything better too by apologising for his part – for saying things that just didn't need to be said and sometimes not seeing how hard this is for me also. We had a long tight hug where I buried my head into his neck and breathed in his scent and he pulled me in, stroked my hair and told me everything would be OK (at that point I wanted to thank Pat, the girl did good raising her son).

I apologised to everyone at the dinner table this evening. I explained I wasn't making an excuse for losing my temper, that my outburst was wrong. As I was just getting into full swing of my speech Jamie interrupted and told everyone that right now things are hard with everything going on and although it accumulated into me having a wobble then losing my cool we may both be a bit distant, snappy or tired at the minute but we are trying our best not to be any of those things. It ended with Belle making a joke to the little ones that I'd been wobblier than a jellyfish eating jelly, and suddenly we were all smiling and laughing. Belle looked up at me and rolled her eyes to the ceiling while smiling as if we both knew she had saved me from my awkward speech.

Ruby stood up, walked round to me and wrapped her arms around my neck and buried her head into my cheek and said, 'I love you, Jo.' It made a hard lump immediately form in my throat and made me feel shit. These five babies have had enough abandonment and rejection between them to last a lifetime; they need nothing but stability from me, not to see me having a meltdown.

I caught Jamie's eye and he gave me the look, followed by a leg squeeze and a wink, and I knew we were OK. I felt such a sense of relief, and a wave of more guilt that I had behaved like such a dick when he does nothing but love me.

I just want us to always be OK. Always.

\*

## Wednesday

I got a call just before 7am from Lou's husband David. He was really sweet and apologetic for calling and I was embarrassed as his call had woken me out of a deep sleep I shouldn't really have been in at that time of the morning, considering five kids needed sorting for school. He explained Lou had been up all night with the most horrendous sickness bug so couldn't make it in today. He asked if I was OK to work alone as he couldn't get any other cover at such short notice.

I agreed immediately – knowing we were out of cakes and wondering how I would manage *totally* alone as I had always had Belle with me. I didn't want to ask David about the cakes, as I was worried he would ask Lou and it would just cause her more stress. I thought about calling Jen and asking her to come and help, but then I felt bad as she has a demanding job and might be on shift, or off work and wanting to spend time with her son.

Just then, Pat knocked on my bedroom door, armed with the cup of tea she now brought in each morning, and I told her about the call as I was yanking my hair into a ponytail so it didn't get wet in the shower.

'Don't worry,' she said. 'I'll pop a tray of brownies in now and I made a Victoria sponge yesterday.'

I felt a sudden relief. Good old Pat.

I got downstairs just after 7.30am. By the time I'd showered, the brownies were already baking.

'They'll be ready for 8.15am – if you take them into the café they can cool there and I will come straight there after the school run,' she said.

I looked around and saw the house was already immaculate. The kids were tucking into cereal and toast and Belle was just leaving to catch the bus. The washing was blowing away on the line. I felt a sense of sadness and panic. How would I ever manage once Pat left and returned home? I had no clue how I would now do ALL of this stuff without her. Still, we managed before she arrived and as much as it would be a bit more of a shit show with two extra kids to look after, we would manage once again.

The shift at the café was fine. We didn't have a special on but most people voted for a slab of brownie, after the amazing smell of them went through the entire café, and down the road, it would seem, from the amount of people asking about them.

Pat got stuck in too; I could tell she really loved helping and she just knew what to do.

She is a real 'carer' and loves ensuring people are looked after at all times, that you have enough food and drink, that places are clean and that you're comfortable. I imagine she was an amazing wife to her husband when he was alive. From the stories she tells, I can see how in love they were, and from that I understand why she's never gone on to meet anyone else who compares.

As much as Jamie and I have things tough with what we've got going on, and we've only been together a couple of years, he still makes my heart beat faster when he comes in from work and I still get a panic of emotion when I think of what I'd do if anything ever happened to him.

I remember when I was speaking to Megan on the beach about her losing her baby, and out of the two of us, I ended up more emotional than her, because I told her I wouldn't be able to 'cope and carry on' like she has. I said to her that I was in awe of her strength, because I was. A few weeks after losing her baby she was on a beach, making memories with her other children, facing stares and looks from strangers in public. I don't think I will ever forget her response to me that day.

'You know, Jo, you don't ever think you'd cope when it's not happening to you,' were her words. 'It's sometimes harder for the people looking in, imagining themselves trying to cope in such pain, in such an unbearable situation, but when you are the ones in the pain, when you are the ones living in that unbearable situation, you don't have any option but to survive. You cannot drown in it because you have to continue each day for the people who need you; there is no choice, Jo. It's just something that has to be done. You have no option but to survive.' It made me look at things so differently. Losing someone – whether through death or having your husband abandon you – forces you to make a choice. You either stop and go with them, or you carry on, you fight – just like my mum's friend told my dad after the funeral – you somehow have to find a way to cope with the grief and pain and hurt, and you try to resume some kind of normality for the people around you that need it – for the people who need *you*.

\*

## Thursday

Lou still isn't back. David texted today to say she would be off until Monday as he was worried she would worsen if she came back too soon. I replied to him to say I could drop them off a lasagne or something for dinner but he said he had it covered. It's sweet that David has such a high-powered career and yet he still puts Lou above it all.

I think Jamie is really nervous about what's going to happen going forward with Laura; he spoke to Pete yesterday and she's still in hospital. He didn't say where but he said it's private, which I assume means she's there out of choice. He re-confirmed she's still unwell and he would update us as and when he needs to. He was really lovely on the phone, Jamie called him while he was sat with me in the kitchen and the kids were all outside playing so I could hear their conversation. He asked how the kids were, if we were enjoying Cornwall and he told Jamie he had managed to get in a few rounds of golf this week, which he sounded chuffed about. They ended the call on good terms and said they would speak soon.

I get why Jamie is worried, because I often feel it too, not just with Will and Ruby but with my three also. I regularly find myself sitting outside their bedroom door so I can listen to them play or watch them interact with each other; or I just sit, and watch them sit, while they watch a film or do their homework, and I wonder what goes on inside their tiny brains.

Every single child in this house has been let down by one of their birth parents, and although Jamie and I are dedicating our lives to ensuring they have a stable home environment where they feel loved and secure, I can't help but wonder what they actually think about it all. Do they keep their questions or worries to themselves as they don't want to worry or upset us, or are they actually OK?

They seem OK. In fact, they seem happy. And to an outsider looking in, they have the perfect life, but then it's our job, I suppose, as parents, to always question if that's the case, isn't it?

\*

### Saturday

We've had the loveliest day today.

As soon as we woke up, the sun was streaming through the blinds, and with the seagulls squawking outside, I almost felt like I was waking up on holiday. I knew it was going to be a good day; I could just tell. We had plans to spend the afternoon and early evening having a BBQ at Megan's house. I could tell Jamie didn't really want to go. He's not one for male friends and I think he was really nervous about having to socialise with total strangers.

But Megan's husband John is a really lovely guy – he reminds me a lot of Jamie – and the way he and Megan are as a couple, especially after everything they've endured lately, is truly heart-warming to see.

We took all the kids with us, and Pat had been invited too. Megan and John had their two kids at home as well as John's elder son, Jacob. They are in the process of slabbing part of their garden to get a hot tub fitted and they have a huge play frame and tree house, on which the younger kids played all afternoon. It worked perfectly and they all got along so well together.

Belle was an absolute weirdo and stuck beside me like glue for the first few hours, and I soon realised that she'd taken a shine to Jacob. He is ridiculously beautiful and they both played the 'awkward teenager' game until John needed more hot dog rolls so he sent them to the shop together. When they returned, they announced they were going back out and disappeared down to the beach together.

The sun was shining. We ate the most amazing food and sipped on iced G&Ts.

Pat came along and after we had eaten, she, Megan and I returned to their huge swinging bench seat and as we rocked slowly catching the final bit of warm sunshine, Pat, as usual, blew me away with her words of wisdom, this time for Megan. She has the knowledge and understanding to support people in any circumstance and speak such sense to them, even ones she's only just met. She took Megan's hand in hers and told her stories I'd never heard as we slowly rocked. I sat in silence and listened, and it was amazing to see the ability Pat has to heal others, and, although Megan shed a few tears, I could tell she was so grateful to have Pat there to talk to about it all.

As we left to stumble home, John thanked us for coming. 'We don't really have many friends,' he said, 'and I have to be honest, I was dreading this, but it's been a great day – just what Meg needed.'

Belle and Jacob still weren't back so I texted her and we agreed she would be home for 10pm.

When she walked in just before ten she said Jacob had walked her home and when I asked if she liked him, she told me to not 'be gross' and trotted up the stairs to bed absolutely beaming.

I looked at Jamie and he smiled, rolled his eyes and said, 'Now the fun starts ... '

I wondered how this new chapter for Belle – and us – was going to pan out.

# CHAPTER EIGHTEEN

......................

# SAME BUT DIFFERENT

## Sunday

Molly came over this evening to sleep. Her mum, Jaclyn, dropped her off and I made a point of going out into the drive to introduce myself. She was dressed in a beige trouser suit with a crisp white shirt and black patent stilettos. She's really attractive, with an ash-blonde bob that sits sharp on her jawline, piercing blue eyes and a Swedish look to her. I asked if she'd had a nice day and she said she'd been busy catching up with work from her office at home.

I felt sad. I knew from Belle that Jaclyn had been away on business all week and yet she didn't seem to see anything wrong with the fact that on the one day she could have spent with Molly she had chosen to work again. And I think I would understand that more if she was a single mum trying to earn a wage to pay bills and make sure there was food on the table, but they live in a huge stately home, she drives a brand-new Range Rover, and she was stood there popping her electric boot to fetch Molly's bag in a designer suit and Louboutin heels.

How could our lives be so different when so many of the features were the same? Teenage daughter? Check. Home in an idyllic seaside resort? Check. Absent baby daddy? Check. Check. Check. I know that everyone is different, and you never really know what's going on in someone's life, etc., etc., etc., but I do find it hard to understand why, if you had a kid like Molly, you wouldn't be carving out more time to spend with her. She must *really* love being a solicitor ...

Before she drove off she wanted to know the ins and outs of all of Molly's plans: where she was going, who she would be seeing and speaking to. Then she gave her a wad of notes and even when Molly protested that she didn't need money, she refused to let her stay with us unless she accepted it. It's not my style – even if I could afford it – but I guess we all show love differently.

She did try to make conversation with me, but again it was all work-based. She said she was working from the office locally this week although she would probably be back late most nights. I told her Molly was welcome at ours whenever she wanted to stay and she thanked me. It was a genuine thank you and for a moment it looked like there was a sadness behind her smile, and I couldn't help but feel a bit sorry for her and the life she had. She was missing out on so much with her daughter, and in just the small amount of time I'd spent with Molly, I knew what a shame that was.

\*

## *Monday*

Lou was back at work today. She looked different. Her hair was usually a mass of untamed wild curls, but today it was pinned to the back of her head with her crocodile clip and she looked frail. I went in and gave her a huge hug and it felt like she had lost weight.

She apologised for being unwell last week and asked me how I'd managed while she had been away. I told her it had been fine, and it had. I mean, I needed Pat to help, but we had managed perfectly. Lou gave me a white envelope, told me to pop it in my bag and open it when I got home and keep it between us. I agreed but felt uneasy.

I had brought in a tray of Pat's brownies today as I wasn't sure if Lou would definitely be back and upon her trying one, she asked if Pat would be interested in earning a bit of money and doing the baking while she was staying with me. I said I'd ask, but was sure she would.

By 10am a huge bouquet of flowers had arrived for Lou, with a card that read 'Thank you for being the best wife to me and mum to our boys'. She looked embarrassed, but I told her the flowers were beautiful and divided them up and scattered them around the café in the quirky little collection of vases we had accumulated from bottles and other items the kids had found on the beach.

Jen came in at lunchtime, greeting us with the line, 'Ooh, that quiche looks to die for, and I need a treat today. I'll have a big slice please, with salad.'

I delivered it to the table she'd chosen right by the counter and noticed that she looked ruffled.

'All OK, Jen?' I asked her.

'Yeah, kind of,' she said with a shame-faced grin. 'It's been a bit of a morning. I dropped the kids off at school and nursery this morning then on the way back a man in a white van pulled out in front of me. I beeped my horn at him but that only riled him and he gave me the middle finger. I overtook him on the dual carriageway and gave him another hand gesture but then he started following me.'

Jen lives near a farm, down long winding roads that get minimal traffic, and when the guy in the van was still following her, she went into a panic and called the police. They told her to keep driving and so she drove past her driveway then watched the van turn into her house, massively freaking her out. She kept driving and by now was in a total state. A few minutes later her husband called her to say the plumber had rang him to say he was outside the house to fix the leaking tap but no one was home .... .

Lou and I cried with laughter at the way she told the story. She was so mortified that she'd called the plumber a wanker that she couldn't face going home and she made her husband leave work to go and let him in while she sat in her car up the road and waited for him to leave. Only Jen ...

*

## Wednesday

I woke up this morning and suddenly remembered about the envelope Lou had given me. I opened it and there was a card in it, which read: 'Thank you, you have no idea how much you have helped. Please keep this between us two, Much love, L'. There was £500 in cash. Five hundred pounds – ridiculous. I told Jamie and Pat immediately. They said it was a nice gesture, she could afford it, and reminded me I had been running the café on and off, so I should gracefully accept and not worry about it.

I arrived at work and went on a meltdown as soon as I walked in, saying to Lou that I couldn't possibly accept the money.

'Nonsense,' was her response. 'Remember, it's just between us,' she said.

I decided to accept, gracefully – and I felt secretly chuffed at the appreciation she had shown me.

We still haven't heard anything from Laura or her parents and it's slightly unnerving, and, in a way, makes me worry more, but at the same time it's so nice to just be able to raise the kids without any drama.

Pat, as usual, reminds us that 'everything will work out for the best', and I can't help but worry that maybe she's wrong on this score. She's so calm, and convinced the children will be looked after, and I'm not sure how she always remains so positive and happy.

I catch her squeezing Jamie's shoulder after dinner as we're collecting the plates off the table and I see him reach up and hold her hand in his. The kids don't pick up on it, but it's heart-warming to see: a mum looking after her little boy, her only child, who's now a fully grown adult and dad, who's trying his best to look after his children; and him responding to her touch to thank her.

It reminded me of a chiropractor I'd visited years ago when I was pregnant who had told me that her teenage daughter had met her first boyfriend. I'd asked her if she liked him and she'd told me that she'd treated his nan for years before meeting him. She'd said that this lady had always spoken of how she loved spending time with her daughter and her grandson, doing the school runs with him and hanging out on weekends with them. I remembered her words from that day: 'When you know someone has been raised feeling that much love, by such lovely people, chances are they're going to be a good person'. Her words flooded back to me tonight when I watched Pat and Jamie.

\*

*Friday*
David called Jamie this morning and said he'd received a letter from Laura's solicitor's firm agreeing to us keeping the children with us for the foreseeable future. It stated that Laura has accepted she has 'issues', which she is currently getting help with. The letter was just a few sentences long

but ended thanking us for all we had done and continued to do for the children.

David said we had two options, to apply to court now to make the children living with us a permanent thing – chances are the courts would wait on her treatment plan, etc., anyway and it would be a long drawn-out process – or we wait. She could get treatment, and recover – and ultimately, this was in the children's best interest in the long run anyway. It could potentially save a stressful costly battle and tens of thousands of pounds, or there was the other option that she wouldn't get better, the children would remain with us for a longer period, then if she did decide she wanted them back we would have better grounds to keep them residing with us as it would disturb them too much to uproot them again.

We decided to wait and instructed David to reply asking her for an update in a month's time.

I called Jen and spoke to her about it all – she's sweet and offers good advice, and she texts regularly to ask me how things are and just check in on me. I haven't had that before, and it's a nice feeling when my phone pings and I know it's a message from her.

We've arranged to go on a spa day on Monday. It's my day off from the café and Pat offered to ferry the children to and from school so we could enjoy the whole day without watching the clock. The spa is in a hotel on a cliff that overlooks the whole town and has huge sheets of glass as one of the walls to show the view across the beaches. We invited

Lou but she'd got the boys off as they school privately so have different/longer holidays, meaning that she can't make it. But I'm looking forward to just spending time with Jen.

*

## Sunday

Jamie and I went for lunch today, just the two of us. We walked into town and ate at a pub/restaurant on the harbour. It's quite exclusive, done out in an industrial theme with matte silvers, brass and coppers and wooden décor that looks old, battered and funky, but the food is amazing. I had a pint of prawns to start and a trio of pork for main and Jamie had steak, and we shared a bottle of wine.

Belle and Molly went and met Jacob and his friend – I wondered if I should have informed Jaclyn that they were hanging out with boys, as although Molly is allowed to sleep at ours she comes armed with a strict set of 'do's and don'ts – but I thought about it, and by telling her there was every chance she would have come and collected her and locked her back up in her tower like Rapunzel, and actually I don't think there is anything wrong with fifteen-year-old girls hanging out with fifteen-year-old boys so I decided against it. Rex and Ruby went to Meg's and played with her kids, and Pat took Art and Will swimming.

I realise, when it's just the two of us, how much I miss Jamie. Time alone with him is something I love but don't get very often.

When it's just Jamie and me, we get to be us. We get to talk about everything and nothing and giggle at stupid stuff, and I learn so much more about him every time we're alone. I think I know it all and then he will tell me a tale from his childhood or a story of a holiday or something that happened to him at work years prior to meeting me and it makes me laugh until I cry. I love learning about him; I love knowing what he likes and dislikes. I never want us to stop talking and being interested in one another, no matter how old we get or how stressful and busy our lives are.

We finished lunch, had a wander round the little shops in town, and then wandered back up the hill with an ice cream. We got home late afternoon and Pat had roasted a chicken with salad and crusty bread for tea.

All the kids were dotted around the house, watching films or on their tablets, and Belle was in her room chatting to Jacob on FaceTime. When I went in, she whispered to me that Molly was staying at her own house tonight then ushered me out. As I was closing the door, I heard her say, 'Sorry. I muted you because my mum came in.' Like Jamie said, this is where the fun starts ...

After the kids were fed, bathed and in bed, Pat went out to the summer house with a cup of tea and a book, and Jamie and I opened a bottle of red wine and got on the sofa together. He rubbed my feet and smiled along to the TV and I got one of 'those' moments again, and I haven't had one for a while. The one where I thought, if this all goes wrong one day – if it all ends in disaster somehow – I will remember how I felt right now and it'll be worth it for this feeling here, today, because some people never feel this happy in their entire lifetime.

# CHAPTER NINETEEN

. . . . . . . . . . . . . . . . . . . . . . . . . . . .

# ABSENT FATHERS

## Monday

I met Jen in town today, as we both live a ten-minute walk away but from opposite directions. We got the bus up the hill to the spa as it's a real trek but also because Jen suggested having a prosecco or two with our lunch, so we left the cars at home. Jen's husband is working from home today and Pat is at mine so they're doing the school runs this afternoon. For once there is no rush for us to get back, which feels lovely, and unusual.

The spa was ridiculously stunning. The view of the beach over the cliffs was breathtaking (although it made me have a quick horrid flash of Laura and I wondered what she must have been thinking on 'that day'. I quickly stopped myself and remembered I was here to rest and relax!).

The spa décor was dark, all plums and navy. The ladies working there had matching uniforms – some navy, some plum and a mix of buttons, collars, skirts and trousers. The smell was divine, the standard of cleaning was amazing and they had dispensers of drinking water dotted about with berries and slices of cucumber and lemon in.

From 10.30am until 4.30pm we swam, steam-roomed, saunaed and lazed about on the plush beds chatting, snoozing, people-watching and reading the books we had brought along. I brought *The Star Outside my Window*. It's a book about domestic abuse, written from the innocent child's point of view. Jen asked me if it's good, I told her heart-breaking, but amazing.

Jen was reading *The Secret* by Rhonda Byrne – I was intrigued as she explained how it had changed her life, she reads passages regularly as a self-help book, which is what she was doing today. It focuses on the law of attraction and teaches people how positive thinking can lead to happiness, health and wealth. I wasn't sure if it was true, but she sold it to me and I could do with more positivity, so it arrives Thursday.

We ate the loveliest lunch which came on a china stand full of tiny sandwiches, with the cucumber and salmon being the best. We had lots of dainty cakes which we washed down with a bottle of prosecco then we strolled to have our pedicures in a fit of the giggles because the fizz had gone to our heads! Bliss.

I walked in at home to everyone sat round eating dinner. Pat gave me a huge hug and asked if I'd had a lovely day. Jamie was making all the kids laugh delivering crap accents on their orders of whatever country and city they fancied choosing.

I have spent tonight buzzing. I have had the best day, going out away from the house and kids and just having a friend that I can speak to about stuff is the nicest feeling ever and just before I came up to bed to write this Jen messaged: 'Had the best day in a long time today, thanks for making me laugh so much. Must do again soon and drag Lou along.'

Made me smile because she was right, and I know Lou would feel exactly how I do next time we go.

## Tuesday

I met up with Megan this morning for a coffee on the beach. I brought the flask and she bought the most delicious homemade flapjacks that I have ever tasted.

She told me that she's really struggling at the moment and feels isolated. Although she can always talk to me about what happened, having a stillbirth isn't something you can stop and chat about to the supermarket checkout girl or an old friend in the street – and sometimes, she feels desperate to talk about it. She doesn't do social media, and although I've never been one to understand people that declare war and peace across their social media pages, I did mention to her about joining some like-minded groups on Instagram or Facebook.

At first, she didn't seem sure, but I explained to her that after Mark left, I found my evenings utterly boring once the kids were in bed, and joining social media had given me a support system just when I needed it most. I had read some horrid internet stories, but after joining Instagram and Facebook, I'd found quite a community of people who were going through the same thing as me – pages set up by women who help and support other women.

I had a look today after speaking to Megan and found a baby loss support group that looked really good. People have set up accounts to share their stories, to raise awareness and to let others know it's OK to talk. I think that it may help Megan to speak to other women who have been through what she has and she said she would think about setting up an account.

I can't imagine what it must feel like to go through an entire pregnancy then be met with nothing but devastation. I keep thinking about when her milk must have come in, but her having no baby there. It's just soul-destroying. And you have to just carry on for the children you do have.

I finally emailed my sister Kitty tonight to tell her about my plan to visit Dad. The time difference in Hong Kong means she will probably respond tomorrow. I haven't heard from her in a few months, she tends to message me a batch of pictures and quick update every eight weeks or so. She always asks how the kids are; she would have made the best auntie if things had been different. She was always way more natural and maternal with kids than I was when we were growing up and it's ironic that I'm now the one surrounded by them 24/7, and she's still showing no signs of settling down or having kids.

I think, for her, teaching kids every day but then being able to do what she wants when she wants is a life she's got used to and enjoys ... and who can blame her for that?

\*

## Thursday

Lou seemed really quiet today at work.

I invited her, David and the boys to a BBQ at our house with Megan and John next weekend, but she didn't seem sure. I thought it may be a bit weird with David advising Jamie about the issues with Laura, but they seemed to get on fine and it's not like we would start talking about child access arrangements over hot dogs and beer.

She said she would speak to David and let me know, as she wasn't sure what plans they had. I asked what stuff they did together on weekends, but it seems like the boys have a lot of sports clubs, so they mainly spend their time ferrying them about, which I understand. I wondered if she has any other friends; no one other than Jen ever comes in to see her at work and I don't think they socialise much together out of the café. Some people, though, myself included, just like being at home with their families. Social lives and large friendship groups are not something that interest them, and David and Lou are always together doing stuff on weekends and in the evenings, so it must just work for them.

*

## Saturday

I don't even know how to write this … I feel like I'm in a dream. A daze.

My brother called at 7 o' clock yesterday morning to let me know that Dad had passed away.

'Jojo,' he said, using a name I hadn't heard in forever so I knew something was wrong, 'Dad's neighbour, Mavis, has just called me. It's bad news. Dad had a heart attack. He didn't make it … '

As I write this, I should have been on the train for three hours already, travelling to see him to somehow try to make things right – at the very least make peace with him. Only now it's too late.

I don't know how to feel, but I feel a huge amount of guilt. I can't get the image of my dad, my elderly dad, all alone, dying on his own with no one he loves near him. Jamie keeps telling me it isn't my fault, that I *was* going to go and make amends, but that almost feels worse – that it took me so long. That I never got there and he never knew I was coming. He died not knowing, after not speaking to me for well over a decade.

Joseph asked if I wanted to tell Kitty or if he should. I explained I had emailed to tell her I was going to see Dad today, but that I'd had no response. When I told him that, he said, 'I'm sorry, Jo. He would have loved that,' and my heart throbbed again.

Kitty is six hours ahead of us, and it was the weekend, so I agreed to make the call knowing she's off work. Joseph sounded OK, and he comforted me for ages as I just sobbed down the phone. I was sobbing for everything – for Mum, for Dad and for the lost relationship between all of us. For not being an aunt to Joseph's kids, for him not being an uncle to mine, but I also sobbed because I still had no idea why we had ever been adopted in the first place and right now, for some reason, I sobbed for the unknown more than ever before.

Kitty broke down when I told her. Her tears then followed for Mum, and Dad, and the fact that everything we had known as children had fallen apart. We cried together and she told me she would speak to her boss and arrange a flight home ASAP.

We have a funeral to plan for a man who had once been the perfect father, yet who we now no longer know. It all just feels so wrong.

*

### Sunday

Kitty's flight gets in on Tuesday. I'm going to meet her at the airport with Jamie; we have agreed to stay at Dad's house together until Joseph gets in from tour on Thursday as it's not far from Gatwick so it makes sense. He wasn't due home for another seven weeks but the army have allowed him to leave this week so he can be home for Dad. We have to sort the funeral, the house, etc.

I feel like I'm still in a daze; I feel like a fraud – planning a funeral and sorting stuff for a man I have made no effort with for so long, but one who once gave up so much to give me a childhood that was the opposite, I imagine, to the one I could have had if we'd stayed in care. The guilt is unbearable.

I am, however, looking forward to seeing Joseph and Kitty, as shit as the situation is. The three of us haven't been together for years as it's been a case of 'out of sight, out of mind'. Now, the thought of seeing them is nice – because once upon a time the three of us were the best of friends.

*

### Tuesday
We're leaving shortly to go and collect Kitty from the airport. Jamie is driving up. Pat is having the kids and has been her usual amazing self and just taken control of everything, not smothering me but just loving me enough to make me feel like this shit situation actually isn't all my fault and it *will* get better.

Yes, I probably should have made contact with my dad way before sixteen years had passed, but I was a mum, prioritising my kids. I'd had a wanky husband who'd left me and these were all things fed back to my dad by my brother and sister, so he could just as easily have contacted me but he'd chosen not to.

As hard as it is, it's utterly pointless re-living the 'what ifs?' and the things that we could have and should have done. Obviously that's easier said than done, and right now all I'm doing is walking around feeling like the world's worst daughter, the realisation has hit that my children will never know their grandad, who was once the most amazing dad.

Mark's parents have lived in Spain since the kids were babies and his relationship with his parents was always odd, and distant, so other than Pat they've never experienced life with grandparents. I can't help but wonder if they would have somehow turned Dad back into the 'old him' if they'd met him, the Dad we'd lost the day Mum died.

Belle is so reassuring, telling me repeatedly not to worry and that she will take care of the little ones and help Pat, and I know she will. She's so good and I feel so lucky that I don't have the typical stroppy teenager at times like this. I often wonder when that child will appear, but I hope it never will. I don't ever want to lose the relationship we have now because even though she is just fifteen, there are times she makes sense of situations I just don't understand and she helps me to see things in a different, more positive way.

# CHAPTER TWENTY

## SOME LIGHT IN THE DARKNESS

*Saturday*

Well, this week comes a close second to the most drained I have ever felt in my life since the aftermath of trying to cope when Mark left us.

My head is still spinning; I haven't even been able to take in what we've been doing, seeing and reading, and I'm pretty sure Kitty and Joseph feel the same.

Jamie was amazing; he got on so well with both of them, and I feel utterly devastated at how much we've missed out on. Despite the shit circumstances that have brought us back together, we have had so much fun, spending our days laughing until we cried and crying until we laughed. Joseph is still as sarcastic as ever and his dry sense of humour made Kitty and me give each other numerous side smiles like we once did. I think we've all come away wondering why we lost contact; why *we* allowed the death of our amazing mum and the change in our dad to destroy the relationship that the three of us had, which was once so precious.

Seeing them has made me realise how much I miss the three of us hanging out, talking about memories only we have, and being in a home together for a few days that holds so many special memories – of the best parts of our entire childhoods.

Kitty has come back to stay with us in Cornwall for a few days until the funeral, and the kids already love her. She tells me her life abroad is lonely at times and she didn't realise how lonely until she was surrounded by us. She is career minded, a grafter, but I think with Dad dying and spending time with me, Jamie and our family, she's perhaps wondering if there's more to life than what she has right now.

Kitty is sleeping in with Belle. I wondered if it would be awkward at first, and I had made up the spare room for her, but Belle embraces anyone and Kitty said she wanted to hang out with her niece rather than go to bed on her own early. Belle is intrigued by people's stories, and Kitty and I are really alike – both in looks and personality. It's 11pm now and I can see the night light is still on in Belle's room and I can hear their whispered chats and giggles across the hall. It makes me feel both happy and sad that this 'could' be their relationship. I wish this was a permanent thing where Belle had a cool boho aunt she could tell her hopes and dreams to and find out more things about her mum that I've either locked away or forgotten, and I wish I had my sister here with me to remember a life I once had, before I became the me I am now.

There is so much paperwork to go through, so much still to sort.

We have agreed the house will go on the market. Dad had a lot of savings and everything will be split equally between the three of us. It's an odd feeling – knowing that financially I will always be OK now with the house sale from Mark and now Dad's death; despite the reasons for being financially secure, I still feel lucky – some people never get a break like this.

The funeral is on Tuesday and Kitty is trying to speak to as many people as she can to let them know the details, but Mum and Dad didn't have many friends and I have a feeling Dad hasn't seen anyone they knew together since she died. The neighbours told Joseph he would go out every morning at 9am, for an hour, returning with his daily paper and a bag of grocery shopping, but other than that he was always home, alone.

The house is exactly the same as when Mum left, although not up to her immaculate standard anymore. It was just the house of a man, with a broken heart, who'd spent the last decades of his life not living, but surviving, so keeping his once family home clean was probably the last thing on his mind. How devastating is that ... ?

While Jamie and I were there, we made a promise to one another that if the worst was to happen, we would always try our best to 'carry on' as best we could for the sake of those around us and if we felt we couldn't we would then try our best to seek help, to engage with our kids, to be focused and to keep plodding. I also know that now, going forward, I will make more time for people struggling. I could have, I SHOULD HAVE done far more to support Dad, to make him better, to force my children into his life to try to make him smile again – he was never going to find himself again without our support and that's something we now have to live with. Mum would have never wanted Dad to spend the last seventeen years like he did. My only consolation is a hope that they're reunited again, back together – smiling and laughing and cooking curries, pottering in the garden and looking at new cars. I hope that in him going from here he's back to being happy with Mum ...

What we did find when we were sorting and bagging and cleaning the contents of our once-beloved home, is bundles of paperwork from when we were adopted. Kitty went to the post office and made two copies on their printer. Joseph gave his to his wife and said he wasn't interested in reading it. Kitty has read a bit of the paperwork and warned me that if I do read it to be prepared, as some of it makes for a devastating find.

I'm not sure if I will; for now, it's hidden at the bottom of my chest of drawers in my bedroom. Part of me is desperate to sit and read through it all; to find out who I am, where I came from and what happened in the short time I had with my biological parents and brother and sister before I was adopted, but then the other part of me feels a huge guilt towards my adoptive parents for wanting to know. And I also worry that, once I know, it will have such a huge effect on me that I will wish I didn't know. Jamie told me just to 'sit on it', to take some time to think about it all, but it's a total head fuck.

Joseph has promised to come and stay with his wife and kids and we have all promised, the three of us, that we will stay in touch more. We have set up a WhatsApp group where we will message each other – no excuses! Our children are cousins yet strangers, and there is no decent reason for this. The last death we went through made us absent from one another, so I am going to ensure that this one does nothing but bring us back together.

\*

## Sunday

We took Kitty out to explore the Cornish coast today. The weather was glorious, so we picnicked on the local beach and took the kids out on a peddle-boat, before we went home where we sipped gin cocktails and Jamie did a BBQ.

A day like today could convince anyone that they're happy, but I wanted to check on my sister so I just came out and asked her.

'Would you say you're happy, Kit? Overall?'

She does what no one ever does, and she pauses and really considers the question. No hurried off 'fine, thanks' for my sister.

'Do you know what? On balance, I'd say that I am. Of course there are good days and there are bad days, but taking everything into consideration, I am. Yes, I'm happy.'

She asks me the same question and I try to give it as much thought as she did and start counting my blessings. I can tell, as dysfunctional as our family is, that she's proud of what I've made here. And actually, her being with us has made me proud of us too, if that's the right word. When someone is visiting or staying with us and I see how kind and loving all our children are towards them, how much we laugh and mess about and how genuinely, truly happy we all are, it really does make me proud.

Pat made a reference to her and Digby going back to Canterbury over the dishes tonight.

'Washing up will be a much quicker job when we get home, just the two of us, hey Digs?'

I felt like I'd been punched in the stomach and within seconds tears pricked my eyes. I have loved having her here, being around Pat makes me happy. I wonder if she feels now that Kitty is here, that she needs to get out of the way, or whether she felt it would be easier for her to sneak back unmissed. Either way, from my reaction that I blatantly couldn't hide, she now knows that her going home is not something I want. I feel wracked with guilt at my selfish response, but I really couldn't hold it in. I'm aware I can't hold her hostage here forever, but I'm not ready to let her go quite yet.

I spoke to Jamie about it just now in the bedroom. He's so non-committal. He's happy if she stays, happy if she goes. 'We'll manage,' he says, when I have a meltdown about trying to cope without her. 'They'll be fine,' is his response when I tell him how much the kids will miss her. I feel like I won't cope though, without her voice of reason, her loving hugs and the way she is just there, making things better for all of us whenever we need her, which of late has been more often than not.

However, I am aware that she has her own life, her own home and friendship group, and I have kept her from that for too long. So, we agree that she will leave on Friday, after we get back from Dad's funeral. We confirm the plans and she pulls me into her sweet-smelling warm neck and wipes my tears off my cheeks whispering, 'Come on, my sweet girl,' in that posh accent of hers that makes me smile even through my sobs.

# CHAPTER TWENTY-ONE

* * * * * * * * * * * * * * * * * * * * * * * *

# GOODBYE DAD

*Monday*

Lou left the café as I got in today. Her eldest son was unwell at home so she couldn't stay long and she looked massively stressed out – still as glamorous as ever though, back to her old self – wearing huge Prada sunnies, her mass of wild red hair and nautical clothing to match the weather and the café. As she ran out the door, she said she would message me.

Kitty came down to the café and hung out with me. She drank coffee, ate Pat's carrot cake and left her dirty dishes scattered about for me to pick up after her, but her company is epic and she made me giggle constantly with her stories, and I realised being around her makes me feel like me again, the me that I was before kids, before I became an adult and before I put everyone else before myself. Being around her makes me miss that me.

She also sat with Oscar for hours and listened to him talk about his wife, his son and daughter. She studied him as he recounted all the memories of them growing up and the highs and lows that came with it. It was heart-warming to see. I wondered if it made her think of Dad. He reminds me so much of the dad we had when Mum was here.

Jen popped in just before lunch and I introduced her to Kitty. They got on well, but Jen could see the café was busy, so she shoved her bag and coat in the back room, popped on a pinny and helped me with the rush hour. She made it more fun being there and was smiley and happy and interacted with the customers with confidence and ease. A natural. I imagined having a baby delivered by her would make the process a darn sight easier.

Jamie is driving us all back up to London as I write this. The funeral is tomorrow and this afternoon we are meeting Joseph to go to the solicitor's and sign all the paperwork for Dad's estate. I had no clue what paperwork, but I am told this is the 'normal' thing that we need to do. The house has to go through probate and will be split between us all.

I feel like I am in a bit of a blur. Am I now an orphan? I don't know. What if my biological parents are still alive? What if they've resolved the issues they had when we were removed from their care and could now play a positive part in our lives? But they can't be decent people because of the comment Kitty made about the adoption papers – and surely, they would have reached out to try to contact us by now?

Then I think I am a mum myself, a fully-grown woman, in my thirties, and I have managed without the input of any kind of parenting for over fifteen years – emotionally, financially or physically – yet all of a sudden, the thought of not having anyone parent me is really frightening. Maybe that's why I'm trying to cling on to Pat so desperately?

We meet up with Joseph and I immediately feel safer. I forgot how safe my big brother always made me feel. He has a way of just caring for Kitty and me without actually seeing that's what he's doing. I wonder if Kitty sees it too? I wonder if she feels safer because he just copes with stuff, without getting stressed out, and he has an understanding of things we don't – and if he doesn't have an understanding, he isn't afraid to ask questions to find out, whereas Kitty and I have never done that – we have always just looked at each other and pulled faces as if to say 'What the fuck ... ?' and continued to plod on. Joseph isn't a plodder; he's a 'doer' who needs to understand the ins and outs of everything to be able to make choices and decisions, and being back in his company has made me see he was always there doing that for me and Kitty as we grew up. I miss that role he played with us and I wonder how far things would have got with Mark if I had kept Joseph close to me. Not very, I imagine. Hindsight – such a wonderful, devastating thing.

*

## Wednesday

We're home now, and I can't even describe my feelings.

Obviously I was at the funeral, but I didn't feel like I was *really* there, if you know what I mean. People I vaguely recognised told stories I vaguely remember hearing before, but mostly, things just happened around me today.

Joseph had stood up at the front of the church and said in a strong confident voice that belied what I knew was going on beneath his surface, 'Thanks Dad. Thanks for giving the three of us a life, together, that we wouldn't have had without you and Mum.' It made me wonder if he had read the adoption paperwork, or if he knew something about our 'life before' with our biological parents.

Either way he was right. Because of our parents we got to stay together, to be raised as siblings in a home where we were met with nothing but love and care. We had no guarantees of ever having this without them and as much as it all went to shit after Mum died, we were raised as babies, into our adult lives, being loved, cared for and protected and that makes me see how badly we had all failed Dad after Mum died.

A few neighbours came to the funeral, Dad's old work colleagues and a couple of faces none of us could place, they left straight after the ceremony with nothing but a sympathetic nod or handshake, but that was it.

Kitty didn't know who else to inform. Mum's green address book that she was forever pulling out when she was alive was nowhere to be found, and as far as we could tell, our dad had disassociated himself with everyone and everything for almost twenty years.

It was sad to see only a row and a half of seats taken in the church to say their goodbyes to him. At Mum's funeral, people were having to stand at the back it was so busy. It made me see how people have the ability to totally stop being who they once were because of grief and heartache and because of that they lose everyone around them, and it's frightening. Frightening and sad, because it should never have been like that for Dad. It wasn't him.

Being back with Kitty and Joseph has been amazing, despite the circumstances. It's made me see how I want them in my life; how I need them. They make me me again. Even Jamie said he has seen a side to me that he didn't know – and he got on so well with them too. Saying goodbye to them broke me. I have emailed Kitty a load of local teaching jobs, which I know she will giggle at when she opens, in the hope she might move back over and be with us.

And now I have to try to work out what to do when Pat leaves on Friday.

I'm wondering about giving up my job at the café. I love it, but with everything that's going on with Will and Ruby, and with the money from my house and my dad's house about to come through, financially I can afford to be at home more. I've been lucky of late, as Pat just picks all of that up, but the reality is, without her here – and with five children who all need individual love, time and attention – I'm not sure how fair it is on them.

*

I popped down to the café to speak to Lou and fill her in on everything that had happened and my thoughts about giving up my job. But one of the Saturday girls was working and said that Lou had been off sick all week again.

I texted her to see if she was OK, but she didn't reply so I decided to pop over to her house with some flowers and check on her. I knew where she lived because you can see her house from the café, it stands alone – on top of the hill overlooking the whole town. It was really odd when I got there. The house is something else. It's huge and looks like it should be in the middle of a celebrity street in LA or Hollywood. It's really modern, all white – mainly glass, no blinds – odd. The grounds that surround it are pristine, with tennis courts and a pool and hot tub. I could see Lou through the upstairs window in the distance as I made my way up their driveway – you can't miss her with her wild mane of red hair – but when I rang the bell, she didn't come to the door. Her car was there and I one hundred per cent know she was in. I shouted through the letter box so she knew it was me but still nothing but silence. It made me feel really uneasy. I left the flowers on the doorstep and sent her another text, but it's now 10pm and I haven't heard anything. She probably just feels like shit and maybe didn't want to pass on her lurgy but it just seemed very strange. Hopefully she will be back in work tomorrow . . .

\*

## *Thursday*

I needn't have set an alarm today as I woke up at 7.20am to my mobile ringing and vibrating on my bedside table. It was David. Again.

'Hi Jo, me again. Sorry to do this – *again* – but Lou is still off-colour and really not well enough to be in. Are you OK to hold the fort for the next couple of days?'

'Of course, anything to help.' I paused, wondering how much I could pry. 'I am worried though, David. Are you able to tell me what's wrong?'

David explained that Lou is suffering really badly with migraines and hasn't even got out of bed for almost three days.

Weird.

I asked if she had got my flowers and he sounded surprised – it was clear he knew nothing about them.

'I left them outside yesterday as there was no answer at the door.'

'Oh, in that case our cleaner must have picked them up and put them in water. Thanks so much for doing that, I know you've had a tough time recently too – we were both so sorry to hear about your dad – and we really appreciate it.'

He said Lou would call me when she's feeling better and we finished the call. I'd have to hurry even more now that I was opening up alone.

I spent twenty minutes multi-tasking getting ready with googling migraines and trying to find out what I could get her to help. They sound pretty dreadful when they're that severe and there is literally nothing you can do other than lie in a dark room and wait for it to pass. Bless her …

The café was fine, really busy but manageable. I feel better for being at work, not thinking about Pat leaving, how much I'm missing Kitty or questioning everything about my dad and what I could have done differently. Joseph sent us loads of pictures of his kids on the WhatsApp group and we've been chatting all day, which has been nice. He's home for another three weeks so he and his wife are going to come down and stay for a weekend with their boys before he goes back on tour.

Jamie has told me that if the café is too much now that his mum is leaving, we can get by OK without my income. He knows it's not just about the money though, and he tells me he'll support my decision either way. That is the problem; I really enjoy working there, and it makes me feel like I'm someone other than just a mum who has no one but her kids and her crazy dog for company.

I do like earning my own money; even though it's not a huge amount it's still a bit of independence and it's great to not only be relying on the house money for my contributions to our family. I think I'll just see how things are over the next few weeks.

# CHAPTER TWENTY-TWO

## THE RUINED FLOWERS

*Friday*

I woke up this morning and immediately felt shit as I knew Pat was leaving this afternoon to catch her train back home. I'm going to miss her so much. The kids said a tearful goodbye before school, which made me feel worse, and Ruby had to be dragged into class by her teacher, which hasn't happened for so long that it made my heart break after everything she's been through. Pat as always was amazing – kissing the tops of their heads while whispering reassuring words into their tiny ears. But they know, like me, that we are losing more than a grandma for a while. She has been so much more than that to all of them.

After the school run, I went and opened the café and discovered the entire kitchen was flooded. The ceiling from the flat above had collapsed and it was a total shitstorm. I called Lou's mobile, which was switched off. I called her landline – no answer. I called David's office but was told, before I could even give my name, that he was in a conference out of town and unavailable all day, even for emergencies. I had no clue what to do.

I left the closed sign on the door, locked up and decided to drive up to Lou's house, in the hope I'd get an answer. I didn't know what the situation was with the flat upstairs, and who was responsible for what, so I didn't want to start making the situation worse by calling people I shouldn't.

I parked the car on the road and went round to the side gate, which was locked, so I pressed the buzzer, and I pressed it again – but nothing. I decided to take my chance and hop over the side gate to see if I could get up to the house and knock on the front door.

As I walked up the driveway, I could see Lou through the kitchen window, she had her head down and, as I got closer, I could see she was doing the dishes. Weird, but maybe the buzzer wasn't working. I approached the house and could see part of the bouquet of flowers I had bought her hanging out of the industrial-sized wheelie bin; the heads of some of the flowers had been ripped off and scattered around their beautiful red-bricked driveway.

I felt sick and wondered if I had done something wrong? It was clear she was now avoiding me and had obviously hated the flowers I'd brought her. I wanted to turn round and walk back down the drive but there was every chance that she would look up and see me, and the thought of that made me feel even sicker. I got to the kitchen window with her still washing up, not noticing me, and tapped gently on the glass. She must have jumped two foot in the air in shock and, as her face met mine, I thought I was going to vomit . . .

Her left eye was totally closed over – purple and misshapen – her right was black with bruising but still open. Her nose was fat and the left-hand side of her jaw was yellow and black and swollen. She looked like she had been in a car accident and I don't know out of the two of us who was more shocked.

I pointed to the front door, to gesture her to let me in, but she shook her head from side to side and pointed back down the drive as if to tell me to leave. I could feel I was going to cry, and a genuine prick of fear sprang up in my throat. I had no clue what I had just walked into and I was scared. Really scared. I said in a firm, loud voice, 'Let me in *now* or I will call the police.' She began shaking her head and crying, but I walked around to the front door, still feeling like I was about to be sick, and waited for her to open it.

When she did, she immediately started begging me to leave in a whisper. Begging. Like an addict begs on the streets for money for more drugs. It was a frightened, desperate beg.

I asked her what had happened, but she was in such a state she wasn't even taking it in. She just kept saying, 'Please, Jo, please go.' Her desperation was now screaming at me from every inch of her body.

I whispered to ask if there was anyone else in the house and she shook her head to tell me no.

I had no clue what to do here. Her sleeves were rolled up from washing up and the bruising round her wrists looked fresh – purple and raw. I took her hands in mine and she quickly pulled her sleeves down and looked back at the floor. She was trembling.

'He did this?' I asked. She didn't answer.

It was enough.

Enough for me to almost fall to my knees. All the obvious signs I'd missed! I thought back to all the times I'd felt a pang of jealousy at David rocking up to the café with beautiful bouquets and mistaking her fear for shyness. The amount of times her wrists had been bandaged, and I'd taken the piss that she wasn't allowed to use the coffee machine any more because I'd believed her when she'd said the burns were from the steam. The constant calls where she was sick, the injuries to her body ... I wanted to eat my own fist in anger at my sheer naïvety and the fact I had totally missed that this beautiful woman was being subjected to horrific abuse by a man who's held in such high regard as a pillar of our community.

It was all a bit of a daze as adrenaline kicked in. I remember just repeating the words 'Oh, Lou' while my head was reeling, trying to catch up, but I felt so nauseous.

Then the sickness came.

As all the little incidents and injuries kept flashing into my memory, the bile rose in my throat, and I ran back to the front door and vomited on the perfect red-bricked drive. I pointed to the flowers in the wheelie bin, and she whispered, 'I tried to hide them from him yesterday so he wouldn't know you'd been here, but then you told him on the phone and he found them.'

I had caused this. That bouquet of flowers I thought would make her feel better had caused the fresh black eye and the lacerated wrists, as well as god knows what other injuries that were going on underneath her tracksuit.

How does this stuff even go on without us seeing it? How have I spent most days with this woman for the past few months, yet I had absolutely no idea she was in an unhappy relationship let alone an abusive one?

Lou spent the entire time I was there in a state of panic that he'd catch me. I have never felt so much rage, devastation and genuine disbelief at a situation in my entire life. I told her we needed to go to the hospital, but she kept assuring me she was fine. Her jaw looked like it was broken to me, but the worst thing was she kept saying, 'No, it's been worse before, it will go down in a few days.' It was totally as if she knew the drill.

Seventeen years they've been married for.

Seventeen years.

How many beatings has she had in almost two decades?

I didn't know what to do. I wanted to call the police but she begged for me not to, again, just like she did when I asked her to let me in the house. I told her she could stay with us, and her boys too. Her boys. I can't stop thinking of her boys and when I asked her what they thought of all this, she told me that she'd told them she'd fallen. I thought that they'd never believe that, but then I look back on all the times I've believed her stories about her injuries and sickness over the last few months. David has forced her to be convincing with her lies.

She begged me to leave. Again.

I begged her to come with me.

She refused.

As I pulled my phone out of my back pocket, she became utterly hysterical, screaming for me not to call anyone, tell anyone. She was like a frightened, injured wild animal locked in a cage who was being prodded with a stick by a big scary human.

I made a deal with her – I would leave and keep it secret if she let me photograph her injuries. I swore to her, on my children's lives, that I would not take them to the police but I wanted them there in case she ever changed her mind or in case he killed her.

She told me that won't happen, that he wouldn't ever do that, and I looked at her face, the fact she can barely see out of one eye, that she only just managed to talk because of the damage to her jaw and the fact her nose is mangled across her whole face – and I wondered how one human who is supposed to love another can ever inflict such devastation and pain upon them. And then I wonder how the human who was stood there, in front of me – with their entire body broken and battered – can defend the person that did this and say the words 'he wouldn't kill me'.

I took sixteen pictures in all; her face, her scalp where there are fresh lacerations and whole chunks of hair missing, her wrists. I asked her to lift her top so I could see her back and chest. The begging started again, and I knew from her reaction it would be bad. I told her unless she did it, I would call the police. The entire time I was doing it I was holding more vomit down, in shock. She unzipped her tracksuit top, naked underneath – I imagine trying to put a bra on would have been too painful.

I sobbed. I couldn't hold back the tears. 'My god, Lou. This is … ' Actually there were no words. Her breasts and shoulders were covered in bite marks. Angry, red, bite marks. Bite marks so bad you could see the indentations from his teeth. What human *bites* another human? There are more cuts and deep bruises that cover her, and she looks back to the floor again, utterly ashamed at what she is being forced to show me.

Now it was my turn to beg. I begged so hard. I repeatedly begged through heaving sobs that my knees ached from falling to them on the expensive, gleaming, hard, cold tiled floor.

Two women, sobbing together; the occasional desperate wail from Lou and the reassuring lies of, 'It's all going to be OK' from me.

Neither of us have a clue how it will be.

I left.

I had to.

He was due back and it was too risky. I didn't want him to hurt her more because of me. She wouldn't leave with me and I didn't want to force her for her then to reject me and have him get away with it all. She closed the front door quietly while repeatedly whispering, 'I'll be fine,' as if I'm somehow going to believe that.

I walked down the drive to my car, crying like a child that had just been dragged out of their own birthday party before it had finished. I was dripping with sweat. I immediately drove off but as I got a short distance down the road, my hands and legs began shaking uncontrollably and I had to pull over and open the car door to be sick again.

I realise I hadn't even told her about the leak at the café.

I needed to tell Pat. Jamie would just call the police – and I was worried. Lou's husband works with the police all the time. What if he talks them round? What if he gets away with it? Pat would know what to do.

I got back to the house just before 12pm and she knew something was wrong as soon as she glanced at me. I couldn't speak. I was trying to let out a sob but was just breathing in, then in, then in like I was going to combust in panic. I handed her my phone, open on my camera roll, on 'those' pictures.

'Oh my goodness.' She must have said those three words one hundred times, while her other hand was over her mouth and the look of shock and devastation spread across her face.

'I'll stay,' were her next words. 'Don't worry, I'm not going anywhere … '

# CHAPTER TWENTY-THREE

## BEHIND CLOSED DOORS

### Saturday

I've stopped crying, just, but I feel utterly broken. I feel like my heart has snapped and I have no idea how to make it better.

Pat called a plumber yesterday about the leak. She went to meet him at the café and when she arrived, so did David. The ice cream shop next door had called him to check on things because we were closed. I have no idea how Pat managed to act normal and stay civil to David, but I was so glad I wasn't there. There was no way I'd have been able to do that.

Pat explained to him that I'd tried to call his office but was told he wasn't contactable. She said he had asked if I'd spoken to Lou, she told him she didn't know. Thank God. He hopefully couldn't trip her up with an 'I don't know' answer. Pat told me what concerned her the most is that if she hadn't have seen the pictures, or spoken to me, she would have thought what a nice man he was. A man who loved his family, was attractive and kind, business-like without being stuck up about it.

She asked David how Lou was with her migraines and he stuck to his story, she'd had one today and she had 'worsened' so was having tests at the hospital to rule out it being anything more 'sinister' so, most likely, she wouldn't be back next week as planned.

Totally convincing, Pat said. If she didn't know what we know, all she would have seen is a husband who idolises his wife and was pushing for hospital appointments to make her better.

He knew full well she wouldn't be back in the café next week. Those bruises he caused weren't going to heal over the weekend. Those cuts and burns and bite marks he had inflicted over her entire body weren't disappearing within the next two days.

I have no idea what to do. What if he's found out that I've been to the house? What if he's hurt her again? What if he's killed her?

Pat is also out of her depth on this one.

She wanted us to call the police to start with but then after meeting with David she agreed that the reality is that Lou would most likely cover for him. Then what if there was a chance, even if Lou did speak up, that the police wouldn't believe her because of who David is – how much danger would she be in then?

Now it's the weekend and I can't get through to her without him being there and I'm worried that by me not calling she will feel like I've abandoned her, but if I call and he's listening I could put her in more danger. I feel like I'm losing my mind with all this and I take comfort in the fact that I'm safe, loved and secure, but what the hell must she be feeling like?

Jamie thinks I'm in this state because of my dad, and Kitty leaving, and I can't let him know the real reason just yet.

Maybe I should call the police, because if David kills her, I will have to live with the fact that I knew and did nothing to protect my friend. And I don't think I'd be able to handle that. It is such a mess.

\*

## Sunday

Today Rex turned five!

We had a party in the garden this afternoon and invited some of his friends from pre-school. Meg and John came with the kids and Jen and her husband too. We got a bouncy castle and Jamie did hot dogs on the barbecue for them all. The kids basically spent two hours running round the garden until they were dripping with sweat and their faces turned scarlet while downing too many sugary drinks and ice poles!

I did wonder when seeing his friends from pre-school if I had made the wrong decision in holding him back a year. He could have started last September, which would have been three months after his fourth birthday, but he still seemed so tiny then, and perhaps now, selfishly, I didn't know how I would cope without his company in the day – we did so much together. We have clubs and activities that we attended most days and I just knew I'd never get that time back, and he was my last one at home, but I definitely noticed how much older he seems than his 'friends' from his pre-school class today. They were all still four – but when he starts school in a few months I know he will also meet kids much closer to his age, so I'm sure it will be fine.

Mark didn't call, or text. He didn't send a present, or a card. Which was fine, I actually felt OK about it. Rex didn't notice, he didn't ask, neither did Belle or Art, which was strange. After the clear up of the party and everyone leaving Jamie and I sat in the garden and I felt myself getting wound up, I suppose for Rex really. I said I felt like messaging Mark to inform him it was his son's birthday and tell him he was a fuckwit, but Jamie asked what it would achieve, and said that this would only in time affect him. I remembered what Jen said about her ex, and I took a deep breath, watched my beautiful five-year-old crying with laughter at his big brothers and sisters who had made his day special and thought to myself 'bite your tongue, Jo'.

On a shitter note, I got a text off Lou first thing. Then another.

The first one said that the café would be closed for around two weeks as the insurance firm needed to send an assessor out to look at the damage then get it all repaired. She said she would be in touch about when they were re-opening.

The second one said, 'I am fine, please do not text me or tell anyone about what's happened xx'.

When I replied to the first text, I tried to write it as if it was two days ago, before I knew her husband had beaten her close to death. I tried to respond in a way that didn't draw attention to the fact I knew, in case he was reading our messages.

> 'Hi Darling, what a bloody nightmare! No worries, I can finally do some ironing with my days off! Pat and I are around if you fancy coffee, we can always come to you. Take care, J x'.

I got a reply almost immediately: 'That would be good, maybe we could do a BBQ with Jamie and David. Will be in touch'.

No kiss.

It was him. He was either writing or dictating that text. I felt the bile rise in my throat again.

All I've done is spend the last day looking at every domestic abuse website known to man and googling things such as 'My friend is being abused should I call the police?'

Of course I should call the bloody police. Why am I not calling the police?

I've then spent the rest of the time googling David. His firm, the work he's done, the testimonials of what an amazing man he is. Seeing his pictures on the internet makes me feel nauseous. He's so convincing.

I keep thinking of her injuries. Her eyes were so black, she must have been beaten so viciously. Bite marks. Who bites like that? I can't help but think there is a grim sexual element to it, and that makes me feel even sicker.

I need to keep plodding on. I have the photos on my phone, and I will check in with her every few days. I just feel like my brain is going to burst with it all.

I feel like the kids are ready for the summer holidays, which are going to be here in just a few weeks. Time flies so quickly it feels since we moved here. I think it's because of the change in schools and homes/areas, plus now it's really hot, so they're ready for a long break to just chill out and relax. I am excited for it too. Things have to be run like a military operation to get through each day, with arriving to the schools on time, homework, etc., so it will be lush to just have lie-ins, lazy days and no plans at all.

\*

## Monday

Today started as a good Monday. I woke to a text from the bank to inform me I had received a payment of £237,000. The house sale money had gone in. I felt happy, and I have logged onto my banking app over fifty times today just to take in the fact I have almost a quarter of a million pounds in my account. I sit thinking about the weeks I was adding up shopping on the calculator on my phone as I walked round Lidl to make sure I had enough to cover it. Living in a house worth so much money yet struggling to get the shopping each week. But now I have enough money to ensure we are OK. I never ever thought back then I would be here today.

I took the kids to school today then came back and spoke to Pat.

She told me that last week while I had been away at Dad's funeral there had been an 'incident'. There hadn't been a good time to raise it with me with everything else that had gone on, but now I was at home more she wanted to mention it.

She said that Molly had stayed over and she had allowed her and Belle to go to the beach with Jacob and his friends. She had given them a curfew of 10pm, the same as what I would have said. She said Jaclyn called the house phone at 9.20pm to speak to Molly as she wasn't answering her mobile, and Pat had explained that the girls would be back at 10pm. Apparently, Jaclyn had lost it and had called Pat irresponsible, demanding to know the 'exact location' of her daughter's whereabouts – which of course Pat didn't know.

Pat had explained that Molly and Belle were sensible girls and that they would be back at 10pm, as they always were, and when Molly got back Pat would ensure she called her mum straight away. But when they arrived back at 9.55pm, Jaclyn was already waiting outside the house and she went crazy at Molly, screaming through the car window at her that she was a liar. Then she kept saying that Molly knew how 'dangerous' it was to be out at night and reminding her that she 'knew the rules'. She ordered her to fetch her things and get in the car. Molly ran in the house, stuffed her belongings into a bag in tears, apologised to Pat (who repeatedly told her she had nothing to apologise for) and left in a hurry, saying to Belle and Pat, 'This is all my fault. I've ruined everything.'

I wondered what Jaclyn would do if she did ever find out about the time Molly had sex. It made me sad to think how Molly must be desperate to ensure her mum never finds out something that had such a huge effect on her mental health. I went into Belle's room and again reassured her if she ever needed to tell me anything that worried or upset her, if she had made a mistake she was ashamed of, I would never judge. She looked up from her phone, rolled her eyes, smiled and said 'I get it'.

I was seething with Jaclyn. I told Pat I would call her, but she told me not to. She assured me that she had dealt with far worse parents when Jamie was a boy.

It's funny how we perceive things before we know about them. Molly's mum is a successful, wealthy career woman, and when we think of successful wealthy career women who are mums, we just expect they'll get it right and their kids will be happy and healthy and go on to have successful careers themselves – because as a society it's what we are trained into believing. Only when you are then faced with these situations in real life do we discover that it's so very different.

Children who live wealthy lives aren't always privileged. Parents who are looked on as pillars of the community aren't always child-focused. Sometimes, children who are raised in poverty and live with neglect get more support and help from outside services and agencies than those that are 'invisible' like Molly, because no one sees the issues at home. People just see wealth so they can pretend things like this don't happen. And the issue now is that you have a teenage girl who's growing up with no one to talk to or confide in, and the only family member she has bans her from doing stuff other teenagers are doing, which as I see it, only causes them to rebel and lie about their whereabouts.

After I had calmed down later in the evening I spoke to Belle again. I apologised that I haven't been there much of late, and she told me it's OK, that she knows I'm not in a good place because of everything, but I tell her that still doesn't make it OK. That she's my daughter and she and her siblings are my priority, but I feel like they don't feel like they are right now.

She wasn't on her phone, and rather than roll her eyes, smile and give me one sentence she actually spoke back to me for a while. She tells me she can't get hold of Molly. She's had her phone taken away and hasn't been at school this week. My heart sinks. She hasn't even done anything wrong to be punished. I wonder if I should call Jaclyn or go round; maybe she needs some support as a mum.

Since we moved here in the last few months, I've done nothing but 'feel things'. I constantly think about Megan losing her baby and it makes me feel so lucky that my children are healthy. I think of Lou, every minute of every day, and feel grateful my partner does nothing but care and protect our family. I look at Molly and the fact she can't talk to her mum, and it makes me want to be a better mum to my own children. A mum who is always there for them, without judgement, to make things better. And, although life lately seems a bit of a shitstorm, and all I do is 'feel things', I'm grateful, because those feelings have made me aware of situations going forward – they've opened my eyes to things I didn't even know existed and they've made me want to change things for other people as much as I can.

# CHAPTER TWENTY-FOUR

............................

# A PROBLEM SHARED

*Tuesday*

I drove to Molly's today after I did the school run. I wanted
to check she was OK after speaking to Belle last night. An
older lady answered the door wearing a pinny and with a
perfect white set perm. She reminded me of Mrs Doubtfire.
I asked for Molly and she looked taken aback. I explained
I was her best friend's mum and had come to drop some
bits off.

I was invited to step in, and waited as the woman I
assumed was the housekeeper went to call Molly.

I noticed that the walls were covered in pictures. The
ones I first spotted were of Molly's mother at various award
ceremonies and events. She was even prettier in pictures; she
had a beautiful smile – with her white-blonde hair, her tan
and gleaming white teeth. She was immaculately dressed in
every picture, and she looked happy, gripping onto various
trophies, award cups and smiling with other men and women
as immaculately dressed and beautiful as her. There were
others of Molly, mainly as a little girl – they looked like they
were taken on holidays, in swimming pools with beaming

smiles. I could only see one of them together, Molly and her mum. It wasn't recent – but they were cuddling; they looked like they were laughing together. It was a beautiful picture and my heart skipped a beat wondering what their relationship is truly like.

Molly came walking down the huge walnut sweeping staircase. She was pleased to see me; I saw that instantly. She shouted my name then ran towards me, wrapped her arms around me and hugged me tight. She was wearing grey pyjamas. She smelt good, of fresh washing powder and nice shampoo, but looked exhausted and pale. I gave her the carrier bag full of chocolates, grapes and some books that I'd brought from home, although I doubted she would ever read them. She told me her mum was away on business until Friday and had left to go on Sunday night.

The lady that answered the door hovered close by and I could see she was uncomfortable with my presence. Molly picked up on that too, ushering me towards the kitchen and closing the shiny solid walnut door behind us. She offered me a cup of tea and I accepted. I don't think Belle has ever offered me a cup of tea; despite us growing up drinking tea together out of matching mugs most days, I don't think she actually knows how to make a cup herself. It made me smile.

It was scorching today so we sat outside. The gardens were huge and there was a swimming pool. When I commented on how beautiful it was, Molly looked unimpressed and said the swimming pool hadn't been used in years by anyone but her in the summer months, but was cleaned every week by the maintenance team her mother employed. Like every other part of this huge home, it all looked so pretty and perfect.

Sitting here, in this pristine tranquillity, I can't help but compare Molly's home to ours. We're constantly fighting for the bathroom, or rinsing knives and forks off under the tap before we eat because we've run out of clean cutlery, and it feels like we live in chaos. But what does Molly see when she looks at us?

We spoke lots about what she's been doing – nothing. Who she's spoken to – no one. She said she missed staying with us, I told her she was welcome anytime, so she called her mum to ask if she could stay – there was no reply so she left a voicemail. She was quite convinced it would be fine, I wasn't – and I wasn't sure if she was either. She might have just been trying to convince me so I took her with me, either way my heart hurt at the thought of leaving her, and the worst-case scenario was that I could drop her home later if her mum didn't want her with us.

'Get your stuff,' I said. She beamed. 'Your uniform, bag and books and some clothes.'

She ran – no, sprinted – to her room and I poured my drink from the china tea cup down the marble kitchen sink, picked up my car keys and politely asked Mrs Doubtfire to pass a message on to Jaclyn to give me a call, and that her daughter would be staying with me until she returned from her business trip. As we walked out the front door, I saw Molly give her a look. It was a look I imagined she had never given to anyone before – because no one had ever made her feel like this before. No one had ever listened and protected her. It was a bit of a 'fuck you' look, to the housekeeper, her absent mum and her huge stately home, but one that hopefully made her feel better.

I'm writing this while I await the phone call from Jaclyn, which I feel more than ready for …

\*

### Thursday

Lou called today. She tried to put on a brave face, if you can even do that down the phone. I asked how she was, how her injuries were, and she kept saying, 'Fine. Honestly, Jo, I'm fine.' She said she was calling from her mobile, stood on the tennis courts, because she knew there were no hidden cameras or bugs out there. It felt like I was speaking to someone in a film. Cameras and bugs? Surely this shit only went on in America?

She said David was away on business. She didn't know for how long; he never told her. The 'element of surprise' always kept her on her toes. She told me she knew he had thirty-six pairs of socks and underpants in total and that four pairs were missing. He'd left on Tuesday so she expects he will be back today or tomorrow. I wonder if he knew that his wife had counted his socks and pants so that she had some idea of when he was likely to return. Probably. I also imagined there were times he took a few extra pairs just to really mess with her already damaged mind.

She said he's booked to take her and the boys away this weekend. They're going to Devon to a holiday cottage there. He has been 'lovely' since 'it' happened and she assures me, again, that everything will be 'OK and fine'. I tell her we will discuss it when we are back at the café together but in the meantime all she has to do is call my mobile and hang up or send me a blank text and I will call the police to her address. The fact that she thanks me before hanging up tells me that the reality is anything but 'OK and fine'.

I spent the rest of the afternoon back on websites researching domestic abuse some more and, upon reading real-life stories and statistics, I got through half a box of tissues wiping away tears.

I feel so ignorant to this situation now it's been shoved under my nose, and I've come to realise that domestic abuse in the UK is an epidemic.

I can't help thinking about Lou's boys. What have they seen in their little lives? What have they grown up witnessing? I can't imagine their dad abuses them – that would be more difficult to hide and I know Lou would do anything in her power to protect them – but after the horror stories I've read today of decent, caring, loving women, who are mothers, and have been abused so relentlessly that they choose their perpetrator partners over their own children, I can't help but wonder what is going on.

They are definitely seeing the injuries, even if they're not witnessing the abuse. I realise my mind has thought of nothing else since last Friday. I've barely thought of my dad, or the funeral, or anything that goes with it.

What I do need to find some time to consider, though, is the adoption papers Kitty gave me – all the notes and the records and the detail I now have, which explain why we were removed from our birth mum. I decided to speak to Pat and asked her if she would be happy to go through them, and then tell me if she thought I would want, or be able, to handle the content.

Her response was so right: 'If I was to tell you that I didn't think they'd help you, do you think that would make you want to read them even more?'

Yes, of course it would. Because my mind is fucked up and I have no idea what I actually want. Still, I wasn't ready to read them without someone else reading them first – just to prepare me. I don't think Jamie would cope if there was anything in there about abuse or neglect, and I really have no idea what they contain.

I handed Pat the thick black file and felt the anxiety whir in my tummy, but I know I need to know, and at least she can be there to hold my hand through the bad bits.

*

## Friday

Friday the thirteenth today ... It certainly felt like that when I answered the landline at 7.24am and it was Lou's husband.

'David,' I said when I heard his voice. I wanted to bite the handset in rage and vomit at the same time, but instead I decided to kill him with kindness to throw him off any scent and keep Lou as safe as I possibly could.

He was calling to tell me the damage had now been assessed and the builders were in the café. They were hoping to re-open in ten days' time – bang on the start of the six-week holiday – ideal.

I asked how Lou's migraines were and he told me much better. He went on to inform me he was taking them to Devon for the weekend as she 'needed a break'.

I wanted to say, 'Yes – a permanent one from you, you fucking psychopath.' Instead I told him that is probably just what she needs, to have a lovely weekend and I would look forward to returning to work. When I hung up, it confirmed all my fears. This guy was a total charmer ... how would anyone ever believe Lou was a beaten wife?

I got a call around 11am from Jaclyn. She didn't shout, or rant, surprisingly. Instead she did an amazing job of speaking down to me. She acted like I was something she had just scraped off the bottom of her shoe – which came as no surprise but all the same conflict wasn't something that sat well with me. I said to her that Molly had tried to call her and we assumed it wouldn't be an issue but if it was I was happy to drop her home immediately.

I think Jaclyn was expecting me to argue with her or go back with a negative response, but the reality was I didn't have the energy. I didn't have an understanding of some things Jaclyn did as her mum. And who am I to judge with how things are with our family? I feel sorry for Molly and I enjoy having her around, but ultimately she is a child and Jaclyn is her mum, which I said out loud to Jaclyn on the phone. Surprisingly, she really changed her tune, she sounded upset but like she was trying to hide it from me. I asked her if she was OK and told her I have issues going on with our kids so I would never judge. She assured me she was fine and said she would speak to the school about Molly's return. She agreed that Molly could stay with us until she was back but asked she was not out past 9pm, or further than the beach at anytime. Before I could agree to her rules she said 'I know I may seem crazy, Jo, but I promise there are reasons for this' and my heart hurt for her, because even though I had no idea what they were, I knew there was something going on.

\*

## Sunday

I come down the stairs on Sunday morning to see Jamie standing at the kitchen sink, doing last night's washing up. I find myself constantly loving him; putting my hands up the back of his T-shirt and wrapping my arms round his warm torso. Standing on my tiptoes to bury my nose into his neck from behind and just generally being more appreciative of him. The father he is, the loving son and amazing partner. I feel safe when I am with him, he's such a steady presence, but I imagine he couldn't say the same about me right now and I'm sure he's wondering what's going on. I know that I should have told him everything by now – this is an open and honest household – but I swore to Lou that I'd keep her secret and then I just kept quiet about *every*thing through fear of saying the wrong thing. I also feel like talking about it would only make *me* feel better, and wouldn't actually help anyone else so why cause Jamie additional stress? I feel lucky to have him. I've spent the last week faced with so many realities of the bad people we have in this world that I feel so happy I have a good one.

Molly went home a few days ago. Jaclyn collected her while I was out doing a shop. Pat said she was pleasant when she arrived, she also apologised for how she had spoken to Pat the night Molly went out. I asked Pat what she said and she said she had a chat with her and thinks she made things feel better for her. Molly texted Belle yesterday to say she was going shopping with her mum, so fingers crossed things are better for both of them.

# CHAPTER TWENTY-FIVE

# OUT OF THE MOUTHS OF BABES

## Thursday

Belle and Molly have been going straight to the beach from school and getting back around 7–8pm. They stay together most nights and Belle stayed there on Monday this week. She said they got Chinese and watched Netflix in the lounge. Jaclyn was there, Belle said she was working next door in the office but she kept popping her head in to ask if they needed anything. My opinion of her is quickly changing and I feel like a cow for misunderstanding her so badly.

I've asked Belle if her and Jacob are boyfriend and girlfriend as he's been down the beach with the girls most afternoons too – to which she bit my head off and informed me this wasn't how it was done any more. I asked her to explain how it *was* done now and she awkwardly just said they were 'getting close'. When I tried to understand this a bit more and queried who decided 'when' or 'if' they want to become boyfriend and girlfriend, she bit my head off again and told me to 'stop being gross'.

I was going to go down the route of contraception and being safe. She is only fifteen, but I know I can't bury my head in the sand – better safe than sorry. I didn't feel emotionally ready for the chat, though, and she would probably cringe so much she would vomit, so I called Megan and left her a message to call me back. Maybe she could get some more answers from Jacob about what was going on – highly doubtful though. Parenting teens, I've come to understand, is a total minefield.

The kids broke up for the six-week holiday. Pat is going home tomorrow for a month then returning to help us with childcare as I'm back to work for the last two weeks in August. I'm supposed to be doing three days when the café re-opens as there is an air show on locally so it will be heaving and Lou has asked me to help. I want to go in anyway; I'm hoping she will be there, and we will get the chance to talk about everything. My mind is still so busy with it all. I feel so many emotions and it isn't even happening to me.

*

### Friday

I dropped Pat and Digby at the train station early this morning. Rex and Ruby came with me while the others were still sleeping. Just before she got on the train, Pat turned to me and said, 'I've read the adoption papers, Jo, and I want you to think long and hard about whether it's something that you want to visit right now. Some parts of it are going to have a huge effect on you and once it's done, you can't undo it,' she told me. It felt like I'd been winded – and it made me never want to read them and feel desperate to read them all at once. I took a deep breath and said 'I know, and I am considering it. There's just so much going on right now and I don't have enough brain space to process it all. I'll give it some thought over the next month and hopefully by the time you come back, I'll see things a bit more clearly.'

We had a group hug with Rex and Ruby and then I squeezed in one of my own before watching Pat climb aboard the train and move through the carriage looking for her seat. We waved until the train was out of sight. I swallowed away the hard painful lump in my throat, squeezed both the kids' hands and skipped back to the car park to make them giggle, then we headed for home.

The drive back to the house, with the kids being unusually quiet, gave me time to ponder. To be honest, knowing that Pat knew the truth about my adoption and wasn't yelling at me to not open that can of worms made me want to go home and read the papers straight away – but I know that at this moment in time, with everything I have going on, I don't need to be adding any more stress, upset and pressure by looking into why I was adopted. I decided I would look, but in the future one day, when things were calmer, when Pat returns, and is there to help me get my head around things.

Jamie brought home some paperwork tonight from the estate agents on four houses that were for up for sale, two of which had granny flats attached. When I questioned this, he said he had spoken to his mum about moving down with us permanently and she seemed keen, depending on what I thought. I was made up. Pat doesn't interfere or get in the way. She also makes the kids so happy because she makes all the time in the world to do everything, from explaining impossible maths sums to teaching them how to sew or plant in the garden. They bake all the time with her and Belle is now able to make the best brownies and understands the importance of leaving the kitchen tidy afterwards, which is heaven!

I have five children, a partner with a demanding career, a large house and a part-time job. Yes, I can manage, and I will – but ultimately if my children can be raised with the support of a loving grandmother, and if Jamie and I have her support and if she has ours – it can only be a benefit for us all.

I called Pat immediately – she's only been gone twelve hours! – and asked her what she genuinely thinks of the idea. Her main concern is putting stress and pressure on Jamie and I. She did mention though that she's been thinking of getting a cottage close to us. That way she isn't 'under our feet' but close enough to still help and also have some of the children at hers overnight to give us a break. I asked her how she feels about leaving Canterbury – she's been there all her life – but she assured me there's nothing there for her now, and her getting home tonight has made her see even more that it doesn't feel 'like home' any more.

She said that she missed the busyness of our house, and being with us made her see how much time she spends alone, and how she tries so hard to fill her days in Canterbury. Whereas, when she was with us, she didn't need to do that. It just happens without her having to join new clubs to make friends.

We carried on chatting for over forty minutes, about everything and nothing, and decided she will contact the estate agents up there in the morning to get the house valued and get it on the market. I told Jamie once I was off the phone and he shook his head and smirked; I could tell he was pleased, his little beam gave it away. I know he worries about his mum being so far away, as well as worrying about me coping here with so much while he is so busy at work, so for him it's a godsend that his mum and I get on like we do, and it means life for all of us is better.

I have spent the rest of tonight looking at houses, it feels surreal to be able to do this now and I keep thinking of Lou and how once upon a time I never thought I'd be in this position again after Mark left, so I hope, in time, she can see there could be life away from David with her boys.

I also had a thought about approaching the landlord to buy our house now. It just feels like home, it's safe and is a perfect size for us. The back garden is huge so we could make a second summer house for when Belle is older or just a playroom for the kids. I need to discuss it all properly with Jamie, but I'm excited about settling down in a proper home with our family around us.

## Saturday

Today was the first time I'd had the kids all day without Pat or Jamie with us in months. I feel like we've really been making the most of our quality time since I've not been at work. Maybe it's just because I've had the time to spend with them again now things have calmed down.

We went to a local green, with a river running through it, and met with Jen and her kids, and had a picnic together. The kids paddled about and jumped in the water and there was a tree swing to play on and we took a dingy along.

Belle brought Jacob and it was odd to see them together. I can see they're really fond of each other and they're forever tickling each other and messing about. She suddenly seems so grown up and the realisation kicked in that she isn't a baby any longer. She's now finished secondary school and is making plans on her entire future. I hope I've raised her well enough to cope in the big wide world but to always know her home is with me. I don't think children ever stop being your babies, no matter how old they get.

I've been thinking for a while now about possibly telling Jen about Lou, but I worry she would say something, and I couldn't risk losing Lou's trust. It's so hard as I feel like I could do with the support and someone to talk to who knows Lou too, but I made her a promise and I can't go back on that so I've kept it a secret.

Ruby turned to me at lunch, apropos of nothing, and, in front of everyone, said, 'Jo, will I ever see my mum again?'

I didn't know where the question came from or how best to answer it. It was asked in the same way she would have asked for a drink or a bag of crisps, no emotion and she didn't seem upset – it was just a simple question she wanted answering.

I felt like Jamie and I should have a script for this sort of thing but it's never been mentioned before so I did as best as I could, and said, 'Sweetheart, I know it's strange to not be spending time with her right now, and you're doing so well. I think we have to remember that even mummies and daddies become unwell sometimes, and that can mean that it's difficult to look after their children until they're better.'

Ruby then asked if her mummy was in hospital. I said no, but then I thought there is no possible way I can explain to a six-year-old the difference between mental health and a broken leg, and would it be fair to try to do that?

'Your mummy needs some help from people to get better, and until she gets that help you and Will are going to be staying here, living with us. We love having you here and you're very lucky to have so many people who love you.'

She then asked if I liked her mummy, in exactly the same way she had asked if she would see her again. I wondered what went through her tiny busy brain and I was aware Will was watching, looking as awkward as I was now feeling. I wanted to cry for her innocence and confusion – and probably because I had no clue what the future held. I told her I did like her mummy, and so did Daddy – and we all wanted her to get better.

Her response was, 'I like living with Daddy and you anyway.' She then stood up, planted a kiss on my cheek and ran back to the river, where she hurled herself in the water and was soon squealing with Belle. I wished there was a way these five children could have childhoods where all four of us, as their parents, were on the same page. Where we could be civil and amicable and put their needs above anything that we felt. I hope, with everything I've got, that this will be the case one day.

*

## Sunday

We had Megan and John over for a BBQ today with all the kids. It was really lovely. Belle stayed at Molly's last night and they both came back here today, Jacob came too, and the three of them spent one of the hottest afternoons we've had watching a film indoors with the curtains closed, but the rest played outside. Jamie got a big inflatable pool, which they spent the entire afternoon in, and they overdosed on hot dogs and burgers.

Megan and I got quite tipsy and ended up having a heart to heart. She told me John isn't sure about trying for another baby. The grief I imagine they've felt over the past three months is enough to make you question ever putting yourselves through that again. She asked me if Jamie and I would ever have a baby together and I immediately answered no – life is stressful enough!

I realised though, after she left, and now I've sobered up, that it's the first time I've ever thought about that question. It's not ever been something we've discussed, and I suppose with the issues both of us have had with our five children it's put us off having more. I feel slightly gutted though, that we will never experience that together. Having our children together would have been something I loved, but we need to focus on what we have: five beautiful babies who need us to focus on them.

God – maybe I'm still pissed.

# CHAPTER TWENTY-SIX

* * * * * * * * * * * * * * * * * * * * * * * * * *

# PRETENDING EVERYTHING IS FINE

## Monday

I woke up with a hangover from yesterday's gin and my head was banging for most of the morning.

I arrived at the café to find Lou waltzing around at the speed of lightning, putting small vases of wild flowers on each table and humming along to some weird folk music I'd never heard before.

'Morning,' she sang, as I walked through the door.

'Morning,' I replied, confused. With that, David came strutting out of the kitchen wearing an apron and holding the salt and pepper pots on a tray.

'Morning,' he sang in tune, as if he was harmonising with the wife that he adored. I wanted to headbutt one of the tables in sheer disbelief as hard as I could and scream, 'WHAT THE FUCK?!'

Lou looked totally normal. No bruises on her face, but I did see she had long sleeves on despite it being another baking hot day. David hung around all morning like a bad smell. Under his apron he was dressed in rolled-up chinos, boat shoes and a designer white shirt, the top few buttons undone and his sleeves rolled up. If I didn't know what he secretly was I'd have thought he looked attractive – and well dressed. Now every single thing about him repulsed me.

Jamie arrived with the four youngest children just after midday. They came in for ice cream and when he saw David they acted like long-lost friends. Patting each other's backs, calling each other 'mate' and joking away. I wanted to vomit. I felt like David was making way too much effort – clearly for Lou's benefit.

I was convinced I'd see through this behaviour now even if I didn't know the truth of their situation, that I'd question his behaviours as weird, over the top, false, but the reality is I probably wouldn't. I'd probably be stood there laughing along at the conversation, thinking he was an amazing husband and a 'fun family guy' just like Jamie.

And that's what the customers had thought for years, wasn't it? I often overheard them telling Lou … 'Oh, he's so lovely; he's so kind; isn't he nice?'

And she'd spend the day agreeing, smiling away about what a great chap her husband was, and I'd smile on while she'd answer, happy at how good they had it together. Only now it was different, and as he stood in front of me, ruffling my son's hair and discussing the tide times with my husband, I watched his wife slyly watching him, and I wondered what scars and fresh injuries were hidden under her sleeves.

As Jamie stood up to leave, David told me I could finish for the day. I saw Lou shoot me a look – although I couldn't work out what it was for. Did she want me to stay on and protect her or was she encouraging me to go, telling me she would be fine. I said I was fine to stay on, but David insisted, saying he and Lou would manage fine. I felt a dagger of panic and wondered if he somehow knew that I knew. I worried that he had seen a look between us, if I had been too obvious with my hatred for him. I saw him turn to Lou, but he had his back to me, and I couldn't see his face. She immediately started assuring me I was fine to leave and I knew. I knew at that point things weren't OK. He didn't want his wife out of his sight for a single fucking second. I told Lou I would see her tomorrow and, as we were going, Jamie decided to invite them over for dinner this weekend. A BBQ if the weather was nice; if not he would cook steak indoors. Brilliant.

Lou was immediately hesitant – saying she wasn't sure of their plans. David spoke over her, said that would be lovely and he would text Jamie once he had checked his diary. I hoped he was also stalling and he was also going to confirm they were busy and had plans they were unable to change. That he had no intention of playing happy families either in my back garden or round my dining table and it was another one of his games to mess with his wife's head. The thought of having to spend the evening watching that fucker play the perfect dad and husband while chowing down on a sirloin steak and sipping cold beer like he had no cares in the world made me want to eat my own fist.

\*

## Tuesday

As I got ready for work this morning, Art appeared beside me. He perched on the edge of my bed as I pulled on my leggings and flicked the GHDs through my hair in an attempt to make it look like I'd made some kind of effort.

'Will we ever see Dad again?' he asked.

Jesus. First Ruby, now him . . .

I cope far better when the kids are silent about their missing parents. If anything, when they don't say stuff, I can almost pretend we're OK. That we're normal and happy and the kids are fine and coping with life as it is. I can almost pretend that my kids' dad and Jamie's kids' mum don't exist – even though I think about them several times throughout every day. I think the same things, over and over. I question how they can live without seeing or speaking to them every day. How they cope without knowing they're OK, what they are doing or what they've been up to. I wonder what they'd think now if they did see them. They change almost weekly with how much they grow; their personalities are different to the last time they saw them, and I have no understanding of how they live without them. Not having my children with me would be like cutting off my oxygen supply . . . then I spend the rest of my time reminding myself they're 'not like me'. They must be unwell, Mark must have something wrong with his emotions to be able to shut off, and I make a promise I won't keep to stop overthinking it all constantly.

I sat beside Art and kissed the top of his head. Part of me wanted to lie to him, tell him that he would be seeing his dad soon and he had just been busy at work ... but the reality is that we've been on this merry-go-round for five years now and I feel the more I continue to protect him with lies, the more I'm fucking up my son ...

'I don't know,' is how I answered. I then went on to explain that, since we've moved to Cornwall, I've stopped contacting his dad, because I've realised since seeing how Jamie is with his kids that it's not normal that I have to beg and plead for Mark to spend time with his children. I try to explain that I don't understand why he doesn't contact them. As I'm doing so, I see Art ripping apart a piece of tissue in his sweaty palm where he's trying to stop himself from crying. I tell him it's OK to cry – and he does. He doesn't want to, but he can't stop. It's a frustrated, hurt cry. One where he sheds tears because he cannot fathom out why he isn't enough for his dad. It's the same cry he did the last time he saw Mark. He doesn't understand why his own dad has chosen to reject and abandon him, and for the first time in half a decade I've admitted that I don't either.

I told him how much I love him, how I would die and kill for him without question and how my heart is so full every time I lay eyes on him. I tell him how much Jamie loves him, no differently to how he loves Will. That all we see is that the five of them now are 'ours' and we try our hardest to make this situation as normal as possible for them. And then I tell him I'm sorry. I'm sorry I picked such a shitty dad for him, I'm sorry I didn't know what I was doing when I did it and that I feel responsible because of how much he has been let down and hurt, but I tell him I am also so glad I did because him, Rex and Belle are the best achievements in my life and I wouldn't change that for the world. He repeatedly mutters, 'I know, Mum,' but the tears have turned into choked sobs and the tissue is now in a thousand tiny damp pieces scattered all over my bedroom floor.

I want to send a text to Mark more than anything, telling him what a shithead he is. I wish I had a way for him to see the damage he's caused his son. I want to call him and lose my mind or get in the car and drive to his house. I want to scream and shout and ask him why. Why is he such an appalling father? My heart is beating through my chest and I feel sick with anger watching my baby so utterly devastated, but the reality is that it's pointless. Me doing any of that is totally pointless. You cannot force, bribe or threaten someone to love their own child. It's either there or it's not, and for him, it's not. And on reflection I don't think it ever has been, not really. It's just another harsh reminder that Jamie and I need to prioritise these five kids above and over anything and everyone.

The chat came to an abrupt end when Rex appeared at the bedroom door holding a used tampon applicator. 'What is this?' he asked – and, as he did, Belle arrived behind him and lost the plot, screaming that he's gross.

I reminded her it would be best to pop these things in the bin and she started screaming that she had put it in the bathroom bin and that Rex is a weirdo to have found it. Will and Art then asked what it was and I found myself stood in the hallway attempting to explain to three young boys and a golden Labrador how it's perfectly normal and healthy for girls to bleed from their minis once a month and this is what they use to absorb the blood. I also pointed out it can make them slightly moody – perfectly timed as Belle was in her room screaming, 'JESUS ACTUAL CHRIST!', in sheer embarrassment.

Art and Rex both made grossed-out faces and giggled and said yuck loads. Will was really grown up and said, 'Alisha in my class started her periods already. She told us all they're really heavy.' I then had to explain what 'heavy' meant – cue more screaming from Belle and me beginning to panic-sweat a little. I rushed downstairs to escape this conversation and when Ruby looked up from her iPad and asked the question, 'When will I start bleeding out of my mini?', I wondered what my life had come to …

I arrived at work slightly late and explained to Lou I'd had a bad morning with Art. Her eldest son Harry was sat at the table and I said hello to him and asked if he had come to work, Lou replied he had come in to help and he looked up from his iPhone and snapped, 'No. Dad made me come.' Lou scuttled back into the kitchen and I knew that this was his way of control, spying on her through their fourteen-year-old son.

I followed her into the kitchen and saw that she was a nervous wreck, scurrying around doing stuff that didn't need doing.

'Lou. Are you OK?' I asked. She kept saying she was while continuing to hurl herself all over the place doing pointless jobs at the speed of light. I walked behind her and as I put my hands on either side of her arms to get her to stop, she jumped out of her skin. She then began profusely apologising.

'Calm down,' I kept saying in a hushed tone, but then the tears came. I tried asking her if she wanted to leave David and come and stay with me, if he had hurt her again, but she was just shaking her head and repeating the sentences 'I'm fine' and 'I'm so sorry' in a whispered tone. Heartbreaking.

I told her this wasn't OK. That she and her sons were in danger and that David was extremely warped and dangerous.

She took some deep breaths while looking up to the ceiling and fanning her face with her hand and told me he had now agreed to get help for his anger and that he had changed. I struggled to see how a man in his position had suddenly willingly agreed to get help, but at least he was trying. Lou told me that there hadn't been any further incidents since I'd been at the house, which I was at least thankful for. If she was telling the truth.

After ten minutes of me begging and pleading, informing her about all the research I've done and the stats on domestic abuse, she was still not having it. Her marriage, she told me, *would* work. Her husband, she told me, *is* a good man. Her children, she told me, *are* fine. Part of me felt really angry towards her, that she wasn't protecting her children, that she was staying with a man who caused them and her such damage, but one thing I've now learned is that supporting a person who is being subjected to domestic abuse is one of the hardest, most frustrating things you can ever do, but I know I needed to do it. She had no one else to turn to; he had isolated her from every other person in life, so for now I would keep supporting, and listening, and just being there – however infuriating that may be at times.

As I was clearing tables out the front, Jen appeared. She ordered a coffee and asked where Lou was as she hadn't seen her for so long. I said she was busy baking but would be out soon. I said it loud enough for Lou to hopefully hear and after five minutes she appeared as fresh-faced as was possible. Jen still spotted her tear-stained face and asked what was wrong. Lou brushed off Jen's worries and started complaining about hay fever and the pollen count.

I stood and watched her lie and lie to one of her best friends, who was, by now, totally convinced by her, and was sharing stories of her friend's daughter who's also currently struggling with hay fever. Jen went onto enquire how her migraines were, about which Lou then gave a whole new account – she was waiting for test results but the hospital hadn't been that great, etc., etc.

It became so clear watching Lou turn into an Oscar-winning actress that the websites I'd trawled were correct. If I hadn't walked up her drive that day and seen those injuries for myself, I'd be stood here now, alongside her and Jen sharing stories about migraines and headaches and hay fever, while still thinking Lou had one of the most supportive husbands and strongest marriages I've ever come across. The victim of a domestic abusive relationship really does learn how to lie and cover for their perpetrator – and the fact she can now do it so well and she's so convincing tells me she knows, more than I do, that her situation is very much a matter of life and death. I need to turn my research more to what I can actually do to help. It's all well and good me learning the stats but we need this to stop. There must be advice out there and I'm sure that being outside of it, I'll be able to see a way to break the cycle more clearly than Lou will.

\*

## Wednesday

Jamie went into work today for a meeting even though he had planned to be at home, so Belle and Molly looked after the kids while I was at the café. We all had breakfast together before I left for work and I thought it would be nice to have some quality family bonding time, so I decided to cook pancakes. But they were like rubber – too thick so still raw after cooking or too thin and I had to scrape them off the pan as black as coal into the bin. The kids were in hysterics watching me attempt to cook them. In the end I was late for work, the kitchen was a haze of black smoke so I chucked three boxes of cereal and milk on the table, thanked Belle for clearing up the mess – in case she wasn't planning to – and ran out of the door.

Jaclyn called this morning to say she is finishing early tonight so wondered if it would be OK for Belle to stay over and she would take them out for dinner. It was really nice, from what Molly said to Belle her mum had never done anything like this with her and it seems like she was really enjoying it. Belle liked Jaclyn too, she said she was posh, but a 'nice posh' – whatever that meant! I wonder about Molly's dad; she's never mentioned him since the day I asked, and Jaclyn never has. I think about if she does actually know who he is and if not does she not want to track him down? Maybe it wouldn't be a bad thing. I don't know.

I called Belle to check in on home and she said Jacob was on his way over and they were going to take the little ones down to the park before Jaclyn collected her and Molly, then she would be staying at hers for the night.

It seems so weird now that she has a boyfriend – well, not a boyfriend because God forbid we call him that – but I often find myself thinking back to the days when we snuggled up on the sofa with our cups of tea when she toddled about, and I never envisaged this. You never look 'that far' into the future. One day you're arguing with your baby, who is adamant they've put their wellies on the right feet even though they're on the wrong ones. Your heart melts when you hear them counting to ten and throwing in random numbers or when they try to sing the rainbow song and add in some weird colours for extra effect, and you think – this is it. You don't see life past this, past them needing you and you needing them to need you. Then one day it just becomes so clear that the reality is you only have them as 'yours' for such a short time.

Our job, as parents, is to raise them so they can go out into the world and cope without us – and when that happens it's really daunting because no one ever prepares you for this part. When you're carrying your baby inside you all you are told is how to cope with the pain of breastfeeding, how to get through the sleepless nights and when to wean your baby. No one ever really gets to the teenage years let alone the time after that when they go to uni or leave home, and the closer I'm edging to that the more I'm realising that perhaps this is the hardest part of motherhood, and actually having a baby that needs you constantly and is with you twenty-four hours a day is the easy part . . .

# CHAPTER TWENTY-SEVEN

# THE SHIT HITS THE FAN

*Thursday*

I've felt sick with nerves all day long and my tummy is in knots constantly. David popped into the café this morning – clearly just to 'check' on Lou. He's bought himself a brand-new convertible Mercedes, bright red, 'just for the summer months', he told a customer at the counter, who was admiring it out of the window. As soon as I saw it, he reminded me of Mark. The knob. Who would spend that amount of money on a car for a couple of months? And what middle-aged father rocks around in a bright-red two-seater soft top?

It's funny, but now 'I know' what he is, and what the situation is, it's so easy to actually see this purchase for what it is – power and control. As he was leaving shortly after, he said, 'See you Saturday, Jo.' When I asked him what was happening on Saturday, David reminded me of Jamie's offer for dinner and that they would definitely be able to make it. I exchanged glances with Lou and she looked as shocked as me.

What. The. Fuck.

I laughed (out loud) and went totally over the top with excitement in case he had picked up on either of our 'What the fuck' faces. I started getting a notepad out of my pinny to make a list of what they wanted to eat and drink like I was hosting a grand celebration. I caught Lou's eye again and her shocked face was worsening at my now weird over-the-top behaviour. I could feel the adrenaline pumping round my body, my face was flustered, and I felt so angry at Jamie for dishing out this invite that I wanted to cry with anger and frustration.

David said Lou would let us know what they liked, he was as cool as a cucumber – he said he had to leave for an urgent meeting. He gave Lou a goodbye kiss on the forehead, one that if I had seen 'before' I'd have thought was cute – but this time I noticed the grip on her chin and a little head movement from her where he held her just that bit too tight to ensure 'she knew'.

As he drove off in his twat-mobile, I passed her an ice pack from the freezer for the now-visible pinch marks on her face and told her it would help with the bruising. As the tears pricked her eyes and she walked back into the safety of the kitchen, I heard her mutter the words 'I fucking hate him', and I felt a little burst of hope that maybe, just maybe, she was getting stronger.

*

### Friday

After we put the kids to bed last night, I asked Jamie why he had asked David and Lou to dinner without speaking to me first and he looked genuinely confused. He reminded me I had constantly tried to plan something with David and Lou for 'months' and all I had done is moan that it was weird that they never wanted to meet up and had a go at him that I'm the only one that ever invites them and he makes no effort. He thought I'd be pleased that he had finally managed to pin them down.

I quickly realised he was of course right to be totally confused that I was pissed off, but I was crippled with nerves about having to spend that amount of time in David's company. It made my tummy do flips and I felt physically sick at the thought of having him in our home. I apologised to Jamie and made the excuse I was hormonal, to which he giggled and planted his usual kiss on my forehead followed by an eye roll.

I called Pat and cried. I missed her so much when I heard her voice.

She asked me to speak to Jamie and to let her know when we wanted her to come back. She had got her house valued and it was already on the market. She had definitely come to the conclusion that her home in Canterbury was no longer home and she wanted to be nearer to us.

We agreed she would come back next week, and we could make a plan and start looking at properties for us all to get finally settled. I felt a wave of relief wash over me that she would be here again.

Jamie and I spent the evening sorting the garden. He mowed the lawn and cleaned the BBQ while I tended to the plants I'd ignored since Pat left and decorated the bushes with some fairy lights that had been sat in the shed for weeks. I mentioned to him about approaching the landlord to buy this house, but Jamie didn't think it would be big enough for his mum to live with us permanently. But he has spotted two cottages for sale down by Lou's café, which are in her price range, a five-minute walk from us – and beautiful.

I've just got into bed and the butterflies are still flying inside my tummy at the thought of tomorrow. I'm not going to have a drink; I can't trust myself not to say or do something to David if I'm not totally sober.

*

## Saturday

We decided on a BBQ for Lou and David seeing as the weather was glorious. We have been so lucky with it lately, and it definitely helps make everything feel better when you wake up to warmth and sunshine. They arrived bang on time at 4pm as we all wanted to make the most of the sun (and I hoped they'd then leave earlier). David was armed with a crate of vintage wine and local ales to impress us and I managed to act as well as Julia Roberts in *Sleeping with the Enemy* when I greeted him.

I hadn't mentioned the BBQ to Belle as she had already told me that she, Molly and their friends were going to a flume park out of town, so I wasn't sure if they'd be back.

David got tipsy quickly. Lou didn't drink as she was driving. Jamie was drinking beer but was relatively sober. I imagine his nerves weren't playing up quite the same as domestic abuser David's.

I noticed a shift within the first hour of David's behaviour towards Lou. The 'looks' were there from the start to shut her up every time she spoke and it was as if he purposely did the opposite to everything she said – for instance when George said he didn't want salad, she skipped past and popped some chips on his plate, but David snatched the plate off her and boomed at her that he *would* be eating salad. He then threw a shitload of lettuce on his plate, bellowed 'EAT IT' at him and looked at Lou for a further reaction. She didn't give one. She just began reassuring George in a flustered voice that 'Dad was right' and he should 'Eat some greens'. I saw him look down at his plate, probably knowing what was to follow later, and my heart hurt.

Jamie continued sizzling steaks – under the hopeful eye of Stanley, who was salivating at the thought of a dropped sirloin – and chatting away to the kids like everything was absolutely normal, and I wondered if I wasn't aware of this awful situation whether I'd be totally oblivious like he is now too. It was hard to believe that I wouldn't notice the fact that George was sticking to Lou like glue and not interacting with his dad at all ...

Around 7pm Belle, Molly and Jacob came home. As soon as they walked in the garden, Molly went bright red. I introduced them all and Molly seemed even more awkward. She said she wasn't hungry and went straight up to Belle's room. I took Belle into the kitchen and asked if everything was OK, to which she said she had been fine up until coming in the house. I assumed she was probably just not used to having so many people around, it being just her, her mum and the housekeeper at home. Belle stayed in the garden chatting to Lou, George and Harry, and, as I studied them, I saw that George was such a sweet lad, which seemed like a miracle given everything he was dealing with at home.

About half an hour later Jamie made a plate of food up for Molly and as I went up the stairs to give it to her, I saw David at the top leaning on the railing with Molly stood in front of him, sobbing. He sounded like he was speaking to her in a firm whisper voice, and I immediately panicked. I asked him what he was doing, and he said looking for the toilet.

Molly went back into Belle's room and quickly shut the door behind her. I told him the toilet was downstairs and he pushed past me down the stairs and sang, 'Thank you, Jojo,' in a sarcastic voice.

I went into Belle's room to find Molly on the bed. She had stopped crying and was smiling – trying her hardest to make out that everything was OK – but she looked like she was in shock and when I asked what had happened, she repeatedly shook her head and said, 'Nothing,' with an even bigger, falser grin, over and over again, she said she felt unwell and had called her mum to come and collect her. I asked her if she was sure and she assured me she was.

I felt out of control, and even more sick. Something was really weird.

Belle came up and we tried our hardest to convince Molly that she could tell us anything, but she was adamant she was fine, she just had a headache and that David had just met her in the hallway while looking for the toilet and she had already been crying as she had started to feel unwell. I thought about calling Jaclyn but I figured she would be here in a minute so I would speak to her and ensure no one had upset Molly.

Belle and I left Molly to rest alone and went back outside. On the way downstairs we agreed something was definitely really odd. David was by now right at the bottom of the garden on his mobile phone. He was pacing up and down and every now and then I would hear his voice raise in an angry tone then quieten back down. I couldn't make out what he was saying but I knew it wasn't good. Lou was still chatting to Belle and Harry and seemed calm and happy. She was smiling away and engaging in conversation, seeming totally oblivious to how utterly weird and angry her husband was. David came back up the garden, looking half-cut and sheepish and said to no one in particular, 'Sorry. Business,' before grabbing his gin and tonic off the table and downing it in one. My stomach was doing flips, but Jamie still seemed totally oblivious, Lou was still chatting away to the kids, and I wondered if I was being crazy and making this all up in my head.

I went inside to stack the kids' plates in the dishwasher and fetch the trifle out the fridge when the doorbell rang. It was Jaclyn. I opened the door and closed it behind me to try to speak to her and explain something wasn't quite right but she seemed massively agitated and started saying she was in a rush and could I fetch Molly as she needed to leave immediately.

Molly came down the stairs and as soon as she saw her mum the tears came, I started really panicking then because I knew something wasn't right and Jaclyn started repeating 'We just need to leave, Molly, now, it will all be fine'.

Before I could even ask what was the matter the front door was swung open with such a force and David appeared. He looked me up and down and sniggered, then ordered me to 'get back in the house' as he had things to sort, before pushing past me. He began following Jaclyn and Molly down the drive to their car, swaying as he went.

I called out to him and asked what he thought he was doing – it was clear now that he was so pissed. He told me to go back inside. Molly looked at me in sheer desperation and Jaclyn looked panicky but said, 'We're fine here, Jo, honestly' and I felt genuinely worried for them both.

I had no clue what was happening, but I rushed into the back garden and told Jamie he needed to come to the front of the house.

'Is everything OK out there?' Lou asked in a trembling voice that reminded me of the day I found out about David's abuse.

'Yeah, I'm sure it's all fine. Molly's mum has arrived and David is talking to her. I didn't realise they knew each other, is all.'

Lou was really blasé at that point and told me they knew each other well since they were both solicitors and often met up for business stuff. Of course they did. That explains it.

'Molly is really upset, though,' I told her, 'and I don't think David being out there right now will help.'

To my surprise, Lou was willing to put herself into the throng. 'I'll go and see what's going on, and see how Molly is.' Her voice was still shaking.

Was Jamie really oblivious to this?! I had a very tense situation unfolding on the doorstep and he's basting steaks with olive oil and a home-made herb brush like he doesn't have a care in the world!

I watched Lou go to the front and as she called David over, he bellowed, 'GO AWAY, LOUISE.'

I knew I was going to be sick. I could feel it coming.

Ruby was in a deep sleep on the sofa. All the boys were kicking a ball down the bottom of the back garden, and Belle and Jacob were still chatting to Jamie while he was flipping his sausages. It looked like the perfect picture of a nice family BBQ – but the music in the back garden was drowning out the shitstorm at the front of the house, and I was feeling like a yo-yo in between.

I watched Lou continue to try to persuade David to come back inside. And then watched in horror as he stormed over to her, grabbed her throat in his right hand and said in a calm but threatening voice, 'GO AWAY, SLAG.'

That was it. The switch flipped in me. FUCK THIS!

I went out the front and shouted at Molly and Jaclyn to get in the house. David told me firmly that Molly was leaving with her mother so we could continue to 'enjoy the party'.

'Just leave it, Jo, please,' Lou begged me. 'Molly and Jaclyn are going.'

'No. Sorry, Lou, but I will not "just leave it".'

Molly was in a state. Jaclyn was incapable of parenting her or making any decisions right now because she was also in a state, and I could see David was gearing up to lose it with one of the four females in front of him, but I still stood my ground.

By this time, Jaclyn was dragging Molly into her gleaming bright-white limited-edition Range Rover. Molly was pleading, begging with her mum for them to come inside, which was making Jaclyn even more panicky. David then bellowed, 'Take that fucking kid home now, Jac.'

With that Jamie appeared and looked like a rabbit in headlights. He asked what the hell was going on, as calm and rational as ever, still holding his BBQ pinchers. Better late than never, eh, Jamie? By this point David had gone into a full-blown rant about 'interfering fucking bitches'. The only part I could make out was him repeating something about 'getting that fucking kid out of his sight' while Lou was wiping away silent tears. Molly was uncontrollably sobbing and Jaclyn now looked like she was bordering on a panic attack.

Jamie tried reasoning with Jaclyn and Lou, asking them what had gone on and what needed to happen now to resolve things. Molly said that she didn't want to go home, and David then screamed, 'Well, you're fucking going home,' before striding towards her in a rage. Lou ran after him to stop him and as she grabbed his left wrist he turned around and punched her full on in the face with his right fist.

He might have been slow to react earlier, but I couldn't fault Jamie's response time now. He was on David, holding him back from throwing any more punches, before I'd even fully processed what had happened.

Lou's head flew back and all of a sudden there was blood everywhere. I couldn't tell which part of her face the punch had landed on but it had hit hard. I heard screams but couldn't work out where they were coming from until I saw Belle stood at the door. I have this vivid recollection of Lou repeatedly reassuring everyone that everything was fine, exactly the same way she had done with me that day I found her at her house, while wiping the blood out of her eyes and off her cheeks. As she tried to pull herself together,

David shook Jamie off and ran forward, kicking Lou as hard as he could. It was a kick on her bum, from behind as she was trying to get up off the floor, which sent her flying back down on her face, knocking her out. She was unconscious. Was she dead? Jamie called to me to ring 999 as he struggled again to restrain David's flailing body.

I had never in my life witnessed anything like this and my hands and legs were trembling so badly I could see them moving but couldn't physically stop them. Molly was now screaming, and I shouted for her to go into the house with Belle and lock the door. I shouted at Jaclyn to help Lou, and, as I ran in to grab my phone, I saw that all the boys were now stood at the front door watching this war unfold.

I called 999 and asked for an ambulance and the police, and when I came out, Jaclyn was helping Lou. She had come round slightly but there was blood everywhere – pouring from her mouth. I could see how frightened Jaclyn was, trembling like me, but she was so kind to Lou, reassuring her, stroking her hair and telling her everything would be fine.

Jamie was rolling round on the floor with an intoxicated David, both covered in blood, though I had no clue whose it was while David continued to shout about 'that fucking kid'.

Molly and Belle were looking out of the upstairs hallway window so I pointed to the lounge window so they could go down and try to calm the little ones, who were still looking out at this absolute shitstorm unfolding in front of us. I saw

Jacob appear at the lounge window and pull the curtains shut. Shit, Jacob. How would I explain this to Meg and John?

*

## Sunday

Snuggled up on the sofa, with Stanley across my lap, it's hard to believe that what happened last night actually happened. As I write this now, replaying it in my mind, I struggle to put the pieces together and figure out how we got from hot dogs and overly polite chit-chat to a bloody attack – because an attack is what it was – in the driveway, culminating in the arrival of an ambulance and two police cars. The situation spiralled out of control within seconds and no one understood why or saw it coming. There's that saying where 'everything can change in the blink of an eye' and that really is so, so true.

The police arrived before the ambulance and arrested David, who had totally lost it by that point, screaming obscenities that no one could make any sense of.

Belle helped me and Jaclyn with Lou. We managed to get her to sit up, but her face was in a state. The ambulance arrived shortly after and I went with her to hospital. Her face seemed to be swelling more and more by the minute and her left eye was closed over already. She didn't say much in the ambulance. I think we were both in shock about what had just happened.

The police arrived to take a statement and Lou kept saying she didn't want to 'cause any trouble' even though she had just taken a punch so vicious it had probably broken something. I sat and explained to her that her children had witnessed this, my children had witnessed this, other people's children had witnessed this. This man, her husband, had done this to her in front of other people. This was no longer a case of him just bullying her behind closed doors; it had escalated and had to be stopped. Nothing had calmed him down and she had to see that he was terribly dangerous.

Finally, whether through relief or shock, she seemed to finally acknowledge that it was done – it was a secret no more. We both gave full statements to the police and then they went to my house to get further statements from Jamie and the others. I wondered if they would speak to all the kids, and what effect it would have on them. I wondered if then that may reflect badly on Jamie with Will and Ruby. I couldn't believe it had happened at all and I was still in shock, so God knows how they were feeling.

By now it was 11pm and we were shattered. They kept Lou in overnight because she needed to see a surgeon. I overheard the doctors whispering about 'old injuries' when they were inspecting the X-rays and I saw Lou look down, making it clear she had heard them too. They confirmed she had a broken jaw and she would need an operation immediately. I took her hand and squeezed it and a tear ran down her cheek. I knew she knew this was it.

It was over.

It had all gone on for too long.

Lou began crying about the boys and the practicalities of what would happen next. I tried to slow her down, and suggested she speak to her parents, because she really needs a support network so strong that she won't ever go back to that man, no matter what.

The police said David was still waiting to be interviewed but it was likely he would be released under bail conditions that stated he wasn't to go anywhere near Lou. I had no understanding of why he wouldn't be remanded in prison when he was clearly dangerous; he could have killed her.

Lou agreed to let me ring her mum and explain things to her, and I asked Lou to leave everything – including the boys – with me and concentrate on healing.

When I finally got home, all the kids had dragged their quilts off their beds and had snuggled up on the sofa and floor in the lounge together. Jacob had Ruby on his lap and I was relieved she had slept through everything that had happened. As soon as Belle saw me, she began to cry, and Molly looked like she wanted the ground to swallow her whole.

Jamie and I joined them all in the lounge and I felt overcome with emotion when I looked at Lou's boys. Both staring at the floor of a stranger's home not knowing if their mum was OK or where their dad was.

Jamie told me that Jaclyn had stayed for a few hours last night. She had cleaned up all the front drive after the police left and helped him get the kids settled and sort the kitchen. He told me she was surprisingly good with the kids, calm and nice – reassuring them and fetching them drinks and snacks. He said she was also extremely affectionate towards Molly, which Molly embraced. That surprised me too. He said she seemed reluctant to talk about what had happened, but he asked her what she knew of David and she told him he was a horrid man, but in a warning kind of way – as if to tell Jamie not to get on the wrong side of him.

'She asked me to tell you that she'll explain things in detail to you in the week.' I replied by saying, 'I owe an apology too, to you, Jamie. I'm really sorry that I didn't tell you what happened that day at Lou's. I shouldn't have kept it a secret – we don't do secrets. This felt too big and too scary and I know now that I should have spoken to you.'

Jamie told me that he understood. I'm not sure he did because I'm not even sure I do, but he didn't give me a hard time, just a hug, a reassuring kiss and a promise that 'everything would be just fine in time'.

When Jaclyn left, Molly was asleep so she agreed to leave her and said she would call in today to pick her up. We were to call her if either of us needed anything at all, she'd apparently said.

Jamie then took Will, Rex, Art and Ruby out of the room and I sat with Lou's boys, Molly, Belle and Jacob. I was really honest. I explained that David had done some bad things to Lou and he was now in custody. I explained that

Lou was still in hospital, but that she would be fine. George looked so frightened and began to cry, and my heart ached, watching his pain, so visible.

Harry told me that their dad always did this – lost his temper and hurt their mum. I asked if he had ever done anything to the boys and he said he hadn't – but they were often shut in their rooms when 'things were really bad'. They also admitted that David had told them that if they ever told anyone they would be put into care and wouldn't see their mum again.

'That's just not true, Harry, and I don't want you to ever worry about that,' I told him. I didn't know how Lou wanted to handle things with the boys, what she was and wasn't going to tell them, but I thought I was on safe ground sticking to the facts and doing my best to reassure them.

I realised at that point just how affected children were by domestic violence – even if they never actually see the violence take place. This family had so much wealth, they were beautiful to look at, and seemed to have it all – but now everything had been ripped apart because their father had destroyed all their hopes and dreams.

Molly didn't say a word. If anything, she looked totally withdrawn and just kept staring out of the front room window. When I asked if she was OK, she just kept saying, 'I'm so, so sorry.'

I told her she had nothing to be sorry for and that we would get her some help and support too. I know that something else isn't right here. The interactions between her and David last night, her mum turning up so suddenly, 'the incident', and her behaviour now, apologising for what happened. It didn't make sense. I can also see she's not in a good way right now; she's fragile and things are too raw, so I will just keep my eye on things, speak to her mum, then make a plan.

Later, I called Jen and asked if she was free for a few hours as I needed to speak to her. I left the kids with Jamie, drove and picked Jen up from hers and started making my way to Lou's house. I tried to tell her what had happened, but the emotion got the better of me and I had to pull the car over. As I explained everything, from when I had gone to Lou's house and seen her injuries up until everything that had happened at our house last night, Jen looked on in horror. 'Oh my god' were the only three words she repeated throughout. She had never suspected a thing.

Jen asked why I hadn't told her before and I said I was so annoyed at myself that I hadn't, but that I'd promised Lou and I was worried about somehow worsening the situation. But I know now that the situation was already as bad as it could be. I honestly thought by me keeping quiet I was protecting her more, but really I was only protecting David.

We arrived at the house and tapped in the code that opened the electric gates, which Lou had given to me. Everything looked so perfect. A perfect home where a perfect family resided. Wealthy and happy and healthy.

I felt so sick.

We got to the front door and when we opened it, we silenced the beeping alarm with the other code Lou had given.

Inside it was immaculate.

A bunch of fresh lilies stood as a centrepiece on the wooden table in the middle of the Spanish-looking entrance hall.

'Look at this place,' exclaimed Jen, open-mouthed.

I ripped the list in half. Jen took the bottom and I took the top.

Lou had told me there were bags, ready. Packed. Hidden. To go.

She had this planned 'just in case'.

She had known this day was coming.

Jen went off to fetch the boys' bags, which were hidden on the top shelves at the back of their wardrobes behind quilts, and I went to fetch Lou's. It made me realise just how desperate and unhappy she was, to want to leave all of this wealth behind and continue her life with just one holdall full of clothes and one crammed full of paperwork and photos of the boys as babies.

I went into the safe as instructed and used the code to open it. I took out two brown padded envelopes stuffed with cash labelled 'CAFÉ'. There were also tens of thousands of pounds in the safe, rolled up in wads of notes with elastic bands around them. I had been told not to touch them, they were his – I didn't believe her, I think they're the takings from the café as it's exactly how we cash up. I questioned where a solicitor would get that much cash from. If it was his I imagine it wasn't legal, so I decided to partly respect her wishes and partly take care of her – I took half.

She hadn't made reference to the jewellery in the safe – and there was so much jewellery. Emeralds and diamonds, necklaces and rings.

Bollocks. There was no other female living in this house of horrors and I couldn't picture David strutting about dripping in diamonds, so I scooped them all up and put them in the zip part of the holdall. Next, I took hers and the boys' passports, a big file labelled 'Café' and two photo albums as instructed.

I went into the utility room next to the kitchen and took two sets of the boys' uniforms, hanging, pristine, where she said they would be.

And that was it.

We left a home worth well over a million pounds full of almost twenty years' worth of memories with nothing other than four bags, three envelopes and a few sets of school uniform.

I dropped Jen at the hospital and drove home. Belle said the boys wanted to see their mum, and although I wasn't sure it was a good idea, Jamie said I should take them so that they didn't worry more than they already were – and it wasn't like they hadn't seen her injuries before now.

I agreed to take the boys, but before I did, I knew I had to call Lou's mum and fill her in on what had happened. The phone gave a foreign dial tone and when a man answered, I realised I didn't even know her mum's name. 'Hi. I'm looking to speak to Louise Metcalfe's mum,' I said.

The man asked who I was several times as if he was hard of hearing and I heard a lady in the background with a thick northern accent say, 'Just pass me the bloody phone, Tony.' It made me giggle despite the news I was about to deliver.

She came on the phone and immediately sounded concerned, asking if Lou was OK. I told her Lou was in hospital and explained that David had beaten her up, several times, over many years, and that things weren't good. I told her the boys were staying with us, but I thought they may be better with her and her husband, as we weren't very familiar to them. She told me they'd both get the first flight over and sort things out. She thanked me for my help. Her voice sounded shaky, but I had a feeling she would take some control here – I also felt she knew what she was dealing with in David. He hadn't quite fooled everyone completely, it seemed.

Lou was sleeping when we arrived at the hospital and George ran over and buried his head into her chest. Harry was more reserved and pulled up a chair next to the bed. As she came round, she said hello to them and she had a big smile on her face, but Harry replied with a simple, 'Hey Mum.' I couldn't work out if he was angry with her, or sad, but he showed her no affection, he just sat awkwardly –

staring at the floor and nervously chewing the skin around his fingers. For a minute I thought there was a chance he could be siding with his father, but after she had ruffled George's hair and reassured him, she was OK, Harry asked, 'That's it now, isn't it? We *can* go this time. We are leaving?'

Lou didn't answer; in fact she totally ignored the questions as if Harry wasn't there and continued fussing over George, telling him his hair smelt beautiful and asking if he was behaving for me.

Harry repeated the question – only louder each time until it turned into a high-pitched wobble where he was about to crack. Lou told him they'd talk about it later and made eyes towards him as if to warn him this 'chat' wasn't appropriate in front of his brother, but it was clear Harry didn't care.

He was now overcome with emotion and as much as he had tears running down his face, when he spoke, I could see he was absolutely, resolutely, done with this situation.

'NO, Mum. Enough!' He was tired and frustrated and hurt and angry. He began ranting and threw all sorts of accusations at his mum – the false promises she'd made to leave over the years, holdalls packed and hidden so they were 'ready to escape'. I realised that Harry had been living with this for a long time, long enough to hate his father and want to be as far away from him as humanly possible.

I think Lou knew the game was up. The choice wasn't hers any more. Her eldest son wanted out and if she said no, I knew that chances were social services and authorities would now intervene.

She silently nodded at her son. Tears ran down her cheeks, and she said, 'We're done, boys. That's it. No more going back.'

Harry stood up and leant into his mum. The three of them clung to one another and sobbed together. I felt utterly devastated – none of this was their fault. They'd wanted to be the perfect family. They'd tried so hard to fit that mould, and to the outside it looked like they had it all, but one man – their husband and father, the person who should have been their protector – had totally destroyed that, yet it was now them left to pick up the pieces and try to somehow heal and move on. It made me question how this world managed to shaft so many decent people while the bad ones constantly seemed to land on their feet.

I got home late. Molly said her mum had agreed she could stay again as she was working away most of this week and she couldn't cancel appointments. I sent her a text because of the time. I apologised I hadn't been in touch but had spent most of the day at hospital and I thanked her for last night. She replied immediately apologising for it all and asked if I could maybe pop into hers for a cup of tea when I was free. I said I would love to. I feel more positive that we can sort things out. Our girls are like sisters now and it's clear things have been massively misunderstood between us in the past.

# CHAPTER TWENTY-EIGHT

······························

# GROUNDED

## Tuesday

Jamie and I sat at the kitchen table last night and spoke about everything that had happened over the weekend. We agreed that I should have told him what I knew, but perversely, him not knowing and inviting them over ultimately resulted in everything being let out into the open at last. She and her boys are finally free of the bullying monster they live with. He pointed out that I've lost weight and I know I have; my clothes now hang off me but I've been so stressed with everything it's hardly surprising, especially finding out about Lou and with what's happened since Dad, so the thought of eating just isn't there. I promised him I would start taking better care of myself and getting back to being 'me' and we would make the most of this fresh start once and for all, without any more drama getting in the way.

I went to see Lou and told her that her mum is on her way and that she's OK with everything. She just looked up to the ceiling – as if it's all finally getting better – somehow. The police went to see her this morning to tell her that, as we expected, David has now been released on bail with conditions not to approach her or the boys. He has a court date next month.

We chatted some more and Lou told me that one of the reasons she hadn't left David sooner was that he had told her constantly that he would kill himself if she did and she genuinely believed that. When I looked into domestic abuse last month, I read that a victim can feel so much guilt that this is one of the biggest reasons they don't leave or tell anyone. She also told me that because he has the best family law firm in Cornwall, she was scared to death that he would apply to get the boys taken off her in court.

I don't think David will commit suicide and I don't think he will get the boys. I don't even think he wants the boys. The more I speak to them the clearer it's become that he pays no attention to them. If anything, he seems jealous of them and the love Lou showers them with. I also know from looking into the situation that, if he ever did decide to take her to court, they are both of an age where their 'voices will be heard' and once a court hears how they've watched their father beat their mother half to death repeatedly for their entire childhood, I'm pretty sure no one is going to force them to see him ... well, I can only hope.

I look at George and Harry and I wonder if anyone ever picked up on what they were going home to. Their mum constantly had injuries on her – I've seen that, but I cannot imagine what they've endured and witnessed at home. From the outside they appeared to have the perfect life, with all the trappings, but peel a layer away and you'd have seen that they were actually living in hell.

Lou's mum and dad came to collect the boys this evening. Jamie answered the door and invited both of them in. Her dad wore beige chinos with a white linen shirt and a straw hat; he looked really cool. Her mum was the spit of Lou, same wild red hair and freckled nose, but slightly shorter and rounder than Lou. She looked glamorous, wearing a blue polka dot dress, a funky orange wooden necklace and matching orange leather, expensive-looking, ballet pumps. They introduced themselves with a hug – Tony and Jane. Jane gave me a huge, tight hug and I was enveloped in a cloud of Chanel No. 5. I knew it instantly because it was my mum's perfume, and breathing it in hit me like a truck and I had to fight to hold back tears.

It was clear they knew what David was; maybe not to the extent of it all but they were aware of some of his behaviours and the control he held over their only daughter and grandsons. They were good people, kind and genuine, and when we shouted the boys down, they gave their grandma and grandad the biggest hugs. It was clear how much they all loved each other and it made me happy that the boys would be well looked after in their care.

They have a house here that they rent out via a firm in the summer, and luckily the changeover day is Monday so they called them when I originally rang to cancel all future bookings. She said they've had to pay a fee due to the short notice but they are fine with that. Their house, they tell me, is big enough for them all to stay in and they will be safe there.

When they left Jamie told me he had already gone to see Megan and John to explain what had happened on Saturday and to apologise as Jacob had been here. They were really good about it all and Jamie said they were totally shocked. Like the rest of the town, they thought David and Lou were the perfect couple and that he was a decent guy. Another lesson of how we really have no clue as to what goes on behind closed doors ...

I didn't eat again this evening, despite today's promise to Jamie. My anxiety is just causing me to feel so sick and I can't stomach anything. Once Lou is out of hospital and settled, I know I will feel better in myself and get back to normal – if 'normal' even exists any more; I think I've forgotten what that looks like. Living on adrenaline and nerves is no good for anyone.

\*

### Wednesday

Lou hasn't heard from David, which is good, but I'm wondering if she misses him. He's all she's known for half her life and I imagine getting her head round everything while being stuck in hospital away from the boys is really shit.

I've attempted to blitz the house tonight for Pat's imminent arrival but it's difficult. I haven't had time to catch up with anything since the weekend and – to borrow a phrase from the woman herself – I feel like I'm just shovelling snow while it's still snowing.

Jamie has been so good. I've noticed that with him being around more to walk Stanley, our four-legged friend behaves so much better when I take him out and is now enjoyable to walk with. Nine times out of ten he comes back when called and he's walking to heel most of the time. I take him to the beach almost every day and I find it clears my head as if I've done an hour of meditation.

Laura has moved back in with her parents. She has visits from the crisis team through the week and has been diagnosed with personality disorder. She is on meds and attends therapy. Pete speaks to Jamie regularly. They take the kids out for dinner and a round of crazy golf every Wednesday. They have said Laura doesn't look good at the minute, and still 'isn't well'. They don't elaborate any more than that – but they're sure the children seeing her right now wouldn't be a good thing. I think it's reassuring for Will and Ruby to see their grandparents weekly though, and that there is no animosity between any of us when they come to collect them. They leave the car in our drive and walk down into town. I know from Pete that the kids ask lots of questions about their mum which they answer as best they can, always assuring them how loved they are by her, but she's unwell right now and is trying to get better. I believe Will and Ruby know they are good people, and their mum is in the best care – so for now, it's all we can do.

Jamie is working so hard and when he gets in from work, no matter how chaotic it is or how loud the kids are, he's just loving and attentive to us all. He cracks jokes at the dinner table, and he's gone out of his way to make everyone feel OK. I've always found him to be the most grounding presence in my life, and now relative calm has been restored to our lives.

I catch myself looking at him and wondering what I did to deserve him, and when I say this to him, he just brushes it off and says he is equally as lucky to have me. I think that, despite us living in the eye of a storm right now, we're all still doing OK ...

# CHAPTER TWENTY-NINE

# FRESH PAINT, FRESH START

*Thursday*

I am so bloody grateful my mother-in-law rocked up with a tray of brownies this evening to make things better.

I called Jaclyn this morning to arrange going over. Molly had stayed at our house so I thought I could pop in when I dropped her home. She didn't answer. Molly assured me it would be fine to turn up, she was certain she would be there alone and expecting us.

We arrived and the electric gates were closed. Molly knew the passcode for the side gate, so we parked the car on the road and walked up the drive. I'm sure the gates were the same as Lou and David's. Maybe all rich people had the same electric gates.

As we started walking, we heard a car coming down the drive, leaving the house. As I saw the car approaching, my heart started beating faster and, as it came closer, I saw that it was David, in his twat mobile with the roof down. He did the most patronising slimy smile I've ever seen, glided out of the gates then roared his engine so hard to fly off up the road I jumped out my skin.

'What. The. Fuck,' was all I could muster to the fifteen-year-old girl walking beside me. She didn't reply, didn't look shocked, confused or worried, just bowed her head to the floor, almost looking ashamed. I asked her if she knew why David would be at her house, but she didn't reply. I realised how inappropriate it was to ask so I immediately 'remembered out loud' that Lou had said Jaclyn and David sometimes work together, so that's obviously why he was there (the reality, in my brain, was that that was absolute bullshit, but I was just hoping I had convinced an already damaged and confused teenage girl).

Jaclyn was stood at the door when we arrived, and it was clear she had been crying. I couldn't make any sense of this situation and Molly was still silent – giving nothing away.

'Molly!' Jaclyn beamed, and looked genuinely happy. She walked quickly towards her and put her arms out to embrace her. It was the first time I had seen this side to her, and after what Jamie had said about how affectionate they were to each other after Saturday's incident, I felt relieved, but Molly just looked down at the floor and didn't show any affection back.

Jaclyn invited us in, and she seemed giddy, nervous. I asked her why David was at the house and she told me it was just business; that they attend many meetings and events together and he had visited her to 'make peace'. What a cock. I wondered if he had threatened her, hence her tear-stained face. Maybe she was just frightened of him; I know I am after seeing what he's capable of. As Molly took her bags straight past the huge vase of flowers and up the sweeping staircase, I whispered to Jaclyn, asking her why he was really there. She stuck to her story, saying how she despised him, but it was easier with 'men like that' to be pleasant than fall out with them, as he has a lot of clout in town because of who he is. David Metcalfe, she told me, is not a man you want to get on the wrong side of. I thought of Lou in her hospital bed post-op and knew Jaclyn was right.

I suppose, being Jaclyn in a small town like ours when there are very few solicitors, it would be pointless going to war with one another when you have to work either alongside or against one another, as I imagined they sometimes do.

'I hate him,' Molly said out loud, walking back down the stairs without her bags.

Before I could stop myself, I hmphed and said, 'I think we're all with you there, Mol,' before biting my tongue.

She surprised me then and said, 'No I really hate him.' Jaclyn gave her a look, as if to tell her to stop being rude, and said, 'That's enough, Molly.'

I asked Molly if I could speak to her mum for a little while alone and she agreed, smiling, as if this was something she was happy about – and she went back off upstairs.

Jaclyn offered me a cup of tea and we sat on the patio, in the same spot I had sat with her daughter just weeks before. She told me how the pool is only used by Molly, reluctantly, in summer. It was the first time I actually felt sorry for her.

I tested the water of our new understanding and delicately said, 'Well, I know you work incredibly hard. It mustn't be very easy to be home with Molly as much as you'd like … ?'

I'd pitched this right and she started to open up, telling me that it was just the way it had always been since Molly was a baby and it was now normal for them. She said that her long hours and long absences from home had only become a problem in the last two years, due to Molly rebelling and 'playing up'.

I tried to explain, again delicately as I didn't want her to feel like I was attacking her parenting, that she wasn't doing those things; she was just being a normal teenage girl and maybe if she trusted her more then perhaps Molly wouldn't feel the need to lie to her mum. Jaclyn kept going on about there being 'bad people' in the world and that she felt safer when Molly was at home where no harm would come to her.

It was sad really, because, despite my first impressions of their dynamic – a rashly drawn conclusion that taught me an important lesson in kindness and understanding – it was clear to me that Jaclyn really loved Molly and wanted to protect her, but she wasn't letting her live and I still couldn't work out why. We spoke for a long time. She cried and I felt desperately sad for her and the life she had created for her and her daughter. Crying, I could tell, is something she doesn't often do in front of people and she tried so hard to hold it together, then when she couldn't, she was so uncomfortable getting upset in front of me. It was clear that she was as unhappy as Molly and they were both here in this huge beautiful home, yet it felt like a prison to both of them.

She asked me about my background and I told her about the kids, Mark and Jamie. She seemed genuinely interested and told me that she hadn't met anyone since Molly's dad, who had broken her heart. She'd found out he had been engaged to another woman when she was pregnant with Molly and he had left her on her own to raise the baby. Jaclyn told me that she didn't ever want to risk being hurt like that again, hence why she threw herself into her career so she could always look after Molly financially.

'I have regrets now; of course I do,' she told me. 'As time has gone on and Molly has grown up, I've come to see that, actually, it isn't about the money I earn – Molly doesn't need a swimming pool in her garden, for crying out loud – it's about time spent together, the love we have and the life lessons we take the time to teach them. If I'm honest, I've probably spent fifteen years in denial, convincing myself that what I was doing was right while knowing deep down that it was wrong.'

I suggested that we do something together, us two and Belle and Molly – the four of us. Her face lit up and I could tell she liked the idea. I wondered if it was because she felt some relief that she didn't have to do it alone, that I would be there to take the pressure off her, or maybe she actually was excited to have someone to do something with that didn't involve her career.

Before I left, I said goodbye to Molly and told her to have a chat with her mum about what they wanted to do. I could tell she was really chuffed and she gave her mum a hug. We had a plan, so it was progress. More progress.

Jaclyn agreed that Molly could come over to ours for the day tomorrow to see Belle while she was working. I gave them both a hug, and said my goodbyes. It felt good.

When I got home, Pat was there, and I was so glad to have her with me. Her presence alone just made everything a bit calmer and easier to cope with. Jamie must have inherited it from her.

*

## Tuesday

Lou is moving into the empty flat above the café and I think it will be the perfect safe haven for her and the boys. Although her parents have the space she said she wants to be on her own with the boys, she can't live with her parents and she doesn't feel it's fair to them, they had already flown back from Spain to take care of them. The flat is beautiful from what I've been told. Light and airy and the views are magnificent – across the entire beach. There are huge sash windows and it's all been maintained to a high standard. I'd planned to pop by today to double-check she has everything she needs for when she leaves hospital.

We've had all the locks changed on the café and extra security bolts fitted. The police have fitted alarms and given

Lou a personal one to keep with her at all times. It seems pretty drastic but as I've read that the most dangerous time for a victim of domestic abuse is when they're planning to leave or when they've just left – that's when the perpetrator is at his worst, when he comes to the realisation he's losing control.

When I got to the café, I wandered straight up the stairs to the flat and I was absolutely blown away. Jane, Lou's mother, had gone to the flat after she left the hospital and, with the help of Pat, had made it look so beautiful, with fresh bunches of peonies and roses in huge stunning vases. There were loads of little touches too that just made it look like home for when Lou walked in. When I arrived, Jane and Pat were sat at either ends of the carpet in the lounge, leaning against the walls with the coastal wind blowing in through the huge windows, both looking exhausted, but jabbering away with a pot of tea from downstairs like they had been friends for years.

Jane told me that even though Lou is in a terrible state, she believes that she's happier now, lying in a hospital bed, black and blue with no idea of her future than she was trapped with David. Her life is hers now and she and the boys are safe at last, and that made me feel better, much better. Looking around this space, with its blank walls crying out to be filled with their photographs and the boys' drawings, I couldn't help but feel full of hope for Lou and the bright new future that she and the boys would have here.

# CHAPTER THIRTY

## OUR GIRL IS BACK

*Friday*

It was a beautiful sunny day today, perfect for a girls' day out, so I took Molly and Belle into town and over lunch, complete with enormous ice-cream milkshakes, the girls asked all about Lou.

Molly was really concerned over her injuries and why David had done such an awful thing to someone he's supposed to love. As much as it was difficult to see her confused and sad, I was relieved she was opening up and talking about stuff. I explained that in life, sometimes, terrible things happen that make us question the world and the people in it, but that we should use those experiences as a good thing to make us be better people – be grateful that we don't understand it, and be kinder and more supportive to others.

Belle asked why none of Lou's family had seen what was going on and stepped in to help. I explained that she only had her parents and they lived abroad. It led on to us discussing family and support networks and I asked Molly what family she had. I knew her dad had never been on the scene, and I asked if she had any aunts, uncles, grandparents, but Molly told me there was no one. Her mum led a life with just Molly, she had worked so hard to become a partner of her firm, hence why she needed staff to help with childcare and the house, they lived away from anyone else.

It was so sad. I imagined her being the age Ruby is now, a little girl, stuck in a house, day and night, with an absent mother and her only company a supply of house staff. I then felt awfully sad for Jaclyn as she had done all of this mother stuff alone from the start, with no dad on the scene or any support from anyone to show her how lovely it could have been if she had done it differently – how hard must that have been for her?

Jamie got back that night with a chippy dinner and Lou's parents came over with the boys for a G&T. They walked down the beach with Jacob, Molly, Belle and Art to get an ice cream and have a paddle in the sea. I put Ruby and Rex to bed as they were shattered from the heat and we all sat in the garden. It was a warm night and the sky was a burnt-orange colour. As much as I was learning to love our unique brand of chaos, this moment of peace, without a child or a dog leaping over me, was just what I needed.

Tony had been a builder before he retired, he owned a huge firm where he employed all tradesmen. He sold it before he retired. He discussed with Jamie what we could change if we did buy the house. It made me feel warm and happy inside as buying this house was clearly something Jamie was thinking about. I really did love it. It was perfect for us as it was and it already felt like our home even though we hadn't done much to make it ours. The walls were still the same plain colours they were when we had moved in and we hadn't hung pictures or changed anything as we knew we wouldn't be here longer than six months. A year, tops.

The thought of buying this home and adding our touches to it makes me happy – happier than the thought of us looking at more properties and moving us all again, and I'm determined to get Jamie to speak to the landlord.

Jane and Pat sat on the swinging chair next to the BBQ, sipping on gin filled with berries and elderflower tonic, and snacking on a platter of peanuts and crisps that Pat's prepared. I liked seeing Pat chat away with someone her own age, but I know she can hold a decent conversation with anyone about anything, and I love that about her. Jane and her got on well and I felt they could share stories about their lives and experiences into the night.

The kids got back from the beach full of life, clutching their sand-covered shoes. Molly and Harry were in a world of their own in the conservatory, chatting away and giggling together watching things on his iPad, and it was so heart-warming to see.

We've had a lovely evening and when everyone had left or gone to bed, Jamie and I sat on the sofa with the fan blasting out cool air at both of us. The windows were wide open, and I could hear the crickets in the bushes outside. We shared half a bottle of red and I felt genuinely grateful for what we have. Despite some days feeling like this life we've made is a total shitstorm, it's a shitstorm I'm glad we're part of, because even though life is far from perfect, I am happier than I've ever been.

The children have a life filled with their friends and they have fun together. They live on the beach and have a beautiful home and they are loved, secure and stable, and that's all we can ask for from life. We can only do our best. When I looked round our living room tonight and caught sight of what we have created, I felt pretty proud, and happy, so happy.

\*

## Saturday

Pat and I collected Lou from the hospital this morning while Jamie stayed at home with the kids.

It was another boiling hot day and I woke up for the first time in ages without the knot of worry in my tummy; instead I had a good feeling about the day ahead. When you feel sad and you wake to grey skies and rain, you feel sadder, but when you feel sad and the sun is shining there's something that lifts your mood, even if it's just slightly ... well, it always has for me anyway.

We drove Lou to the flat and Pat had filled the fridge with lots of things for her and the boys. She had made one of her famous lasagnes and a tin of brownies. Her parents were bringing the boys over later so that Lou didn't feel too overwhelmed at seeing her new home, and realising how different things were now going to be compared to what she had been used to. She also didn't want her getting upset in front of the boys when we're all selling this to them as nothing but a happy occasion. She told me to text and keep her informed of how Lou was, and they would bring the boys across when the time was right.

Lou seemed happy during the drive, but when we got to the flat and walked in, she sobbed, really sobbed. I felt like I'd been punched in the stomach and I didn't know how to stop that feeling of panic. Before I could reassure her that this was all temporary and she was going to be OK, that we could find them a bigger forever home once things had settled, she grabbed hold of me and hugged me so tight. Tighter than any of Jamie's or Pat's hugs had ever been and as she continued to sob, she just kept repeating the words 'Thank you'.

She was happy. She was genuinely happy that she was not returning to a mansion with tennis courts and a heated pool. She was happy that she would now be living in a flat, above a café, where her boys would have to share a room. I wondered what she felt to be so grateful to me. Freedom? Relief? Maybe both, but the main factor was that her tears were nothing to do with sadness. She was now free from David's abuse and control and undoubtedly relieved that she didn't have to return to 'his' house. This was hers. Hers and the boys, and there was no trace of him here. He had finally lost his power over them.

I text Jane, 'Come whenever. She is so happy', and the thumbs-up emoji. Twenty minutes later I heard her boys come charging up the stairs and, just like their mum, they were so grateful and happy and excited. Harry gave his mum the biggest hug in the world and they just held each other and cried. I looked at Jane and she held her hand to her mouth and began to cry too. Tony wrapped her into his arms and said, 'She's OK, it's OK, we've got our girl back.'

I tried my hardest not to get emotional, but watching them all get to this from what I had first witnessed was something I didn't think I would ever see, and it was amazing.

They'd done it. The three of them.

They'd escaped and they were free.

My family and I spent the evening after today playing Junior Monopoly. I wanted us to all do something together. After what had just happened and realising that we actually should celebrate being a family more, I thought a family board game would be fun.

How wrong I was.

It was hell. Belle cheated repeatedly and sent the boys over the edge. Ruby was bored within minutes so I was playing with two counters and getting totally confused and Jamie was half cut on red wine so had no idea how to add up or subtract and therefore made the shittest banker in history.

Next time we'll stick to Twister or Connect 4.

# CHAPTER THIRTY-ONE

* * * * * * * * * * * * * * * * * * * * * * * * * * *

# WTF?!

*Tuesday*

I should have known better than to think all of our drama was over for the summer ...

Pat and I dropped the kids to summer camp this morning and nipped out to do a food shop. When we got back, we had a cuppa and unloaded the shopping and I could hear a phone repeatedly vibrating but I had no idea where it was. I started looking under piles of paperwork and magazines, but couldn't find the thing anywhere. Pat could hear it too and when it happened again, she said she thought it was coming from the kitchen bin and, sure enough, when we opened it, there was Molly's iPhone buzzing away.

I laughed that she hadn't noticed it was missing – usually it was attached to her hand permanently – but as Pat handed it to me across the table it buzzed again and a message came up.

'I mean it you little spoilt bitch'

I looked down and on the home screen I saw more abusive messages. My instinct took over and I started scrolling. There were over thirty messages of abuse from an unsaved mobile phone number. I couldn't read the full message or get into the phone as it had a password on it but even from reading the beginnings of these messages it was clear these weren't OK. They started off asking Molly to call the person sending them, then telling her to call her mum, which seemed odd. The person sending the messages then got angrier and angrier that they were being ignored and the abuse towards Molly worsened.

Just then the phone started ringing and it was that number on the screen. I took a picture of the number from my phone before I answered, but as soon as I said hello it went dead.

I changed the settings on my phone to make my number withheld and I tapped in the number. I decided at that point I was wasted serving coffee – I should be a detective, if I'm honest.

It rang out for a long time and I realised they weren't going to answer and just as I was about to hang up an answerphone clicked in: 'Hello, you have reached the voicemail of David Metcalfe ... '

David.

David had sent Molly all these texts.

What. The. Fuck?

I felt the colour drain from my face and my heart was pounding. I recall Pat repeatedly saying, 'Jo, what is it? Jo?'

I stood up without saying a word and walked past her – I went straight up the stairs, phone in my hand; I can visibly picture myself now shaking with adrenaline. I just knew there was something more to all of this. His reaction towards Molly on the night he had hit Lou had seemed strange then and I'd had a feeling there was more to this story. It had just been confirmed.

I walked into Belle's room, trying to look calm. Molly was lying on the bed playing on her iPad while Belle was scrolling through her phone next to her. Molly looked at me, then saw her phone in my hand, and her face immediately dropped.

'What the hell is going on, Molly?'

Belle clearly didn't have a clue what was going on either and Molly started to cry and kept saying, 'Please, Jo, just leave it.'

Pat came up the stairs behind me and asked, calmly as ever, what was going on.

'Thirty-seven messages, Molly. And that's just in the last hour, from David the fucking psychopath!'

Pat and Belle looked at Molly and she started begging them not to ask her anything more. The same beg that Lou had used that day at her house when I had mentioned calling the police. A desperate beg where she would have done anything to not be in this situation.

Pat told me to go downstairs, and I tossed the phone on the bed and did as I'd been told. I had a huge lump in my throat that I knew would turn to tears if I tried to swallow it away. I felt so guilty that I had shouted at Molly, but I couldn't understand why a man in his forties was texting a teenage girl – the reasoning that could be behind it made me feel truly sick. And David! Could that man sink any lower?

Belle appeared behind me as I got to the bottom of the stairs and said that Pat had asked for a few minutes alone with Molly. Belle swore to me she had no clue what was happening and that Molly hadn't mentioned David since 'that' weekend. She promised me that she had no idea why he was texting or calling her and she was as weirded out as I was.

Pat stayed upstairs for what felt like forever, but there was no shouting or crying – I couldn't even hear them talking. Eventually I heard Pat tiptoe down the stairs. She walked into the kitchen and gave us both a smile and said, 'This *is* going to be OK.'

I felt the bile in my throat at what I was about to hear and how I would have to act in front of my daughter.

Pat sat at the table and beckoned me to sit down, next to Belle.

'He's her father,' she said.

Belle and I looked at each other in shock.

'What do you mean?' I asked.

'David. He's Molly's father. Molly has known for the past six years and has been sworn to secrecy by her mum. That's why she got pulled out of private school when she was seven because Harry started there, and David didn't want them at the same school for fear of Lou finding out. Jaclyn never wanted Molly to know but David has followed her and kept track of their every move so she had to tell her.'

George. Harry. Lou.

Jesus Christ. How would they take this news?

My head was suddenly swimming with so many questions.

'David has been threatening Molly because he thought she would tell Lou the truth as she has been spending so much time with the boys of late.' She went on to explain that Jaclyn met David at uni in their final year, fell head over heels in love. She then found out about Lou when she was six months' pregnant with Molly. David and Lou were already engaged, living together with a wedding planned and paid for by her parents. Jaclyn begged David to stay with her, raise their baby together, but he'd refused and got nasty, as nasty as we had seen him be on our driveway, while she was pregnant, so she'd stayed away, qualified as a solicitor and raised Molly alone.

Jaclyn had moved here for a fresh start, but David had enjoyed the power and control and had moved his family close by shortly after, started Harry at Molly's school and forced her to leave. He would 'pop in' every time he felt like it and by all accounts from Molly, he bullied her mum a lot of the time – threatening to ruin her career if she didn't do what he asked. It seemed he had total control over her too.

Belle ran upstairs and I heard Molly sobbing like a baby.

I sat at that table for over an hour, my head spinning, and the same questions kept coming out of my mouth. Questions Pat sat and attempted to answer, unfazed, as always.

She told me Molly felt she was to blame for all of this coming out. She was in a real state.

I had no clue where we went from here. How would I tell Lou, and the boys? Would Jaclyn be angry with Molly? What would happen now with this entire situation?

As my head was still swimming, I heard Jamie's key in the front door and when he walked into the kitchen, he greeted me with a kiss on the forehead and a shoulder squeeze. He asked if everything was OK and I went to answer with a lie that everything was fine, until I remembered our promise to each other, and, as Pat flicked the switch of the kettle, I replied, 'I think you'd better sit down, darling.'

*

## Wednesday

What a difference twenty-four hours makes ...

Jamie was amazing after last night's revelation. After hearing Pat and me explain that Molly is David's lovechild, and Harry and George are her brothers, he shook his head and muttered, 'You couldn't write this shit,' and yet here I am ...

It's clear to me more and more since we've moved here that he's inherited so much of his mum's amazing traits and so he has a way of not only taking it all in his stride but also of making things better and not as bad as they actually are.

We agreed with Molly that she could stay at ours and we would work out a plan, together, with Jaclyn.

More than anything now, Molly needs to know that she's supported, that we are all here for her and her mum, and that we will make things OK for them and for Lou and the boys – ultimately, they're all the victims here.

*

### Thursday

Mark called today. I almost didn't answer but curiosity got the better of me. When I did he was sleazily nice.

'Jo, babe, how are you? How's Jamie? How are our babies? New house good?' He didn't give me chance to answer each question before delivering a new one so I knew that he didn't really want to know the answers. I played along, though, wondering where the call was heading, and trying not to be sick in my mouth at how revolting he was being, then he asked to come and visit the kids to take them all out.

I told him Belle may not want to see him due to how he'd behaved recently and that the other kids all had prior arrangements over the next few days, but he replied with, 'Just see what you can sort.' Brilliant, as always, Mark – you fuck up and I'm the one left to sort your mess.

We agreed on a date and that he would take the kids out for the day and drop them home at tea time.

I told Jamie and he was really positive, saying hopefully he had sorted himself out and him being positive around the boys could only be a good thing.

I ignored the voice inside my head that told me he'd let them down again as I told the boys before bed. I *was* going to be positive.

Art was excited; Rex couldn't give a shit. I then went in and spoke to Belle. She was annoyed that he was coming and refused to see him. She was annoyed that Art was excited but I explained the boys needed to grow up more to reach their own conclusion about their dad, and maybe he had changed.

But a sick feeling rose up then and hit me, about how it would go in reality. I had to remember what Jamie said – it *could* be a good thing.

# CHAPTER THIRTY-TWO

## FEELING POSITIVE

### Friday

This week has been as crazy as ever, but fun. I've helped Lou re-design areas of the café because of the water damage from the flat upstairs, but it's been something for her to get her teeth into and I know she's excited about the prospect of a proper fresh start when it opens. It's also kept her mind busy after I delivered the news that her husband had a secret love child, and that Molly was the boys' half sibling. She took the news extremely well, considering. I mean she was shocked, she called him a few choice names, but she was more concerned for Molly and how she was. Her decency as usual just shone through.

Jaclyn and I went out for dinner the other night. I told her I knew about David and Molly and she said it felt like a weight she'd been carrying for sixteen years has been finally lifted. She was upset, embarrassed, ashamed, but it's almost like this situation has stopped her from loving like she should, from being the mum her little girl needed.

She told me the whole story about David. About how he'd seduced her, promised her the world, then tore it out from under her as his double life was exposed, leaving her pregnant and alone. He really is a piece of work and I felt so desperately sad that she had also lived for so many years totally under his control. Now the secret was out, hopefully she could manage him far better because she wasn't living in fear any more.

Lou and Jaclyn are going to meet up next week, to speak and sit the kids down to explain. There are no hard feelings between them – why should there be? No one is at fault other than David. I wondered how Harry would take the news. On reflection now I see Molly was spending time with him and loving it because she knows they're her brothers – but the boys don't. I wondered if Harry likes her in another way and if this will upset him more. They've been through so much already; I can't bear to think of them getting hurt even more.

*

### Saturday

Jamie had booked a little village pub in Devon for us tonight that has amazing food on the menu and local beers, but I've come down with something that I can't shake off so we cancelled. He's instead spent the day cleaning the BBQ, mowing the lawn and pottering around the garden. I've slept on and off most of the day. I've felt exhausted. I think it may just be the events of the last few weeks catching up with me.

The kids have just pottered around too, making TikToks and playing games. It's nice every now and then to have a full day at home, doing nothing, watching how they interact with one another – the games they make up and the conversations they have really make me smile. Rex had me chuckling at his pirate impression as he and Art pretended to set sail across the seven seas in a big cardboard box – he wouldn't have it that it was a *parrot* he should have on his shoulder and had made Art bring him a carrot from the kitchen ... I was with him on that; it was funnier that way.

\*

## Sunday

Pat took me to the out-of-hours GP this morning. Yesterday's nauseous feeling has turned to full-blown sickness overnight, and I've had a banging headache all night.

The doctor took some bloods and asked if there was any chance I could be pregnant.

'No,' was my immediate answer. Definitely not.

We left the doctors and called into the supermarket to grab some bits for the week and when we got home Pat handed me a pregnancy test. I laughed and asked her what she was doing and as soon as she said the words, 'Just do it, I have a feeling,' I knew.

I didn't want to do the test. I was scared of the result. Scared of the outcome if it was positive.

I did the test.

It was positive.

I am pregnant.

I am shit scared of what happens now.

Pat snuggled me into her perfumed neck scarf and told me I'd be fine, we'd be fine. This is a baby that will be born into a family that's full of love. She told me she has never seen so much love under one roof.

Jamie came into the kitchen and asked what was wrong, and Pat told him it was just all a bit too much with everything that had gone on this week. He immediately asked his mum if she would mind watching the kids one night so we could re-book the pub night away – he felt we needed a break from the kids.

I remembered right then about the promise I made not to keep a secret from him again. I asked him if we could go upstairs and talk. I could tell he knew I was about to drop another bombshell but he played it cool and said 'of course'.

Pat said she would watch the kids and, as we walked out the kitchen, she said out loud, 'You will be fine.' I couldn't work out if that was reassurance for me or a warning for Jamie on how he needed to accept the news he was about to be given.

We got to the bedroom and I asked him to close the door. My hands were visibly trembling and I kept doing that thing where you start to talk but your nerves take over to the point you can't catch your breath and you trip up on your words and keep swallowing mid-sentence.

Before I could get past the 'I don't know how to say this' he blurted out, 'We're having a baby, aren't we?'

I recall instantly thinking that he said 'we're having a baby' not 'you're pregnant'. Like it was already 'ours' and a baby, not 'mine' and a pregnancy.

The feeling of relief came immediately, and as I began to cry I was also laughing. He pulled me onto his lap and was just beaming. He wiped away my tears, then asked me why I was being silly, followed by an excited giggle.

As soon as I saw his response, the relief turned into excitement for me too, and it was the first time I had thought: 'we're having a baby'.

I had pictured this going so differently as I always seem to think the worst, me begging to keep the baby, trying my hardest to convince him we would 'be OK' or the worst-case scenario of accepting it was all a huge mistake and working out a 'best plan' together – but now Jamie's response meant that I didn't have to think of any of that … and it showed me that although this wasn't planned, it all of a sudden felt like a happy accident.

*

## Monday

I walked round feeling like I was on cloud nine today, as did Jamie, and Pat. Despite feeling sick until tea time, I still felt happy. I imagine that's because I now know the reason behind me feeling so sick all the time.

Pat is so happy for us. We sat at the breakfast table after the kids had eaten and I did the whole 'how will we cope', 'is it unfair on the others' questions and they both batted them away, reassuring me that we would be just fine, and all the kids would be over the moon to have a sibling they could fuss over and share – it would be a little piece of all of them – a different kind of happy to what we have now, but one I hoped would be amazing.

\*

## Tuesday

Jamie came home just after 2pm and announced the two of us were going away for the night.

In all honesty I just wanted to climb into bed and sleep. I am so tired and sick. I don't remember feeling like this with the other three, but then I wonder if I just wasn't 'allowed' to feel like this and actually I put on a brave face and convinced myself I was feeling fine because I was so aware to be 'grateful' of the life I had.

We set off in Jamie's car. I asked where we were going, and he told me it was a surprise. He drove for about twenty minutes to an area I didn't even know existed. It was like moorland but had a stream running through it. The sun was low and there were those hovering flies over the water, which was glistening bright gold. It really was beautiful; he had brought a big blanket and some scatter cushions and the thought of snoozing on his chest, breathing in his amazing scent next to the sound of the water in the warm air, was perfect.

He passed me the blanket and pulled out another huge bag from the boot then took my hand. We started walking and I had no idea what was going on. As much as the sickness was still whirring away, I got the giggles because nothing like this had ever happened before. This was not Jamie's style and it felt a bit weird ...

We got by the edge of the stream and opened the bag. He pulled out a little brown wicker hamper and speaker. The way he had thought of this was just the cutest. I did worry about what food he'd packed considering I was now nil by mouth with the morning sickness.

Morning sickness. I have no idea why it's called that when it's all day and night sickness; kind of makes it sound far less dramatic than it is.

He put the speaker on and started playing the Stone Roses. I'd never heard any of their songs before we met – yet now I could recite the track order of most albums. I loved how he had introduced me to so much music that made me feel so many things. He asked me to close my eyes. I was just there thinking, *Oh God – what if he pops an olive in my mouth and I hurl over him.*

When he instructed me, I opened them and he was holding a small black box and had a huge beaming smile on his face. I felt my heart thud. I opened the box, feeling like a total fraud, and then I saw his grandma's engagement ring – three huge sparkling diamonds in a row on a platinum band. It was a ring Pat always wore on her right hand, which had been left to her by her mum, who I'm told was as amazing as she is. I sobbed. This was NOT what I was expecting.

He then pulled out some pregnancy multi-vitamins and anti-sickness wristbands. The beam across his face had doubled.

I can't remember his exact words, but it was something like: 'Jo, I want us to have this baby. I want us to get married and complete our family. This all makes sense to me and I've never, ever been happier than what I've been since I met you and your kids.' He went on to tell me that he had been speaking to the landlord and they'd agreed a figure for the house that was now well within our budget. His mum has had an offer on her house and she is looking at the two little cottages tomorrow afternoon. It just all felt like it was coming together. Finally.

I cried so hard that I had snot dripping from my nose and I think I may have dribbled, just to make me look even more attractive.

I think I said yes over a hundred times to his proposal and I felt so, so happy. I still feel so happy. I'm buzzing.

His reaction to the pregnancy news made me realise how much I want this – and how happy I am – for the baby, for us to get married and for our future together, the eight of us.

The engagement ring is beautiful. Wearing it gives me feelings I've never felt before; nothing has ever compared to how happy this has made me. The ring shines so bright constantly, and I feel honoured that I've been trusted with it – that Pat and Jamie trust me to take care of something so special.

When we got home, Jamie called all the kids to the kitchen and told them that we were getting married. I held up my hand and wiggled my ring finger and they all jumped up and down. Belle wiped a tear from her cheek and as she hugged Jamie, I saw her whisper, 'Thank you,' into his ear. Ruby asked when we could go and get her bridesmaid dress and the boys started planning a wedding party with football goals and a rodeo bull to ride on.

Pat had a little sob with me over a late-night cuppa on the swinging chair in the garden. She linked my arm in hers and thanked me for making her son and grandchildren so happy. I wasn't sure how I'd managed that. Life seemed to have been one shitstorm after another since we'd been together, but it was clear that had just made us stronger.

# CHAPTER THIRTY-THREE

## A DIFFERENT KIND OF HAPPY EVER AFTER

*Thursday*

We spent today on the beach. I met Meg, Lou and Jen and we spent the whole day sat on the sand while the kids played together building sandcastles and running through the waves. The kids were getting along better than ever today, and even Belle, Molly and Jacob came.

As we walked down, I kept my arm wrapped around Molly and told her how proud I was of her. She didn't say a lot, but she grasped my hand tight on the top of her arm and she thanked me for everything. She said she was nervous about seeing Lou, but I explained Lou thought she was amazingly brave and was excited to see her.

They sat on a blanket together, down by the tide, and I saw Lou drape her arm across Molly's shoulders as they talked to each other. I watched Molly rest her head on Lou's shoulder – perhaps she was crying; I couldn't see – but they were together chatting for a good hour, and when they came back to join us they both seemed happy and at peace.

Molly also still hung out with Harry as she had before so I was pleased that the situation hadn't changed their relationship; and, actually, when you take away the sheer shitshow side to all of this, a young girl who was drowning in loneliness has just gained two brothers and their amazing mum.

I was really feeling the love today and my three new friends were over the moon when I told them about mine and Jamie's engagement. I'd been worried about telling them since the end of Lou's marriage was so traumatic and still so raw, but she was nothing if not ecstatic. She said we all needed more love in our lives and was pleased that we had something to celebrate. So much has changed for me in the last few months but these women coming into my life is one of the changes that I cherish the most. We've been through so much together, in so little time, and we've forged a bond that will last a lifetime. I'm so proud of us and am so grateful for them.

And to top it all, we had the best day today.

\*

### Friday

I went for a coffee with Jaclyn today, just to a café in town on the high street. She had been over to see Lou on Wednesday evening and she seemed totally different now to the Jaclyn I had met originally.

She seems so much calmer, and upon speaking to her in more detail, the leash she kept tightly upon her daughter was to keep her away from David and the damage she knew he was capable of. Now that their secret was out, she seemed almost at peace. She was totally fine with allowing Molly to have a life like a normal teenage girl – encouraging it even by asking me about the curfews and allowances Belle has in place so she can do the same with Molly. It was clear it was never about not trusting her – it was always about protecting her – and I felt a pang of guilt for how badly I had mistaken the entire situation and judged her in such a negative light.

Jaclyn said that she was going to speak to Lou about Molly seeing the boys and how it will work because she doesn't want to upset her or overstep the mark, but she knows Molly is desperate for them to come over and spend time with them. I know from speaking to Lou, and watching Lou speak to Molly, that she will be fine with this – she knows the boys having a big sister is something they'll love, and the issue they have with their dad, who funnily enough has been silent and invisible since this situation came to light, is already enough for them to contend with without adding more issues in with Jaclyn and Molly – and perhaps now, finally, the swimming pool will get the love it deserves.

*

### Saturday

I'm knackered! Jaclyn and I took the girls up to Exeter today and I had to pull the car over twice to be sick. Belle kept saying we should go back as I was poorly, but finally we managed to get there and the girls were excited about the shopping trip.

I ended up confiding in Jaclyn about the baby when the girls were trying clothes on. I worried she would think I was maybe contagious and also I thought it may be obvious. She seemed really chuffed for me, like it was nothing but a good thing. That made me feel better. I worry people think Jamie and I are mad to have another one when we already have so many children.

How strange – I really had my doubts about this woman when I first met her and now she had been the first to learn I was pregnant.

The girls had an amazing day and the dynamic between Jaclyn and Molly has already changed; they are so much closer and it is so beautiful to see. Walking past a card shop, Jaclyn pulled me aside and pointed to one of the more risqué cards on display up on a top shelf. I thought she was ready to make a complaint to the sales assistant that a card with a penis joke was on display where our girls might have seen it, but instead she elbowed me gently in the ribs and snorted with laughter until I found myself joining her. It turns out she actually has a wicked sense of humour and I like her. I really like her.

We spent too much money on clothes for the girls to wear when they start college, but they've had a tough summer, and they're good girls, so it was nice.

We got back around 7pm and I've come straight up to bed. Mark is coming tomorrow and I'm dreading seeing him.

Jamie is as reassuring as ever, but Belle is still adamant her dad's a dick and she doesn't want to go but at the same time she feels she has to so she can protect Art if (when) Mark fucks up.

*

### Sunday

So today didn't go to plan.

Belle didn't come. I went in to wake her and she just opened one eye and said, 'No, Mum, I've decided I'm not doing it.' I didn't really know how to feel: relief that he wouldn't upset her, but upset she didn't want to see her dad – I just didn't know.

We got to the beach just after 10am and Stanley was running up and down loving the boys chasing him. It got close to 11am and Mark still hadn't arrived. I tried calling him, but he didn't answer. My heart sank at the prospect of him not turning up, but I thought even he wouldn't be that cruel this time – although I knew deep down from past experiences there was every chance he would be late, or not show at all. I knew that if he was on his way he would have his brand-new top-of-the-range phone synced to whatever penis extension he was driving and he would have answered the call. When he didn't, I just knew he wasn't coming, and

I got butterflies in my tummy – the bad butterflies that flit about from the pit of your stomach to your throat making you go physically jittery and people notice the panic in you.

The boys were bored by now and there was a chill in the air. I worried Art would get upset so I suggested visiting Lou and the boys as they hadn't seen their flat yet. They were instantly excited and I prayed that Mark would either turn up, or this would take Art's mind off it if he did call and drop the bombshell I knew was coming.

We walked in and both my boys were so lush – as they nosed around they kept saying how amazing it was, how lucky they were to see the beach out the windows and that they loved the boys' bunk beds. I could see Lou's face light up and it made me so happy that they were so kind when I imagine she worried what people's reactions would be after what she was used to.

She made us a coffee and Jamie and I sat with her in the front room while the boys played on the Xbox in their room. Stanley sat in front of the huge sash windows watching everyone on the beach. Lou seemed really happy and relaxed. She had a book on the sofa next to her and a cashmere blanket, and she told me she'd been thinking about getting a dog for the boys. They'd always wanted one but David hated them, so it was never an option. It made me so happy she was already making choices for her and the boys, confirming she wasn't going back but also planning for their future, together, the three of them.

I kept trying to call Mark, but got no response. By now it was midday and time for us to get back to the other kids. We'd told Pat we would only be half an hour.

Just as we stood up to leave, Mark called back. I answered the call, my hands already shaking with adrenaline and anger, and he immediately began with the excuses. Art and Rex were stood in front of me getting their shoes on and although the phone wasn't on speaker, they could hear Mark's patronising tone clearly. Art took the phone off me and asked what time he would be coming. Mark immediately went into great detail about a deal going wrong at work, meaning he'd had to rush into the office and had got stuck in a meeting so he would have to 'postpone'.

A meeting. First thing on a Sunday morning.

'Postpone' – as if it was a football match that couldn't be played because of bad weather.

I wanted to kill him. I was so unbelievably angry. I waited for Art to lose his temper, to break his heart and start to cry but he didn't. He just stood, holding the phone, listening to the shit pour from his dad's mouth. He then said 'OK' and ended the call. I instantly switched it to silent in case he called back, which he did, immediately. I ignored the flashing phone and got ready to reassure a devastated little boy who had been rejected by his dad again, but amazingly it didn't come.

Instead he looked up and said, 'I knew he'd do that,' and I realised that his heart had hardened to his dad, and, even though it shouldn't have to do that, he was learning to protect himself. Before I could apologise for his dad for the millionth time, before I could pretend that I believed him and he would come visit soon, Jamie began playfighting with both boys and said, 'Looks like you're stuck with me today.' As they got carried away clambering all over him, he asked what they wanted to do and they decided upon swimming. He walked out of the flat with them both hanging off him in fits of giggles and I realised this was Mark's loss.

I didn't return Mark's call and I've decided I am no longer going to accept his. His number is now blocked. In order for him to contact me he will have to get in his penis extension and make the drive down to knock on my front door. He knows where we are. Part of me thinks, *oh great, here we go again*, but really I know that it won't be like the other times because things are different now. We're different now. I'm different, and my children are different. We know our worth. I am no longer going to engage with someone who cannot prioritise being a parent to their children, and I pray that my silence is so deafening it makes him want to be a dad – but if not then I am finally at peace with the fact they have everything they need right here with us.

I've been thinking a lot lately. I sat here in the garden this afternoon and thought about how crazy things have been since we moved here. But although things have been hard since Jamie and I made this move together, it was never hard between 'us'. We have always been OK – it was just everyone around us that caused these feelings.

And although I've cried more tears that I have ever cried before, and felt extreme emotions of happiness, sadness and devastation, I know now that I didn't 'feel' anything when I was married to Mark – I just bumbled through, isolated from friends and family with no highs or lows. And despite feeling some really low lows in the last six months, I've also felt some ridiculous highs, and I've come to the conclusion this is how you live – this is the right way to do it, where you feel things, experience things, rather than just plodding ... I feel like for the first time in my life I now understand the saying 'life is like a rollercoaster'.

There's been a lot of soul-searching this year, and a huge cloud that's been hanging over that is the prospect of what I might find out about myself in my adoption papers. At first I was waiting for Pat to come back to hold my hand while I took it all in, but now I'm starting to think that, actually, I don't want to look at all. Who I am isn't tied to how I came into this world and how my life began. Who I am is who I have made myself into. It's the little things, like how I like my coffee, and how that one part of my hair on the left side will never lie flat. It's the big things, like my family and my friends. It's knowing that I'm loved and knowing who I love, and I'm more aware of that now than ever. I'm not going to be reading the papers any time soon.

Right now, today, even after this morning, life is good. We've built an amazing life here, full of incredible friends who would do anything for us and make us want to do likewise. They've had me crying with laughter and in sadness recently and I'm so pleased we've had those experiences together – good and bad. I've learnt a lot over the last few months – I can always be kinder, relationships aren't always what they seem, and I need to always remember that there are so many different ways to be happy. If I can find one way every day, and if my children can do the same, then I can't and won't ask for more than that.

I'm now sat in a home that we will soon own, planning the changes we will make to fit a tiny new bubba, while I am surrounded by happy kids and a devoted fiancé who is the most amazing daddy and stepfather, and it's made me see that, sometimes, the most dysfunctional families are the happiest and the ones that look like they have it all really don't.

Jamie wanders over to where I'm sat, carrying two cups of tea, so we can grab five minutes' peace together before the next drama begins. He meets my eyes then floors me with a smile.

I wouldn't change a thing right now ... not one thing.

# ACKNOWLEDGEMENTS

To my circle, which is now somewhat smaller than it was during my first book in 2017.

Thank you to each and every one of you for your love, your support and your loyalty.

For always listening to my crazy, rambling voice notes, reading my weird WhatsApp messages and supporting my hopes and dreams, however crazy they may seem.

Thank you also for the understanding that some days I'm just 'too busy' but I've not changed. I will never change. I will always be me and I will always do whatever I can for you.

To my circle, if you're a part of it, and I know you will know if you are.

To my circle. Smaller. Smaller but stronger.

I love you all endlessly.

rofessor. He could write a book on memories alone. He could
rite about the things he had seen and heard and not take one
ing from his imagination.

He wanted to see her, but the nurse said that he could do so the following day.

When they were walking home, Lester said, 'Well, you must be relieved now.'

'Yes. But the police should do something about these hooligans. Is no joke to have them swooping down on innocent people like that. The police should do something about it.'

'It's not as simple as that,' Lester said. 'Much more is involved than action by the police.'

'Stephanie could have died, or the baby. We have too many hooligans in this city. Too many idle, ignorant people.'

'That is true,' Lester said.

'The police should do something about them, or the government if it comes to that. Something must be done.'

'Something must be done,' Lester said. 'But what?'

'I don't know. But that is why we have a police force, that is why we have a government, to protect the people. Look, tonight they even cut off a boy's hand, his mother crying and throwing down herself in the road. The police should be harder with them.'

'You can't blame the police. Already they're overworked,' Lester said. 'And I'm not sure that you could attach all the blame to the so-called hooligans, either.'

'Who'll you blame, then?'

'All of us have some share in the blame,' Lester said.

'Well, that's a fine one. That's a damn fine one. A setta young hooligans come down with guns and knives and iron bolts, wounding and chopping people, and you say all of us have blame in that. That's a fine one!'

'You see, Walter,' Lester said. 'We have to help them because we can't punish them. There's no way to punish them.'

'What you mean, we can't punish them?'

'It's like this: punishment is punishment, is effective only when the person punished is conscious that he has done wrong,' Lester said.

'You telling me that they don't know it's against the law to walk with knives and guns and iron bolts and shoot and wound people? That's what you saying?'

'Against what law?' Lester asked.

'The law,' Walter said. 'The law of the land.'

'But that's just what I'm telling you. They don't accept the law. They have their own laws, and the laws of the society are not necessarily their laws.'

'I don't see why the laws are not their laws. The law is for everybody,' Walter said.

'I'll tell you why they don't accept our laws. They don't accept the laws of society because, in the first place, society doesn't accept them. It appears to them that society wants to crush them. How can they accept society? And if they don't accept society, how can they accept the laws of society? This is quite simple, but many people don't consider this side of the problem.'

'They have to accept society. If you have to cat them and throw them in jail, they have to realize that the law is the law,' Walter said.

'No, Walter. You have to teach them; you can't force them.'

'You making joke, yes, Lester. I say teach them in jail, teach them with the cat whistling on their backside.'

'You're saying so because of what happened to Stephanie. If you look at the thing squarely, you wouldn't talk like that.'

'But I don't know how you'll teach them. If they don't learn in jail is because they don't want to learn.'

'Jail only makes them harder,' Lester said.

'What way they'll learn, Lester? What way?'

'I say, give them a purpose in life, give them a worthy goal, and give them a fifty-fifty chance to achieve it; try to understand and encourage them. That's the only way,' Lester said.

'What goal can we give them? What goal is there to give them?'

'That,' Lester said, 'is the problem. There seems to be nothing of lasting value that is at the same time sufficiently tangible. As a matter of fact, the goals of the supposed well-adjusted persons are nothing to shout about… And that's the truth.'

And that time he was silent and thoughtful, for there was much in what Lester had said.

Lester was right, the youngsters had no valuable goal. What goal can you give a young criminal, a young delinquent who has nothing, who has the whole big world against him, squeezing him, pushing him, telling him to move on; with the whole police

force geared to fight him, with the whole lot of citizen for him to make a false move? What laws can you ask h when you hold no law dear? When you accept laws it is convenient to you, when you flout those not interest, you, leading citizens of the nation? L What was to be done? What could be done? Wha was a hell of a situation.

Now he remembers how happy he was to se well and to see his little daughter, so tiny and Stephanie came from the hospital, he wou work just to look at his little baby.

And he remembers how good Mrs Wal helped Stephanie with the washing and t' not well enough to take care of them he the letter Stephanie received from Anna was in England and it asked about To bottle of home-made pepper sauce a

And he remembers that time whe Sears and he went to the square to how he stood there with his eyes heard the politicians tell about th development of the land, askir legislature. And he remembe home, he saw the beggars cr pavements and passed the w' hawk-eyed for customers, woman selling oranges, sle stuck on the wall, a poste candidate, marked, 'Vote showed it to Mr Sears, N day.

And he remember christened, how his li employment, and rer he didn't get a job, back home…

So many thin

It is evening now. The man Walter Castle is looking through a window of the living-room of the apartment which he tenants on the third floor of the tenement building on Webber Street. In the sky, where the clouds have lifted, there are patches of blue, but the sun is hidden and dampness still hangs like a wet garment over the city.

The sky curves downwards to the sea of muddy blue, in which ships lie at anchor without tossing; the hills rise up, on one side dark-green, mysterious and silent, and on the other side, where man has been at work, houses stand out on the hillside above the road of brown earth.

The man sighs after a while, then looks up Webber Street. There is the gambling-club; and there is the snackette with the blaring jukebox, with the tesses drifting in and out, drinking beer, talking and laughing; and there is the grocery – closed today; and next to the grocery is a gateway leading down to barrack rooms from which prostitutes emerge at night. There are one… two… three… there are four such gateways, and then there is the laundry. The laundry is shut too. Some tesses sit before it, talking. After the laundry is the bridge. Tesses hardly stand around by the bridge any more. The police jeep passes around regularly and before the police can say 'Move on!' the tesses move. The man can see no further than the bridge.

Now he looks down the street. Here, the three-storeyed tenement buildings range. They are all of one size, same colour and pattern of construction. One is as ugly as the next and the paint is flecking off the front of all of them. Further down the street is the sports pool, and next to the sports pool the tailor shop, and next to the tailor shop is a grocery and then the inn, and just past the inn is a cross street where taxis are parked.

'Walter.'

'Yes.' He turns from the window. 'Yes, Stephanie.'

His wife is dressed up.

She is looking good.

'We're ready to leave.'

'All right. What time you coming back?'

'About nine,' she says.

'Nine? Well let the taxi drop you right in front the house. It's not safe to walk home in the night.'

'All right. But I have the baby with me and Carol, nothing would happen. But I'll do as you say.'

'And Stephanie.'

'Yes?'

'Take one of the keys with you. I might go out later and you'll have to open the door yourself.'

'You going out?'

'I might go up by Ruth. Take one of the keys all the same.'

'Ask Ruth when she coming down here. Since last month she promised to come.'

'All right. And tell your mother good-evening for me.'

'Good. I made tea for you. All you have to do is warm it. I'm going.'

Carol, his little sister, comes into the living-room, holding the baby by the hand.

'You have the baby bottle, Carol?' Stephanie asks.

'Yes, it's in the bag. Ready, Stephanie?'

'Yes. Come, Cherrie. Kiss your daddy. Give her a kiss, Walter.'

'Fix that hat on her head properly,' Walter says. He bends and takes hold of the child. The child smiles and encircles his neck with her small hands. Walter kisses her. 'Now, who's a sweet girl? Let me fix your hat.'

'You can't fix that hat, she's always at it, just can't keep her hands still,' Stephanie says.

'Look, she wants another kiss. Give her another, Walter,' Carol says.

Walter kisses the child again. 'All right. Good. Sweetheart, behave a nice child.'

'What about mine?' Stephanie says.

'Your what?'

'My kiss,' his wife answers, pouting her mouth and leaning towards him.

'All right.' He kisses her. 'And I guess you want one too,' he says, looking at his little sister.

The girl smiles.

'We're going,' Stephanie says. 'You think we should carry an umbrella?'

'That old thing,' Carol says, wrinkling her nose. 'Rain wouldn't fall again.'

'You'd better carry it just in case,' Walter says.

'Take the umbrella, Carol. All right, let's go,' Stephanie says. 'Walter, we're going.'

'Okay.'

'We're going, Walter,' Carol says.

With a clattering of shoe-soles, the females walk through to the door. The man turns to the window, watching for them when they reach downstairs. After a while they appear. They look up and wave to him; he waves back and watches them walk down the street. He looks fascinated at the awkward steps his little girl-child takes.

Now Mr Cross comes into the yard from up the street. Mr Cross looks up; their eyes meet.

'Hello, Mr Cross,' Walter says.

'Hi, Castle. What's happening?'

'Cool.'

'Like you just sent out the family?'

'Yes.'

Mr Cross leans on his crutches. 'Quiet evenin',' he says. Then he jerks his head in the direction of the pavement and says, 'Look at them.'

Walter looks across the street and sees the tesses sitting in front the laundry.

'They're not so bad, you know.'

'Who?' Walter asks.

'The boys. Look at them sitting there on the pavement, talking quietly. Nothing to do. Nowhere to go. A young fella's a restless creature. I grow up in the country. When I was their age, something was always jumping under my skin. Boy, I would hunt and play all-fours, play stick, play cricket. But cricket's an expensive game now – white clothes, boots, bat, gloves. Long time we play windball-cricket on any little patch of ground that could hold three wickets… Nothing to do here. Only to look on: look at the girls passing and motor cars passing. A young fella don't like to look on. But what to do? No wonder they get real restless after dark and find themselves in mischief. People talk about the steel-band. I don't know what woulda happen if it wasn't for the steel-band to keep some of these boys occupied.'

'Trinidad woulda been a battle zone,' Walter said.

'But steel-band alone won't do,' Mr Cross said. 'Castle, these boys want something more.'

'It's employment too, Mr Cross. You can't do a thing without having funds.'

'Employment is like hell here in this city. Hell,' Mr Cross says. 'That's why I say you can't put all the blame on these boys. I don't know what's going to happen.'

Walter says: 'And a man can't help himself, far more help somebody. Cost of living – '

'Don't talk about that. Cost of living so high, and is I alone.'

'I tell my wife, let's leave and go to the country. No, she says. Wait and fight. Well, it's her life too. I can't drag her away if she doesn't want to go.'

'Maybe it's a good thing, Castle – waiting and fighting.'

'Ha, Mr Cross, waiting on what? The second coming? And fighting with what?'

'Personally, I would like to form something or other, give the boys something to take their minds off their immediate problems. But no help. The people won't co-operate. They're too busy or too tired or they just don't give a damn. Selfishness. People're too selfish. I would really like to do something, Castle, but no co-operation, no encouragement. I give up now. Castle, I give up,' Mr Cross said.

'What you had in mind?'

'So many things that I forget them. I had to forget them.'

Walter is silent, hoping that his silence will encourage Mr Cross to continue speaking.

'I tell you it's hell here, Castle. I thought about the boys reading a little poetry, doing a little drama, a little singing, going on excursions – the same old things.'

'People can't read poetry on empty stomachs, and it's not nice to sing about poverty and hell,' Walter said.

'I know it could've worked. It's hell anyway. But I give up, Castle. I give up. Leave such thoughts for a younger man. I give up.'

For a while neither man speaks. Darkness comes haltingly like a blind man upon the city. The street lights go on.

'Maybe you're right, Castle,' Mr Cross says. 'Maybe the best thing is to leave this goddam place.'

'And maybe I'm wrong to want to leave,' Walter says consolingly; for he notices that Mr Cross feels some hurt over the state of the city and his own failure to assist in solving the problems involved.

'I don't know,' Mr Cross says.

Walter says, 'Things can't go on so.'

'I don't know, Castle. Ah –' he exhales loudly – 'this is my land. Well, night is falling and I'm a bachelor. I have to make my own supper.'

'All right, Mr Cross. I'd better go and eat something too.'

Walter turns and goes from the window. He goes into the kitchen, warms his supper, sits and eats, and when he is finished eating, goes into the living-room and turns on the radio and sits, listening to the music. Now there's a knock on the front door. Damn, he thinks.

He opens the door and finds Ruth, his sister, and Lester, her husband.

'Hi, Ruth, Lester. Come in. I was just thinking of coming up by you.'

'True?'

'So help me.'

'Where's Stephanie?' Ruth asks.

'She's gone to Arouca by her father; taken Carol and Cherrie with her.'

'Oh, so you're keeping house,' Ruth says. 'We came down-town to go in the square to listen to the faith-healer from Canada.'

'Don't make joke,' Walter says. 'You people interested in that?'

'Ruth insisted that we come and hear the man,' Lester says. 'I think she's getting religious.'

'You know I go to church every Sunday,' Ruth says. 'Except those I miss.'

They laugh and sit down.

'How's everything with you, Walter?' Lester asks.

'Funny.'

'What's the matter?'

'I don't know how to begin.'

'Begin anywhere,' Lester says, leaning forward interestedly. 'Stephanie?'

'Not Stephanie, it's me. I want to leave the job and leave Port of Spain and go and live in the country.'

'You must be crazy,' Ruth says.

'Why?' Lester asks. 'Why you want to do all this?'

'Well, first, it's the job. I've been working donkey years and I'm stagnated and I can't get promotion. They've passed over me time and again. And I know it is not because I'm incapable. I'm an efficient worker, still they pass over me. I can't stand that no longer. I don't want to stand it another year. They tell me they're looking into my case. I've heard that a hundred times, still the same story; so I decide to go to the country and work a piece of land, give up the damn foolish fight. I mean, what's the use? I am being used there in the office to show new fellows the work and they get the promotion and I remain nothing. Look, I've thought this thing out, and I find that life's nothing unless you put a meaning to it. I'm just a slave on that job. There's nothing in it for me. At the end of the month, I can hardly pay the bills. It can't be worse in the country on a piece of land. It can't be worse, and there I'll know that whatever I make is mine, what I put in that I will get in return, not this one-sided slavery here. And then, I'll be able to consider myself free and to hold myself up with some pride, because what is life if a man can't at least consider himself free?'

'Freedom is a funny word,' Lester says. 'In the strict sense, a man can never be free.'

'I know a way. If a man has no desires, he's free,' Walter says.
'What? You're a beatnik or something?'

'I don't know what you call it. And the second part is this Webber Street. Last night there was a big riot here, police with guns. I had to wait till police come before I could run inside the house that I paying rent to live in. All about the place is violence. People can't walk the street without being afraid. Gangs, gangs, gangs. Little boys just out of school creating terror in the place. I know they alone not to blame, but the fact remains that a man frighten to walk the streets, far more a woman or a girl. When it isn't robbery it's rape, and when it isn't rape it's big riot with shooting and cutting and police coming with guns and hardly arresting anybody, because they not waiting on police to come to arrest them. I was telling Mr Cross this morning, it's like a sickness passing over the place. Too much crime, too many criminals. I can't fight the criminals, I can't fight a gang man with iron bolts in his pocket and a cutlass or a gun in his hand. Remember what happen to Stephanie? And anyway, when things happening all around you, any time you could get your share – when your brother beard catch fire, the best thing to do is to wet yours.

'Boy, I tired-tired with this town. I tired-tired with the job and with this Webber Street. I see no future here for me. Just now I was talking to Mr Cross again. Mr Cross telling me how the boys not so much to blame and I agree with him. They not to blame. You have unemployment, you have this wicked environment, you have no one caring what happens to them, you could call a hundred factors, but calling factors don't solve the problems. Things going from bad to worst and I tired.'

'You have some strong points there,' Lester said. 'But you have to think about many things when you want to leave a job, and not a job alone, but a whole way of life. I'm a slow, plodding fellow and I find myself caught up in a world from which I can't escape, so I try. I try to mind my own business, to pay my debts and to do no harm. But I'm a slow, plodding fellow and not full of fire like you.'

'If I could find something here, something big enough to make me forget myself, something high enough to make me want to reach up to it, then perhaps I could bear the kind of existence I'm leading here,' Walter says. 'But there is no point in this kinda living, there is nothing to hold on to here. A man finds himself looking within himself for something.'

'I see that you've been doing a great deal of thinking, Walter,' Lester says. 'Like I said, I'm a slow, plodding fellow and I mind my own business; but I've done a little thinking too. This condition is not something that's particular to you or your situation in life; it is something that's common in this part of the world today. We have no God, no religion, no ideology to live by; we have nothing to sink our teeth into. In the past the priests gave us something, that was good for a time; then the politicians gave us something, and that has its limitations. We keep on looking for the priests or the politicians to give us something, but I'm afraid we'll get nothing from them. We have to do something for ourselves. The ball is in our corner… Like I said, I don't allow myself to be too entangled in this sort of thing in a practical way. All this is just an academic exercise to me. Perhaps that's some sort of advantage, because with that kind of approach I am able to view things more objectively. You know, what I want to say is that we, the people, must now come out with a philosophy of life, something strong and uplifting, something positive, something that will save us. As it is now, the world is broken up into races and classes and creeds. Then, more and more, the individual is being pushed off the scene. Man wants to retain his individuality, and yet we know that unless others are involved, a man's contribution isn't worth much. So the thing, the God, whatever it is, must cater for the exercise of individuality as well as the participation of other human beings. This is my roundabout way of telling you that you're making a mistake if you leave the town and expect to find peace by yourself in the country. In the first place, I don't think you're as interested in peace as you are in – let's say – righting the ills of this city, or in getting a square deal on the job. At least, that's my impression. You want life, as you put it, to mean something – really mean something. You'll fall far short of your expectations if you leave and go like a hermit in the country… We must get together and talk, Walter. You hit on a very interesting topic there. Very interesting.'

'I have quite a few years' service on the job there. If I leave now, I'd lose all that,' Walter says, like he's thinking.

'Yes, and if you go to get another job, you'd still have to start from scratch,' Lester says. 'But I won't tell you don't leave. There're some things inside a man which can't be satisfied with money… And yet, a man has to think many times when he has a family to support – you know?'

'Yes, I know… I know.'

'Better come with us and hear the preacher in the square,' Ruth says. 'By the way, what time is it?'

'Nearly time to leave if we want to be early and get a good place in the front,' Lester says, looking at his watch.

'Then you'd better leave now. I wouldn't like to keep you back.'

'Will you be coming?' Ruth asks Walter.

'I might do that, but I'll take my time.'

'Walter, we'll have to talk again,' Lester says, rising. 'Think we'd better leave now.'

'We'll see you in the square,' Ruth says.

'Hardly likely in that crowd,' Lester says. 'Say hello to Stephanie for me.'

'Okay. Stephanie was looking out for you-all for the whole month.'

'Why don't you-all come up by us on Sunday? Tell Stephanie I'm expecting her,' Ruth says.

'All right. 'Night, Ruth. All right, Lester.'

'Right-o, Walter.'

The man sees them to the door. After they go, he takes a bath, then changes his clothes. Perhaps he will listen to this man in the square. He locks the front door and drops the key into a pants pocket, walks down the steps, through the yard and reaches the street.

The street is well lighted. Here and there, at gateways, young men and young women (and men not so young, and women who look as if they were never young) are talking. A woman laughs scandalously, a tess hugs her and they both rock and laugh.

Swing across here. Next street.

Vehicles cruise with park lights on. People move – up the

pavement, down the pavement, across the street. Going to the movies. Going to a dance. A party. Going visiting. Going God-knows-where. Here is a snackette. The jukebox moans: Ray Charles, 'Born to lose'. Four young men walking down the pavement; walking fast, talking so fast you don't hear what they're saying. Walking fast. Walking slowly, a woman, big bottom, nice figure; her perfume trails behind her – going somewhere. Here's a recreation parlour: pinball machines. Men lined up by the machines push ten-cent pieces in a slot, pull back spring levers, shoot balls, stand goggle-eyed and watch the balls go where they will. Idiotic. They look at the lights go on in the machine, they look at the numbers registered. Idiotic. Walk on. Two old tesses recognize each other after a long time. One says: 'Sam!' The other stands, shakes his head, looks at his friend and stretches out a hand: 'Zachy!' A young tess wants to pass. He grumbles that the old men are blocking the passage. The old tesses don't hear him, they're busy shaking hands and mumbling greetings. Scree-chhh! A motor car brakes abruptly. Somebody says, 'Jesus! Another accident?' Somebody else says, 'No. Lucky. He didn't bounce her.' Walter looks back. An old woman limps out of the street; the motorcar picks up and moves on.

Cross here. Wait. Look up, look down. Cross now.

A boy holds the elbow of his girl, propels her across the street. The boy is taller than the girl, he bends and whispers in her ear. Nice couple. A fat man waddles drunkenly across the pavement. He stops and holds on to a telephone post. A dog comes out a gateway and sniffs at his legs. The man kicks at the dog and falls. People laugh. He curses the man who tries to help him to his feet. 'Drunk,' the fellow says, and continues to help him until he has regained his feet. A beggar is asleep on the pavement. She doesn't turn. She doesn't snore. She is silent. She is accustomed to the constant tramp of feet near her head. She is accustomed to the sudden screech of vehicles' brakes and the snore of vehicles' engines in the night.

Up here.

A little boy stands looking at one of the display windows of a store. His mother and two sisters continue walking, but he stands and looks at the toys in the showcase and doesn't notice his family going down the street. A woman is selling oranges on a tray. Another woman is selling mangoes. Another woman is selling apples. They look at each person as he passes. Two fellows stop. They ask the price of the oranges and don't buy, they ask the price of the mangoes and don't buy. The woman selling apples looks at them walk up to her.

A Baptist preacher is at the corner. A crowd surrounds him. If you want to pass, get off the pavement and walk in the street. Listen to this man. Listen and hear what he says. He is a tall black man and his head is tied with a yellow cloth. When he says something, his followers repeat after him. Sometimes they do not repeat the actual words, but amplify the meaning of his words. Listen to him. Listen to them. Stop a while and listen.

'Bretheren an' sisterin. As I lay sleepin', I heard a voice.'

'Sweet voice,' the congregation of followers sing.

'I heard a voice, Lord. An' I see the lightening cuttin' 'cross…'

'Glory halliyew-ya!'

'Lightening cuttin' 'cross heavens an' fire catching the sky.'

'Oh, Jesus.'

'An' I heard a mighty thunder…'

'Mighty thunder, Lord.'

'An' I hear a moaning an' a crying an' a shouting from sinnerman…'

'Sweet Jesus. Tell them, brother. Tell them, leader.'

'Yee-es, an' I was praying near a river in a dark-dark night.'

'Night, leader. Night, Lord. Night.'

'An' above the thunder an' the moaning an' the lightening an' the fire, I heard a voice…'

'What voice, leader? What voice?'

'I heard a voice saying. Cryin' out an' sayin', "Damnation for the evil. Slaughter for the children of evil." '

'O God!'

'An' I see a ball of fire, an I see a river of blood, an I hear voices bawlin', callin' to the Lord. I was there prayin' by the river an' the fire…'

'Yes, yes, yes, yes. Say it, leader. Say it, pastor. Yes, yes, yes.'

'The fire. The fire whistle like a cravat an' it moan like a dove.

An' people was runnin' an' people was bawlin' an' me on me knees prayin'.'

'Sweet Jesus. Pity, Lord.'

'An' now I tell yuh. That a time is a' comin'. A dangerous time. A time of fire an' a time of thunder an' a time of slaughter an' a time of blood.'

'Oooh Lord. Mercy, Jesus. Mercy.'

'For I get a message an' I get a call an' I hear the thunder an' I see the fire an' the blood. Bretheren an' sisterin, repent!'

'Repent!'

'Pray!'

'Pray!'

'Have faith!'

'Have faith!'

'Cease from evil!'

'Cease from evil!'

'For tha' day is a' comin'...'

'Oh, Jesus!'

'When tha' voice shall be heard...'

'When tha' voice. Mighty voice!'

'An tha' trumpet shall sound...'

'The trumpet, Lord!'

'An' the names shall be called over yonder!'

Clink! Clink! People dropping pennies in the bowl near the lighted candles flickering at the preacher's feet. The preacher preaches, and now and then, casts an eye to see how the coins are coming in the bowl.

Vroom! Vroom! Motorcycles. Five of them. They take the corner very low. The one behind takes it lower than the rest. All the riders wear crash helmets except the last one who is wearing a bee-bop cap. Passing the preacher, they rev up the engines and the girls riding pillion giggle.

Time to leave. Time to see what's in the square.

People, people. Woodford Square is jam-packed with people, and people are entering still. You stand right there in the street and you hear the preacher coming over the loudspeakers. Yes, there are many loudspeakers, all turned to the streets.

Listen to the preacher coming over the loudspeaker.

'…And I say unto you that it is better to give than to receive. It is nobler to forgive than to seek vengeance, and far greater to love than…'

Nothing new, Walter thinks. Nothing new. Words, words, words. You are fed with words puked and swallowed and puked again… Gotta decide whether I'm going to work in the morning. Gotta try to keep holding on to my balls. They're all I have. Can't let them go. Gotta try to keep hold of them. Now this life. What it is? What does it mean? Where does it lead? Eh? Death? Eh? Where did it begin? Why? Hell! Better walk up the road. Yes. Walk up the road.

The voice of the preacher comes over the loudspeakers: '…Through the world today, man stumbles, seeking for a light, seeking something to be guided by, seeking meaning in darkness. Today, man tells himself that he's free. I'm free! he boasts. I want to be happy. I want to be rich. I want to be glad. But he isn't happy and he's not rich and he is not made glad; so he turns round and asks, Am I free? Is he free? Are you free? What is this thing, freedom?…'

Walk on up the road. Let the preacher preach. Walk. Up Frederick Street. Two lovers looking at gifts in a lighted display-window. One watchman in a khaki suit sitting on a box and, between coughing, thumping his stick and singing a toothless hymn:

> 'Are you washed in the blood of the Lamb?
> Are you washed in the blood of the Lamb?
> Are your garments spotless
> Are they whiter than snow,
> Are you washed in the blood of the Lamb?'

One woman talking and laughing with herself. As he passes by her she looks at him and says: 'Pss-st!' He walks by. She says: 'Boo! Boo!' And laughs. The old watchman singing 'Are you washed in the blood of the Lamb?' stops singing, coughs and calls out to the woman: 'Mad 'Arriet, c'me 'ere.' The watchman is a Barbadian. The woman runs past him, up the street. She stops when she sees a policeman standing at the corner. The policeman stands with his toes well apart, his heels touching.

He pulls at the edges of his tunic, then folds his hands behind his back and rocks on his heels. His baton is in his pocket and the strap of his helmet right under his lips.

Park Street. Bright. Vehicles moving, people moving, music playing, nightclubs alight. A tout talking to four American sailors. 'St James,' a taxi-driver calls out as he stops his vehicle at the red light. No, Walter shakes his head. Not goin' St James, he says to himself, without opening his mouth.

'COME UNTO ME ALL YE THAT LABOUR AND ARE HEAVY-LADEN AND I WILL GIVE YOU REST, FOR MY YOKE IS EASY AND MY BURDEN IS LIGHT.'

That's what painted right there on the wall. An arrow points to a dimly lit drinking-spot. Clever… 'Come unto me all ye that labour and are heavy-laden…' Better go in and get a drink. Better take a drink. A good stiff one to burn your insides. Yes, better take a drink. Go in the spot. Go on in.

Not a bad place. Nice set-up. Females, slant-eyed, red-lipsticked, thin though, haggard and thin even under these lights. But who said this is heaven? Jukebox, stingy-brimmed men, fried chicken, rum, beer.

'Gimme a nip,' he says to the bartender.

'Whatyuhwant, Shorty?'

'A nip.'

'Rum? What kind?'

'The white one.'

'Okay. Soda? Ginger? Coke?'

'Gimme a Pepsi.'

Walter takes his change and finds an empty table near to the jukebox. He sits and begins to drink his liquor.

A fellow with an unshaven face sits on a tall stool before the jukebox guzzling wine from a bottle he cradles in his arms. He drops another coin in the slot and the jukebox gives out the tune 'Georgia on my mind'. The man has a drunken, pain-twisted face. He cocks his head to one side and listens. He pushes the bottle against his lips and some wine falls and reddens his soiled white shirt. When the tune is played out, he listens to it play again. Maybe he'll play that tune all night. Some tune. Some fellow. Some problem.

One nip done. It didn't even touch him. Try another. Walter goes to the bar.

'Another nip.'

'Whatyuhwant, Shorty?'

'Nip.'

'Rum? What kind? Soda? Ginger? Pepsi? Coke?'

'The white one and a Pepsi.'

'Right. Here.'

Walter pours a drink but adds no Pepsi. He drinks. That was all right, he thinks. All right.

A fellow with two front teeth missing comes over to where Walter's sitting. Watch it. Bum, he thinks.

'Good night, Mr Castle,' the fellow says, smiling and showing the open spaces in his mouth.

'Hello,' Walter says. He's sure he doesn't know this man.

'Bet you don't know me,' the fellow says.

'As you mention it, yes. I'm not sure I know you.'

'Yes,' the fellow says wisely, 'I coulda bet that you don't know me.' The fellow looks at the nip and draws up a seat and sits down. 'Is just what I does say. People livin' one place an' they don't know one another.'

'Where you livin'? Webber Street?'

'Well, not exactly, but I have a lady-friend living downstairs by you there – you know?'

'Yes. You takin' one?'

'Well, yes,' the fellow says, lazily, like he doesn't care but since he is forced, okay. 'Lemme get a glass.' He sits right there and shouts at a waitress going by, 'Irene, one glass and ice.'

Well, lemme introduce myself. Willie Brand.' They shake hands. 'I know yuh good-good. You on the third floor, you have a brown-skinned wife and a little baby.'

The waitress returns with the glass and the ice. They drink.

'Never see you here before,' the fellow says.

'Never was here before.'

Nip finish. Could take another, Walter thinks. He gets up and goes to the bar, returns with another nip.

Commotion in the place. A tess wants to play a tune on the jukebox, but the records don't stop spinning. 'Georgia on my mind' by Ray Charles is all that's coming out of the jukebox. Maybe the fellow did punch that tune so it plays all night. Helluva fella. The tess who wants to play the other tune stands looking at the other fellow by the jukebox as if he wants to fight him.

'Want to fight me, pardner?' the tess who has been playing 'Georgia' all night says softly.

'I have me worries too.'

'Wife left you?'

'No. The bitch come back.'

'Funny world. Take a wine?'

'Yeah.' He takes the bottle and puts it to his head and some of the wine runs down the corner of his lips.

'Funny world,' the tess who says his name is Willie Brand says.

'Yes,' Walter says. 'Funny world. Last drink an' I going home.' He measures the remaining rum in the bottle with his eyes.

Willie says, 'Yuh know I ent drunk yet.'

Walter says, 'Well, I feeling drunk like hell. Last drink for me.' He pours some of the liquor in his glass and passes the bottle to Willie Brand, who pours the remainder into his glass. They drink.

'Home now,' Walter says.

'I think I goin' in too,' says Willie Brand. 'Let's go.'

They walk out the place, saying nothing.

Outside. Cinema over already. Place quiet. Tesses up and down. Whores leaned up near gateways and at club entrances. Cars slow. Policemen alert. The odd fellow picks his way home, with his hands deep in his pockets.

'Place quiet,' Walter says, breaking the silence.

'Yes. Cinema over already. Yuh went an' hear the fella in the square, the healer?'

'I passed 'round there.'

'I went last night. He's a helluva man. I see 'im heal a cripple woman from Belmont. I know the woman dragging on she bottom since I going to school.'

'Yes?'

'Yes, man. Funny how yuh di'n know me all the time, eh? That's how it is in town. A man don't even know his neighbour. That's the town for you.'

200

'You're right. People not interested in others.'

'You know, that's a true thing yuh say there.'

Spice Street. Swing down here.

'A lotta police out tonight,' Willie says, observing the four policemen by the corner. 'An' all of them have dawgs.'

'Yes, they have revolvers. Wonder what happen.'

'Big thing! A setta teenagers beat up and kill a man in town.'

'Where? Around here? Webber Street?'

'No. Down in town, but some of the fellows from up here.'

'Helluva thing.'

'Man, I don't know what wrong with them young tesses. I don't know what happen to them with this knifin' an' shootin' an' beatin'. Yuh think a man like me have time to study violence? Me! I studyin' how in the mornin' I gettin' up without a blasted cent in me pocket. I studyin' about goin' to hussle for a job, or go up in the club an' hussle in a whappie game. I don't have time to think 'bout violence.'

'You not workin'?'

'Six months now. Six months, not a stroke to make.'

'I can imagine.'

'No, yuh can't imagine. Sometimes I does wonder what the hell I doin' in this blasted world.'

'Look! More police. Like boys from around here involved.'

'Yes. I tell you some of the tesses from round here.'

Webber Street. Very quiet. No vehicles. Two policemen. No tesses.

'You feel any of the boys from Webber Street?'

'It must have been boys from Webber Street involve. Must have.'

'Real serious,' Walter says. 'Not even the jukebox playin'. An' the snackette close.'

'Well, we reach,' Willie Brand says.

'Yes. I feelin' upset. Glad I reach home.'

'Well, I goin' round in the back.'

'I goin' upstairs. Hope I can make the steps. Okay?'

'Okay.'

One two three four five six… Feeling real drunk now… up… Second floor… Steps… Third floor. Key. Have the key in my pocket. Key. Nice. Praise God. Walter stumbles inside, locks the door and stumbles to the bedroom and falls on to the bed. He doesn't have the strength to change his clothes. Drunk like a blasted fish, he thinks.

## 12

Monday morning.

The woman enters the bedroom, the man turns, sighs and opens his eyes.

'Here, I brought you some coffee.'

'Coffee?' the man asks, like he's groping to establish connection with his surroundings.

'Yes. Sit up and drink it.'

The woman rests down the cup and watches the man struggle to a sitting position. 'How you feeling now?' she asks.

'Rotten. Head's splittin'.'

'You drank too much. Why'd you have to drink so much? Last night I had to take off your clothes and put you to bed.'

'Thanks,' the man says. 'What time is it?'

'Past seven. You goin' to work this morning?'

He disregards the question. 'Hand me the coffee.'

'Here. Drink it, you'll feel better. Hold the cup.'

'It's scalding hot.'

'I know. It's better hot. Drink it. If you want, I can ring the office and tell them you're not coming this morning. I can tell them you're sick.'

'Don't worry with that.'

'You're not going back to work?'

'I didn't say so.' He drinks and hands the empty cup back to her.

'Heard what happened last night? It just came over the radio,' the woman says.

'Somebody murdered somebody?'

'Yes. They held five of them and the oldest is not yet nineteen.'

'I hear some of the boys from around here,' the man says.

'Well, I don't know. I would hardly know them. I don't know the boys around here too well. But that's bad, eh? Think about their poor parents, how they must feel this morning.'

'You don't see this city's no good? You don't see it's better that we leave here?' the man says.

'Walter, let's not start that again. Please.'

'Facts, facts. You don't want to face facts.'

'I don't want to talk about it now,' the woman says.

'All right,' the man says. 'How's your mother?'

'She's all right. Daddy says he might pass here today or tomorrow.'

'You told him?'

'I just asked him if he thought it was a good idea to leave town.'

'And what did he say?'

'Said that was for us to decide.'

'Someone's at the door,' the man says.

'All right. Let me see who it is.'

Good woman. A bit stubborn when she thinks she's right. Maybe she's right. Maybe anywhere a man goes life's the same hell, Walter thinks.

The woman re-enters the bedroom. 'Walter,' she says. 'You'd better come. Something's happened to Mrs Walls.'

'What?' he asks, getting out of bed.

'I don't know. She's just there crying an' wringing her hands. She can't say a word. Something's wrong.'

'Okay. I'm comin'.'

'Come quick. Don't worry to change.'

Mrs Walls is a thin-faced woman. She stands with her hands twitching before her and tears rolling down her lined cheeks. There is fear about her and great sorrow.

'Mrs Walls,' Walter says.

The woman makes no answer.

'Get some coffee for her, Stephanie, and let her sit down,' Walter says. 'What is it, Mrs Walls?'

'Sit down, Mrs Walls,' Stephanie says. 'I have some coffee there, I'll get a cup for you.'

Mrs Walls sits like she's in a dream.

'If we don't know what's wrong, we can't help you, Mrs Walls,' Walter says.

Stephanie goes out and returns with the coffee. Mrs Walls's hands shake, holding the cup. After the coffee she seems to gain some possession of herself.

'Now, what's wrong, Mrs Walls?' Walter presses.

Tears come into the woman's eyes and she shakes her head. 'Trouble,' she says. 'Big trouble.' And begins to tremble.

'Try to control yourself, dear,' Stephanie says. 'Try. What trouble?'

'My son. Ruben,' the woman says, shaking her head and trying hard to keep the tears away. 'O Gawd!'

'What happen to Ruben?' Walter asks.

'Ruben. Ruben. Ruben…' Mrs Walls says, as if she is willing to say what must be said, but doesn't know the words to use.

'What happen? He get in a fight? He's in hospital? What happen?'

'Worse than that. Ruben… Ruben. O Gawd! The police just come again… The police come an' gone with Ruben.'

'What happen? Why the police gone with Ruben?' Walter asks, like he's talking to a child.

'The police come…' Mrs Walls begins, and can get no further. She begins to cry.

'He's in trouble?' Stephanie asks.

Through her tears, Mrs Walls nods.

'Bad trouble?'

'Trouble. Real trouble,' Mrs Walls laments, panting, trying to gain control of herself.

'He involved in… in the…?' Stephanie asks.

Mrs Walls nods. 'Oh Gawd, yes,' she bursts out. 'O Lawd, Gawd, Jesus!'

'He was in it?' Walter asks.

'Ahhh-Awwww-Ohhhh!'

'Oh God!' Stephanie says, sucking in her breath sharply.

'This town,' Mrs Walls cries. 'This town. This bad company. This bad company that Ruben follow in this town. Lawd! Lawd, Gawd. Now look whey the boy reach! The boy reach in the prison. The boy reach to the hangman rope. The police just leave

205

with him. They come askin' me question an' gone with him to the jail. Hell. Is hell when a woman don't have a man to help she raise she chillren. Is hell when a woman so small an' so poor she can't fight the town, can't prevent she boy-child roamin' out with gangs. Is only trouble they could meet. Only trouble walkin' behin' them like a shadow.

'But yuh don't have nutten to offer them. Yuh don't even have words to advise them, an' even if yuh have words to tell them, what is words? Chillren today want more than words. Oh Lawd! They roamin' the town like is high woods they roamin'. They roamin' the street like is a forest they huntin' in. Poor parents don't know what to do again. When they reach a stage, is only God to help them. Only if God bless his eyes on them, they get lucky an' stay outa trouble. But it hard. They have nutten. They seeing so much an' they have nutten. Temptation to thief, temptation to rob, temptation to kill, temptation to hit back at the world that squeezin' them so. Too much people lookin' on an' not doin' nutten, like if they don't know is only bad these chillren headin' for. Like if they don't know is something these poor chillren want. Is something that we can't give them. I poor an' what I could give Ruben? What? In the beginnin' I send Ruben to college. Ruben had to leave college. Times was too hard. I couldn't make it. Since Ruben leave college, all Ruben ambition wash away. Ruben gone. Ruben vex with the world. Ruben vex with himself. Ruben reach the stage where he don't care what happen. I see it. Lord, yuh know I see it comin'. I pray, but I couldn't prevent it. It was like fire.

'Ruben used to play football in college. Ruben even stop playin' that. He drinkin', he smokin', he even lookin' for woman an' fight. Ruben is a gang man with a gang jersey. Oh Lawd! And now Ruben reach. He reach the hangman.'

'Mrs Walls,' Walter says. 'Don't blame yourself too much, don't blame the boy too much, either. It's this city where everybody is busy, everybody thinks only about himself.'

'Not the city, Mr Castle. It's the people. Somebody should care. When you can't take care of what you have, somebody should care. But who cares? If yuh not lucky you don't survive. Years now I alone. I come down here from Arima with Ruben

206

father an' then the man pick up with a jamette woman an' gone America. Leave me alone to battle with the chillren in this town.'

'Is not your fault, Mrs Walls. Don't blame yourself,' Walter says.

'Well, who fault it is? Is not the boy fault. Is not Ruben fault. Ruben is a little boy. Who fault it is?'

'The society, perhaps?' Walter ventures.

'We have no society. We not social folk. An Gawd, Ruben have two sisters goin' high school. What a shame for the poor chillren. What a shame! Why this had to happen? Why he couldn't stay home last night an' keep conversation with his sisters? Why this had to happen to me? Trouble, yuh not tired with me? You not tired harassin' a poor woman with nobody?'

'You know, Mrs Walls, it's not anybody's fault,' Walter says.

'Not anybody fault! Is everybody fault. Everybody,' Mrs Walls says bitterly.

'You sure he's really involved in this thing?' Stephanie asks.

'How you mean sure, Mrs Castle? Ent the police take him?'

'I know the police take him, but are you certain that he's actually involved in this thing?'

'No,' Mrs Walls says. 'I not sure.'

'Well, you can hope and pray that he's not,' Stephanie says.

'The police take him. The police take him; the police would know. But me, I 'fraid. I 'fraid to pray an' to hope. I use to pray that nothing like this happen to him, an' look it happen.'

'You mustn't give up hope, Mrs Walls,' Stephanie says. 'When you going to see him?'

'I can't go alone. I can't face him alone, I would bawl,' the woman says, as if she would bawl right there.

Stephanie looks at Walter, appealing to him. Walter is silent, thinking. He looks at Mrs Walls.

'Tell me when you going to see him and I'll come with you.'

'You will come with me?'

'Yes, Mrs Walls, I'll go with you.'

'I want to go later in the mornin'.'

'I'll go with you,' Walter says.

'Perhaps he isn't really involved,' Stephanie says.

'You just sayin' that to cheer me up. But don't cheer me up. I don't want to hope an' then get bad news to throw me back down.'

'Walter will go with you to see him,' Stephanie says.

'I have nobody around here. No family, nobody. If they have to give the boy bail, I have no money to bail him. If I have a lawyer to get for the boy, I have no money to pay lawyer. This is something, Lawd! Livin' in town. Livin' in town. Livin' in misery in town. An' you have no money an' you not lucky. I don't know why I ever leave Arima. I don't know why I born. Hell, hell, hell. Is only hell I seein'.'

'Don't say that, Mrs Walls. God is love,' Stephanie says.

'Madam, I don't see no God in Port of Spain. I don't see no God in Webber Street. The God who love is not in Webber Street. God somewhere around Elleslie Park and up in St Clair where people seeing well. God is not 'round here where poor people ketchin' hell. If this is hell, this is where the Devil is; it can't be heaven where God is. God don't be in hell. This is hell.'

'God hearing you, Mrs Walls,' Stephanie says.

'O Gawd, if you hearin' me, hear me. I only seein' hell, hell, hell. I only seein' Satan leading away the people here, leadin' away the chillren here. I don't see no God here. So, Gawd, if you hearin' me, hear me. Come an' show me that you hearin', 'cause I waitin'.'

Now, Mrs Walls falls on her knees and bends down, touching her face to the floor. 'Forgive me, Lawd. Forgive me, Jesus. But my boy, my son, involve in this big trouble. Forgive me, Lawd, 'cause I can't see your face. I really can't see your face. An' is only your face to save the boy.' She remains on her knees sobbing until Stephanie helps her to her feet.

'I am sorry,' Mrs Walls says.

'We understand,' Stephanie says. 'Walter will come down in a while and he'll go with you to see the boy.'

'Thank you, Mrs Castle.'

'We wish we could help more, Mrs Walls,' Stephanie says.

'All right, child. I will go and prepare myself.'

'Have courage, Mrs Walls. I will pray for you and for the boy.'

'You will pray for the boy?'

'Yes, Mrs Walls,' Stephanie says. 'I will pray for him.'

'God bless you, child. I'm goin'.'

'All right, Mrs Walls. Walter will come to meet you in a while.'

The woman walks slowly towards the door. Stephanie walks with her.

Troubles, troubles. Everybody have troubles here in this Webber Street, Walter thinks. Now, what can I do to help that boy? He goes into the bedroom and takes up a towel, then goes to the bathroom.

After bathing, he returns to the bedroom and finds that his wife has laid out a clean white shirt. Good woman, he thinks. Smart, too. He dresses, then goes into the living-room and has breakfast. While he is having breakfast, his wife brings in a newspaper.

'Thought you might want to see it,' she says. 'The story's there.'

Yes, good woman, smart too, knows how to get around her man. He opens the newspaper slowly, as one who is afraid.

MURDER IN CITY STREET

TEENAGE YOUTHS HELD

'Here,' he says, handing the papers to his wife. 'I cannot read it.' He pushes aside the remainder of his breakfast and stands.

'You are ready to go with Mrs Walls?' Stephanie asks.

'I am ready.'

'Try to cheer her up,' the woman says.

'I will try. It will be hard.'

'Try your best.'

'All right. I am goin'.'

He walks through the door, down the steps and on the second floor, turns and knocks on the front door of the apartment occupied by Mrs Walls. Mrs Walls appears at the door in a faded blue dress.

'I am ready, Mrs Walls.'

'I am ready, son. Let me just get my hat.'

He waits while she gets her hat and handbag.

'Let us go,' she says. 'Let us go.'

Mrs Walls goes before him. They walk down the remaining steps and into the yard. Some of the neighbours know. They look up at Mrs Walls and seem to be afraid to say good morning. Mrs Walls walks with her head straight.

Say something. What conversation to make?

'Few people on the street this morning,' he says.

'Yes. Few people,' she adds as an afterthought.

'Shall we take a taxi?'

'Let's walk. No taxis around here going that way.'

'I can get one to carry us. It will be much quicker.'

'All right then.'

He stops an empty taxi and tells the driver where he wants to go.

The walls around the jail are brown and thick and tall. It is very quiet around here. Mrs Walls reaches into her handbag, takes out her handkerchief and sniffles into it.

'Don't cry now, Mrs Walls,' he says. 'Not now.'

The woman daubs at her eyes. 'All right,' she says in a small voice. 'I'll try.'

'Good. Let's go.'

They pass through the gate and enter the grim place. The officer at the desk is a fellow Walter knew at school. He explains the situation to him and asks for his assistance. So it is arranged. Mrs Walls and he are taken to a room. They sit and wait.

The boy comes out, followed by a guard. The guard explains to them that they must not speak in whispers and they must not hand anything to the prisoner. They understand. The boy sits facing them.

The mother looks at the boy. The boy holds his head erect for a moment, then bends it as if he is thinking. The mother looks at her son and reaches into her handbag for her handkerchief. She shakes her head from side to side and clutches the handkerchief in her fingers.

The mother speaks. 'Ruben.'

'Yes, Ma.'

'You in jail.'

The boy does not answer.

'You in jail, Ruben,' the mother says, very close to tears. 'Eh, Ruben?'

What can the boy say?

'You reach where you goin',' the mother says in a voice hoarse and strange with grief. 'You reach where hardness an' rudeness an' bad company lead. You reach.'

The boy bites his bottom lip and shakes his feet.

'Answer me. You reach, eh, Ruben?'

The boy says, 'Ma…'

'You had plenty things against you. No father, no job, nobody to really take care of you. Because I wasn't able. I just wasn't able. You had plenty against you; but you coulda do better than this. You coulda do better than gettin' yuhself in this big trouble.' The woman wipes her eyes. 'You know you in big trouble?'

The boy does a funny thing. He smiles. What is remarkable about the smile is that it is not one of self-pity, rather it is as if he's smiling at his mother and at Walter and at the whole world.

'You know you in big trouble?' the mother repeats.

The boy nods his head.

'You know I don't have no money for lawyer to fight yuh case?'

The boy bends his head. His face grows ugly, his chest heaves, he begins to cry.

'Why you crying for now?' the mother asks, torn with grief and anger.

'Ma…'

'Ma what?' Mrs Walls says roughly, anger mastering her.

'You didn't even ask,' the boy says.

'What, Ruben? What?'

'You didn't even ask. You didn't even ask if I guilty. You didn't even ask.'

'You not guilty, Ruben?' the mother asks with too much hope.

'You didn't even ask,' the boy moans.

'Ruben, talk to me. You not guilty?' the mother asks in a voice new with hope.

'No, Ma. I wasn't there. I went down the road with the boys an' I left them an' went to the cinema an' when I come back I meet them in Allum tea-shop.'

'You not guilty, Ruben?'

'No, Ma. I wasn't there.'

'If you wasn't there, how come the police hold you? How come? Answer me that, boy.'

The boy is crying silently. The mother looks at Walter.

'If you not guilty, they'll let you go,' Walter says.

'Let me go?' the boy says as if he doesn't believe it.

211

'You told them you wasn't there?' Walter asks.

'Yes. But they don't believe me.'

'They will believe you, if you're speaking the truth,' Walter says.

'I tell you they won't believe me.'

'Why? Why won't they believe you?' Walter asks.

'Because they don't feel to believe me,' the boy says sharply.

'And why should they just feel that you're guilty?'

'I know why,' the boy says. 'I know why. Because once you from a particular area an' you in a particular company, anything you do, you wrong. You never right. You never innocent, always guilty.'

'Look, wipe yuh eyes,' the mother says.

'They have to prove you guilty. That is the law,' Walter says.

'That is the law for them. That is not the law for me an' tesses like me. They don't believe you. They don't care about you. They don't want you in their world. They don't give you a chance. Nobody comes out to speak for you. You have nothin' an' you mean nothin' to nobody.'

'You can't believe all that, boy,' Walter says.

'I can't, mister? You don't know, but I know. I tell you they'd like to get all the tesses on a rap like this an' hang the whole lot.'

'You mustn't believe that,' Walter says.

'It's all right you sayin' so. It's me who's behind bars. It's all right the whole world sayin' what they want to say, but it's me behind bars, waitin', waitin'.'

'Don't talk so, boy. Mr Castle come here to try to help,' Mrs Walls says.

'But, Ma, I talkin' the truth. Even people right there next door to us on Webber Street don't know how we living. They don't know and they don't care. Some people tell a tess good mornin' or good evenin' not because they want to but because they 'fraid. They 'fraid you throw a bottle in they face. People not interested in you because you in trouble or because you poor, but because they 'fraid what you will do. They only tryin' to keep you off with a smile, not help you,' the boy says hotly.

'Talkin' so won't get you nowhere now,' the mother says.

'I don't know, Ma,' the boy says.

'An' Ruben,' the mother says, 'if you know so much, if you know how people don't like you and don't care about you, an' they glad to see you get yuhself in trouble – if you know all that, boy, why you come an' get yuhself in such company to come now an' get yuhself in trouble so big that you can't carry? Why you get yuhself in such company, why you didn't look for other company? You went to college, it wasn't hard for you to find better company.'

'What other company, Ma? Is Webber Street I grow up, where to get the other company in Webber Street?'

'Well, why you didn't stay by yuhself? Why?'

'You can't ask me that, Ma,' the boy says.

'Why I can't ask you that? You self say how people don't like people of a particular company. Now why you go an' keep that same company that people don't like, company to get you in trouble, an' can't help you when you get in trouble? Why I can't ask you that?'

'Because, Ma, is not natural for someone to stay by theyself when so much people around him. And Ma, I grow up with the fellas, I just like them.'

'An' you say you not guilty?'

'Yes, Ma.'

'Tell me what happen,' Walter says.

'The same thing I say already. I was with the tesses an' I skip out on them 'cause I wanted to see the double at Royal. I went an' see the picture an' when the picture finish I went by Allum tea-shop where the tesses does be. I meet them an they tell me how they was in a fight with a man. While we there, we get a wire that the police lookin' for the tesses. Every man scatter. I shoot home. They come home an' ask me where I went an' who was with me. I tell them I went cinema alone. They ask me where I went afterwards. I tell them I went Allum tea-shop. They want to know why I went there. I tell them I always does go there. Who was with me? I tell them, some fellas. They want to know the names of the tesses. They want me to tell them the names of the tesses.'

'You didn't tell them?'

'I can't remember all who was there, I tell them. They say that they hold four fellas an' the fellas say I was with them an' how we

213

get in a noise with a man. I tell them I wasn't in any noise with anybody. They lock me up.'

'That's the truth?' Walter says.

'That's the truth, Mr Castle.'

'I don't have money for lawyer,' the mother says. 'But you have to get a lawyer. I don't know how… Look whey you find yuhself, eh. Lord, Jesus, what to do?'

'What you goin' to do, Ma?'

'I goin' to do what I could do.'

'I sorry, Ma.'

'You sorry?'

'Ma, I wasn't in it.'

'I don't know what I goin' to do,' the mother says.

'You won't get no help, Ma. I know. Who goin' to help you? Who goin' to help me? People don't even know if we livin'.'

The mother begins to cry. 'Pray, Ruben.'

'Ma,' the boy says and begins to cry.

'I don't know what I can do,' Walter says, 'but I'll try for you, Ruben.'

'You?'

'Yes.'

'Why?'

'Ruben!' the mother reprimands sharply.

'All right, Ma.'

'Sorry,' the guard says, 'Time to leave now.'

'I will come tomorrow,' Mrs Walls says.

'You will get a lawyer?'

'What you askin' me now, boy? Pray. If you use to pray now this wouldn'ta happen to you. Is true, this generation have no God.'

'We didn't meet any, Ma. That's why.'

'And you couldn't find one? You look for gang life an' violence, but you didn't look for God. Time to go now. I goin'. I will see you tomorrow,' the woman says.

They turn and walk out the room and the guard leads the boy away in another direction. Now, the woman and the young man pass out of the grim place. They walk down the street and away from the high, thick brown walls of the prison.

214

'Oh Gawd,' Mrs Walls says after a while. 'Poverty. Not even money to hire a lawyer for the boy.'

Walter says nothing. He is thinking.

Downtown. Quick-stepping pedestrians, traffic lights, automobiles, shoppers, quack salesmen eagle-eyed. Look! A blind man at a corner. Nice of that woman to take him across the street. Think. The good fellow from Samaria came and helped the plundered fellow after the Levite and the priest hurried by on the other side of the street. Who is my neighbour? Who is my neighbour? Who is neighbour to the people of Webber Street? Think.

'You goin' straight home, Mr Castle?' Mrs Walls asks.

'Yes, Mrs Walls.'

'Good.'

Yes, and the fellow, the one from Samaria, put the wounded man on his beast and carried him to the inn and told the innkeeper to keep him well and put the charge incurred on his account. Think. Nice cathedral here. Stout and holy-looking, but where is God? Mrs Walls told the boy to pray. Pray, boy. I have seen the savages naked like fish – remember Mr Reggie said that, and how he saw them civilized too; and Lester said that the criminals have their own law. Think 'fore you put yourself in this; said you'd help but you have no money for lawyer either, no strings in government or in the Party, you don't know one senator personally. Think.

Divine and sweet, an idea comes. He twirls it about his brain.

'I-have-an-idea,' he says.

'An idea?'

'Do you think the people of Webber Street will help, Mrs Walls?'

'You don't know them people, son.'

'What you think?'

'Give them something, they will take; sell them something, they will buy: but, help, I don't know.'

'I could make a try.'

'God be with you. If the position wasn't so bad, I would tell you don't worry with the people. They don't care about anybody. But the position so bad, I will try anything… An' tomorrow when I go to see that boy he'll want to know what is the position about a lawyer, Lawd Gawd, don't know what to say.'

Webber Street. Like soldier ants, the people. Tesses by the corner stare and pick their teeth with matchsticks. Jukebox in the snackette blares.

'I'll see you later, Mrs Walls,' Walter says in front of Mrs Walls's apartment door.

'All right, Mr Castle.' She turns and fits the door key into her front door.


Walter mounts the steps. When he reaches his door, he knocks.

On the other side of the door, his wife asks, 'Walter?'

She unlocks the door and he enters.

'Afternoon, Stephanie.'

'Afternoon, darling. How was it?'

'Not so good.'

'Daddy's inside. He was just about to leave. We were talkin' about it.'

'Let me go and see him.' He walks into the living-room and his wife follows.

'Good day, Mr Sears,' he says.

'How're you, boy?' Mr Sears says, standing to shake hands.

'All right,' Walter says. They both sit.

'I hear you're a lawyer,' Mr Sears says, smiling.

'Oh no. I only went with the boy's mother. She lives downstairs, you know.'

'How was it?'

Before Walter can answer, his wife asks, 'Is the boy guilty?'

'He says he wasn't there. Says the police picked him up because he was with the other fellows.'

'See what I told you this morning. The boy isn't guilty. And I told you, Daddy.'

'Yes, you said the boy wasn't guilty. What's the mother doing?'

'Praying, I think. The trouble's to get a good lawyer.'

'They don't have any money, you know,' Stephanie says.

'That's bad,' Mr Sears says. 'Bad.'

'How much does a lawyer take on a case like this?' Stephanie asks.

'I have no idea,' Walter says.

'Me neither. But I'm sure it's a nice sum,' Mr Sears says.

'I guess it would be. Murder. I'm sorry for poor Mrs Walls,' Stephanie says.

'Look, I was thinking,' Mr Sears says. 'If he wasn't there, it's simple. All that's necessary is for the other fellows who were there to say that he wasn't there.'

'Perhaps they won't be too keen saying that,' Walter says.

'Well, well,' Mr Sears says, disappointment in his tone.

'But I have to help. I promised.'

'What can you do, Walter? We have no money either.'

'You promised?' Stephanie asks, flashing a look at Walter.

'I have an idea.'

'I'd like to hear it,' Mr Sears says.

'It concerns the people.'

'Now you're going to get yourself mixed up with these people,' Stephanie says.

'When I told you about leaving this city, it was you who told me that I cannot get away from people. Well, darling, you're right. If you want to live and life is to mean something, you must be involved with people.'

'You know I didn't mean these people, Walter.'

'These people, Stephanie, are the people around us. They are the people we know and have to know. You don't remember that Mrs Walls pulled you in from those hooligans and helped you when you were having the baby?'

'I remember, but I didn't mean that you had to live among these people and get yourself involved with them,' the woman says. 'And what can you do?'

'I'm getting involved with them as of now,' Walter says.

'So you're staying?' Mr Sears says.

Walter looks at Stephanie.

'Yes, she told me how you wanted to leave. If you're not going, I think it's sensible. You don't have to talk of it. Yes, but you were talking about this idea of yours.'

'As I was saying,' Walter says, 'it involves the people of Webber Street. If they can contribute to a fund to provide a lawyer for this boy, I think that would solve the problem.'

'You think they will?' Stephanie says.

'I have know these people to make contributions towards hurricane relief in the other islands and many of them spend large sums on costumes for carnival. I think if they're made to understand that they have a personal responsibility in this matter, they will be prepared to help the boy. But I guess the important thing is how to go about interesting them in the idea,' Walter says.

Mr Sears says, 'You have a good idea there, Walter. If this thing is properly handled, it can achieve much more than you imagine.'

'If it is properly handled,' Stephanie says. 'If.'

'Yes, *if*. If you can get across to the people, then I think you will have started something much bigger than a fund for providing a lawyer for a boy accused of murder. Of course, it won't be easy, but if you can do it… if you can do it…'

'It can be done,' Walter says.

'Yes, it can be done,' Mr Sears says. 'What is needed in the national community is a sense of responsibility. We are just a bunch of individuals. That is bad. We must develop a sense of pride in our community. We must feel grand when we accomplish something worthwhile and we must feel shame when a mean act is done in our community. In everything, we must feel personally affected. We must be involved. We can only be involved when we participate. Right now you are participating. That is good. That is the only way a community spirit can be brought out. And if you can get the people of this area to contribute, that in itself would be a form of participation. And I think participation is the fundamental pillar upon which to build a strong nation. If people are to save themselves, they must be interested in themselves. Interested, not in a narrow, personal way, but interested in the community as a whole. You understand me, Walter?'

'I understand.'

'Just the other day I heard one of the ministers saying that this land is as much the next man's as it is his; he was saying nothing new. The calypsonian said that: "This is your land and also is my land; this is your place and also is my place." That is what we must think. That is what we must live. So you see the whole range of possibilities your suggestion gives rise to. But, as you say, it must be well handled,' Mr Sears says.

'This is a big thing I put my hand to,' Walter says.

'Yes, quite big,' Mr Sears says. 'And you must be commended.'

'Don't commend me as yet,' Walter says. 'I'm not sure that the people will be interested. Do you have any ideas, Mr Sears?'

'Well, first, I think you shouldn't try to do this thing alone. Include people. As many as possible. And second, when you are planning, work with a small committee. That way you do more work and you do it faster. The idea is good. If the people go for it, they will not only be doing the boy a favour, they will be doing themselves the biggest favour that they have yet done. Look,' Mr Sears says, glancing at his watch, 'I hadn't intended to remain here so long. But you know how I like to talk on these subjects. I always get carried away. Anyhow, it's time for me to leave.'

Mr Sears rises.

Walter rises. 'Thanks for your advice, Mr Sears.'

'I only hope it's of value, really.'

'It will be.'

'I hope so. I must go now.'

'You leaving, Daddy?'

'Yes, dear. Good evenin', Walter. And you must tell me how this thing turns out, you hear?'

'All right, Mr Sears.'

'Good evenin', Daddy.'

Now his father-in-law leaves, and his wife is smiling.

'What are you smilin' about?'

'I must be happy,' she says, her smile broadening.

'Hey! You're getting beautiful,' he says.

'In this old dress? With this big belly?'

'Come.'

She walks over to where he is standing.

'Now, will you please allow me to plant a kiss on your – er – chin.' He kisses her, with exaggerated gentleness.

'Thank you, sir. And now, will you please kiss me as a wife should be kissed.'

'And how should a wife be kissed?'

'A wife should be kissed like this. First, you hold her like this and then she holds you like this. No. Bring your head over here. Yes. And then – Walter?'

'Darling?'

'I love you.'

'Wonderful.'

'No, I mean it. I love you.'

'Kiss me.'

She lifts her lips and closes her eyes in anticipation.

'Wait, I hear something,' the man says. 'Someone's knocking on the door. You hear it?'

'Yes. Well, kiss me before you go.'

He smacks her hurriedly and they go to the door together. It is Walter's brother Andrew in his police uniform.

'Andrew!'

'Hello, Walter… Stephanie.'

'Come in. What's up?'

Andrew steps inside. 'I rang your office.'

'What they said?'

'Said you didn't come out this morning. Sick?'

'I wasn't feeling so good when I got up.'

'Feelin' better now?'

'Yes. Siddown, Andrew.'

'What about the baby, Stephanie?'

'She's all right. Inside sleeping. What about the wife and your little one?'

'Fine, Stephanie. Fine.'

'You know about the murder, Andrew?' Walter asks.

'The one in town last night? Some teenagers were involved, eh?'

'Yes.'

'Yes, I heard about that case. I understand the fellow who got it is a homo. He got into some kinda argument with this boy an' the others came up an' beat 'im up. You know how it is with these homos. They try to encourage these boys. Well, he got a good beating. What happen? Some of the boys involved from around here?'

'Yes. There's a boy who lives right on the second floor,' Walter says.

Andrew shakes his head sadly. 'When you intend to move from this area, Walter? This place not good, you know… How long you livin' here now?'

'How long we living here, Stephanie?'

'Three years and some months,' she says.

'Three years, Andrew. But I'm not thinking of moving now.'

'Suit yourself, but I know this isn't a nice area.'

'The boy I was telling you about,' Walter says, 'the boy on the second floor: I went to see him this morning, went with his mother. He isn't guilty. Says he wasn't there.'

'Alla them say the same thing. Who will believe that?'

'I believe.'

'How you know?'

'I spoke to him.'

'Well, if he's innocent he'll get off. Trinidad is one place they don't hang innocent people. I come here this morning to tell you something too.'

'Well, I'm listening,' Walter says.

'I don't know how to begin,' Andrew says. 'All the time I sit down here, I've been thinking of a way to tell you.'

'Well, tell me. You don't have to look for a special way.'

'Is about Chris.'

'What happen to Chris?'

'He done a foolish thing.'

'What happen? What he did?'

'Chris stowaway.'

'Little Chris? Where to?'

'England. Five of them, but they catch them before they reach and they sending them back.'

'Chris!' Walter bends his head. 'You mean Chris, little Chris stowaway?'

'A little boy like that,' Stephanie says.

And now, they all fall silent.

'I'm damn sorry about it,' Andrew says.

'It's our fault,' Walter says. 'We didn't give him a thing. We just lived by ourselves, for ourselves. We gave him nothing.'

'I didn't think about it so. I did what I could,' Andrew says. 'I couldn't do more. And anyway, what did we have to give?'

'At least we could have given him guidance. We could have guided him.'

'I tried. He's a funny fellow to understand.'

'Well, I didn't try hard enough. We didn't try hard enough.'

'No good blaming yourself, Walter. These young fellows not like us. They don't listen.'

'They don't listen because we never give them nutten to listen to. We just want them to accept our way, our style, and when they don't, we say something's wrong with them. You tell Ma yet?'

'Not yet. Ma will be cut up like hell.'

'And Carol wouldn't like it.'

'Don't take it on too hard. Nothing's wrong with him. He's on his way back, safe.'

'What I am thinking is how we didn't give him nutten,' Walter says. 'We gave him nutten, so he had to run away. He didn't feel wanted, so he had to strike out on his own.'

'He didn't kill anybody,' Andrew says. 'It coulda been worse.'

'That's true, but...'

'Well, we can't do a thing about that now. And we still have a chance to help when he returns this time.'

Walter sits, shaking his head. 'This is a helluva world.'

'Well, I just dropped by to tell you about Chris. I have to go on duty in a while.' Andrew stands.

'Wait, Andrew. I wanted to know who's a good lawyer.'

'For a murder case? What about Wattley?'

'Wattley?'

'Yes, he's one of the best. Some people say Fitzgerald, but I think Wattley's the best. But I don't know if you can pay him.'

'Expensive?'

'Very.'

'All right.'

'Well I'm moving,' Andrew says. 'Stephanie, I'm leaving. Keep well.'

'All right, Andrew.'

Walter walks with his brother to the door.

When he returns to the living-room, he sits. He says nothing. His wife, who had gone to the kitchen, returns and sets his lunch on the table.

'You're thinking about Chris?' the woman asks.

'He's such a little fellow to stowaway.'

'It sounds bad, eh? But these things happen.'

'Yes, these things happen. Stephanie.'

'Yes, Walter.'

'We'll keep our children together, eh?'

'Yes, darling.'

'I mean – If I should die, you'll try to keep them together, eh?'

'I will try, Walter. But sometimes children go away,' Stephanie says. 'They grow away and then go away.'

'The parent's duty is to prevent them from growing away. Is this growing away that sent me to this town when I was just a boy and is the same growing away that made little Chris stowaway.'

'Families not like they used to be, Walter.'

'Yes. That's why so many people are lost. That's why we have so many criminals, wanting to hit back, feeling to hit out at something. No family, nothing to belong to, no one to care and no one to care for.'

'We will keep ours together,' she says. 'But you'd better eat now, darling.'

'I almost forgot about lunch.'

He gets up and goes to the table.

'It's funny,' he says. 'Just yesterday I wanted to leave this place and go to the country. And now…'

'Now you want to join with the people of this street.'

'Funny, eh?'

'Yes.'

Now she sits and looks at him eat.

'What are you going to do about the lawyer for the boy now?' she asks.

'First I have to tell the people what I have in mind.'

'You'll have to do that at a meeting.'

'Yes. And it'll have to be a special meeting. We don't have much time.'

'You don't even know the people around here.'

'I know a few. I know Mr Cross and there are others who I don't know so well. There's Alpheus, the captain of the steel-band – '

'That's the boy with the motorcycle?'

'Yes. And Mr Woodley. He's some kind of official in the Party Group around here.'

223

'You know Mrs Roach? She's a nurse at the hospital, lives in the next building. Though she's a woman, she has good ideas about this kinda thing.'

'Good. Well, darling, we have enough to start with. And they can recommend others. Now, we'll have to hold that meeting tonight. The boy's case will go before the magistrate during the week and we have to know how the people react to the suggestion before we really know where we stand.'

'Walter, don't you think that people will say we're meddling in what doesn't concern us?'

'They might, but this does concern us. What we have to do is to make people realize that it concerns them also. This is not something that's happening in Japan; it's happening right here, understand, darling?'

'Yes, but will they understand?'

'That's the job, to make them understand. Now, you'll get in touch with Mrs Roach later and I'll see the others. Okay?'

'But what time and where?'

'Perhaps here. I'll discuss it with Mr Cross. But the meeting must be held tonight.' He begins to get up.

'Okay. You finish eating?'

'Yes. Can't eat more now. I'd better go and see Mr Cross.'

'All right. How do you feel?'

'Excited. Excited like a hen that has just laid an egg.'

'Hold yourself together,' the wife says.


So Walter holds himself together and goes downstairs and knocks on the door of Mr Cross's apartment.

'Come in,' Mr Cross calls.

He enters the room and Mr Cross has to remind him to close the door behind him.

'This radio is givin' me hell,' Mr Cross says, indicating the radio he is repairing, with a gesture. 'People turn an' twist, an' turn an' twist hell outa a radio trying to fix it, and after they finish spoil everything, they bring it to you in a rush and want you to fix it in a rush – the hell with that! I should be running a school of magic, not a radio repair shop. Looka this radio. You feel I could finish repair it this evening? The man bring it Saturday night an' he want it today. He don't care how many people have radios to fix; he want it today. And after I done finish bust my brains to get it ready for him, you know what goin' to happen? I goin' to see him next three months, an' he telling me how he was in a jam an' couldn't call for it before. Now, put it down an' don't fix it, next thing you know he coming knocking down the door. He want his radio. A tradesman always in some kinda jam with people. An' you know why, Castle? You can predict the weather, you can predict anything; but you can't predict what a human being will do. Siddown, Castle. I can see something on your mind.'

Walter lifts a radio cabinet off a chair, rests the cabinet on the floor and sits. 'Yes, Mr Cross, I have something on my mind. But though I come to tell you, I don't know where to begin.'

'Anywhere you begin is the beginning.' Now Mr Cross turns to look at him.

'You heard about the murder?' Walter asks.

'Everybody heard about the murder. When I heard about it, I say to myself, Castle was damn right to want to leave this jungle. This is no place for decent people to live in. Half-a-dozen boys involved in this thing an' four of them from around here. You want no more proof than that to know that something wrong, not only with the boys, but with the whole area, the whole Webber Street. You damn right to leave if is leave you leaving. I have my shop here, an' anyway, I old already and alone, otherwise I pack up and go too.'

'I've been thinking, Mr Cross.'

'That's good. People don't think in the city. They just hurry with the crowd. What've you been thinking?'

'About many things. About this city and this street and about the murder. You know I went to see one of the boys involved – Mrs Walls's son?'

'Yes.'

'Yes. And I was thinking about the young people, and the older people in this street, and about myself and where I stand in it all.'

'Where do you stand, Castle?'

'Right now, somewhere in the middle, I think.'

'I don't understand you. I thought you wanted to leave this place.'

225

'Well, I was thinking, Mr Cross, and I changed my mind.'

'Changed your mind?'

'Well, the long and short of it is that I want to help. I thought that maybe the people of Webber Street would also like to help the boys around here and themselves.'

'What you driving at, Castle? You not making sense.'

'Well, I think that the boys around here who commit crime are not alone to be blamed; that maybe we, the other citizens, never gave them anything.'

'What to give them? You tell them good evenin' sometimes and that they don't want to accept. They look at you, deaf. I know that they're not alone to be blamed, but what to do? Tell me exactly what you want to do, Castle.'

'I think that the community can do something about the boys involved in this murder case.'

'All the boys? Or just one boy?'

'As I think now, it will have to be all the boys.'

'Good. You want the community to do something for all the boys involved in the murder case.'

'Yes. I think that the factors of poverty, lack of jobs, general oppression, the attitude of more fortunate people, all contribute to push these young fellows to rebel, to want to hit out, to hurt someone, to want to make people shame and even to want to kill.'

'Well put, Castle, but I know all the facts. What you want to do is to ask the people to contribute in some way to help these boys in this case?'

'Look, Mr Cross, at the outset I had no idea that I would either be in this, or want to be in this, but I went to see one of the boys in the prison, and I thought that I was in some way responsible for what happened, not to that boy alone, but to all the boys in this area, because I have never done anything to assist them. So I thought that the people of this area should help this boy because his mother is poor and has no money for lawyer. Now that the question of other boys come up, I think we will have to assist all, if we assist one. I don't know what are the resources of the others, but all that is not so important at the moment. What I think we can do is to help get a lawyer for these boys.'

'You know what you saying, Castle? You know you're asking people to encourage these fellows in their crime?'

'You know that is not so, Mr Cross.'

'I know that, but that's what people will say. But go ahead, tell me how you hope to encourage people to do this thing.'

'Well, I came to you because I thought that you're someone who'd help.'

'Look, boy, I don't want to let you down, but maybe you came to the wrong man. I'm tired with these people. I'm here now fifteen years, was here before some of these buildings went up, and I tried to open a singing group. That fell through. Afterwards, I tried to interest them in opening a co-operative shop. No. They'll have nothing to do with that. Perhaps the only thing they'll join is the Party Group and that because of one man, the Prime Minister. I'm here fifteen years an' I know these people; and some of the children I knew as babies, and I am ashamed to see how they come. I thought when these houses went up, people will get a little dignity, think a little higher than the ground, but, Castle, take it from me: you can take a man off the ground, but you can't prevent him from looking down. Your idea is good, Castle. Good, but to tell you the truth, I'm tired – tired with these people.'

'I was hoping that you'd help, Mr Cross. My idea is really a raw, crude one, but I thought that you'd see the good points in it and try to push it across.'

'Boy, your idea is good, has good possibilities. It might work, but... but...'

'But what, Mr Cross? Perhaps the reason why you never got across to the people before is because the time was not ripe then.'

'You feel the time is ripe now?'

'Yes.'

'Castle, I say to myself and I say it in public, "Cross, you done with Webber Street." I livin' here fifteen years and I kinda accustomed with the people and the people accustomed to me, but I don't like it here. It's too exciting. Long ago was bottle an' stone; now is iron bolts an' home-made guns. I got only one foot. I've thought about moving, but I make my living here, and besides, where in Port of Spain I'll go? But I tell myself an' I tell

227

the people, "I finish with Webber Street." You young, you could try, you might be lucky, but me – Boy, you don't know.'

'You owe it to yourself, Mr Cross, and you even owe it to the people here, because you make a living by them. And Mr Cross, times changin'. The attitudes of people changin'.'

'I can tell you about these people, boy. They might say they changing, they might look like they changing, but I know them. They not changing one bit. I tell you I here fifteen years now and I tried to open a singing group once; they say I want their daughters, and now I live to see the same daughters whoring on the street. I tried to interest them in a co-operative shop and they thought I wanted their money. Now not one of them have the smallest share in any business around here.'

'You have to put all that behind you, Mr Cross. But if you don't want to help, well…'

'Listen, Castle, you know what people will say? They'll say, if these young boys playing robust, let them stand their grind. Let them meet the hangman if is that they want. Maybe that will stop some of the crime in this place.'

'People will say anything, Mr Cross. But the thing is that the people will be helping themselves. You know that.'

Mr Cross turns on his crutches. 'I don't want to make a fool of myself, Castle.'

'You won't be making a fool of yourself, Mr Cross.'

'Man, I know these people.'

'You won't be making a fool of yourself, Mr Cross.'

'And anyway, this thing involves plenty work – plenty hard work. And what thanks these people have? I had dealings with these people, boy. I tired with them. Try somebody else. Who else you had in mind?'

'Well… Mr Woodley, the secretary of the Party Group, and Alpheus, the captain of the steel-band, and Mrs Roach. I thought you would get the others.'

'I sorry, Castle. Better try one of the others. Try Woodley; at least he will be getting something out of this. Yes, you'd better try Woodley. I give up.'

'Mr Cross.'

'I sorry, Castle.'

Walter rises tiredly from the chair. He forces a smile on his lips.

'All right, Castle,' Mr Cross says, without looking at him.

So Walter leaves the room, and does not forget, this time, to shut the door behind him.

With the silly smile etched on his face, he walks.

Failure like a jagged-edged knife twists teeth into his chest. Frustration chases anger down the streets of his mind. It is only left for him to weep – weep for the times and for the people of Webber Street; weep for himself and his dream. Weep, for one ageing man has words and no deeds, and another is stiffened by pride and galled by previous failures; and young women are prostitutes before their breasts are fully formed, and the young men are angry and violent, angry at street corners, ready to stick a knife in God's ribs. And a mother prays, and a son knows that he must hope; and in this city, in this island, the gods are falling and there is nothing for the young people to look up to – nothing for anyone to look up to. The leading citizens are wrapped in their self-centredness, and life is the extension of the individual's personality – a sort of emotional masturbation; and love is something that you can crease and slip into your wallet; and pride is something that on Sunday morning you wash with a garden hose and shine, having polished. It is not only unemployment and shanty-towns and overcrowded houses, not so much crimes of violence and sex; it is that there is nothing decent and valuable to hold on to. Out of the land has come asphalt and oil; from the bosom of the peasant the bongo and the limbo have come, and a wealth of song; from the tesses the calypso and the steel-band. But out of the others, the leading citizens, the good and the rich and the educated folk, what has come?

Step step step, Walter walks, slowly tiredly. And what has come out of him? What has he contributed? His own brother stowed away to England. And didn't he, just a day or so ago, want to leave Webber Street and run, run away to the country? And what would he do now? Turn again into the lane of aloneness?

He turns and mounts the steps leading up to where he lives. Mud thick and deep, frustration, weighs down his shoes; he walks in a fog. He doesn't know the answers to his questions.

He walks into the living-room. His wife looks up as he enters; her expression is a question.

He lets himself into a chair.

'You saw Mr Cross?'

He nods.

'And what did you-all decide?'

Walter looks at her, shakes his head and smiles crookedly.

'What is it?'

'I am a fool,' he says. 'A damn big stupid fool.'

'What did Mr Cross say?'

So he tells her everything, and she doesn't interrupt him at all.

'You know, I told Mrs Roach,' Stephanie says. 'She wanted to know where we'd keep the meeting, and because I think you said something about keeping it here, I told her here at seven tonight.'

'Well, you'll have to tell her it's cancelled.'

'But, Walter, how will it look?'

'I don't know. Tell her, and she won't bother to come.'

'You mean I have to go now and tell her the thing's off?'

'She'll understand. Tell her. Tell her Mr Cross won't have anything to do with it.'

'Then, Walter, maybe we'd better do without Mr Cross, what we can.'

'You crazy? I don't know these people well. They'll wonder what I'm doing this thing for. And besides, I can't be chairman. I can't talk.'

'How you mean, you can't talk?'

'You know what I mean. We'll have to scrap the whole thing. Too bad.'

'Because of one man? No.'

'Be reasonable, Stephanie. I tell you I alone can't do it.'

'And what we'll tell Mrs Walls now?'

'Tell her. Look, Stephanie, you know I alone can't do this thing.'

'You can try, Walter. And what about you? What about us? We going to pull out and go back and live in the country now? We going to leave Webber now? I thought you said you'd remain and – '

'Look, if you want I'll remain here and go back to the job. Nothing would worry me. I'll work hard and kiss the boss arse and get through. I had a nice dream… Maybe it's good it happen so. Now I know what I have to do.'

'You know you don't mean that, Walter. You know you can't stand that. Maybe you'll go back to work; and maybe you'll try to get through. But for how long? How long before you come again and say again that you want us to pack up and get out and go and live somewhere in the country?'

'You have to be hard in the world. Hard and sharp. And that's how I'll be.'

'At least Mr Cross tried a couple times before he gave up. And poor Mrs Walls depending on you so much. Only you she depending on. And the boy in jail? Poor innocent boy.'

'How you so sure he innocent?'

'You self told me so.'

'Stephanie – '

'Wait. Listen! A motorbike. I sure that's Alpheus coming in.'

'Why don't you just forget everything? Mrs Walls will have to understand.'

'Why you don't go and talk to Alpheus?'

'And what can he do?'

'Talk to him. You don't know. Maybe something will crop up. Try. That's what *you* have to do.'

'You doing as if I alone could change this city. As if I alone could change the world.'

'Walter, Alpheus downstairs. You could go and talk to him. I'll call him for you,' she says, going towards the window.

'You know, without Mr Cross the whole thing dead.'

'I'm calling the boy, eh, Walter.'

'Go ahead if you think it will do any good.'

'Just a little patience, darling. You can't give up at the first difficulty.'

'Okay.'

Stephanie lifts the curtain at the window, pushes her head out, looks downstairs and calls out to Alpheus. She tells him that Walter is coming to speak to him.

'The boy is waiting,' Stephanie says, turning from the window.

'I'll go and talk to him,' Walter says.

Downstairs, he meets Alpheus.

'You wanted to see me, Mr Castle?'

'Can spare a few minutes?'

'Yes.'

'It's about this thing with these boys.'

'The killing, you mean?'

'Yes.'

The young man called Alpheus bends his head.

'I was thinking maybe we could help these boys, Alpheus.'

'You think we can help them?' Alpheus asks, speaking slowly and raising his eyes to Walter's.

'I was thinking. I don't know. I'm not sure.'

'If you know how these boys make me shame, Mr Castle. I'm the captain of the steel-band, and as soon as people hear these boys involved, they say, "The steel-band boys kill a man." But mosta the steel-band tesses quiet. They don't look for noise unless somebody trouble them. We was bad. But the young tesses now hot like pepper. They crazy. They lookin' for kicks. They lookin' for devil-play. They don't know what they lookin' for. Trouble! They always in trouble, 'cause trouble's the easiest thing to find. Older tesses talk to them. Tesses who do time tired tell them that this badjohn business don't pay. They don't understand. Sometimes one fella stop playin' the fool an' settle down quiet. That's the signal for three-four young tesses to come up an' try to take his place in the criminal world. I don't know what to say. Now they gone and kill a man. I went to see them. Alla them in jail bawlin'. You's a badjohn but you bawlin'. Badjohn don't cry. They realize too late. I don't know what to say. You talk to them an' like is not them you talkin' to.'

'I was thinking maybe if the people of the area assist in providing a lawyer for them…'

'People! Lawyer! What you want to do that for?'

'All of us live around here,' Walter says. 'People should help the boys, try to keep them out of trouble. Now they get in trouble, it not too late. We can still make a start. If the boys know the people willing to help them, then maybe they'll try to do better.'

'Why the people must help them?'

'Well, you see, we live in a community. People should live together in a community. They should participate in community life. They should help. This is a start. We don't want the boys to feel that every time they in trouble like this we going to agree with them. We'll try to help. But they have to help themselves too. This is only a beginning.'

'Well, it will be a good thing if people could live like human beings in this place.'

'And you feel providing the lawyer is a good start? Yes, Mr Castle. I'll tell the boys about it.'

'I don't know how it will work now,' Walter says. 'I spoke to Mr Cross a while ago. He wasn't really keen.'

'Mr Cross? But Mr Cross – '

'You see, Alpheus, Mr Cross has been trying to do one thing or another in this place for a long time. He never got co-operation.'

'So he fed-up now?'

'I guess so. And then, he believes that the people not inter-ested.'

'You mean if he know that the people interested in this thing he'd – ?'

'I think so. And he's a good man to have on it.'

'Mr Cross is a good man.'

'And what you think about the idea?'

'Well, I support it. You think if I talk to Mr Cross – ?'

'I don't know. Maybe. It will have to be quick, though. My wife told Mrs Roach that there'll be a meeting at my place at seven tonight. It'll have to be quick. I don't know what the three of us can do. I was hoping that Mr Cross would bring Mr Woodley.'

'I'll talk to Mr Cross. You want me to bring the tesses to hear for themselves?'

'Not now. If the meeting comes off and we agree on this lawyer business, then we'll have another big meeting and everybody will be invited. At the moment we must keep the group small. And we want ideas. You'll come?'

'I'll come. And I'll speak to Mr Cross. And maybe he'll speak to Mr Woodley. Seven?'

'Yes, Alpheus.'

'All right, Mr Castle.'

So Walter leaves the young man and returns to his apartment and tells his wife what has taken place. She sets about fixing the furniture for the guests that she hopes will come later in the evening. Walter looks at her, out the corners of his eyes, and wonders if much of her preparation will not be in vain. But it isn't long to wait. Seven o'clock will come soon enough. It will come, and with it another crisis or… Or what? What will come out of the meeting, even if it takes place?

## 13

Walter sits on a chair in a corner, Stephanie sits on a chair near a window, Mrs Roach sits in the middle of the room. She looks at her watch.

'Oh my! Look at the time,' she says.

Stephanie says, 'We Trinidadians can never be punctual.' She stands and looks through the window for the umpteenth time. Nothing.

'I cawn't bear to be late,' Mrs Roach says.

'I wish more of us were like you, Mrs Roach.'

'Did they say... I mean, are you sure they're coming, Mr Castle?'

Before Walter can answer, Stephanie says, 'I'm sure they'll come. Walter spoke to Alpheus just this evening.'

'But it's twenty-five minutes after.'

'Twenty-five minutes,' Walter says.

'Maybe something happened,' Stephanie says. 'Well, let's wait five-ten minutes more, and if they don't come we'll call it off for the night.'

'But I cawn't understand them. I mean, this matter is important,' Mrs Roach says.

'Ten minutes, Mrs Roach,' Stephanie says.

'All right.'

Long seconds tick-tick slowly by.

Mrs Roach says, 'But it was awful wasn't it, Mrs Castle?'

'Yes.'

'Murder is an awful thing... And so young.'

Now there is the sound of a motorcycle in the street below.

'Alpheus!' Stephanie exclaims, and looks through the window.

The motorcycle swings into the yard.

Mrs Roach sighs, removes her spectacles, squints, and polishes the lens with a small lace handkerchief. '*It's time*,' she says.

Walter stands.

'I think everything's prepared for them,' Stephanie says.

Walter goes across to the door.

'Sorry we're late,' Mr Cross says.

'It's all right, Mr Cross.'

'Woodley,' Mr Woodley says, extending his right hand.

'Castle,' Walter says. 'Come right in. Come in, Alpheus.'

The men walk into the living-room.

Walter performs the necessary introductions.

'Is everyone here?' Mr Cross says.

'Yes, everyone,' Walter answers.

'Good. We can begin.'

'You sit there Mr Cross. Right there.'

'Most comfortable chairman in the world,' Mr Cross says, putting aside his crutches and sinking into the chair.

'Ladies and gentlemen,' he announces, bringing to an end the little smattering of conversations in the room. 'Ladies and gentlemen, all of you have been told that the chief reason for this little meeting is the – er – formulation of plans for providing a lawyer for the defence of certain young men of our area involved in that unfortunate case in which a man was beaten to death on Sunday night – last night – er.

'I understand that one of the boys claims that he's innocent – er – innocent. That is not the most important consideration here tonight. Even if they are all guilty – I am using the term guilty quite loosely – I think we should still want to make this effort on their behalf. For to my mind, they are nothing more than the victims of our society, if we can use the term society to mean the... the individuals who tenant these buildings of Webber Street. And I think that the act for which these unfortunate youths now stand accused could more rightly be laid at our doorsteps. It is the society, or pseudo-society of this island, and more directly of this Webber Street, which faces the accusation of murder.

'I know we can enumerate many factors which contribute to

crime in the area: poverty, lack of employment, and other factors over which we have no direct control. But what about broken homes? And lack of parental control? And poor use of leisure-time? What about a complete absence of example? And an absence of discipline? And a falling away from religion? And a lack of ideals to which the young people can aspire? There is no meaning to living here. There is no God here.

'We have direct control over most of these factors. So notwith-standing the fact that we can and do blame unemployment and poverty, we must take the lion's share of the blame. The trouble with us, ladies and gentlemen, is that we do not really live as a community. We do not have the good of the community in which we live at heart. The trouble is that we are too self-centred, too selfish. Instead of trying to better our environment, we think of leaving it. Every day you hear people saying, "I'm going to leave Webber Street... Port of Spain... Trinidad." We think of leaving instead of trying to improve. And you know what happens? Very often people find that for one reason or another they cannot move. Five years, ten years, fifteen years afterwards, they're still at the same place, still wanting to move. Only now, conditions have worsened because we never tried to do anything about improving them. We think of what the community can do for us and not of what we can do for the community. And this has been our downfall in this area, and perhaps the downfall of many other areas here and abroad.

'Notice! We lived here in barrack rooms, and there was crime. We left the barrack rooms and came to live in three-storeyed tenement buildings, and there is more crime. Why? The build-ings have changed, but the approach of the people hasn't changed. The buildings have expanded, but not our minds. We are too concerned with what we think are our own interests. And what are our own interests? If we would look, we would see. If we would think, we would realize that our interests must be closely bound up with the interests of the community. But we do not look and we think too narrowly.

'If this area had produced doctors instead of gangsters and schoolteachers instead of prostitutes, we would be rightfully proud. But we have not produced doctors and we have produced few schoolteachers, so we are ashamed of the community. For deep within us we know and feel that in some way we have been responsible. Now, we must face that responsibility. It is time.

'As I said, the first consideration is the provision of a lawyer for these boys. The object is not to prove them innocent or to condemn them. The real object is to set in motion a force of community consciousness and community participation which in time will solve, if not all, at least the majority of our ills. If the killing of the man has been a tragedy, let us turn the tragedy into a vehicle that will carry us to victory over crime and vice.

'I have spoken too long, perhaps, but I wanted to express my own sentiments. I welcome your suggestions now.'

Good so far, Walter thinks. Now, watch.

'You want to say something, Mrs Roach?' Mr Cross says.

'Well, first, I think we should have someone taking note of the suggestions which might be made.'

'What about you, Mr Woodley? Would you care to – er – ?'

'I don't mind.'

'Good. We can continue. Mrs Roach… No. You needn't stand. All this is quite informal, you know.'

Mrs Roach swallows, perhaps to tune her voice to the correct key. 'Well,' she says, 'actually this is the first time I've been called a murderer to my face. And I can tell you it's quite an experience. But Mr Cross brought out the points so – you know – so very clearly that we have no alternative other than to agree. I can tell you that I for one am a hundred per cent behind the idea of an improved community consciousness and it is true that we should think more of what we can do for the community than of what the community can do for us. I know many of the women in this area through my profession of nursing, and I feel sure if we hold a meeting and invite the people and Mr Cross tells them exactly what he told us, they will listen and be convinced that the time is ripe for each and every one to make a contribution. I would like to suggest that we keep a meeting as soon as possible and invite the people, and secondly that we form an organization whose object would be the general improvement of Webber Street, with the emphasis on prevention of crime. I think if the young men can find important and valuable things to do with their leisure-time, they would keep off the streets. With respect to the lawyer for the boys, I think the idea is a good one and I support it because this endeavour will bring us closer as a community. I will suggest that we ask the people to contribute. I know that we're not rich in this area, but we are not so poor as to be unable to do this. That is all I want to – have to – say at this moment, thank you.'

'You see, ladies and gentlemen, how we are moving forward. Thank you, Mrs Roach,' Mr Cross says.

'If I may be permitted,' Mr Woodley says, 'I prefer to stand.'

'By all means, Mr Woodley – er – if you wish the exercise,' Mr Cross says. 'Go ahead and – er – stand.'

Mr Woodley is a short, yellow man. He stands.

'First, I want to say that the Party Group in this area, of which I am secretary, has been alarmed at the increase in crime. I have personally given the matter some study and have found that there are a few basic factors which are responsible. But these factors give rise to many secondary factors, one factor leading to another. It is a vicious circle. You see my argument. And although it is more comforting to blame circumstances, it all has to come back to the individual in the end. Two men might find themselves in the same unhappy circumstances, but one man drinks and the other prays. It is the moral fibre of the individual. The problem is with the individual. You follow me?

'How do we make the individual a good citizen? The good citizen is responsible. Responsible both to himself and to society. What I mean is, you must realize that you affect others with your actions. Since you do, it is obviously better that you affect them favourably. Yet we find this lack of personal responsibility. And we find this lack of morality. Governments are blamed. We can and should expect a government to provide a proper economic and political climate. But it is too much to ask a government to provide a moral climate as well. Morality is a personal matter. The trouble is that we confuse morality with economy. We tend to measure morality in dollars and cents. We feel that morality, like so many of the goods of the world, is controlled by the rich; and that the poor can do without it. No one can do without it.

'Colonialism, it has been repeated, has been the cause of a great number of our ills. With colonialism, not only was our economy subject to foreign control, but so were our minds. We evaluated ourselves for very little. And perhaps because of the poor evaluation of self, we tend to value others even less. A human being is not simply a complex animal. A human being is a divine being, a beautiful and sacred achievement. Here again, much as I would like not to do so, I must give colonialism its fair share of the blame. But attaching blame, though useful, is not solving the problems. I am the first to agree that these need to be solved before crime is eradicated. But of the problems, I think the most important is the individual's approach. We must do something. We must find something to look up to. Something outside of self, something bigger than self. I am in agreement with this proposal here tonight, not only because it will cause the community to sleep easier, but because I believe that with the proper guidance and direction those who are now potential criminals will turn from crime. It is as true of governments as it is of crime – the community gets the type of criminals it deserves. Until we become really involved in the community and think beyond ourselves, we will continue to have this terrible criminal situation here.

'This is a very small meeting. I note that we are all agreed upon the existence of the problem and on its urgent nature. I am one hundred per cent in agreement with the suggestions. One of the first things we must press for, after this matter of the lawyer for the boys is dealt with, is the provision of a community centre to serve the area.

'Ladies and gentlemen, if I go on, I will merely develop the points that I've tried to make. But I could not resist the temptation to try to state some of the feelings that I've held about crime in this area for such a long time. Before I take my seat, I must thank Mr Castle for taking the initiative in this matter and for inviting me here so that I might make my contribution. Thank you.'

Now Mr Woodley is pausing, as if he expects applause before he takes his seat.

'Thank you, Mr Woodley,' Mr Cross says. 'Thank you.'

Alpheus clears his throat and looks around.

'Mr – er – Alpheus,' Mr Cross says. 'Yes – er you – er…?'

'I mean,' says Alpheus, 'that I'm very pleased over all this. I mean about the efforts to help the tesses generally. I can tell you that most of the tesses are sensitive to help. They want to know that you're serious, that you really want to help them, not just to show off for the newspapers or something. So I think if you are planning something for them, it shouldn't be something too easy. You know? It shouldn't be something too hard, either. It should involve a certain degree of challenge. Dare them to do something and they'll want to do it. And it will have greater value for them. Mosta the tesses own nothing. I mean nothing. Most people have families and so on, most tesses have nothing. You have to make them realize that they belong to something, somewhere. They have to know that they're a real part of the community. You have to make them know that, else nothing you do will be really successful.

'I mean – er – tesses play football, cricket and games, you know. And tesses play carnival and beat pan. But mosta the people around here don't go and watch the tesses play anything and they leave them here, some of them, and go and play carnival with another band. I mean, that more than anything else shows the tesses that people aren't interested in them. If you could go and watch the tesses play football or cricket sometimes and cheer them on, support them. And if for carnival you play with our band, then the tesses know that you trust them and you are behind them. I mean, they'll get a greater sense of belonging. They'll know you're behind them when you're supporting them. Then you put the responsibility upon them not to let you down. They'll think twice before they commit an act.

'You can't do anything for the tesses until and unless you accept them. That's the only way. And the trouble is that you can't fool them. They're so sensitive about belonging that you can't just say we accept you, boys, and expect that to be all. They have to realize that you accept them. So you have to show them you do. They'll know if you accept them when you accept them. Anything less than acceptance is not going to work. This is my opinion. And I want to support the business about getting the lawyer for the tesses. I will tell the boys and ask them to make what contributions they can. I will also tell them about the meeting when it is decided to have it. And thanks for inviting me tonight.'

So Alpheus settles back in his chair, and Walter knows that it's his turn now. Christ! I'm shaking all over, he thinks. Like a leaf, I'm shaking. Knees too. My knees are like when I had the fever, that time when Stephanie and I planned to go to the dance. Know what it is: I have too much to say. In such a short time I've discovered so much and I want to relate everything. When I had the idea about the lawyer, I really had no idea that it would trigger off such a movement. Better begin and say anything that comes into your head. Read that outa a book once. Say anything that comes into your head and forget that the occasion is important.

'Mr Castle is to a great extent responsible for this meeting,' Mr Cross says. 'He exemplifies the spirit which must prevail if we are to get any place with this undertaking. I was ready to give up when he approached me on the matter and convinced me that it is necessary to participate in the affairs of one's community. And now you will all want to hear what Mr Castle has to say on the matter. Er – Mr Castle.'

'Ladies and gentlemen,' Walter says, 'I am very pleased to see the way in which you have responded to the idea...' Nice. Keep it up. Goin' good. My voice. Gotta hold on to my voice. What is Stephanie looking at me like that for, making me so damn nervous. Hell... 'When I had the idea of the lawyer, I really had no idea that it would turn out to something like – I mean, a movement so full of promise. I have been a long time in and around the city and I have lived in the country and I think I have a fair idea of the way we on this island live... Just this morning I was remarking to myself that the gods have fallen in this city. I was saying that there is nothing to worship and nothing to look up to. I wanted to leave town. Leave this area of crime and uneasiness. I am glad now that my wife did not agree with me. And I am glad that I remained because I've discovered something.'

How do you explain that now? It isn't as if you discovered something new. Maybe you didn't really discover anything. Maybe you had it in you all the time. Maybe each one of us have it in us, only it's stifled by fear or greed, and then something happens and it comes out like a shoot from the dark earth.

'I've discovered – er – if I might use that word – discovered that there's no escape for man within himself. And I've learnt that freedom... I mean, if freedom is anything, if it is to mean anything, it must be used for some good purpose. What I mean is that you don't store it like money in the bank, you don't store it, you invest it and you invest it in others. You're a bird and you sing for you're free and you make others happy…

'Ladies and gentlemen, I cannot really express how I feel. I really would like to but you see,' Walter says, 'you see…' He stammers now, stretching his fingers as if he would hold some invisible thread in the air. Lord! A big man like you mumbling so. Can't get out what you want to say. Lord!

'You see, there is so much inside of me that I want to bring out and – ' he smiles, consciously – 'I don't seem to be able to. But to get back on the track, to be practical, I suggest that we expedite this matter of the lawyer immediately. We should try to hold the meeting with the other people of the area tomorrow, and I suggest that we contact the lawyer even before we see the people. We can explain the situation to him and ask him to hold on for a while until we meet the people and finalize the details. That's all, thank you.'

'Well, you have heard Mr Castle, and now, ladies and gentlemen,' Mr Cross says, looking at his wristwatch, 'it is still relatively early so perhaps we should see if we can do some more planning in a concrete way. Mr Castle suggested that we contact the lawyer even before we meet the people. What do you think of that?'

'You see, Mr Cross,' Walter says. 'I – er – made enquiries and I've been told that Mr Wattley is a good lawyer for this type of case. The boys go before the magistrate some time during the week, perhaps tomorrow, and although the people might eventually decide to assist, the assistance might come too late unless we contact the lawyer now. In any event I think we will be saving time.'

'But don't you think,' Mrs Roach says, 'that we might get a lawyer to do this case for free?'

'Interesting,' Mr Cross says. 'Mrs Roach suggests that we explore the possibilities of getting a lawyer to do the case for gratis. I don't really know if such altruism exists in the legal profession in this country, and my impression is that the object of this exercise is to rope the people in, to make them aware of their ability to contribute. And perhaps this freeness might defeat that purpose. You see…'

'I think the people should be asked to contribute. That is really the whole purpose of this meeting. We want to involve people in the affairs of the community,' Alpheus says.

Mr Woodley says, 'The exact position is that the case comes up quite early before the magistrate and we need a lawyer, but we have no money in hand. Therefore, I think we should contact the lawyer, as Mr Castle said, explain the situation to him, and I feel sure that he will take the case and wait until we have collected his fee from among ourselves.'

'Do you think you can contact Mr Wattley, Mr Woodley?' Mr Cross asks.

'I can do that.'

'Early tomorrow. You see, we don't know exactly when the case is going before the magistrate,' Mr Cross says. 'It might even go tomorrow.'

'Yes, I think tomorrow,' Alpheus says. 'There's some law that says an arrested man must be tried so many hours after arrest. I'm not sure, but it might be tomorrow.'

'Well, that settles that,' Mr Cross says. 'Mr Woodley will contact the lawyer tomorrow.'

'And will we have the meeting of the people tomorrow night?' Mrs Roach asks. 'I think we should have it then.'

'I am wondering,' Walter says, 'if Mr Woodley can use his good offices to get the school for the meeting. That would solve the problem of venue.'

'I can try. But I think the manager will want something in writing.'

'That will be arranged,' Mr Cross says.

'What about publicity?' Alpheus asks. 'We should do something to get people interested in what's going on. And to let them know too.'

'I don't know what people will say, what they'll think,' Mr Woodley says, 'but I think I can get something in the papers.'

'But, Mr Woodley, we can't worry with what people think now. We are trying to do something, that's what important,' Mrs Roach says.

'I'm glad you think so, Mrs Roach, but you know people.'

'I think it will be all right,' Mr Cross says. 'We must have publicity. If you can get something in the papers, Woodley, all right. What I am thinking of is some posters. We should have some posters.'

'I can see about the posters,' Alpheus says.

'I can help,' Mrs Roach says.

'I can make some too,' Mr Cross says.

'We forgot something,' Mrs Roach says. 'We forgot words for the posters. I think all the posters should have the same words.'

'We can settle that right now,' Mr Cross says. 'Can you suggest the words the posters should carry, Mrs Roach? It doesn't have to be elaborate. Something simple and to the point.'

'All right,' Mrs Roach says. 'What about: "Citizens of Webber Street, you are invited to attend a meeting tonight at the Webber Street school. Come and hear and discuss the problems of your area. This is most important." '

'That's all right,' Mr Cross says. 'Well, shall we adjourn until tomorrow? We all know what we have to do. And all of us must publicize this matter as much as possible. And yes, the article in the papers. That's on you too, Woodley.'

So the meeting is finished. One by one, the persons say good night and take their leave. First, Alpheus, then Mrs Roach, then Mr Woodley, and last of all, a smiling and satisfied Mr Cross.

'We might as well close up and go to bed now,' Stephanie says.

'Yes,' Walter says. 'I'll go and call Carol from downstairs.'

Now the man and his wife are in bed.

'Walter,' Stephanie says, softly.

'Yes.'

'You're not sleeping?'

'I'm not sleepy.'

'You thinking?'

'Yes.'

'About the boy?'

'Not that alone.'

'You thinking about this Webber Street and the plan you and Mr Cross and Mr Woodley and the rest of you have?'

'More than that.'

Silence.

'I'm thinking about how a man… About how it makes no sense a man thinking only of himself. And I'm thinking how a man never really knows himself. I mean, really knows what he's capable of. And how it is that a man is always discovering something new, and only when he discovers who he is he knows what life is, what life means.'

'That's what you were trying to say at the meeting?'

'Something like that.'

'Walter?'

'Mmmmm?'

'You think it will be a boy?'

'Yes.'

'You know I can feel him moving. Put your hand here. Put it here… You feel him?'

'No.'

'He don't want you to feel him. As soon as you put your hand he became quiet. Walter?'

'Mmmmm?'

'Why you think it's going to be a boy?'

'Because. Because it has to be a boy.'

'You think you'll want to go away again, Walter?'

'No. I don't think so.'

'Even if this thing doesn't work out?'

'It's going to work out.'

'Look! He's jumping again. Put your hand here.'

'Leave him alone. He doesn't want me to touch him.'

'Darling?'

'Darling.'

'I love you.'

'And I. I love you.'

'You'd better hold me. I can't fall asleep unless you hold me.'

'Yes, we'd better go to sleep. I have to go to work tomorrow.'

'Hold me tighter.'

'That'll be strangling you.'

'Strangle me, then.'

Now the wife settles into the husband's arms.

'All right now?' the man asks.

'Yes.'

This is Tuesday morning. This is the morning after. You know that morning when you awaken and hurry outside to look upon the ordinary day, expecting to see extraordinary change, and are disappointed. Yes, disappointed, for there are intricate ways about change and subtle ways about people, especially the thoughts which they people live by. These things do not change overnight. These things do not change with one meeting. Sometimes these things do not change after many, many meetings. Time, time, and more than time is necessary to bring about change in them. What can you see above the earth the morning after a seed is planted?

Clouds drift lightly and lazily across an almost blue sky over an awakened city; dogs trot on pavements; people walk, each individual in his own way, with his own familiar rhythm, with his own thoughts in his own brain; cars move down the street, engines rumbling, horns tooting; cyclists perched on bicycles pedal, ring bells, pull brakes, swing in here and swing out there and continue down the street; near a dustbin on Webber Street a cat devours a mouse.

The bandy-legged little man standing on the third-floor landing of the three-storeyed tenement building there on Webber Street is Walter Castle. He is just about to leave for work. Looking down and seeing the usual face of Webber Street staring back at him, he feels a little disappointed; not too disappointed, for he is a man. A man knows what hope is and he knows what is patience. He can wait. The woman standing next to him is his wife. She will speak now.

'You're leaving?'

'Yes, darling. And, sweets?'

'Yes.'

'I won't be home for lunch today.'

There is concern in her voice. 'Why? What're you going to eat?'

'I'll pick up a snack downtown. You see, I want to go down by the courthouse to hear what's happening with the case against those boys.'

'They go before the magistrate today?'

'Yes. Didn't you hear it over the radio?'

'Suppose the case finishes before lunchtime?'

'I can't help that. If you hear anything, phone me and let me know. I will only hear good news, so if the news is bad, don't waste your time. All right?'

'You think they'll commit Mrs Walls' son to the assizes?'

'I don't know what to think. Anything can happen.'

'You don't have confidence in the law, then? If the boy's innocent, they'll let him off.'

'I don't know. I don't know any longer.'

'You always say that a man should have confidence in the law.'

'Saying is one thing.'

'Well, I have confidence. If I telephone you, it'll be to say that Ruben is free.'

'Good for you. Come, lemme kiss you, I'm goin'.'

'All right.' She turns her lips towards his.

The man walks briskly down the steps. On the second-floor landing, he meets Mrs Walls who is now from seeing her daughters off to school.

'Good morning, Mrs Walls.'

'Good mornin', Mr Castle.'

'So it's today, eh, Mrs Walls?'

'Yes, today. I'm goin' to get ready right now to go down by the courthouse.'

'Well, I'm hoping for the best.'

'I pray and pray that everything will be all right,' the woman says.

'Don't be afraid, everything will be all right.'

'You goin' to come to hear the case too?'

'I have to go to work, Mrs Walls, but I'll pass around there at lunchtime to hear what is what.'

'I wonder what Ruben thinking now,' the woman says.

'He must be saying, thank God I have a mother,' the man says.

'Is my only son,' the woman says softly.

'I know. Don't be afraid, Mrs Walls. Keep courage.'

'I'm not afraid,' she says, brightening, 'I cannot be afraid. So many people try to help me. It's not nice for me to feel afraid now. You help me a lot, Mr Castle.'

'That's all right, Mrs Walls. Mrs Walls, you will tell my wife what happen, as soon as you return?'

'I'll do that. God bless you, son.'

'I'm goin' now.'

'God smile on your way, Mr Castle, and make it bright.'

In the yard, Walter unlocks his bicycle, mounts it, steps on the pedal and is off to work. A little way down the street he meets Alpheus and some tesses sticking up posters for the meeting. Alpheus calls out to him.

'Mr Castle, you see we're at it,' Alpheus says.

'I see you. How's it?'

'Not bad. We have only four more.'

'What you think will be the turn-out at the meeting tonight?'

'Good. I can feel it.'

'Really think so?'

'I tell you I can feel it, sir. As fast as we put up a poster, we tell the people what's it about. They're interested.'

'And you think they'll come tonight?'

'I know it.'

'Good. You goin' to listen to the case this morning?'

'I want to do so. That's why I'm trying to get up these posters now.'

Walter remounts his cycle and continues to work, riding at a brisker pace now. When he arrives at the place, he parks his bicycle, walks into the office and goes quietly to his desk.

There are the usual faces, the usual helloes and grins. There is nothing here to indicate any change. Nothing in the office changed. It is he that has changed. It is he that is new, if anything is new. There is Mr Purcell in his office, Parris at his desk, Alford at his desk, Miss Regis at her typewriter, and Santo yawning at his table.

Siddown and do your work, Walter tells himself. So he sits and puts his mind to the work before him.

The morning crawls and crawls, there is no telephone call from Stephanie, so at lunchtime he hurries out of the office and rides down to St Vincent Street where courts are held. Just before he reaches the place, he comes upon Mr Cross walking up the street.

'Mr Cross.'

'Hi, Castle. I was just going to get something to eat. Court's adjourned for lunch.'

'You were at the courts this morning?'

'Yes, I was there. You sound anxious to hear about the case.'

'True, I am very anxious.'

'Rest easy. The case has not been called as yet. I should tell you, though, that Mr Woodley contacted the lawyer. He is quite willing to take the case. He said he didn't want any money.'

'But, Mr Cross…'

'We explained the situation to him and he agreed to take the money on condition that he offers it back to us when we have formed a proper organization. What you think of that? Good, eh?'

'Yes. Good. And what chances does he think the boys have?'

'He didn't say and I didn't ask. Some people don't like you to ask those kind of questions. He will do his best, he said. That is good enough for me.'

'You think he'll let them plead guilty to manslaughter?'

'Castle, I don't know. I didn't ask. You saw any of the posters?'

'Alpheus and the boys were putting some up while I was going to work.'

'I gave him some to put up for me, and Mrs Roach and some women put some up. And, Castle?'

'Yes, Mr Cross?'

'Woodley got the school for the meeting tonight.'

'So everything is all right, then?'

'Yes. It's left to the people now.'

'You said court's adjourned for lunch?'

'Yes.'

'Well, no sense sticking around here. I'd better grab a snack and get back to work.'

The afternoon drags lazily and without enthusiasm. Now, as the clock registers four o'clock, it is with a sense of relief that Walter hurries from the office. Home. Straight home, he goes.

In the yard he can see no one to give him news of the trial. He parks his bicycle downstairs, locks it, and takes off running up the steps. Now he stands breathless before the door of his apartment. He knocks one, two, three times, in quick succession.

'Who is it?' his wife asks politely on the other side of the door.

'Your husband. Open up.'

'Walter,' the wife says. 'You're early.'

With his eyes he asks, What happen with the case?

'I didn't hear a thing about the case, so I didn't phone,' she says. 'You didn't see Mrs Walls?'

'No. Is she back?'

'I don't think so. Come and eat your lunch. What did you eat today?'

'A sandwich. So no one who went to hear the case is back as yet?'

'No one. Come and eat.'

The woman puts his lunch on the table. Instead of going to the table, he goes over to the window and looks out.

'See anybody?' the wife asks.

'No one.'

'Come and eat. They'll come in a while.'

'All right,' he says, without turning from the window.

'Come and eat. Come before the food gets cold.'

'I'm not hungry,' he says, picking at the food.

'You're too anxious. Go ahead and eat. I'll go and look through the window. I'll tell you if anyone's coming.'

'Anyone?' he asks after a while.

'No. Just the usual people drifting in from work. You siddown and eat. I'll tell you.'

'I hear a car stopping. Who's it?'

'Nobody.'

'How you mean – nobody?'

'It's a girl downstairs and a man getting out a taxi. Eat. I'll tell you when they arrive.'

Then she says, 'I see Mrs Walls.'

He jumps up from the table. 'Alone?'

'No, Mr Cross is with her.'

'And the boy?'

'I don't see him.'

'Let me see,' he says, going to the window.

'Walter, you think…?'

'I don't know what to think,' he says, turning from the window.

'They're coming. Look, Mrs Walls is pointing up here. Looks like she's coming here. Mrs Walls doesn't look sad to me. They're coming up.'

'Oh Lord!'

'What you gettin' so excited about?'

'Who's excited? Who's excited?'

'All right, darling. They're coming up here.'

'Like they didn't release the boy after all,' Walter says.

'You can't be sure about that.'

'I don't know what to tell Mrs Walls.'

'You don't have to have anything special to tell her. You tried your best.'

'It is true what the boy said. They wouldn't believe him. He knew well what he was saying. When you're from a particular area, you start with marks against you. I was hoping they'd let him off.'

'Someone's knocking.'

'It's them. Open the door.'

His wife goes to the door.

'Good evenin', Mrs Castle,' Mrs Walls says. 'I just reach back.'

'Come in and siddown, Mrs Walls. Walter's inside.'

'I just reach back, Mr Castle. I had to come and tell you about the boy.'

'The boy? They didn't… they didn't…?'

Mrs Walls leans and kisses him on the cheek.

'No, Mr Castle, they didn't keep him. They let him off.'

'But I didn't see him come in the yard with you,' Stephanie says.

'He was right behind me. He's there talking to some of his friends. He's coming up here too. But I had to come to say thanks.'

'Siddown, Mrs Walls.'

Mrs Walls takes a seat. 'I don't have words, Mr Castle.'

'It is all right. What are words?'

'But I want words. I cannot speak without words.'

'Then don't speak, Mrs Walls. I understand.'

'That must be Ruben at the door now.'

'I'll see,' Stephanie says, and goes to the door.

'Good evenin', Mrs Castle.'

'Hello, Ruben. Come in.'

The boy walks inside. 'Mr Castle… Mr Castle I came to… I came to say… I came to say good evenin'.'

'Good evenin', Ruben.'

'And I want to say thank you. Thank you.'

'I understand. And what happened to the others?'

'They must stand trial for manslaughter in the higher courts.'

'Ruben.'

'Yes, sir?'

'I want to say something too.'

'Say it, Mr Castle. I promise to behave myself. Nothing like this will ever happen to me again.'

'Ruben, what I want to say is thanks. Thank you.'

'Thanks? Mr Castle, is I to thank you.'

'I must thank you too.'

'If you say so, Mr Castle. If you say so.'

'Yes, thank you. Stephanie?'

'Darling?'

'Do we have anything there to drink? Bring something.'

'I heard about the meeting last night and the one tonight,' Ruben says.

'Who told you?'

'The tesses.'

'They know about it?'

'Most of them.'

'And they will be coming?'

'Many of them.'

'Good. It's a fine night for a meeting.'

It is a fine night for a meeting. The sky is clear. You don't have to be a weather expert to say that there will be no rain. The school is almost centrally placed on Webber Street; if you live up the street or down the street, you don't have to walk very far to get to it. It is almost time for the meeting to begin, yet at windows looking over the street are heads of women. They are not going out for the night. And on the pavements, tesses group and talk and joke, and there are people moving away from the direction of the school, going elsewhere. But some are going down to the school. You know they are going because there are ways about people: the set of their shoulders and the swing of their arms. There are ways about people, yes, sir! And you know who are going to the cinema and who are going down Frederick Street to look in at the display-windows of the stores, and you know who are going to the meeting at the school.

Walter Castle and his wife walk down Webber Street. They are going to the meeting.

'Let's cross to the other side of the street, Walter,' his wife says. 'Those boys at the corner – I don't like to pass near them.'

'Why? Do they interfere with you?'

'Not really, but you never know. It's safer on the other side. You going?'

'No. Let's walk.'

Before them on the pavement is a group of young men standing right next to where a poster advertising the meeting is stuck up. The tesses stand in such a way that anyone wanting pass has either to pass through the group or get off the pavement. Walter continues along the pavement. When he comes to the tesses, he stops and says, 'Gentlemen, would you please excuse me.'

For a moment they hesitate. Stephanie grips her husband's hand tightly. Walter stands, waiting, tense.

'Move nuh, Bottle. You don't see the man want to pass,' one of the tesses say.

The tension melts.

'Pass, mister,' another says.

'Thank you.' Walter smiles and walks through the path they allow him.

'Excuse me,' he says, turning around. 'I was wondering if you-all knew of the meeting at the school.'

'What meetin'?'

'The meetin' at the school, stupid.'

'Yes, right there at the school,' Walter says. 'There is a poster right behind your back. You heard of it?'

'I didn't hear nutten.'

'Look the poster there. Like yuh can't read.'

'You-all are coming?' Walter asks.

There is no answer.

'Well,' Walter says, 'I just wanted to tell you, if you're coming, you don't have much time. Good night.'

As he walks off, he hears them arguing.

'Me an meetin'! Not me.'

'We could go.'

'For what? Only a setta jokers...'

Walter turns to his wife. 'That's all a man can do,' he says.

They walk down the street without speaking. The wife looks back after a while. She grips his hand tightly. 'Walter!' she says.

'Darling?'

'Look. Not there. Look behind us.'

So he looks back and sees the tesses walking down the street, coming towards the school.

'You think, Walter?'

'Yes.'

'How you know?'

'I just know, darling.'

Yes, he knows, for there are ways about people: the set of their shoulders and the swing of their hands and the way they hold their heads. Those boys are coming to the meeting.

'Fine night for the meeting,' he says.

'Yes, fine night.'

Walter looks around him. There are still too many people at their windows; there are still too many of them hurrying to the cinema or to God knows where. He wishes that he was bold enough to shout like a madman so that they would hear him up and down Webber Street: 'Fine night for the meeting! Fine night for the meeting!' But he is not so bold. Not yet. He smiles at the wild thought and automatically quickens his step.

## ABOUT THE AUTHOR

Earl Lovelace was born in the remote country village of Toco in 1935. He worked for a time as a forest ranger and as an agricultural assistant in the Department of Forestry in Tobago. He studied in the USA at Howard University and on Johns Hopkins writing programme. Whilst being mainly based in Trinidad, he taught at a number of American universities in the 1970s. His first novel, *While Gods Are Falling* was published in 1965, followed by *The Schoolmaster*, *The Dragon Can't Dance*, *The Wine of Astonishment*, *Salt*, which won the Commonweath Writers Prize in 1997, and in 2011, *Is Just a Movie*. His collection of short stories, *A Brief Conversion and Other Stories* was published in 1988, and a number of his plays in *Jestina's Calypso and Other Plays*, in 1984. He is one of the few major Caribbean writers who, except for brief periods, has never left the region. He currently lives in the remote village of Matura. He teaches at UWI, Trinidad.

# OTHER CARIBBEAN MODERN CLASSICS

Now in print:

Wayne Brown, *On The Coast*
ISBN 9781845231507, pp. 115, £8.99
Jan Carew, *Black Midas*
ISBN 9781845230951, pp.272 £8.99
Jan Carew, *The Wild Coast*
ISBN 9781845231101, pp. 240; £8.99
Austin Clarke, *Amongst Thistles and Thorns*
ISBN 9781845231477, pp.208; £8.99
Neville Dawes, *The Last Enchantment*
ISBN 9781845231170, pp. 332; £9.99
Wilson Harris, *Heartland*
ISBN 9781845230968, pp. 104; £7.99
George Lamming, *Of Age and Innocence*
ISBN 9781845231453, pp.438; £14.99
Una Marson, *Selected Poems*
ISBN 9781845231682, pp. 184; £9.99
Edgar Mittelholzer, *Corentyne Thunder*
ISBN 9781845231118, pp. 242; £8.99
Edgar Mittelholzer, *A Morning at the Office*
ISBN 9781845230661, pp.210; £9.99
Edgar Mittelholzer, *Shadows Move Among Them*
ISBN 9781845230913, pp. 358; £12.99
Edgar Mittelholzer, *The Life and Death of Sylvia*
ISBN 9781845231200, pp. 366; £12.99
Andrew Salkey, *Escape to an Autumn Pavement*
ISBN 9781845230982, pp. 220; £8.99
Denis Williams, *Other Leopards*
ISBN 9781845230678, pp. 216; £8.99
Denis Williams, *The Third Temptation*
ISBN 9781845231163, pp. 108; £8.99

Titles thereafter include...

George Campbell, *First Poems*
Austin C. Clarke, *The Survivors of the Crossing*
O.R. Dathorne, *The Scholar Man*
O.R. Dathorne, *Dumplings in the Soup*
Neville Dawes, *Interim*
Wilson Harris, *The Eye of the Scarecrow*
Wilson Harris, *The Sleepers of Roraima*
Wilson Harris, *Tumatumari*
Wilson Harris, *Ascent to Omai*
Wilson Harris, *The Age of the Rainmakers*
Marion Patrick Jones, *Panbeat*
Marion Patrick Jones, *Jouvert Morning*
George Lamming, *Water with Berries*
Roger Mais, *The Hills Were Joyful Together*
Roger Mais, *Black Lightning*
Edgar Mittelholzer, *Children of Kaywana*
Edgar Mittelholzer, *The Harrowing of Hubertus*
Edgar Mittelholzer, *Kaywana Blood*
Edgar Mittelholzer, *My Bones and My Flute*
Edgar Mittelholzer, *A Swarthy Boy*
Elma Napier, *A Flying Fish Whispered*
Orlando Patterson, *The Children of Sisyphus*
Orlando Patterson, *An Absence of Ruins*
V.S. Reid, *New Day*
V.S. Reid, *The Leopard* (North America only)
Garth St. Omer, *A Room on the Hill*
Garth St. Omer, *Shades of Grey*
Andrew Salkey, *The Late Emancipation of Jerry Stover*
and more...

All Peepal Tree titles are available from the website
**www.peepaltreepress.com**
with a money back guarantee, secure credit card ordering
and fast delivery throughout the world at cost or less.

**Or c**ontact us at:
Peepal Tree Press, 17 King's Avenue, Leeds LS6 1QS, UK
Tel: +44 (0) 113 2451703 E-mail: contact@peepaltreepress.com